FIVE
FERRIES

FIVE FERRIES

WILLIAM MICHAEL RIED

CKBooks

Names: Ried, William Michael.
Title: Five Ferries / William Michael Ried.
Description: New Glarus, WI : CKBooks Publishing, [2018]
Identifiers: ISBN 9781949085020
Subjects: LCSH: Young men--Travel--Europe--Fiction. | Hitchhiking--Europe--Fiction. | Adventure travel--Europe--Fiction. | Self-realization--Fiction. | Nineteen seventies--Political aspects-- Fiction. | Brothers--Death--Psychological aspects--Fiction. | LCGFT: Bildungsromans.
Classification: LCC PS3618.I39228 F58 2018 | DDC 813/.6--dc23

LCCN: 2018953594

Cover image by Lorenzo Contessa
Cover design by Colum Jordan ◆ columjordan.com

CKBooks Publishing
P.O. Box 214
New Glarus, WI 53574
CKBookspublishing.com

Acknowledgements

Rudolf William Ried, my grandfather, was the son of immigrants from Germany and Denmark. His formal schooling ended after fourth grade, but he went on to become a master toolmaker, raise a family and retire to his dream house on the north shore of Long Island. In his late eighties he began writing in pencil on both sides of the paper everything he could remember, from the decimation of his Yorktown neighborhood by the sinking of the General Slocum in 1904 to bowling in the Rocky Point Senior Citizens League in the 1970s.

Robert Rudolf Ried, my dad, made it all the way to a master's degree, was an aviation photographer in World War II, and over a long career moved from the telephone company shop to teaching employees around the country about mainframe computers. He retired to a house on a golf course in Florida, surrounded by lifelong friends. In his late-seventies Dad used a desktop computer to record his life story, from his earliest memories to the group tours he and my mom took to all corners of the world. He took up writing short stories in his mid-nineties and is going strong at one hundred. He is nothing like Jim Kylemore.

I was not yet through college when I began writing down my thoughts and experiences. I worked my way through Europe before law school and decided to record this as a snapshot of life from the perspective of a twenty-two-year-old. What began as a memoir evolved through the years, was lost and rewritten, and took a back seat to a legal career and raising children, until I concluded it should be the basis for a novel. This meant creating fictional relationships and fitting the course of the trip to a story. In her earliest comments, my editor would question whether an incident was believable and then add, "You're going to tell me this really happened, aren't you?" I had to admit much of the story was beyond my skill to make up, as was what was most important: the hours on the roadside, the search for a safe place to sleep and the next meal, the wonder of friends well met, the laughter and repose, and most of all, the freedom of life on the road. I hope this story sparks memories among my fellow senescent travelers and inspires those coming of age to step off the path for a look at the world and themselves.

Beyond my progenitors I must thank many people who have helped with this book. The two months I spent sorting through editors was well spent, because Christine Keleny, of CK Books Publishing, has been instrumental in taming my unruly manuscript into a novel. I also owe a debt to David Sobel for straight advice about editing and publishing. Early readers included my brother, Greg Ried, a novelist in his own right; Ann Marshall, who may be the most well-read person I know; and Philippe Durant, my expert on France and through the years my most faithful reader. More recently I have had help from the author Mary Behan in keeping it real and distinguishing Irish from "Oirish"; sparred on grammar, style and all things British with English author Bernard Hampson a/k/a Sam Boyd; and received assistance from Sven-Eric Huhn, a professional colleague who helped me tell east from west in Germany, and details about Switzerland from Mattias Ernst. I also must thank Carolina Rodriguez Garcia, a young friend who helped with Spain and Catalonia; Willeth (Chip) Miller III, a master of the piano, whose enthusiasm was infectious; the author Vicki Goodwin; and my niece Jennie Ried Samoska. Karla Heller also helped enormously with proofreading and fact-checking. I also owe special thanks to Drew Dawson, for his companionship and his perspective and help on Australian dialect. Remember, Drew, it's fiction and thus deniable.

While the counsel of my country experts has been invaluable, I have not heeded all their advice and all errors of language, custom and topography remain mine alone.

In the post-editing phase, my daughter Katie Ried has been my guide through marketing in the age of social media.

The cover image came from Lorenzo Contessa, who took this project to heart and put up with my many vacillations, and Colum Jordan designed the cover.

Finally, eternal thanks to Megan, the love of my life, who has helped me through the final stages and has so long and gracefully put up with me.

New York, July 2018

FIVE
FERRIES

Chapter I

Bedford Falls

"You bastard!" Pam shouted, pitching a deck of cards at my head. I ducked and the cards spread over the room, the mess a metaphor for our relationship. But cursing was not in her nature, and she quickly became calm, which was scarier.

"So you want to meet girls?" she asked with a voice like ice water.

"No, that's not it!"

She slayed me with her eyes, which sparkled blue even when her scowl reduced them to angry slits.

"I'll come back," I pleaded, "to you and to everything. It's just not fair to ask you to save yourself while I'm away."

"You've got it muddled," she spat out, "you and your 'heroes.'"

Seeing Pam angry was a shock because she almost always smiled; with her background and brains and looks, she had a lot to smile about. She came from Grosse Pointe, daughter of a big-time surgeon, who both doted on her and preached a serious work ethic. That was why she had to wait tables like the rest of us. But, unlike most of us, she had a plan; she knew she'd go to grad school and then plan the cities of the future.

More important to me she was beautiful and funny and never gave me a hard time. In fact, she was nice to everyone. She still had close friends from grammar school. She called her grandmother every week. She connected with animals, from the dogs playing outside the lecture halls, to birds that, I swore, sometimes sang back to her whistles. She was also curious about people and ideas and receptive, though timid, about veering off the normal track. The first time we made love was in the Arboretum, not far from a footpath. She was scared but also playful, and in the end it was our laughter rather than our lovemaking that passersby noticed behind the bushes.

There was no getting around the fact that I graduated and she would spend two more years in Ann Arbor. She couldn't go off with me on an unstructured trip. She didn't have unlimited time and wouldn't sign on for my kind of trip even for a few weeks. I understood this, but the trouble was she thought I shouldn't go without her, or at least that I should put a time frame around my trip. She saw me sailing off the edge of the earth. Leaving with no return date meant abandonment, plain and simple.

"You don't understand," I said quietly.

"Yeah, I know: Thoreau, Mark Twain, your family, your sacred adventure. I've heard it before."

I had no response and she continued. "And how will you get by with no money? You think the merry farmers in the fields will take you in?"

"Look, I know there are questions."

"Questions. Right. And oh, what about being able to speak some language other than English?"

"Well, there's German."

"Yeah, and you learned more vocabulary in two weeks with flash cards than you had in four semesters."

She had a point. My language skills were feeble, and money could be an issue. My old roommates also thought I was nuts. And then there was my father. Maybe they were all right. I worried about the ways things could go wrong. What if I didn't get a job? What if something happened; where would I find help?

The worst part was I really loved her—or thought I did. I'd have been crazy not to. We'd been together for eight months and I knew I wanted to come back to her. But that couldn't stop the trip. This was my only chance to go before life with a career (of some sort) and a wife (maybe Pam) and a dog (hopefully a dog) turned me into George Bailey without the storybook ending.

Part of my travel fixation came, I admit, from reading too many novels. I was obsessed with protagonists who left comfortable lives to step into the unknown. From Wilhelm Meister to Larry Darrell, the hero always left a predictable life behind. I'd read every adventure novel I could find, always starting one before finishing another to avoid the hollowness of having no romantic alternate reality at hand.

My big brother Edward first brought novels to life for me. He did great voices and always read me books I couldn't yet read myself. He wanted to show me the richness of serious literature was worth the effort. Something about thick volumes beyond my ability added wonder to these stories. My father flipped out when he found me in eighth grade trying to read Edward's copy of *Women in Love*. My brother had to assure him D. H. Lawrence was a legitimate author, and I was just trying to expand my vocabulary. In time I read all the books Edward left behind, always hungering for stories more real than life.

Even from Vietnam, Edward's enthusiasm for literature inspired me. In his last letter, he wrote about Patrick O'Brian's *Master and Commander*, a novel about a naval captain and his half-Irish, half-Catalan friend and ship's surgeon in the Napoleonic Wars. Edward liked that the surgeon, Stephen Maturin, had my name.

I fixated on anything Edward liked, so I looked up "Catalan" to learn the place was really Catalonia, part of Spain. When the dog-eared O'Brian paperback came home as part of Edward's effects, I read it in one long night, adding tear stains to the dirt smudges he left on some pages, and Catalonia became a mystical destination of the trip Edward and I had always planned to take. I even spent thirty bucks on an old one-peseta Catalonian coin. Somehow, I thought this would help me remember Edward and I started carrying it for luck. I wondered if I'd be able to visit Spain on this trip.

If not for Vietnam, things would have been so different. Edward and I would have set out together on a real "adventure," the skeptics be damned. I wouldn't be alone, and I wouldn't be afraid of anything with my brother beside me.

My father always thought I spent too much time reading and not enough playing outside and talking with real people. (He accused me of having conversations with fictional characters, which I denied; I was sure I didn't do that out loud.) He said I should be more like my brother: excel at baseball and make everyone laugh. I would have liked that too, but I couldn't hit a fastball and fell on my face trying to play to the crowd. In adventure stories, though, I could be the hero.

When Pam first saw the paperbacks all over my room, she said it gave the place a cloistered academic chic. But what charmed her at the start later annoyed her, and she came to treat books as rivals for my attention. She could never believe I could be so engrossed in a book that I wouldn't hear her speak. I thought this was a good thing, though, because it helped me hide how crazy I was about her. I was sure my occasional distractedness helped me hold on to her.

College was an opportunity to read more novels, and I took all the English classes I could fit into my schedule. This took me far from the accounting or engineering degree my father had in mind and caused a serious blow-up at home.

"The point of college is to get a job!" he often barked. "A high-paying job; it's the only way the cost and the time make sense!" (He had gone to work right after high school, and then came World War II and he signed up to fight in Europe.)

When I declared my major as American literature of the twentieth century, he refused to pay anything more toward school. Luckily, my grandfather had set up an account with enough for tuition, but room and board and everything else was on me. This forced me to take the restaurant job, which turned out well since that's where I met Pam. I guess I should have thanked Dad for that.

My senior thesis—on the suspension of disbelief in fantasy literature—won "best in show" as we called it, and the university offered me a teaching position and a place in the doctoral program the following September. Dad thought more school would be a further waste of time, but when I passed up that appointment, he nearly disowned me. In the world of Trollope or Thackeray, he would have disinherited me as if I had married beneath our family's station. As it was, my next visit home was simply filled with seething silences—the equivalent in our staid household of the honest shouting I heard so often in the homes of my Jewish and Italian friends, who represented the other ethnic components of my home town.

Mom held us together after my brother was gone. She quietly demanded peace under her roof and made clear she'd love us both no matter what. I think her struggle to dampen the combustion between my father and me gave her a purpose that helped lift her from despair. She also found comfort in religion and, until I left for school, I tried to go to church with her on Sundays, all I could think to do to ease her pain.

But the years passed, and I finished college and it was time to go, maybe my only time. In sixteen months another graduate class would start. There was no assurance I'd find a place in the next year's class, but if I found a spot somewhere I could slip back onto a career path without anyone noticing I'd been gone. And when would there ever be another window like this? I truly wanted a career and all that—and hopefully a life with Pam—but just not yet, not until I'd taken this chance.

I was also privileged to be able to take this trip—not in having the money for it but in having the time. Edward and I had often talked about how after college he would visit Ireland to trace the family roots, so he could "show me around" later on, when I was older.

"If you weren't such a squirt, we could go together," he'd tease, and I'd insist I was plenty big enough. I kept at him until he agreed he'd return to Ireland with me the summer after I finished high school.

Edward went to Notre Dame, which Dad loved because the "Irish" thing fit with the Kylemore family name and the brogue he put on after a few drinks as the essence of his ethnicity. But when Edward graduated in 1970, he couldn't go to Ireland. He could only go where Richard Nixon sent him, to the worst place in the world.

Edward's death only a few months later convulsed my world. I was so angry and heartbroken and wanted to lash out against something. I read antiwar books and embraced protest music and wished there was a better way to voice my pain. As time passed, I thought of taking the Europe trip as if we were going together, as a way to memorialize him. So I started preparing in earnest. During college I hitchhiked four times between home on Long Island and school in Ann Arbor, covering the twelve-hour drive in about sixteen. After surviving the middle of the night in Detroit and the dark Pennsylvania mountains, I wasn't afraid to hitchhike anywhere. In the end, no matter how unlikely the circumstances, someone always stopped. People were basically kind, and things worked out. I had to believe Europe would be the same.

As for money, I had a job lined up once I got to Germany, and for the first couple of weeks I could live on the cheap. I could always find a dark corner where no one would notice my tent. I'd just have to move once the sun came up; things would be easy in the light of day.

When Pam and I hitchhiked over spring break in the Florida Keys, the time on the road turned out to be more important than reaching any destination. In her cutoff shorts she had no trouble getting us rides, and when we got tired we simply walked away from the road and camped. It never occurred to us to worry about snakes or whatever else was crawling in the scrubby bush. We simply checked into the "Grand Hotel," as she called it. The tent had no fly to keep out moisture and it always sagged, but that didn't matter. After we made love, she'd burrow into my shoulder and call me her "big air mattress."

Pamela Granger was two years behind me at Michigan. She came to work at the restaurant my senior year and, with her golden hair and long legs, was by far our best-looking waitress. Actually, the Ann Arbor term was "wait-person," which she would be sure to point out. She was innocent about some things—like music and sex—but otherwise confident and strong. She was always on top of school—and work— and soon spent a good deal of time on top of me. Given my generally scruffy appearance and functional wardrobe, my friends found it hard to understand how I had attracted someone like her, and I often wondered about this myself.

The guys I lived with were devoted to a largely British genre of "symphonic" rock, by bands like Yes and Renaissance, which combined the colors and instruments of classical and traditional folk music into complex compositions played with rock virtuosity. Pam listened to us rave about obscure lyrics and complex time signatures, and was a good sport about the music we blasted, but she really preferred happy music or something she could dance to. In the spring she came along to a tacos and brownies party my friends gave before a Genesis concert. Next morning over waffles at a diner, she was dreamy.

"The music swept me up and held me," she said with an ethereal smile.

"That might have been the second brownie," I laughed.

"I don't think so. I kept thinking you prepared me for the concert by playing the album when we made love in your house."

I'd been infatuated with her beauty from the first, but that was the moment I knew I loved her.

*   *   *

I needed to save for the trip so, when spring semester ended, I went on full-time at the restaurant. The manager was happy to have Pam as well, so she decided to stay for the summer. We sublet the second floor in an old house by the stadium.

She was a major upgrade over my prior roommates. The comparison was, of course, unfair since we spent so much time in bed. But she also fixed up the place, cooked meals and twice borrowed a vacuum cleaner from a neighbor. I sometimes missed living in a house with six guys who worked hard but were always ready to party, listen to music and play speed chess. But then Pam's eyes would light up, or I'd notice everyone on the street was looking at her while she saw only me, and I saw the magic of the time we had together.

Working weekends at the restaurant meant cleaning up until three in the morning and then counting tips over brandy and backgammon until four. We'd get a ride home or sometimes walk the dark streets and get to bed just before dawn. I loved waking up beside her when the afternoon sunshine found our windows.

Since it was summer the students were mostly gone. Rent was cheap. We got plenty to eat at work. We took home our tips in cash so always felt flush with money. There were lots of parties and picnics in the Arboretum. I loved how easily she laughed and how she was always doing something different with her hair. Peter, one of our cooks, lived next door and had an old Plymouth. He'd jump at the chance to drive us out to Silver Lake to swim because he'd get to see Pam in a bathing suit. I couldn't blame him.

But May and June rushed by and things began to sour. I saw the dwindling time as a slice of heaven to treasure since I might never again have it so good. But she couldn't enjoy the moment for lamenting I'd soon be gone. These antipodal views on the basic question of embracing life made me wonder whether we'd be compatible in the long run.

Our last happy time together was in late June. As a surprise, she'd bought tickets to see the Yankees visit Tiger Stadium and got two of her friends to give us a ride. It's true she wore a Tigers hat, but she watched with impeccable grace as my hero, Ron Guidry, won the game. She also showed she knew more than I did about baseball, other than maybe the Yankees, just as her dad had taught her more about Big Ten football than I would ever know.

My departure soon after this was painful—Pam and I agreed on that, at least. We both cried through the last night. She got up with me before dawn but disappeared before I lifted my pack and took the first of thousands of steps away from her. Her tear-streaked face from the night before haunted me all the way across Route 80 to New York.

Nothing at my parents' house lightened my mood. The house felt empty without Edward. Mom busied herself feeding me and suggesting things to pack. I kept one step ahead of my father's disapproval.

As my parents drove me to the airline office in Queens the next day, I listed the cities in Europe where they could send letters care of American Express. Dad cringed at each name and stared straight ahead. It was a cinch he wouldn't be writing to me.

Chapter II

Innocence Abroad

My left eye opened on a loop pattern in the carpet. The rest of my face was pushed into the sleeping bag strapped to my pack. I didn't move but took stock of the situation. Jimmy Carter had been in the White House for a year and a half and Ron Guidry was off to a great start for the Yankees. Two months after graduation I was sharing the Freddie Laker Skytrain office in Queens with maybe a hundred other college kids, each with a ticket for a bus ride to JFK and a standby flight to London.

The upstart Laker Airways sold cheap tickets to the UK, but you had to wait hours or days for a seat. That worked for me since I had lots of time but very little money, and London seemed as good a place as any to start. I'd never been to Europe and had only dancing visions of places to see. I had a year to spend and my only target was Grettstadt, a village in Germany. My old boss Victor would be visiting his family there for three weeks in July and said he'd set me up with a job with his relatives. I had worked in Victor's machine shop for a year and a half and he liked what I did enough to try to talk me into putting off college to work full-time. But he understood I couldn't give up a ticket to Ann Arbor and we had stayed friends. Now his offer to find me work filled in the missing piece to my plan. I just had to travel cheaply for a couple of weeks until I found him.

Once I got a job and saved some money, I could buy a rail pass and a hostel card. I could then head south, maybe find my way to Yugoslavia and my mother's family and winter in the Greek islands. Otherwise, I'd have to turn for home once I spent my two hundred dollars in cash and the three hundred in travelers checks I'd stashed away to get me home.

After England I wouldn't be able to speak the language, except the most rudimentary German, but this wouldn't be a problem hitchhiking. Drivers wouldn't know I was foreign and, once I was in a car, no one would throw me out because I could speak only English. To communicate where I was going (once I figured that out), I could always point.

More troubling than the languages or the money was that I'd be alone. Everyone I knew went to Europe through some kind of school program or group or at least with a friend. No one would join me on a one-way ticket to hitchhiking and sleeping in a tent, no one but Edward, which made this trip all the more a toast to him and all he meant to me. We always said we would traipse through the European countryside so, damn it, I would traipse!

I looked around the waiting room. The passengers were mostly dressed like me, in jeans and sweatshirts. It looked like we were about to board a bus for a school trip: an inauspicious sendoff for my grand adventure. But this crowd would dissipate. I was sure they all knew where they were going, if not precisely when they'd get there. I only thought about reaching Victoria Station and then eventually finding my way to Germany.

I had started *The Nick Adams Stories* in Michigan, where they were set, hoping this would cultivate my inner Hemingway. I'd nearly finished the book in the Skytrain waiting room when word spread there would be buses to the airport at five. A girl poked her boyfriend and told him. He raised drowsy eyes under a floppy hat, looking like Arlo Guthrie, which brought to mind another impetus for the trip.

Guthrie's song "Alice's Restaurant Massacree" told how Americans were not subject to the Vietnam draft if they'd been convicted of a crime, even as minor as littering. This suggested to him and his friends getting arrested for littering as a ploy to avoid the army. I figured any means was fair to escape a war that was wrong on so many levels. You could defer for college, but only for four years. You could use a medical reason but how could you fake that? Some boys burned draft cards and ran to Canada, but then they had to live as fugitives. Edward was a stand-up guy; he wouldn't run and hide. After college he had no excuse, so he was drafted immediately and in central Vietnam right after Christmas.

After Edward went overseas, our house was always still. Dad didn't play his records. I often hid inside novels but couldn't help watching Mom wait for the mailman each day, even though she knew he'd come straight to our house if there was a letter from Edward. I ran out of things to say to make her feel better when there was no letter. She cried and I struggled with how this could be right and why we were in Vietnam. I began paying attention to the images on television every night. I couldn't erase the image of a monk burning himself in Saigon or fathom why we fought for a dictator. I embraced the sounds of protest and saw old politicians sending young boys to die where we couldn't tell friends from enemies. We weren't defending ourselves, just "preserving a way of life." Of course, after we lost the war, our way of life didn't change… except for people like my mom.

I argued with Dad every night at dinner but couldn't make him see Vietnam was *nothing* like World War II. This was no noble struggle against tyranny. This time *we* were the bad guys. We propped up a puppet government clear around the world and then burned down the country to save it from communism. We rained down napalm but lost sight of the people in sandals and straw hats fighting for their country. The more I thought, the more politicized I became and the further I drifted from my father. He felt the divide as clearly as I did and acted as if he'd lost *two* sons.

Guthrie's song was distinguished, not for criticizing the war, but for being mostly a monologue running over twenty minutes, yet getting enough airplay on FM radio that I knew it more or less by heart. But what most grabbed me about the song was its story of hippies living in an abandoned church, apart from the world. These people lived in union and joy outside ordinary life. I wanted to know these people.

I returned to my book and was not happy to finish it. I realized I should have grabbed another novel at home because I'd have nothing to read on the plane. I leafed through the book and came upon an underlined quote in the introduction:

> *The only writing that was any good was what you made up, what you imagined. That made everything come true. Everything good he had ever written he'd made up.*

That made no sense to me. Did Hemingway really make up the Nick Adams character and the settings of those stories? Then again, the collection wasn't published until after he died, so maybe he didn't think much of the stories.

What was most important about this book was I had finished it, which meant I was ill prepared for a long flight and the trip to follow. I had to do something about this and carried the volume around the waiting room until, with great relief, I found a guy from Boston College, who was willing to trade me for *The Innocents Abroad or the New Pilgrim's Progress*.

The cover of the Twain book quoted someone saying it was "irreverent and incisive commentary... one of the most famous travel books ever written about Europe and the Holy Land by an American." It was perfect.

After an eight-page table of contents, Twain's fictional "Mark Twain" character prepared for his voyage. The short opening chapters sounded like a typical tourist's journal, made *almost* interesting by touches of wit. I was sure this would improve, however, as it went along.

Buses arrived at the Skytrain office, and I got a spot on the overnight flight to London. My assigned seat on the plane was slightly more comfortable than the floor in the office, and I was glad to have something to read. The food wasn't very good so I hardly touched it. If I'd known what was ahead, I wouldn't have been so picky.

Chapter III

The Anteroom

I had read so many stories set in London that I expected to feel at home. The city was known for its fog, a mixture of the particular soot of the age and the mist natural to a rainy climate. It seemed right, then, to arrive at Gatwick Airport on a fog-filled morning. Unknown on the continent and far from any place I'd ever been, I stretched like a cat after a long nap and looked around.

Waiting at the baggage carousel was all too familiar, although I was pleased to see my backpack emerge intact. I lifted my big pack onto my back. On my belt a vinyl camera pouch held my wallet and passport. My white tee shirt bore a Heineken Bier logo, and I had tied a hooded sweatshirt around my waist.

I was eager to experience something foreign, but the customs officers, who hardly noticed me, were public servants like any others, albeit with public-television accents. Once through the customs gate, I set down my pack and paused to read from my thick paperback *Let's Go: The Budget Guide to Europe*. As instructed, I found a currency exchange and changed fifty dollars for just over twenty-six pounds sterling. I didn't see why I should have to pay a commission to exchange currency, but stowed the banknotes in my pouch and stepped to a quiet corner of the terminal.

Trying to swing the pack from my shoulders, I almost dropped it. It was top-heavy and hard to lean against a wall so its rubber feet wouldn't slide. I untied the top flap and placed half my new pound notes inside a rolled pair of socks.

The English girl I'd met at JFK was nowhere to be seen. That was too bad; she was cute and said she knew London. But we'd been assigned to opposite ends of the DC-10 and I thought I should respect fate at this jumping off point. Anyway, I didn't want to wait to get started and so searched for signs for the train to London. The current of travelers swept me through tunnels crowded with people and ads full of union jacks and tea biscuits.

In a near-empty train car, I sat against the last window with my pack on the aisle seat. After days in open lounges and vehicles, it was a relief to finally be hidden. The worn leather seats gave off a comforting smell and the tarnished brass light fixtures looked a hundred years old. I felt like Michael Caine in a grainy black-and-white film, on my way to London for a date with a "bird." (My obsession with stories extended beyond literature to movies of all sorts.)

The Twain book made me sleepy, and I laid it aside and leaned my forehead against the window. We rolled by a few fields and then industrial looking towns under a gloomy sky.

At the first stop, two young men entered wearing black leather jackets. Each had a long, or rather tall, Mohawk haircut, one black and the other snowy white. They could have stepped off the cover of a David Bowie album. I tried not to show my excitement at spotting my first exotic Englishmen.

The two sat across from me. One poked the other, grinned at me and made a guttural noise. I avoided their glances and ignored the clucking sound, which seemed natural to boys made up as roosters.

At the end of the line was Victoria Station: an enormous shed, bustling and grimy. I pulled the belt on the pack tight and walked into an open space. People streamed across the floor at all angles. Steadying myself against a railing, I looked up to trace intricate ironwork in the curved ceiling. It took my breath away to think Thomas Hardy might have noticed those same designs.

Let's Go said to sign up for a cheap bed at the "Student Accommodations Office." A handwritten sign on an interior office said just that, so I swung open the door, bumping into someone on the other side. I backed up, apologizing through the door, and in another moment squeezed gently through the doorway. I found myself wedged into a room full of kids, denim and backpacks.

The blank stares around the room said I might have to wait for hours. It felt all too Dickensian, as if we were orphans being packed off to the workhouse. One boy with long dark hair tied in a bandana looked up from his seat on a sleeping bag. "Welcome to bloody London," he said.

"What's the story?" I asked, gazing around the room.

"You take a number, then you wait for the next bed. Hey, where you from?"

"New York," I said absently, shaking my head at all the weary faces. I was trying to do the math: six hours ahead of New York, almost two days at it, and all this waiting and flying and driving with more or less these same people. All routes into London could *not* pass through this office. I wondered if it was safe to try finding my own way. Another look at all the tired faces convinced me: I'd ditch Dickens for Lewis Carroll. I, and the great appendage on my back, would jump down the rabbit hole.

I nodded to the boy, who said something about visiting New York City. There was no room to turn around so I backed out the door.

In the open terminal I swung my pack to the ground and opened the guidebook. Below the previous instructions was a list of student hostels. I folded back the page, placed the book beneath one arm and carried my pack on the other arm to a row of wooden telephone booths.

The instructions on the phone were confusing, but one of each type of coin from my pocket got me a dull double ring, followed by a brusque voice with an exaggerated accent.

"Hallo, who's that?"

"St. Cyril's?"

"Yes, yes, St. Cyril's. How may we be of service?"

"Ah, I'm an American student looking for a place to stay. Have you got room?"

"American, you say? Well, you must be under twenty-five and have a student card and a sleeping bag."

"No problem there."

"Yes, good. And how, may I ask, did you learn of us?"

"You're listed in *Let's Go: Europe.*"

"Argh," the man moaned. "One of those, is it?" He paused, cleared his throat and continued: "Well, come anyway; yes, we've room. It's one pound sixty for a cot in the church and breakfast and a shower; you provide soap and towels."

Outside the station I stopped to adjust the pack straps and look around. I guessed it was mid-day but I hadn't noticed any clocks at the station. The time didn't matter anyway, now that the trip had begun. I looked around at the faces rushing past and felt a lump in my throat thinking how Edward would have insisted we toast to commemorate this moment.

The guidebook directions led me down Victoria Street, past a cathedral of brick and stone. Walking in the fog woke me up. It felt both liberating and a little scary to break away from the crowd. I was truly on my own for the first time.

The city was quieter than Manhattan. Tiny cars, large black taxis and double-decker buses drove on the wrong side of the street. Still, it seemed a bit staged, as if this weren't real.

My father and I butted heads on most everything that mattered to me, from the war, to rock music, to my hair. But of all the things I did, my decision to take this journey angered him the most. This trip added an ocean and many miles to the considerable distance between us. He'd been to Italy to fight and still held a grudge against the European continent; I was here to see what this place could teach me.

I was now free of anyone with any hold on me—beyond Mom,

who would always be there. Dad had written me off. Pam had moved on. Edward could join me only in spirit.

In half an hour I turned a corner onto an empty side street. The sidewalk sloped into a curving, solid wall a hundred feet long. Above two heavy oak doors flush with the wall hung a sign with one large "S" beginning three lines: "St. Cyril's/ Student/ Shelter." Ironwork girded the door and formed a point at the top, set in stone and stained with centuries of grime.

The moment I knocked, the door flew open. Filling the doorway was a middle-aged man with ruddy cheeks and thinning gray hair. He was taller than me and his girth strained at the buttons on his tweed vest.

"What, yes; you'll be the American, then?"

"Yes sir, Stephen Kylemore, newly arrived and looking for a bed."

The man wore a watch chain and an appraising expression. He looked me up and down and then pulled the door open and stepped aside. I entered a kind of anteroom, which opened into a cavernous, dimly lit space. As I lowered my pack to the floor, the man passed around me to sit behind a large, cluttered desk. It seemed a bit of English humor that the towering guardian of the gate in a flash became the obsequious hotel clerk. I was thinking of John Cleese for the role.

The man examined my papers through half-glasses perched comically on the end of his bulbous nose. My passport photo showed me as I then appeared, with the short haircut intended to get me rides, but my international student ID pictured a typical U of M senior, unshaven and wearing all the hair I could grow in three months away at school. The cards said my eyes were blue, both of them, which was easier than explaining they were different colors. He squinted, looking again at the student ID until his two eyebrows joined into one.

"Yes, then," he grumbled, jowls shaking. "I am Niall Toodle, the house father. I run the shelter, and I make the rules. I live on the third floor, which is *off-limits to all*. You will pay one pound sixty in advance for each night. Breakfast at eight. Your key will open the door until midnight; thereafter the inside latch is thrown and the shelter is impregnable until seven a.m. Your bag is utterly safe, as we interdict the perfidious element; just park yourself on an empty bed."

I paid for the night and turned for the beds but stopped when Niall continued: "And as to *Let's Go: Europe*, it is quite disturbing we are listed there. No one from *that* publication has ever given us the courtesy of a visit. Consequently, of course, the information listed is inaccurate as to rates, and times, and matters more crucial yet. In any event, posted by the door you'll find a copy of my letter asking the editors at *Harvard* University kindly to delete mention of St. Cyril's until they have had the integrity to research what they publish."

I nodded and glanced at the letter on the wall. It sounded like Niall had a lot of time on his hands. It also dawned on me that, rather than being a character from *Monty Python's Flying Circus*, Niall could have been the model for the proper, feckless Englishman in a bowler hat.

Walking on I found myself alone in a large nave with a high, dark ceiling. Where pews once stood were rows of metal cots. At floor level the room ended with a temporary wall covered with sheets. Long wooden tables lined the right side of the room, and in the near right corner were several cots behind hanging sheets and the sign "Girls Only!!" A dim light showed from high on the walls through panes of blackened stained glass.

I unstrapped my sleeping bag, pulled it from its sack and laid it on cot thirty-nine. It was only mid-afternoon but I was exhausted. With my sneakers off for the first time in a day and a half, I lay back on the sleeping bag, peering into the darkness for the speakers playing a dreamy string quartet high in the air.

The closing of the front door woke me. I jerked up, confused at where I was, and then recognized St. Cyril's and fell back on my elbows. The windows were dark. The stone floors and walls gave off a chill. A bare electric bulb silhouetted two girls through the "Girls Only!!" sheets. Then they stepped past the sheets, speaking softly in what I thought was French. Their angelic laughter echoed around the vaulted ceiling. They appeared to nod at me and, in case this was true, I returned the nod with a big smile. On two empty cots by the wall, they opened bags and exchanged and repacked things, and then they sat at one of the tables.

I unpacked a towel and a bar of soap. With my socks off, the cold of the stone floor took my breath away. I walked quickly past the French girls—smiling again—and stepped behind a false wall to the showers. The fiberglass shower stall opened into a wooden chamber set off by a checkered plastic curtain. As I undressed in the cramped stall, my limbs poked through the curtain and my elbow banged the clapboard wall. Finally in the shower, I bent my neck and placed one shoulder at a time beneath a trickle of water, barely warm enough to stave off the chill.

I peeled the soap from its wrapper, lathered my hair and body and then reached up to put the bar on top of the fiberglass wall. Before stepping back onto the cold stone, I reached for the soap and came down with an empty plastic soap dish. I looked at it intently. This was something I could use, but my impulse was to leave it where it was in case the owner returned. While I dried off, I looked at the dish on the bench. If it were abandoned or forgotten, it would be fair salvage: the law of the sea and all that. Anyway, living off the land might require a suspension of normal civil rules, like respecting other people's property. In the end I decided I shouldn't make this into a moral dilemma. The soap dish coming to hand was simply a turn of luck. I rinsed it and closed it over my soap.

It felt great to be clean. Once I was dressed in jeans, a tee shirt and a fisherman-knit sweater, the trip began to seem worthwhile. I unrolled the suede sports jacket Edward had sent home from Hong Kong, threw it over my shoulder and ventured into the street. But a heavy mist returned me quickly inside to change the jacket for my hooded sweatshirt and Yankees cap.

On crooked back streets, old façades and courtyards were shrouded with mist. It was quiet and dark, except for splashes of chatter and light spilling from the occasional pub. Someone pushed open the mahogany doors of The Prince William and warmth and voices pulled me in. I removed my cap and ordered a Guinness stout.

"We've found our way as far as jolly old England," I mouthed in silent toast to Edward and, looking back at my glass and around the room, added out loud: "And now what?"

"You've got twenty-four minutes to get to Victoria," a gentleman said.

"Well then," his companion responded, "I suppose we should get another round and then see how the fire's going. The train will probably pull out any old time."

They spoke like characters in a film and one of them looked like Nigel Bruce. I really had made it to the source of so many novels and films that had shaped my view of the world. After my stout I returned to the street, wondering where to find companionship. I thought about what Pam might be doing in Ann Arbor but then told myself to stop dwelling on the past. Instead, I concocted a fantasy of a proper English lady taking me in to warm a lonely day or two.

Another pub down the street was busier than the first. The locals were watching a game of darts. I stood at the bar and ordered a pint of bitter, trying to look casual. Two stools down and far from trying to fit in was a middle-aged American couple. They looked like visitors to the London exhibit at Disneyland.

"The place has character," said she, eyeing me.

"I can't believe a 'Seven & Seven' is strictly an American drink," he grumbled.

If I told them I was from Kansas City and had campaigned for Richard Nixon, I thought I might squeeze a beer out of them.

"You know, Ireland would be a fun place to go to a pub," said she. "Wouldn't cost more than a couple hundred dollars. It'd be better than Hawaii."

This *non sequitur* changed my mind about attempting contact. "*Ich verstehe nicht*," I practiced quietly and watched darts until it was time to find my way back to St. Cyril's.

The shelter was quiet and mostly dark. People slept on a few cots around mine. I went to bed and dropped quickly to sleep, my dreams commencing from strings and woodwinds in soft strokes.

* * *

My eyes snapped open and stared into the high ceiling. The sleeping bag was warm and my dreams so soothing that I yearned to return to sleep. But my fellow travelers were already at the tables eating breakfast, so I rose and dressed, finding my sneakers under the cot.

After rinsing my face at the sinks I joined the others with a towel over my shoulder. With a plate filled with hard rolls and jelly and a cup of tea, I turned to look for a seat. A pair of dazzling green eyes invited me to a table.

She smiled when I sat. "Hello," she said with a musical accent sounding Mediterranean. Her black hair set off mischief in her eyes.

"Good morning," I said to the girl and her companion, a thin boy of about twenty with dirty hair and bad skin.

"Mornin' mate," he said.

"You have two different color eyes," she said, gazing at me intently.

"Yes, I do, if you look closely, but hardly anyone does."

"One is a light gray and one a pretty sky blue," she continued, almost clinically, as if examining a specimen on a lab table.

I was embarrassed, as always when someone noticed this, but flattered by the attention. Her friend couldn't care less about my eyes and turned the conversation to where I came from and where I was headed.

Annetta was on a university exchange program from the Polytechnic University of Turin. For an engineer she was striking, and she seemed unaware of this, which made her even more attractive. John had come from New Zealand, to stay as long as it suited him. I watched how they treated each other to decipher their relationship but decided I'd have to see how things unfolded.

When I started a second cup of tea, Niall appeared with a tray and began clearing dishes. "You'll have to be about finishing your breakfast," he said. I noticed I was the only one still eating and gulped down my tea.

"Like he's got anything bloody else to do," John muttered under his breath.

Niall looked up. He'd heard John's aside but hadn't made out the words. "I can't be at cleaning up after breakfast all day," he declared, glaring at John.

I finished my tea and carried the dishes to Niall's tray. Sensing hostility, I soon headed out the door with my sweater and the camera that had been a graduation present from my parents, although I suspected it came only from Mom. As I pulled out the camera, a tiny stuffed animal fell to the floor. I'd forgotten about "Ubit," short for "Ubiquitous." Pam had given it to me as a traveling companion before everything went wrong; he was supposed to take over the job of watching over me. Since I wouldn't be seeing Pam again, it seemed Ubit now had a permanent gig.

Over my long last night with Pam, she refused to make love, insisting it would be dishonest. I told her she was my home and I'd chase myself around the world and back to her, but she looked sad and said I shouldn't bother. Nonetheless, I asked her to write care of American Express, first in London, then Munich in August and Athens in October. I suspected she would *not* be writing.

Snapping to, I barely avoided stepping on a pigeon, which must have been sick because it paid no heed to me. While there wasn't much chance of mail, I made my first destination the American Express office by Trafalgar Square. The office was easy to find, but there were no letters, of course, since I was only three days gone. Still, it made me feel more alone than I'd expected. I began to think my friends had been right: traveling alone *would* be lonely. Still, there was no sense rethinking at this point, ankle deep in the grimy scavengers of the square. I had to put America behind me and focus on making it to Germany.

The National Gallery provided solace in the form of original oils of the prints of sunflowers and water lilies familiar from dormitory walls. More interesting was a tour group of young French girls, who giggled the second *and* third times I passed by. I realized that talking to girls—never my strong point—was going to be a bigger challenge when I couldn't speak the language.

The National Gallery held my attention for a couple of hours, then I bought a sandwich at a small shop and wandered along the Thames. Unlike when I first arrived, London now appeared much like the Manhattan I knew growing up, except there were more tourists, and I was nearly run over each time I stepped from a curb looking the wrong way.

And then there was the relentless drizzle. The day washed over me: soggy air, master paintings, waves of tourists. I wondered if there was space in this city to drum up a game of Frisbee.

Back at St. Cyril's in the late afternoon, I sat at a table reading. The ship carrying Mr. Twain had crossed the Atlantic, and in Morocco the "barbarians" from the New World achieved their goal of finding "something thoroughly and uncompromisingly foreign." Within a few pages they had crossed to France and were "getting foreignized rapidly and with facility."

I shared the desire to embrace something totally foreign, but England seemed the wrong place for it. Things were odd in a British sort of way but still too familiar. Twain's account, as well, was becoming tedious after only seventy pages.

"What have you done today?" Annetta's lyrical voice broke in.

"Not much," I said, pleased to be interrupted. I waved for her to sit beside me. "Went to the National Gallery. Walked in the rain."

She laughed. "Yes, the weather is not so good in England. But the National Gallery is old paintings, yes? I like the Impressionists."

"Oh, so do I. They had some Manet and Gauguin."

"Yes, but I believe the Tate Gallery is best for Impressionists."

"Would you... would you like to go tomorrow?" I said, surprised at overcoming my diffidence.

"Yes," she responded without hesitation. "This would be nice."

I glanced around but didn't see John. She watched me with a knowing smile.

"You look for my friend?"

"Uh, yes," I stammered, surprised by her perception and openness. "I wondered if he will mind your going to a museum with me."

"He is very nice boy, but he is *not* my boyfriend. My boyfriend is on holiday in the mountains, how is it... skiing?"

I nodded and tried to deduce how I might fit into this arrangement.

"John takes me tonight to hear music," she said with fresh excitement. "Maybe you will like to go too?"

"Music? Yeah, great!" I said, adding, "What kind of music?" as if that mattered.

"Oh, punk music, I think. John knows where is a club."

We talked for half an hour about music and rainy London. Not since I met Pam had I been so interested in a girl and sensed she might like me, but her connection to John was an obstacle. When he returned he grudgingly agreed to my joining them for the evening. I left for a shower, and after I dressed found "hotel clerk Niall" at his desk.

"I'd like to pay for two more nights," I said.

Niall looked like he'd bitten a lemon. "Taking an interest in Britannic culture, are we?" he sneered as I slid the money across the desk. "Well, I should exercise discernment in with whom I spend my time, if I were you."

This was baffling. I thought back to John's comment at breakfast and Niall's reaction. Whatever had transpired between them seemed to have poisoned Niall's opinion of me. I simply nodded and returned to my bunk to read until my friends were ready to go. When I saw them, she wore a black sweater and pants with a bright red scarf. I wondered if all Italian women looked elegant in simple clothes or if this was unique to her.

John disappeared for a few minutes and returned to lead the way out the door and toward the underground. On the misty street he told us Niall had kicked him out of the shelter. Next day he'd move to a hostel around the corner.

"What did he say?" Annetta asked, genuinely concerned.

"Ah, the old bugger," he said. "Don't know what got stuck up his bum. He just said I should move on, and I said fine."

This explanation seemed a bit thin, but if John was abandoning the field I thought I might extend my stay.

Annetta walked between us with John at the curb. In a few blocks great rings of light around a street lamp pierced the mist, and I thought for a moment I saw them holding hands. I heard again the concern in

Annetta's voice at John's news and recalled he was not leaving London or even the neighborhood. He was here first, I thought, so maybe I'm the one who should shove off. He'd been nice enough to me, and I had no business trying to steal away his girl.

Nashville was a punk music club on North End Road. We arrived by the West Kensington tube and paid a pound each admission. John made a show of buying the first round of beer. The other patrons were in the uniform of black clothes, spiky hair and safety-pin earrings. A band called "The Bitter Edge" played loud punk rock. Kids danced wildly in the center of a crowd of drinkers.

Finishing his beer at a gulp, John asked Annetta to dance. She nodded and looked for a place to set down her glass, and then handed it to me with a sweet smile.

I watched the bouncing tops of their heads but then tried to concentrate on my beer. None of the other girls in the pub were as pretty as Annetta or even attractive enough to make me want to dance with them. I found dancing fun when I was drunk or loved the music. Otherwise it was strictly a mating ritual, a way to meet girls. With no one besides Annetta of much interest, there was no reason to bother.

The band started a slower song, and my companions stayed on the dance floor. I finished both the beers in my charge and made my way through the crowd to buy more. Looking back while the bartender poured, I was almost sure I saw Annetta and John kissing. This concluded the matter. I turned away and concentrated on how to leave London and get across the Channel.

After the band stopped, Annetta came up from behind me and pulled at my sleeve. I turned and handed her a fresh half-pint. I was baffled she still looked at me with such inviting eyes. John swaggered up like a rooster and magnanimously accepted his new beer. We toasted the queen.

There was a brief changeover and the next band was introduced as "The Molesters." They looked the part, with ripped shirts and gothic makeup. As soon as they finished tuning, Annetta grabbed my arm.

"Now *we* dance?" she asked with eyebrows raised over those pretty green eyes.

I looked to John in my resolve not to get in his way, but he wasn't bothered and went to find the WC. I left my glass on the bar and followed Annetta to the dance floor.

The tempo was jarring. The lead singer leapt and screamed more or less lyrically while the guitarist pounded a few chords, and the drummer pushed everyone on. Annetta's enthusiasm roused me and together we jumped frantically up and down. When the song ended, we were winded and sweaty and fell together half leaning, half hugging. I was sure she wanted to be kissed but couldn't shake the image of her with John. As I pondered that, she leaned in and kissed me full on the lips. I held still for a moment and then stumbled back. She laughed mischievously and pulled me by the hand back to the bar.

John was deep in conversation with an anemic-looking compatriot from New Zealand. The stranger looked as if he had no money at all but bought us all another round. We talked loudly over the music about the punk scene in London and Amsterdam. Annetta directed the same coquettish look at each of us, which left me hopelessly confused.

We arrived back at St. Cyril's just before midnight and met Niall coming to lock up. "Barely in time," he noted, checking his large brass pocket watch and then looking us up and down with a scolding expression. It may have been my paranoia, but he seemed particularly to condemn me for again associating with John. I could imagine him in a Victorian novel dismissing John as that greatest of rascals unhanged.

But I restrained any laughter or over-wide smile. Annetta excused herself to prepare for bed. John and I exchanged cordial goodnights, and he seemed to park himself in wait for her. I went to sleep without catching the next episode in the melodrama my trip had become: exotic girls with distant boyfriends; snubbed suitors cast into the street. I fell to unsettling dreams and twice groped across the icy floor to the WC.

In the morning I confirmed my date with Annetta while John fetched his tea. I ate quickly and went to shower so I wouldn't have to talk with him before he left.

When I was dressed, I lay on my cot with *The Innocents Abroad*. Unlike most of the "great books" I'd read, this one failed to hold my attention. I put it aside and closed my eyes, thinking about how to get my hands on a replacement.

Annetta tapped my arm. Apparently, John had beaten a hasty retreat before she had time to tell him how she'd spend her day. I gathered my things and, as we left, Niall's humming halted and it seemed his comical scowl turned menacing.

In a light fog, Annetta and I wandered toward the Tate Gallery. Within a few blocks she reached for my hand, delivering a charge up my arm. We intertwined fingers and I forgot there was a John from New Zealand or a boyfriend in Italy. Along the river we slowed and veered into a secluded doorway. She leaned back against the wall and looked up at me with those eyes. I didn't know who initiated it but we kissed over and over. She was warm and soft. I wanted to spend the whole day in that doorway, but too soon she pulled me back onto the sidewalk.

The Tate had a grand porticoed entrance through six great columns, and a dome over the central building made the whole structure resemble a temple. A statue of Britannia with a lion and a unicorn stood on top of the pediment under which we entered arm-in-arm before we walked up the central stairway to look for the Impressionists. It turned out we had similar taste in paintings and joked about which priceless oils to hang in our villa by the sea. Running through my head was a quote from Saint-Exupéry: "Love does not consist of gazing at each other but of looking outward together in the same direction." I felt as if I were floating through galleries of great art, tethered to the ground by her hand.

We left the museum and wandered along the Thames across from the Houses of Parliament. The huge gothic structure stretched along the riverfront in sandy-colored stone, from a great tower at the south end to Big Ben at the north. The drizzle let up when we reached Trafalgar Square and so, beneath the gaze of Admiral Lord Nelson atop his column, we lingered to watch tourists feed the pigeons. A Spanish father asked me to use his camera to photograph his family. While she waited, Annetta dried a park bench with a paper bag, and then we sat.

"You will stay how long?" she said, in such an inviting tone I wanted to answer "perpetuum." Instead, I said, "I've paid only for tonight, but if you like, I'll stay another day."

She smiled and kissed my cheek.

Recovering from this, I said: "What are your plans?"

"Plans?" she said, looking into the distance and hugging my arm. "I go home to Turino on the plane. You will perhaps visit me?"

"Sure," I said, but then paused. "But will your boyfriend mind?"

She looked quizzical and then smiled. "Oh, yes, he minds, but he goes to the Alps and does not care if I mind."

This invitation confused me. Would he still be her boyfriend? Would I kiss her one moment and watch them kiss the next? What would the sleeping arrangements be beyond Niall's omniscient glare? It seemed unlikely she'd clear up these questions, so I just took her address and telephone number in Turin. I tried to practice my own philosophy and focus on the time at hand.

"What will you do tomorrow?" I said.

"I will see a friend at his school for part of the day, and maybe you will come with me and then we will go some other place?"

"Yeah, okay," I said and turned her chin with my hand to look into her eyes. "But this 'friend,' this is another boyfriend?"

"He is a boy," she laughed. "But he is not my boyfriend."

This was starting to make me crazy. Still, she was beguiling and I knew I wouldn't leave London while she stayed; it was actually a good thing she was going home so I could start north. *Let's Go* said a ferry for Holland debarked from a town called Harwich, and to get there I'd pass through Cambridge. This would bring a semblance of academic legitimacy to the junket, "which should please Dad," I said out loud and laughed to myself. The guidebook placed Cambridge about a sixty-mile drive from London, which should be an easy morning's trip.

Then Annetta mentioned she'd be having dinner with John. My pique must have showed in the roll of my eyes.

"John is very nice to me; I should say goodbye," she said, kissing my cheek again.

It was clear I had to take what Annetta was willing to give and pouting wouldn't help. We agreed to go to a pub later in the evening. In a few steps, walking again hand-in-hand, I forgot about John and thought only of how electric her green eyes looked against her black coat and hair. We lingered in several more doorways.

When we returned to the shelter, she changed shoes and went to meet John. I caught up with Niall in the anteroom.

"Niall, I'd like to pay for one more night," I said pleasantly.

"You'll do no such thing," he snapped, visibly angry. "I have reached the end of my tether and, having persistently followed the vulgar herd, you shall not stay even *this* night; you shall have your money back and you shall leave as soon as you are dressed."

"What do you mean?"

"I warned you. Now you shall oblige me by leaving directly. You may follow your chum to the hostel on Greycoat Street."

"But," I objected, but Niall turned away and returned shortly with my money. With John gone I couldn't understand why Niall would throw me out, but there was no reasoning with him, so I packed. To get word to Annetta I wrote a note asking her to meet me at the King George at nine. When I turned in my key, I politely asked Niall to give her the note. He agreed, snatched the note from my hand and ushered me out the door.

Following Niall's directions, I found the Gayfere Hostel on Greycoat Street and checked in for a night. Beyond the price and requirement for a student ID, there was little similarity between the shelter and the hostel. The Gayfere's multiple floors opened on twelve-paned windows rather than stained glass, and they were clean enough to see through to the street. The gentleman who took my money was not particularly warm, but neither was he a caricature like Niall. Dormitory rooms filled with bunk beds were designated for boys or girls. I unpacked my bag on an empty bunk and took my jacket and novel along to look for dinner.

Over greasy fish and chips wrapped in newspaper and a heavy

smell of vinegar, I decided *The Innocents Abroad* was boring me and I couldn't finish it. After dinner I exchanged my book in the television room for a dog-eared paperback of *Don Quixote of La Mancha*. Like the discarded Twain, the new book had a scary-long table of contents. But this was a legitimate "great book"; I'd seen it on lists and syllabi. It had to say something important to still be published after three hundred and seventy years.

At ten minutes to nine, I put the book in my pack, grabbed my jacket and walked to the King George. With a pint of ale in hand, I watched a darts game. When I finished my drink, the clock behind the bar said nine-twenty. The bartender asked twice before I ordered another, understanding this was the price of keeping my stool. I became angry with Annetta for keeping me waiting. I wondered if she'd gotten caught up at dinner or had just turned her sparkling eyes on some new friend.

At ten o'clock I gulped the rest of my ale and walked angrily to St. Cyril's. From the dark street without a key, the door was impenetrable. A drizzle started, so I sheltered in a doorway across the street. I didn't want to impose on Annetta, and her shifting affections left me unsure whether I had imagined our connection. Maybe it was all in my head? I also didn't want to see Niall if I could help it, but I finally knocked and waited.

"I thought we'd settled up?" Niall growled, barely opening the door.

"Yes, we have, but I was supposed to meet Annetta. Do you know if she got my note?"

"Yes, yes, she read your note. Now you must be off."

He closed and latched the door. I stared at the ironwork on the heavy oak for a moment, then snapped to and walked off. I couldn't believe how quickly she dropped me after she'd felt so close. I returned to the Gayfere and found John in the television room.

"Hey, mate," he said. "Been out with our girl?"

I tried not to show disappointment. "No, I'm afraid she's moved on."

He looked up with eyebrows raised. "That's funny, she said you two were supposed to get together tonight."

"*After* you had dinner?"

"Yeah, mate, and that was two hours ago."

My anger turned to bewilderment, but the wet street in front of St. Cyril's and its impervious door meant I couldn't solve anything that night—or perhaps ever. Instead, I went to my room and packed for the morning. Two roommates joined me on their way to bed, so I turned out the light and lay staring into the darkness. I drifted to an uneasy sleep, wondering about Annetta.

In the morning the woman handing out the familiar breakfast gave me directions to the Cambridge motorway. I said goodbye to John, threw my pack onto my shoulders and, on my way to the underground, walked by St. Cyril's. From across the street I saw a piece of paper tacked to the door. I crossed and was shocked to see it addressed to me.

Dear Stephen,

Where have you gone? When I return from dinner, shelter was empty and Niall said you decide to leave. He was strange and said shelter would close in one more day but I could stay. He made last two others, girls from France, go to another place. This night I have slept in my clothes close to door and hear him play music loud and then soft. I am scared and wish you were here or I knew where you are. Very early I have ran out to the train station. I hope you are safe and will write at address I give you.

Your friend, Annetta

My legs gave out. I slumped against the wall, astounded and abashed. Then I hit my head with the palm of my hand, recalling the sound: Niall had latched the door! He had closed it in my face and threw the latch, but it wasn't midnight! Guests couldn't get in if the door was latched! I should have yelled through the doorway and demanded to see her. I was a villain to leave her with that psycho!

The note said she went to the train station, so I stood bolt upright, tightened my pack belt and strode to Victoria Station. Inside, I searched frantically but with no hope of success. I could picture those green eyes clearly but doubted I'd ever see them again. Niall had gotten rid of all of us except her. What a degenerate! I felt sick.

In an underground men's room, I brought my pack into a stall. I sat thinking I might throw up and that I'd deserve it. But beating myself up didn't make me feel better. Annetta was gone, and there was no way to set things right. I only hoped she'd get home safely.

Eventually emerging from the WC, I asked directions to the underground running toward Cambridge. A half-hour later I bid London a beaten farewell from a dirty, rattling subway car.

Chapter IV

Parkeston Quay

It was well into the morning, but the sun was hidden behind a carpet of clouds. I tied my sweatshirt around my waist, hoisted the pack and walked to find a spot wide enough for a car to stop. It's about time we got to this, I thought, leaning the pack against a tree and stretching my thumb. It was odd to hitchhike with my left hand.

One short ride got me into the countryside but then I didn't move for an hour, so I walked on with my thumb outstretched. I'd noticed how heavy the pack was on the trip from Michigan to New York, but the quick march to Victoria Station and an hour on the English road tired my legs more than I'd expected.

Noon church bells rang as I reached a cluster of small cottages. There were few people about, but the smell of baking filled the air. In a small shop a woman behind the counter cast a cautious glance at my pack, so I quickly bought bread and Cheshire cheese and found my way to a roadside park. Rows of lush purple and pink flowers against the grey sky made the scene look like a badly colorized film. I ate on a bench, wearing my sweatshirt against the dampness, and found the orange cheese sharp and crumbly. I pictured Annetta's green eyes and hoped she was safely on her flight to Turin. Would I ever see her again? I promised myself I'd write to her as soon as I had a return address.

After lunch I continued walking. Beyond town I rested the pack against an elm and applied myself to the art of hitchhiking. The trick was to focus on drivers who were alone; they were most likely to pick me up—for company. Anyway, unlike the cars in America, many of these were barely big enough for a driver, my pack and me.

An hour later I stood beneath the same tree. It seemed I was destined to become intimate with the local flora. This would make a riveting travelogue: the English byways, one tree at a time.

Through the bushes I could see big houses set back from the road. I wished there was a way to get some tea. I could knock on a back door and ask to fill my canteen but didn't want to take the chance of emptying it first. Besides, who knew what kind of reception I'd get appearing from nowhere with my backpack?

A long time later and maybe a mile up the road, a small white car pulled up. I smiled broadly and leaned toward the window.

"And where are we off to?" said a middle-aged man in a tweed jacket and awful plaid tie.

"Cambridge," I said, meaning that's where *I* was headed, while I had no idea where he was going, "though I'd be happy to go anywhere up the road." By this time, I'd given up the idea of stopping at Cambridge and then continuing on to Harwich. I hoped it would not always take so long to travel such short distances.

"I'll just get the boot," he said and jumped out. The pack fit— barely—and soon we were on the road.

Relieved to be sitting and moving, I turned to the driver. "I really appreciate this. I've tried to get a ride all day."

He looked at me closely. "I say, you're a Yank, aren't you?"

What was your first clue? I thought, looking at the Yankees cap in my lap, but I said cheerfully: "That's right."

"And you're going to Cambridge to visit friends?"

"Not really. Just passing through on my way to the ferry at Harwich."

We drove for twenty minutes discussing the driver's work as a civil engineer and British public opinion about President Carter deferring production of the neutron bomb. He then hesitated and lowered his voice. "Listen, I have a proposition for you. I'm a member of a club for old school chums called... well, you wouldn't know the name. But by the by, you see, we have a tradition that, on a fellow's birthday he must..." He paused and looked at me closely. "This may sound a bit daft, but we have this tradition, you see: on a fellow's birthday he must pull down his drawers at the club meeting and take a whack with a paddle from each other member."

I felt for the door handle, nodding reluctantly for him to continue.

"Well, and the only way to avoid this paddling at the meeting, which is rather ignominious, as you can imagine..."

No thank you, I thought.

"... is for the fellow to find a stranger that day to give him five whacks in return for five quid."

I didn't know whether to laugh or jump from the car. Instead I said: "And you want me..."

"Yes, yes, well, you needn't if you'd rather not, but I assumed that, well, hitchhiking and all, perhaps you could use the fiver? And it would do me a great service, don't you see; and anyway, we could pull off shortly to my office, and it wouldn't take but five minutes, and I'd put you right back on the road in a spot shipshape to catch a lift."

The man was heavier than my hundred and seventy pounds but pudgy and shorter than me. I was also twenty years younger than him and sure I could protect myself. Just then he turned on the windshield wipers, which brought home that I was sitting for the first time all day and I was dry.

He said he'd move me in the right direction, and five pounds was, like he said, five pounds, and would defray some of the cost of London. "Okay," I said, hoping I wasn't destined to start my adventure as a David Copperfield babe in the British woods. "Five pounds for five minutes and you leave me on the road to Cambridge."

"Brilliant!" he exclaimed. He soon pulled off an exit toward a small village.

He introduced himself as Trevor Leach and thanked me again. "You can imagine the ticklish wicket I was in," he complained. "I've been watching all the morning for a hitchhiker who might do."

"Ticklish" seemed a poor choice of words but I let it pass. We pulled into the lot behind an anonymous, two-story office building of white brick, and Trevor led the way through the back door. I was uneasy about leaving my pack in the car but decided it would be safe as long as I kept Trevor in sight. This proved easy, as he led me past an empty secretary's desk into an inner office devoid of people. The whole building seemed deserted.

He took a wooden paddle from where it hung on the wall and handed it to me. "You needn't put your back into it, mind you," he said. "Just five quick swats."

The fact that the paddle hung openly on his office wall suggested some bizarre credibility to his story, but I remained suspicious. I strained to listen for sounds in the building or from the car but heard only birds chirping. With the wooden paddle in hand, I felt sure I could beat Trevor senseless should things become strange. Then I had to laugh at myself for worrying things might *become* strange. A shudder came over me thinking what my father would say if he saw his son, the impoverished English major, paddling a British pansy.

Trevor turned away from me, lowered his pants, and pulled down his boxer shorts decorated with illustrations of horses. He bent over the desk. "Fire when ready," he said.

I looked around once more, wondering where a camera might be hidden. Stepping quickly up to Trevor, I grimaced for a moment at his expanse of blotchy rear end, slapped him five times lightly with the paddle, and stepped back, gripping the wooden handle so tightly my knuckles turned white.

He quickly straightened up and fastened his pants. He looked around with a knowing smile. "I say," he said, "that wasn't too bad, wot?"

I gripped the paddle until Trevor was ready to go, then laid it on a table and followed him out the back door. It was a relief to get outside. When Trevor handed me a five-pound note, I felt absolutely fortunate. I asked him to open the boot so I could get my camera. These Englishmen are truly queer, I thought, as I snapped a shot of Trevor and the white building. I still didn't know if I believed his story or if he was just a pervert or if maybe I should have wiped my fingerprints from the paddle, but true to his word he left me with a wave at a "jolly convenient entrance" to the motorway.

* * *

Another hour left me standing in the same spot, so I hoisted the pack and walked. When I was too tired to go on, I leaned the pack against yet another tree and tried various ways of shaking my thumb, but still couldn't get a ride. It was like *It Happened One Night* with no Claudette Colbert to stop a car by revealing a shapely leg.

Time dragged. I again shouldered the pack but felt a throbbing in my knees. After I had walked another couple of miles, finally, a lorry downshifted noisily and stopped.

"That rucksack looks a weight," the driver said, throwing open the passenger door. My savior had a ruddy, workingman's face and an understated smile. As I climbed up to the seat I also thought I saw something like a halo over his worn cap.

My seat was a cushion resting on a wooden crate. The driver geared up to speed and careened around curves in the narrow road. I held onto the door and watched small towns and patches of woods pass through the windshield like a sped-up film.

In the next town we stopped at a traffic signal across from a red brick building with high windows and a sign reading "Independent Order of Odd Fellows." I wondered if that might be Trevor's club, assuming he actually belonged to one.

To my great relief the driver was passing through Cambridge. This let me relax, while still holding on to the door to avoid sliding off the box. I appreciated the high vantage point but even more so the seat, be it ever so hard. The road was barely wide enough for vehicles to pass each other, but the driver seemed in control, and I was so grateful for the ride that I wasn't concerned.

Where I had learned to drive on Long Island, the demarcation between one town and the next was a line down the center of a busy road. Here you left one village and drove through fields and woods until you reached another, as in the English countryside of my imagination.

After several villages we reached a large town the driver told me was Cambridge. He left me with an affable salute and ground his gears pulling away. Things looked much like what I'd seen from the truck: neat little houses and shops clustered together. But I walked on and soon reached a number of university buildings. Blocks were walled in with gothic structures that must have housed students or classrooms, opening onto central courtyards. Many of the long blocks of stone buildings looked like the law school at Michigan, or *vice versa*, but here the limestone and ivy seemed ancient.

The flyers stapled on a kiosk looked familiar from a distance but up close were quite tame. There was a notice for the Oxford-Cambridge boat race on the Thames, which had been defaced, I assumed, following a disappointing result. I pondered a cryptic notice recruiting for "Gog Magog Molly," with no hint at what that might mean. There was nothing at all from the Socialist Workers or the militant lesbians or even the Hare Krishnas. "More Princeton than Ann Arbor," I scoffed out loud, as two young men with short hair and tweed jackets glanced my way and hurried through a stone archway.

Let's Go said the university, founded in 1209, comprised thirty-one colleges. This was a bit overwhelming and of less interest than the listing of a "backyard with running water" where I could spend the night. I wandered toward this address, asking directions from people on the street. At a tiny, whitewashed house decorated with too much gingerbread trim, Mrs. Peevy came to the door in a print housedress under an apron. She showed me to the "bit of grass" in her garden and said for a pound I could set up my tent and wash with the hose behind the garage.

As my first campsite, it wasn't very scenic, but the price was right and I couldn't wait to put down the pack. The orange tent came out for the first time. I unrolled it on a poncho laid as a ground cloth. I had bought the tent for thirty bucks before Pam and I went to Florida. The lack of a rainfly to keep out the dew assured a rude awakening if you sat up too quickly in the morning. Also, I recalled from Florida that there was no way to stake it down tight enough to stop it from sagging in the middle.

I tossed the sleeping bag through the flap and ducked in to unroll it. It felt great to stretch out. I'd brought along a steno pad as a place to sketch and record thoughts and pulled this out to write to Pam, as if it were a letter I'd mail and she'd bother to read. I fingered the little character stuffed in my pouch with my lucky peseta and wrote to her that Ubit and I had checked into the Grand Hotel in an English garden and we almost didn't know how to set it up without her.

A vision of Pam stretching her lithe form over a pool table stuck in my mind. Living with her had been like a dream. I loved sharing an ice cream cone with her over a game of pinball and got so distracted by the way she filled out her gym shorts when we played racquetball that I often lost track of the ball and she often beat me—or maybe she was just a better player. But as the weeks drew short, she came to resent me. "You mix up writing a novel with being its hero," she complained, not far off the mark. If only she could have lived in the present, our fantasy would have stretched to the end of my time in Ann Arbor.

It grew dark and I set the pad aside. The ghosts of Milton and Lord Byron lured me from repose toward the ancient campus. Outside the tent I unpacked a sweater and jacket. *Don Quixote* and I wandered back to the university buildings I'd passed on my way into town. I wanted to find a way into one of the great stone buildings but instead stopped in a shop along the street for fish and chips, this time wrapped in brown paper and served by a woman with a heavy Indian accent. As I sat at the counter, my left knee throbbed. It hurt enough that I gave up the idea of invading a college or finding a pub. Instead, I headed back to my tent by what I thought to be the quickest route, but which turned circuitous and left me exhausted.

Finally in the tent, I laid my flashlight on the sleeping bag and, by its ineffectual light, stuffed a pillowcase with my sweater and sweatshirt. The night was growing cool. I got into the bag and tried to read Cervantes but soon turned out the flashlight.

In the dark, I cataloged what I knew about *Don Quixote* from pictures and cartoons and one memorable X-rated film. My journey seemed to resemble the Don's. Everyone thought he should stay home and not wander about; my friends said I shouldn't go traveling without a companion, not to mention the hostel card and Eurail pass I couldn't afford. We both seemed to be tilting at windmills. Just as I couldn't remember how the Don's story ended, I had no idea how my story would end. This trifling literary analysis sent me quickly to sleep.

I awoke, tentatively, to pale orange light. Before moving I rolled my eyes toward my pack. After a long moment I remembered the English garden. Sitting up quickly, I hit the tent roof and cold water splashed down my back, jolting me wide-awake.

In my jeans and sneakers I stood outside the tent. Stiffness reached from my shoulders down my back. Stretching, I realized my knee still hurt. I leaned carefully into the tent to retrieve the canteen and the bread left from lunch. Walking around the garden while eating, I decided the great alumni of Cambridge would have to do without me, as I should continue on to the coast. I was eager to reach someplace more foreign than Britain, and hopefully sunnier, and was beginning to feel anxious about reaching Germany and getting set up with a job. In an hour I was on the road headed east to Harwich and the Holland ferry.

*   *   *

Hitchhiking proved easier than on my first day. Uneventful rides with a schoolteacher and in a plumber's van inched me forward without much walking on my sore leg. Small Essex towns and vegetable gardens flowed by a succession of car windows while I politely responded yes, I was American, and no, I hadn't visited England before.

By late afternoon I had covered the fifty or so miles to Harwich, one of the Haven ports on the North Sea. On a rough shale beach facing the bay, the air was cool and salty. An elderly gentleman with an enormous white mustache told me the ferry left each evening at six from Parkeston Quay, three kilometers up the coast.

A shop supplied a bottle of ale, apples and fresh bread to go with my cheese. I set out dinner on a bench facing an abandoned lighthouse over the water from on a small spit of land. Cervantes was a charming dinner guest.

I contemplated where to sleep. *Let's Go* didn't list anything in Harwich. Anyway, if I was going to sleep in my tent, I saw no reason to pay for the privilege. When the light had faded, I took my pack toward a small clump of trees and bushes between the shoreline and the footpath. I looked around to be sure no one could see me and then ducked under the trees. On a flat patch of grass surrounded by bushes and sheltered from streetlights, I quietly set up the tent, thinking this wouldn't be the last time I cursed its bright color. I pulled the pack in behind me and closed the flap. In my sleeping bag I fell back into the company of the Don.

In the morning I remembered the wet shock in store for me and sat up slowly. When I opened the flap, the chill and overcast sky made me glad to be leaving England. The only sound came from waves breaking against the sea wall. The sun was not yet far up in the sky, so it was too early for anyone to be about. I nonetheless listened carefully for sounds while I gathered my things. With the loaded pack on one shoulder I edged toward the path and froze again to listen. Still hearing nothing, I jumped down to the gravel path and nearly toppled over a little woman in a big overcoat!

She jumped back, startled but strangely quiet. A patchy-red hand went to her chest as she peered at me through pink-rimmed glasses. She seemed more curious than frightened. She was maybe sixty years old and no more than five feet tall. Her coat was drab gray and her hair was wrapped in a flowered scarf beneath a rain hat.

"And where have you descended from?" she asked, with no nonsense about her.

"Uh, New York," I said, turning my hands out in a shrug without shoulders.

"Aye, New York is it? And you near landed on top of me in Harwich?"

"Well, no," I stammered. "I mean, yes, I did almost land on you, and I apologize for startling you. You see, I came from America a week ago, but just now I was behind the bushes… sleeping in my tent." I immediately wanted to take back the part about sleeping in the park, but it was too late.

She looked closely from me to the shrubs and back to me again. "In *those* bushes?" she said, incredulous.

"Yes, ma'am. You see, I'm going to the ferry today and needed a place to sleep."

"Well, in all my years," she said and looked around me at my pack. "And you've a *tent* in there?"

"Something of a tent."

"And you're taking the ferry?"

"Ah, yes, if I can find it."

"And you don't know where the terminal is?"

"Well, a man told me it was..."

"Rubbish, a man told you; I'll show you to the station, and you'll take the train to Parkeston Quay."

The lady walked with me the few blocks to the train station, chattering the whole way. She said to wait outside while she made inquiries and then came back, distressed. "Well," she said, "there's no train for an hour, so you may as well walk. I'll tell you what: I'll show you to a path I used to take with my sisters, Sadie and Rebecca."

"That'd be too kind."

"Kind? Oh, nothing of the sort. I'll show you; you just come along with me." She started back the way we'd come but stopped short and I almost walked into her.

"Wait, now," she said, pursing her lips. "That's no good. The path along the river... let's see. Yes, I'll have to show you the way."

"Oh, please, don't go to any trouble."

"Trouble? Oh, dear no, no trouble at all. But we'll stop while I change to walking shoes. Yes, we'll stop," she said and paused, "and you'll do with a spot of tea after a night on the sea wall."

Mrs. Maple led the way to a cottage on a sleepy street. I wiped my feet but worried I'd still leave tracks on the rug. I parked the pack carefully so as not to knock over a ballerina figurine on a spindly table. The frilly curtains and lace doilies said grandmother's house, as did the faint smell of dried flowers and cleaning fluid. She offered a wash-up, at which I jumped, and the hot running water was restorative.

Soon we sat in the front parlor. She set out tea and sweet biscuits. A large tabby cat rubbed against my leg, and Mrs. Maple talked while I ate.

Her father ran a factory at "the Navyard" across the bay until hard times forced it to close. Her eyes brightened and she sat up straight, one hand at her breast, recalling running with her sisters through the woods across from the factory. But she stooped as she recalled that the war had ended, and then there was no work, and everyone went on the dole, though she got by all right with her pension from when she was a teacher and in the house her father had left her.

As soon as I finished my tea (and all the biscuits in the house), Mrs. Maple led me outside, but before she closed the door behind us the cat slipped out.

"Oh, Kitty," she complained. "Oh, this won't do."

"Does she need to stay in the house?"

"Yes, she does, naughty Kitty. She'll be into all manner of trouble."

I took off my pack and leaned it on the fence. Mrs. Maple had followed the cat to the end of the porch, where it hid behind a pile of sacks. I walked around the porch and lifted the docile escapee from behind. The cat hung in my hands and hardly seemed capable of causing trouble. Still, Mrs. Maple was visibly relieved and opened the door, so I could deposit the cat inside.

With the door closed again, I pointed to the sacks of what looked like peat moss. "Mrs. Maple," I said, "can I move those bags for you?"

"Oh, what, those? Oh, no. I've a wheelbarrow and they only need to go round back to the garden." She motioned for me to lift my pack.

"You'll not be lifting those bags," I said and bent to pick one up.

"Oh, you'll injure…" she started to say, but stopped when she saw me holding the bag without much effort. There were three sacks weighing maybe forty pounds each, a good deal less than my pack. They were only hard to lift because they'd gotten wet stacked at the edge of the porch.

"Where do they go?" I asked, and she reluctantly showed me to a shed. In a few minutes I moved the sacks, she secured the shed door and then she led the way across the village and onto a wooded path.

Once we were walking, she kept up a brisk pace and a monologue over her shoulder. She touched on trees and birds but mostly on stories, more or less in sequence looping back to her sisters in summer dresses and pigtails, running the path and laughing, "Da" in charge across the bay where they trained the lads, and how hard times had changed everything.

She didn't hear me ask the fate of her sisters or what the factory had produced, so I simply said, "Yes" and "I see," and smiled whenever she looked back. Her stories of sailors training at the yard painted a vivid image of a bustling home front. Horrific as it was, World War II had been noble and necessary; it had inspired sacrifice and common dedication. I envied the people who fought a "Good War." The war that cost me a long life with my brother wasn't officially even a "war," just a police action to hold the devil communists at bay. I wondered how Edward would have contrasted his war to the one our father fought, and I lamented that I would never hear the truth about his time in Vietnam. I also guessed that, if I had been sent to war, that would have cured me of yearning to seek adventure.

Mrs. Maple again stopped short and snapped my attention back to the trail and not running her over. Then she scampered forward again, saying something about the factory, and I concentrated on keeping up. The little lady hiked at quite a pace, considering she was tiny, pretty old, and never stopped talking. On a dirt path in the woods, we walked faster than my comfortable speed on even ground, and my knee still didn't feel right.

She paused in walking for a welcome moment. "Do you know the saddest place I've ever seen?"

By this, the third time she'd asked, indeed I knew, but I also knew the question was rhetorical. I shook my head no.

"India," she went on, resuming her pace. "It was so sad. The people were all very poor; they didn't have enough to eat. Did you know the British army used to be there? The military men would pay the people to do their washing up and cooking and so forth. What they paid wasn't anything to the soldiers, but it was enough for the people to get by on. And now the British army is gone, and the people have nothing."

This was funny and sad. Granted, when Mrs. Maple was young, Britain had ruled the waves and India, but how could she believe the Indian people had been better off occupied by a foreign power?

After a quick mile on the trail, I was winded. Embarrassed to ask Mrs. Maple to slow down, I instead suggested taking her picture. She was timid about posing but I sensed a flattered blush on her chalky complexion. I lowered my pack against a tree and took my time finding the camera. She posed at the edge of the path where I could include her father's old factory in the background. She paused her stories for one toothless smile.

Barely waiting for me to lift the pack, she was off again. This time we started with the naval facility, which was closed now because of the economy, but one day when she was young it was quite grand, and she and her sisters....

Did Mrs. Maple have any place in the present? She was steeped in another age, with no one to talk to but the cat. Still, she had extraordinary energy. It seemed unfair she should live out her life in this lonely way. She was Billy Pilgrim in *Slaughterhouse Five*, living all the moments of her life simultaneously, or hopefully only the good moments. While she resided with her cat in a prim, little house in a moribund village, she was also a young girl running and laughing with her sisters across from her father's factory.

The prominence of World War II in her perception of the present day made me think about my father. I always attributed his inability to come to grips with Vietnam to a myopic focus on history thirty years gone. But it seemed he was not alone in this and it might be partly my own narrow perception that prevented us from finding common ground about war.

At a break in the woods, Mrs. Maple pointed across a field to a large terminal. She walked to where the path ended at a road. "This is where I leave you," she said abruptly. "I must get back to my Kitty." She seemed like a fairy-tale creature of the woods, who couldn't set foot on the man-made road.

I swung the pack down and leaned it against my hip. "Mrs. Maple, I don't know how to thank you."

"Oh tut, tut," she said, eyes flitting back to the path. "The walk made me feel like a girl again. Now you run along and mind: eat your vegetables."

She turned to go, and I half reached out to her. She paused, waiting for me to speak. But she clearly wanted to get back to hiking pace, so I just waved, and she strode off, saluting over her shoulder. I imagined she had started again the story about the factory and her sisters. I watched her fade into the woods, thinking she'd do as a character in the Beatles' "Penny Lane," along with the barber, the banker and the fireman.

Once more beneath my pack, I started along the narrow road at the slowest pace of the day. The road skirted a field and a quarter mile away passed an unadorned building three stories high, clad in beige metal panels. There were no other buildings and no vehicles or people to be seen. More to the point, there was no boat. Given my early start and the quick march along the coast, I reckoned the ferry wouldn't leave for hours and wondered if I should have brought a watch, but that would have smacked of timetables and betrayed the rules of rambling Edward and I had agreed were required of a true adventure.

As I walked toward the building, a lone figure came into view sitting against its nearest wall. I made out sunglasses and long hair beneath a floppy hat. Must be American, I thought; what use would a Britisher have for sunglasses?

He leaned back in exaggerated ease by a backpack as big as mine. He was also dressed like me. A long weed hung from his mouth. Nice touch, I thought; very Huck Finn. When I was about to pass by, he nodded.

I paused and said: "Want some cheese?"

He raised his eyebrows above the glasses. "Yeah. You want some hash?"

Chapter V

Windmills

Bruce from Montana was twenty, fit and utterly at ease on the road. In slow American diction, with no regional accent I could place, he said the ferry wouldn't take on passengers for hours, and so we decided to pass the time in the woods. We hid our packs behind the ferry building and walked across the near field to where Mrs. Maple had spirited away.

Barely into the trees, Bruce sat upon a stump and waved me to a nearby log. He took from his pocket a ball of foil. With a pocketknife he sliced flakes from a black chunk into a small metal pipe. Lighting the bowl, he breathed in slowly and then offered it to me.

As I inhaled, the embers glowed beneath my nose. I exhaled and was suddenly dizzy. I held onto a tree to regain balance, and then sat beside Bruce and we passed the pipe until the hashish was done.

When I stood again, the blood rushed through my limbs. Stretching my shoulders and neck, I noticed how sunlight stabbed through the branches. The trees swayed with a breeze, opening up intricate patterns of light that shifted by the moment. I wobbled a bit looking up and again steadied myself against a tree. As my head stopped spinning, I heard a far-off, pleasing sound and then recognized it as Bruce laughing.

I joined his laughter, hearty and full, and felt a great release. I didn't know what was funny but that hardly mattered. More important was the aberrant English sunshine, which lifted the weight of struggling for rides under overcast skies.

Bruce stepped beside a tree to relieve himself and I stared at the silver buckle on the back of his hat. *Don Q* was in my head and I was all at once gripped with a sense of the quest delayed. This stoic lad must be none other than "Montana Bruce," who would open the portal to never-before-imagined exploits. Upon Bruce's return, I cleared my throat and formally introduced myself as "Stephen Kylemore, knight errant."

He chuckled and responded: "Afghan hash can take some getting used to."

We walked back to the field, sharing road stories. Suddenly a soccer ball bounced toward Bruce and he trapped it deftly with his foot. I broke for a pass. He kicked the ball to me and I turned, hearing the roar of the crowd. Ten yards away I faced three young girls in plaid skirts and purple school sweaters. They laughed and slapped their knees and yelled for me to kick the ball.

The cagey Brazilian fullbacks blocked my way to the World Cup golden goal. The crowd chanted in some vaguely South American language. I feinted and dodged, stepped on the ball, and fell, ingloriously, on my rear end. The girls laughed so hard two of them fell over. Bruce picked up my cap from the ground and handed it to me. "I hate the Yankees," he said with deep conviction.

Two more girls joined us, facing Bruce and me with a wall of freckles and bangs. Between giggles the girls asked earnestly about our travels and our homes. Their ebullience was infectious. After a few minutes, we moved noisily as a group toward the terminal until a far-off voice called and the girls turned to run, laughing and blowing farewell kisses. The last to leave had curly brown hair and a pixyish smile. She picked up the ball, curtsied, blushed and then chased after the rest. Bruce and I watched them disappear over the field and shared a smile.

Back at the terminal we sat to a lunch of cheese and bread from my pack and wild onions Bruce had as a parting gift from a friend. It was something like an omelet without the eggs.

"Only an onion, some cheese and a crust of bread," I said, half-jokingly, referring to *Don Quixote*: "the sustenance of emprise."

"Yeah, dude; tastes good," Bruce said with his mouth full. After he swallowed, he added: "So where're you off to?"

It was refreshing to speak with someone interested in where I was going rather than where I'd been. "I have a notion," I said, "of tossing a stick in the air and going the way it points."

He grinned, clearly thinking I was nuts.

"Of course," I continued, "I also have to make it to Germany to start a job before the money runs out."

"Well, it wouldn't be an adventure if you had money."

"That's what I've always read," I said, encouraged to find a sympathetic soul.

"So what's the job?" he asked.

"I don't really know yet."

"You have a job in Germany, but you don't know what it is?" he said, grinning skeptically.

"Oh, I know I'll have work doing something. An old boss, this really good guy: he comes from Germany, and he said he'd fix me up with one of his relatives while he was over for vacation."

"So you'll…"

"I don't know: work on cars, clear tables, dig ditches. Doesn't matter as long as he finds me a place to stay and I can save up some money."

He nodded in appreciation of this plan. "Me," he said, "I came over for three weeks for a break and to see some people. I'm gonna crash in Amsterdam overnight and get a flight home. I didn't have much money either, but I brought some Window Pane and traded it for a place to stay and the hash."

"You carried LSD through customs?"

"It was easy, a hundred hits on a little piece of paper. Cost me two months' pay at the filling station."

Bruce leaned back and pulled his hat over his eyes, letting out a loud belch. I appreciated this compliment to lunch but was concerned about the drug smuggling. I wasn't sure what to do so, as usual, sought insight in literature. The caterpillar's hookah hadn't reflected badly on Alice. The Count of Monte Cristo believed hashish both medicinal and edifying. Natty Bumppo would have smoked anything offered in a peace pipe, as a matter of courtesy.

There was, however, the minor concern about landing in a Dutch jail. "You've only got that small chunk left, right?" I asked.

"Huh," said Bruce, seeming to have been awakened. "Yeah, left-right: that's it. Something happens, I eat it."

I saw myself in *Midnight Express*, scratching out a letter from prison: "Dear Mom and Dad, as you can see from my return address...."

With time left before we could purchase tickets, I suggested we toss the Frisbee. His face brightened. We spread a good distance apart on the field. He threw with strength and ease, which allowed me to catch and throw in fluid motion. It felt great to stretch out in the warmth of the sun. The spinning white and blue of the disk blended into the sky and cotton-like clouds. I hurled a discus on a Thessalian plain, my prowess with this distinctly American equipment earning me back some respect after my embarrassment at the World Cup.

* * *

Eventually, there was activity at the terminal. We retrieved our packs and purchased two of the cheapest tickets, which nearly depleted my pounds.

The ferry had five public decks above a level for cars. We walked through several lounges. Bruce kept trying doors until he found an unlocked closet by a stairway.

"Here we go," he said, swinging his pack to the ground and lifting it through the doorway. "We can leave this stuff here. Just take your passport."

I followed his example but also took my camera and *Don Quixote*. He jammed the closet door shut, and we found seats in a lounge. I pulled out my book and read, then soon looked up and smiled. "Hence commences the *viglia*," I said, looking at the book for pronunciation.

"The what?" said Bruce.

"The *viglia*: the ceremony of watching over our arms before we're knighted."

He apparently had tired of my knight-errantry shtick and said he'd go look around. I laughed at how easily I had let down my guard and shared my inner literature with Bruce. I generally worried that people would think my enthusiasm for fiction showed an insufficient grasp on reality. But Bruce and I were the same in a lot of ways, intersecting for one day, and there was no reason to hide my true nature from him.

Back in the book a goatherd told a story to the hapless Don, who apologized for repeatedly interrupting to praise the story and the charm of the storytelling. "May the Lord's grace never fail me," the goatherd replied. "That is all that matters."

*   *   *

When the ship left the terminal for the North Sea, I moved to a window and watched the coast fade from view. There were no white cliffs, like in old English movies, and no ethereal heroine throwing herself onto jagged rocks. The dock and then the bay faded into a regular shoreline. While I could still make out certain hilltops, Bruce returned with a thin, dark-skinned boy dressed in slacks and a dingy button-down shirt.

Bruce introduced him as "Miguel," and I shook his thin hand. "Miguel's from Spain," Bruce said. "His English isn't good but he's gonna buy some wine at duty free, and then we'll find a place to party."

Miguel laughed eagerly. A wild light in his eyes made me wary and I turned to Bruce. "You don't mean..."

"Sure," Bruce interrupted. "We can find someplace no one'll smell it."

Adding a Spanish partner fit with the Cervantes theme and, true to his bargain, Miguel bought a liter of Italian red wine and proudly contributed a bag of pistachio nuts. The three of us then hunted for somewhere our smoking wouldn't be noticed.

Guards patrolled the garage-level. We searched all five passenger-levels but found solitude only on open decks, where steady winds whipped the night air.

We continued to wander the levels to the highest public deck, below only the bridge and its uniformed sailors. "It's too bad we can't do it right here," Bruce said. "Nobody's watching and the wind'd take the smoke."

I felt mostly relieved that we wouldn't be taking any risks, and contemplated returning to my novel or looking for food. "It's no use," I said to conclude the matter. They frowned and shook their heads.

Hoping to placate them, I nodded above the rail. "The only private place on this whole ferry is in a lifeboat," I laughed.

Miguel cocked his head like a rooster. I immediately sensed my blunder. Bruce quickly stepped back to the rail with the lifeboat suspended above it and the sea far below. He looked both ways along the deck and then stood on his toes to glance under the canvas cover of the boat. When he turned back to us, he held the rail behind him with both hands. He looked at us cautiously and then said with a wide grin: "It's perfect."

"*Si*," Miguel said, "*perfecto!*"

"No, no, wait," I said. "We can't do that. Those boats are for emergencies."

Bruce looked at Miguel, who shook his head and said somberly: "*Emergencia.*"

"But how do we know it's secure?" I reasoned.

"They're lifeboats, dude," Bruce scoffed. "What's safer than that?"

I winced and stepped back. Bruce peered through the door to the lounge and waved Miguel to the rail. Without hesitation Miguel stepped up on the rail, scampered over the side of the boat and disappeared under the canvas. The lifeboat rocked on the large mechanical arms holding it over the sea, then steadied. I was stunned, and scared. What if someone fell? They'd never find the body.

Bruce continued to watch through the door and then waved at me. I froze. He looked again and waved his arm urgently. I took a breath, stepped up on the rail and followed Miguel into the boat. In a moment Bruce scurried after us.

My heart was racing. I took deep breaths to quiet the pounding. The boat rocked with our movements, but we settled in and soon swayed with the roll of the ship. Miguel pulled back the canvas at its outside edge. We could hear waves far below and see the dazzling night sky above.

The stars cast enough light for us to see Miguel unscrew the wine bottle and rub the mouth on his sleeve. With great flourish, he bowed his head and offered the bottle first to me. "Is good," he said.

I took a swallow. It *was* good. When I handed the bottle to Bruce, I left off the bow, given that he had tired of traveling with Don Quixote. He took it with a smile and tipped it back; several gulps rolled visibly down his throat.

Bruce busied himself with his knife and pipe while Miguel and I passed the bottle and he gave us the Spanish names for constellations. Soon we sat back and passed the pipe. Staring at the glowing bowl before my nose for the second time that day, I lost any sense of danger. I felt like a babe rocking beneath a resplendent mobile. These were by far the best accommodations on the ferry: legroom and privacy, a skylight view, in-cabin service.

Bruce gazed at the stars and said: "One day a friend of mine came back from a trip to England with his family. He said he'd met a lot of kids who were cool and liked to party but all they could get was hash. He said he wished he'd had some pills or mushrooms or anything and he could've made a bundle. So I saved up, didn't spend money on beer or nothin', and brought all the acid I could to England."

Bruce grinned at Miguel, who shrugged his shoulders, clearly understanding none of this but applauding Bruce's enjoyment in the telling. When Bruce returned to the pipe, Miguel cleared his throat, apparently deciding he too should tell a story. In halting English, fast Spanish and universal grunting and gestures, he got across that he had won the day with the daughter of the mayor of Sabadell, a small city near Barcelona, but in the end had to jump from her window to avoid her father. I couldn't understand much more of the story, but his mention of Barcelona made me think of the character from Edward's novel: Stephen Maturin, the destitute physician, natural scientist and naval surgeon. I had read three more books in this series and came to think of the two main characters as kindred spirits.

"He's both Irish and Catalan," Edward had written about Stephen, "so he mixes facility with beer *and* wine, with also being good-looking in two languages!" I imagined Edward and I toasting Patrick O'Brian in Catalonia. On one hand it was hard to imagine him letting me climb into a lifeboat to get high, but on the other he'd certainly applaud the audacity.

When Miguel finished, we all laughed and Bruce slapped his shoulder. Then we fell quiet. I listened to the waves against the ferry and remembered how Edward and I had watched *The Longest Day* every time it came on television. He declared it the best war movie of all time, so I accepted this as critical fact. I pictured the American soldiers crouching in a landing craft off Normandy. I saw myself as Robert Wagner, bit player in a great—and a good—war.

Edward loved World War II movies, and so I did too. When he had to choose a foreign language to study in school he chose German, so he could understand the soldiers in these movies. That was a good enough reason for me, too, and I also tried to learn the language, although translating simple movie lines marked the peak of my proficiency.

We sat in the boat until the moon rose. Now and then one of us would pull at the bottle or set another match to the pipe. Bruce saw me smiling and laughed.

I reached for the bottle and toasted: "We finally dip our hands to the elbows in the noble game!" I could see him roll his eyes, even in the dim light.

When we finished the wine, Miguel motioned that we should rejoin our fellow passengers. Bruce agreed and knelt to peer under the tarpaulin at shipside. I pulled the tarp back into place on the waterside and felt my heart begin to race again.

But we disembarked, unobserved, from our vessel within the vessel. Most passengers were sleeping. Miguel bid farewell with profuse handshakes and thanks. Bruce and I retrieved our packs from the closet and looked for a place to lay our sleeping bags.

The lounges were crowded, so I suggested sleeping out on the deck to get the full North Sea experience. Bruce saw no point in seeking out "experience" for its own sake but agreed the open deck might be the only place to stretch out. We found a cul-de-sac beneath an overhang on a middle deck. Laying our bags in front of our packs for security, we bedded down on the hard deck. I tucked the camera into my sleeping bag along with my pouch.

Barely had Bruce said goodnight before he was snoring. Although I was exhausted, the spinning in my head wouldn't let me sleep. It was hard to believe I'd spent the previous night on the Harwich sea wall; so much had happened since then. For a few minutes I read by flashlight. Don Quixote explained to Sancho Panza that, in the best manner of romantic literature, he imagined an ordinary handmaid to be the princess Dulcinea, so he could prove himself as a courtly lover. I could easily see Pam as a fanciful princess but doubted I'd get another chance to prove myself to her as a lover, courtly or otherwise.

My eyes tired of reading in the poor light, so I watched solitary figures emerge from the dark deck into the light from the door. It looked like an abstract film noir, appropriate to the black and white film I had loaded. I opened the camera and set the shutter at its lowest speed. Leaning on both elbows, I held the shutter button for several slow heartbeats. The rhythm of the shutter joined the roll of the ferry to lull me to the edge of sleep.

Withdrawing into my bag, I thought about Don Quixote's vision of Dulcinea and his belief that a loveless knight-errant was like a tree without leaves or fruit. I felt bereft of leaves and fruit myself, left with only dreams of Annetta's pouty lips and Pam's strong, slender shoulders.

I awoke to choppy seas and the taste of stale wine. The sun was up but hidden behind clouds. Bruce's sleeping bag was tied to his pack but there was no sign of him. I got to my feet. The ferry rolled, and I reached out and held tight to the rail. Closing my eyes, I pressed fingers against the throbbing in my head, wondering when I would learn to get up slowly in the morning and maybe not drink so much wine. I looked around and saw Bruce by the doorway, grinning. "An hour off Hoek Van Holland," he said with unseemly good cheer. "Time for breakfast."

This reminded me we'd eaten only pistachios the night before, which might have contributed to my headache.

We went into a lounge. Bruce laid the coins in his pocket onto a table. I emptied my pouch as well and then grimaced, embarrassed.

"What is… we won't be able to pass this," he said, holding up my lucky peseta.

"Yeah, I know," I said sheepishly. "It's from Catalonia, something I carry to remember my brother. I took back the coin and snatched Ubit off the table and shoved them both into my pouch. Bruce grinned but gallantly did not ask me to explain the stuffed animal.

We pooled our British coins and bought hard rolls and bowls of coffee, to which we added lots of milk. At our breakfast table I asked: "So what do you do when we land?"

"I'm gonna spend the night at an old circus tent on the outskirts of Amsterdam; they give you an air mattress real cheap. Lots of kids. It's a party."

"Sounds uncomfortable."

"You have a better idea?"

"Well, there are listings in *Let's Go: Europe*."

"Oh, dude, don't tell me."

"What do you mean?"

"Well, first off, you gotta trash that book; it's for tourists."

"And we are?"

"I thought we were knight-errants," Bruce laughed.

"That's 'knights-errant'," I said, feeling ridiculous in the light of day.

"Right," said Bruce. "Either way, we're not college girls on vacations bought by daddy."

"Yeah, but how do you find places to sleep?"

"You ask around. You hear." Bruce lifted his pack to his shoulder. "And you don't stay in *youth hostels*." He said the term the way my father used to say "cod liver oil" in stories of the Great Depression.

"Listen," Bruce went on, "you travel by Eurail; you see train stations. You stay in hostels; you meet Americans who can't take care of themselves. No guidebook'll tell you to party in a lifeboat."

He sounded like he knew how to get by on the road, but I still wanted a bed. I changed only twenty dollars to guilders because I didn't plan to stay in Holland but agreed to travel with Bruce to Amsterdam and then figure it out. By then the ship was approaching shore. Bruce said we should get ahead of the crowd to look for a ride from the passengers. We hurried up to the ramp and were among the first to disembark. On shore I followed Bruce to the road to Amsterdam. Still beneath his pack, he stuck out his thumb and snagged the first car off the ferry.

Bruce and I rode in the back seat. The prim British couple had not picked up a hitchhiker in twenty years, they said, quite giddy, but the bird-like wife recognized us from the boat. Bruce and I grinned at each other, wondering that the good lady could have seen *the two of us* on board and still wanted to pick us up. The woman asked a few polite questions and then fell silent. We sat back and enjoyed the flat green fields laced with colorful flowers. The lonely wooden windmills each seemed a perfect setting for a story of blond children in wooden shoes.

*   *   *

We reached Amsterdam in early morning. Golden sunlight colored narrow gabled houses. Shopkeepers swept sidewalks and watered brilliantly colored tulips. Robust women with rolled-up sleeves scrubbed floors and aired linens. Pretty women with blond hair tied back chatted on street corners, holding groceries and their children, or rode upright on bicycles. I could see Pam in this setting; she had the posture to ride one of those bikes.

The city was laced with stone-lined canals. Not the place to be when a storm blows in from the sea, I thought. Bruce and I wandered over several low pedestrian bridges, vaguely toward the city center. On one bridge he grabbed my arm. "Canal theater," he said, pointing.

A barge was tied up, or not, in the canal below us. It was covered with bright splashes of paint and crowded, among other things, with potted plants, a child's pinwheel, a large naked baby doll, and an overstuffed couch beneath an umbrella. On board a man with wild gray hair and a long beard wore the top of a sweat suit but no pants. The barge drifted away from the bank and three bungling police officers struggled to secure one end or the other. The man jumped from stem to stern, waving a long oar—the valiant captain defending his vessel. People stopped to watch and snap pictures.

This encounter called for a knight-errant response. The man was clearly about an adventure, almost literally tilting at windmills. Still, I hid behind reality and remained a spectator.

"I'm glad we finished the hash last night," I said. "The city is so clear in the bright morning."

Bruce leaned close and spoke quietly: "Listen, about that; I didn't want you to know, in case they found it, but I've got a shitload of hash going back."

I gulped, the recklessness of the lifeboat incident suddenly magnified. But the crossing was done, and I marveled at Bruce's savvy at import-export, so far at least.

The police finally wrestled the old man off the barge, though he kept shouting in what must have been Dutch and thrashing like a landed barracuda. They left the woman with similar wild gray hair but fully clothed in command of the barge and piled the man into a police van.

"Man, I gotta find a bed and a shower," I said.

He gripped my shoulder. "So this is it then, dude," he said. "Be cool."

"Right, and... good luck with everything."

We shook hands, thumbs up, and took opposite directions along the canal.

*   *   *

I longed to be clean for the first time since London. Thinking of

St. Cyril's poor excuse for a shower brought back Annetta and I realized the intrigue had started before I met Montana Bruce. Picturing Annetta in a flowing brocade gown, I wondered if I should confer upon her a chivalrous name but concluded I couldn't improve on hers.

The morning was fresh. I sat by a canal and watched the water ripple against barges. Eventually, I fished *Let's Go* out of my pack. I don't care what Bruce says, I thought, I don't speak Dutch and I need a shower! There was a listing for six-and-a-half guilders a night at a "Christian" student shelter near the Nieumarkt. I found my way across bridges and along tiny streets to the shelter. Pausing at the entrance, I thought about how Mom always said when one door shuts, another opens.

A large, serious man at the reception desk asked for my "card." I handed him my student ID. He looked at me as if I were simple. I let loose a quiet stream of being sorry, not knowing I'd need a hostel card, having a student ID, wishing I could stay, just for one night....

Still overly serious, he cleared his throat and said I was *quite* welcome to stay the night. He also soberly explained this was a *Christian* shelter, but all were welcome, and the curfew was midnight. I paid the money and took the best five-minute, lukewarm, shoulder-high shower of my life. Afterward I dressed, except for sneakers, and lay back to read. The bunk bed felt soft after a night on the ferry deck.

The Don had survived another battering adventure and Sancho suggested it was time for bed. "Sleep," said the Don, "you who were born to sleep, or do what you please, for I will do what I think becomes my profession." I had to see about finding Grettstadt, as I was anxious to start my job. But for the moment I was in a fabled city and, though my body said rest, I got off the comfortable bed to have a look around.

On my way out the door, I met the large man. Something disturbed me about his bushy eyebrows and the way he said the free tea and biscuits would be served at four-thirty, "right before prayers." I had thought of afternoon tea as something distinctly British and wondered about the man's nationality. At any rate, I'd be on time for a free meal and take my religion on the side.

Let's Go said the Anne Frank house was nearby but there was an admission fee and I barely had enough guilders for a meal. Instead of exploring history, I wandered through the Dam, a kind of city center teeming with tourists and thin, swarthy men selling drugs. I must have looked like an easy mark, as a dozen dealers called to me.

I photographed sunlit tulips by the canals, taking great care with composition. The flowers were all shades of red and yellow and purple, but I forgot my black-and-white film wouldn't record the brilliant colors. I saw Oz but shot Kansas.

In the city center, shop windows displayed marvelous chocolates, but I bought only three bananas from a cart to carry me through to tea.

Well before time I found a seat in the shelter dining room. I brought *Let's Go* with the intention of cutting it down to travel size while I waited. I decided to rip out and save only those sections I'd need, to reduce what I had to carry and avoid embarrassment when people recognized the orange cover. I leafed through the sections on Germany, then Switzerland, Italy, Yugoslavia and Greece. This traced my crystalizing plan: make money in Germany, get a train pass and wander through Italy, find Mom's relatives in Yugoslavia, and winter in the Aegean. With two piles of pages, one to keep and one to discard, I reconsidered, recalling Bruce's sneer and imagining what Edward would do and then decided to abandon the whole book. I left all the sections on a card table stacked with religious leaflets, feeling I had done a public service by diluting the propaganda.

At that moment the large man opened a pass-through from the kitchen and he and a young woman set out plates and toast. I was second in line and limited myself to twice as much toast as the boy before me. In a far corner of the dining room, I ate quickly, and was rising for seconds when the young woman began to speak in what sounded like Dutch, then English, then German. She said she would lead grace in Dutch since the Dutch were our hosts. Reverend Graaf, the large man to whom she gestured, then would give a talk in English because many of the guests understood that language.

It was the moment to act, as I felt targeted by the "understood

English" comment. I decided it best not to pass under the reverend's lectern for a second helping of toast. Instead, I slipped quietly out the door, prepared to answer in German if anyone spoke to me and feeling Reverend Graaf's glare on my back.

In the bunkroom I grabbed my pad. Outside, I drifted on golden sunlight highlighting gabled façades on beautiful seven and eight-story houses along the canals. It made sense many of the front doors were up a flight of stairs from the sidewalk, given how close Holland was to sea level and the waterways that laced through the city.

Although the tea was billed as coming with prayers, I was annoyed at being preached at when I all I wanted was food. The juxtaposition of "pray" and "prey" popped into my head. At home I had my fill of debating the Hare Krishnas and Moonies, who hovered on the periphery wherever young people gathered. They all had the same vacuous look and yet they were predators, teaming up on the weak ones who strayed from the herd.

Sitting by a bridge I sketched barges and jotted notes, thinking this all might someday be source material for a novel. I was sure, at least, that whatever lay ahead would develop the story, and the stark differences between England and Holland made me curious to see Germany. At any rate I needed to find Victor and make sure my trip wouldn't be cut short.

Later, I looked for an inexpensive meal. The toast and tea had barely taken the edge off my appetite. I found a half-underground café on Armsteeg called "The Last Water Hole," where my remaining guilder bought a "hamburger sandwich" and a beer. The bar was basic and the jukebox selections good. Then came the band Old Tennis Shoes, playing before a Rebel battle flag. The singer was Dutch and had only an approximate facility with the English lyrics, but the drummer was good, and the guitarist carried the music on his authentically beat-up Telecaster.

Behind the bar a sign said in English and four other languages: "No Dealing, No Hard Drugs." I imagined an opium den in Sax Rohmer's *Dope*, one of the novels I bought on the street in Ann Arbor and assumed no one else had read in the last thirty years. Beneath a separate service window, the handwritten sign read: "Hash Cookies."

The food arrived, and I focused on my first hot meal since fish and chips in Cambridge. Everything was expensive but I had enough cash for one more beer and, as a veteran of the hospitality industry, I had to leave my small change on the table.

* * *

At dusk the city transformed. The crowds thinned, and I was stunned to see curtains drawn back at street level to reveal ladies of the night sitting in windows lining the narrow lanes. There were prostitutes in New York City but they walked the streets rather than displaying themselves in windows. These women were captivating, for their sad eyes and bored expressions more than their cheap lingerie and what it revealed. When any of them looked up, I was embarrassed and walked quickly on. It saddened me I couldn't see through the makeup to the scrubbed faces of my morning arrival in Amsterdam.

I returned to the shelter before eleven o'clock. This apparently encouraged the reverend, now sweeping the floor, to believe I might yet be saved. But I sidestepped the seraphic man with a nod and went upstairs. The lights were out and the bunkroom full of sleeping sounds. I found the cloth bag with my toiletries and walked down the hall. It felt civilized to wash and brush my teeth before bed.

Next morning the bunkroom was sunlit and deserted except for an undernourished boy wearing his pants pulled up too high and thick glasses. He seemed to be talking to himself, but then, without looking at me, said in a manner apparently directed at me: "You're not at the prayer meeting."

I tried to intimidate him with a stare.

"Would you like someone to go to breakfast prayers with?" he persisted. His skin was pockmarked, and he gave off a faint medicinal smell—or maybe it was brimstone.

I cringed at having to eat with someone who ended questions with prepositions but saw no way to avoid it. "I see you speak English," I said euphemistically.

"Yes, and I'm going down to breakfast now. It's free, you know."

"Free" seemed an interesting characterization. The young man rose and hovered. I wanted breakfast but not with my new buddy. I pretended I'd follow him to the dining room until he spun on his heal and marched out of the bunkroom, then I turned back, grabbed my kit and escaped through another door to the bathroom.

Later, I sat blissfully alone with coffee and rolls, butter and jam. However, my new friend joined me. I wondered if he had been assigned by the reverend to reel me in, but in any event his proselytizer had a jammed throttle, and the called-for response was the same: be absorbed in pamphlets while stuffing my face. The poor kid tried to make friends but then faded into the background.

Within two hours I had checked out and walked to the eastern edge of the city. I stopped in a shop for food and directions to Germany, although I lost in translation what part of Germany. I knew Grettstadt was near Würzburg, which *Let's Go* said was in the southeast. I decided to take a Battle of the Bulge route across the border and *then* search for Würzburg. I began to question my notion that packing a map, like bringing a watch, would detract from the spontaneity required on an odyssey.

I stuck out my thumb and before long was headed east in a truck. Mid-day I was outside Arnhem, close to the border. Then a square little car pulled up. A plain, pleasant woman in her forties motioned me to sit in the front seat. The two kids in back were also hitchhikers. The woman asked in German where I was going. Calling on all my schooling and the summer's flash cards, I replied I was headed to Würzburg.

They could plainly hear I didn't speak German and signaled they didn't speak English. Nonetheless, they understood "Würzburg" and, after some discussion, agreed I should continue south when they turned east at Cologne. My course settled, they launched into conversation over a background of *American Top Forty* on Armed Services Radio. It was hard to ignore the irony that I couldn't follow the conversation at all but was the only one in the car who understood the lyrics. Unfortunately, I also understood a brief report that the Yankees trailed the Red Sox by fifteen games.

Chapter VI

Toccata & Fugue

My driver dropped me in Cologne and pointed the way to the youth hostel. I stood with my backpack at the corner of a bank building. The streets were clean, and the buildings seemed new and antiseptic after the colorful structures in Amsterdam. The sidewalk was mostly empty of pedestrians. A large river in the near distance split the city. The sun warmed my face as I contemplated my first move in Germany, left or right.

The youth hostel was down the block and so this was the logical choice. It had been a long day of travelling. However, the Germans took their rules seriously and the woman in charge said in terms unequivocal in German *and* English that I could not stay without a hostel card.

So back at the corner, pack against the bank, I again wondered what to do. Where would I sleep? Where could I change money? How would I carry on a conversation out of a dictionary?

Then something hit me, literally. I reached to the top of my head and felt wet hair. Three stories up a pigeon's tail hung over the edge of the roof. I wished I'd packed a rifle.

I wiped a bandana over my hair and tried to clean it on the white brick of the building. It was their bloody pigeon, I reasoned, so they should share the good luck of being shat upon.

There were few tall buildings but two dark cathedral spires on the far side of the river, which had to be the Rhine. I concluded the train station and its inevitable currency exchange must be there as well. The view was breathtaking, and I thought of taking a photograph. But there were more important tasks at hand, and I'd come to think just setting up a picture etched the image in my mind almost as if I'd seen the print. Also, unlike my actual photographs, my mental images were always in focus and perfectly framed.

Walking toward a bridge across the river I tried to formulate the polite German for "Excuse me, where is the train station?" Although the pack felt no heavier than usual, my legs were saying to sit down while my stomach rejoined "and eat!" I tried singing to drown out the debate, then simply mumbled: "Been down so long, it looks like up to me."

Past a patch of woods, a bridge with a pedestrian walkway crossed the swift, dark water. The woods would do for the night if I could first change money and buy food.

On the bridge I asked directions of a stooped old man. He was amused but simply smiled and pointed the direction I was walking. I stopped a second person to ask if it was legal to camp in the woods I had passed, but he turned out to be some kind of guard. So much for staying alert, I thought, only then noticing the uniform beneath his jacket. Nonetheless, he seemed to answer no, it was not legal, but yes, I could camp "*im Rhinepark.*" On the other side of the river, another man gave me involved directions I couldn't understand but his hand gestures led me to the train station.

At the station I changed forty dollars and my few guilders for about eighty Deutschmarks. In the station there was much activity. I recognized a boy as American by his sneakers and camera and asked if he knew of a place to stay. He said he was waiting for a train, but his guidebook listed a youth center at 4 Georgstrasse. His book didn't have the infamous orange cover, and so I decided to trust his directions. There seemed no better option.

A kindly woman at the Strassenbahn ticket window seemed to say there was a stop at Georgstrasse, and I should stamp my ticket on the train. I boarded with people coming home from work, stamped my ticket and asked the driver in German how far it was to Georgstrasse. He nodded like he understood but his reply was inscrutable.

The Strassenbahn was an electric streetcar powered by overhead lines, made up of two cars with no passage between. At the first few stops, people stepped on and off both cars. Then at one stop two men in trench coats got on my car, stood back-to-back, flashed badges and started checking tickets. I clutched my ticket and waited, but before they reached me they accosted two young men and pulled them off the train. I committed to memory the look of the officers, in case I ever found myself on a streetcar without a ticket.

In twenty minutes the driver rang the bell and said something over his shoulder, which I assumed meant it was my stop. I got off and quickly found Georgstrasse, a quiet street lined with low buildings and overhanging trees leading past a tiny park. My stomach grumbled. I couldn't wait to stow the pack and get some food. The approaching dusk underscored how far I'd gotten from Rhinepark.

Number 4 Georgstrasse, it turned out, was the Church of Saint George, a small Romanesque building of sand-colored stone. It made sense George Street would be named for the church and the church for a saint. What didn't make sense was why my "youth center" was a church. I was done in and needed a place to put the pack down, not a hostel hunt.

An old man saw me staring at the stone building and asked something in a sympathetic voice. He listened to my explanation in quasi-German and motioned me around the corner, where a side entrance to the building looked like it could lead to a youth center. My back and my stomach joined in a "huzzah!" and I stepped through the open doorway, smile on my face and dictionary in hand. A middle-aged woman behind a desk returned my smile and waited patiently for me to put together an inquiry. She then grinned apologetically and explained the "*Altersheim*" sign over her head meant "old folks home." With some effort she communicated I was ten kilometers from any kind of youth center.

Backing out the doorway, I felt spent, and my head was spinning. Across the tiny street, I threw my dictionary into the square, took off the pack and lay face down on a bench. This wasn't fun anymore. I wanted to go home, but was that even possible? How far was I from an airport? Wouldn't my father get a laugh at how quickly his son had given up his boondoggle? And then I'd look ridiculous to all the friends who thought my plan was crazy, and worst by far would be Pam—if she even noticed. I loved most every expression on Pam's face except the rare "I told you so" look, which I'd do anything to avoid.

I wished Edward were with me; he wouldn't give in to despair because we were tired and hungry and a little lost. I could imagine him being disappointed his little brother was so forlorn about finding a place to sleep, in a peaceful German city with no scorching heat, no leaches and no one shooting at him. But being unable to justify feeling beleaguered didn't make me feel any better.

Time still stretched on. I calculated how long it would take to walk back to the woods over the river. I prayed to St. George for deliverance, regretting all those cynical things I'd said about religion. I must also have been crying because my face was moist when I looked up. A young priest in a long white robe stood by the bench, asking if I was all right.

"Just dandy," I said and forced a smile.

He seemed satisfied and continued on his way, hands folded piously in his robe. After he entered a building across the square, I got up, swung the pack onto my shoulders, and tightened the belt. This time no message from my legs reached my brain. I was no longer conscious of hunger. A numbness had cut off internal communications.

I walked in short steps vaguely toward the cathedral spires. Something in me seemed to have died. I didn't know what it was, maybe my sense of romance or my belief in the story always working out. The city grew darker and the pack heavier. All I could think about was how sapped I was. I paused on a corner, thoughts blank....

"You look lost," I heard as if from a distance.

I looked up and stared. It was a guy my age with shaggy hair and wire-rimmed glasses. He looked kind, smiled and repeated himself.

He's speaking English, I thought, and to me. I shook my head and stammered, "Yes, yes I *am* lost. Could you tell me how to get to the park by the river?"

"You will go in the woods?"

"I'll pitch my tent."

"Camping is good," he said. *"Natur!"* He paused and looked back at his companion. "But now you to come with us. We live nearby and have a couch you will use to sleep."

I joined them as if this were prearranged. Wolfgang introduced himself and his friend Hermann. Hermann spoke little English but smiled to my smile. Together they led me onto another Strassenbahn. Wolfgang said I shouldn't worry about a ticket because the inspectors would be on their dinner break.

On the streetcar Wolfgang said he thought I was American from my pack and sneakers and that he was glad to practice his English. He was a student and an *Antimilitarischer*, which meant he had avoided national service as a conscientious objector. Hermann was also a student at the university.

At the apartment Wolfgang introduced his roommate, Olfred, who had a full blond beard and a crooked, infectious smile but spoke no English. Wolfgang pointed out a couch by a large open window, and I laid my pack beside it. Olfred was cooking dinner. I washed up and tried to help but he made me sit and handed me a bottle of golden *Kölsch*, a beer Wolfgang said was special to Cologne.

Their kindness washed over me. They seemed like old friends, like I was meant to be here. Olfred's stew was ambrosial. My whole body embraced the hot food. After we started eating, Wolfgang asked my plan. I laughed and replied in German: "To eat and sleep."

We spoke for some time through Wolfgang and discovered

shared passions: we hated war and loved rock music. After dinner and schnapps, Hermann said goodnight and I insisted on doing the dishes. Later, Wolfgang poured more schnapps, and Olfred and I played guitars. While we couldn't converse in words, we found a common language in the blues in G.

I later told them about England and Holland. They couldn't stop laughing about Trevor and the paddling. I was laughing too hard to argue it was worth a quick five pounds. I eventually told them about Victor's promise of a job, but said I was open to any kind of work if I could find it.

When I could no longer keep my eyes open, Wolfgang found me a pillow. I barely had time to notice my couch was the most comfortable bed in Europe before I was lost in a long and dreamless sleep.

Late in the morning I awoke to a trilling birdsong. Everyone was gone, I supposed to classes. By the coffee pot was a key and a note saying I should let myself in and out and help myself to anything I found in the refrigerator. Wolfgang suggested I see the cathedral and join them for dinner. He said they'd ask around about work.

After a shower and some cold coffee from the pot on the stove, I headed out. I took Wolfgang's advice and even paid a mark forty to mount the stairs in the north spire of *Der Dom*. The climb was long but easy with no pack. The reward was a panoramic view of dark slate rooftops and an array of bridges spanning the Rhine, the most striking being the Hohenzollern Bridge with tied-arch construction looking like three rolling steel hills. Although I had brought my camera, I lacked the wide-angle lens to do the scene justice and so instead recorded another imagined photo.

After the up-and-down I was content to buy groceries for the road and sit by the Rhine with *Don Quixote*. I worried whether ninety dollars and sixty something marks would carry me until I got paid. But Wolfgang and Olfred had pulled me back from the brink, and I knew I could go on. Next time I just had to find a place to stay before my legs gave out.

Wolfgang brought home pasta and vegetables. Olfred bought a

bottle of wine so we could toast to meeting and parting. I tried to be useful washing, peeling and chopping. Over dinner I tried, in German, to say how I'd spent my day. They found it terribly funny I'd climbed the cathedral stairs. I was unable to translate that I understood their amusement because I'd never been to the top of the Empire State Building, where all the tourists in New York went.

After dinner Olfred played tapes while we sipped the last of the schnapps. He was disappointed I couldn't teach him the guitar part in "Rock & Roll Hoochie Koo." He noticed me mouthing the words, though, and asked me to explain them through Wolfgang.

Wolfgang and Olfred said they hadn't found me a job. I thanked them for trying but said I was sure I had something waiting for me, and that I'd be off in the morning.

"Give me your map," Wolfgang said, "and I will mark the way to Würzburg."

"Ah," I replied, realizing how foolish this would sound, "I don't actually have a map."

Wolfgang rolled his eyes and translated for Olfred and they both laughed again. (I was good for nothing if not a laugh.) Olfred said something, and Wolfgang agreed and turned to me. "We think it is good we have found you—to see you on your way," he said with a sincere smile.

I slapped him on the shoulder, and Wolfgang reached for my pad to draw a map of the highways I should take, south through Frankfurt and then east. Then we said goodnight. In the morning I was off to the Autobahn, promising to send a postcard from down the road.

*   *   *

The Autobahn entrance was not far, and I caught a ride instantly, pleased at getting back my touch. The woman driver spoke no English, so following Wolfgang's sketched map I said only "Frankfurt, *bitte*."

After a while I tried my German for "You have a beautiful country," and she seemed pleased. My translation for "I am from the

United States" also got a smile. But her appreciation for my attempts at German notwithstanding, she soon left me at a desolate Autobahn cloverleaf.

The speed of the traffic was daunting and reminded me of run-ins in my teenage years with New York state troopers on the highways leading to Jones Beach. To get a look at my situation, I climbed a hill, but my running shoes were designed for moving straight ahead and my feet slid onto the sides of the shoes. Also, the view from the hill showed nothing but highways in all directions: a distressing panorama of humanity overrunning the land.

Back on the Autobahn I walked, sticking out my thumb. This was a low-percentage strategy, given the speed of traffic, but I saw no other choice. As luck would have it, a man pulled over, mumbled something I couldn't understand, and drove me to where he left the Autobahn and I continued south toward Frankfurt. On the roadside I thought about my Channel crossing and Olfred's blues smile. I tried to picture the Strassenbahn inspectors in Cologne. If I could spot the authorities in time, I could ride public transportation for free, which would stretch my funds.

Between public transport scams and timely connections my trip was becoming a real "ramble," like Edward and I had planned, something like *Don Q* without the insanity. I didn't think I could explain this to Pam or anyone else, though Edward would have understood. I guessed being inexplicable was part of the point; otherwise, it would be in the guidebooks.

I soon found myself riding shotgun in a Renault, screaming south at a hundred sixty kilometers an hour. The driver was proud of his graphic equalizer and told me to pick a tape. In the glove compartment I was amazed to find a cassette of Yes, my favorite band, whose last album had encouraged me to travel when all the people around me had not. Green hills and signs for anonymous towns flowed past and the music told me I wasn't so far from home: "going for the one...."

The music made me think of the summer and our second floor of the house by the stadium. It was disturbing how many topics led back to

Pam. Maybe she was the one for me and I had screwed it up by leaving her behind. She was a stunner, no doubt, and smarter than me in many ways, and yet so soft and vulnerable inside. She really was all I could want in a lover and a partner. I was destined to take this trip, but I'd always regret it had cost me Pam.

The Renault left me outside Frankfurt, still early in the day. I had the impression from Wolfgang that the city was dirty and commercial, so I had no interest in visiting. Instead, I found myself in the middle of another cloverleaf. Wolfgang's directions showed me going beyond Frankfurt and then turning east, so I would continue south, regretting having no real road map.

All around me spiraled a dozen loops of streaming, smoky traffic, but it was peaceful within the railing at the lips of my deserted island. The short, tough shrubs and I were invisible. Drivers rushed by and didn't see anything where they expected nothing. I ate bread and rested and dreamed. The engines sounded like endless waves, blind to the sand they pound. Blue and yellow wild flowers thrived on this life. I took out and fingered my peseta, thinking it was time for this talisman to work its magic.

After lunch I got a ride to Heidelberg, the kind of stately castle town I'd expected to fill Germany. Sunshine lit the red roofs of old buildings nestled along a river beneath a deep green mountain. A part-Gothic and part-Renaissance castle of red stone overlooked the town.

I was sure I could make it across southern Germany to Würzburg in a day, and from there it would be a short step to Grettstadt and my job, so I decided I could afford a bed. I launched into a sympathy routine to get a bunk at the hostel without a card, but I was getting pretty good at that, and the bunk came with bread and a bowl of stew.

After dinner I read in the common room, but the novelty of *Don Quixote* was wearing thin after six hundred pages, so I headed for a shower and bed, hoping to get an early start and see some of the city before traveling. At the end of the room, a fat-cheeked boy who looked American was reading *Steppenwolf*.

"Good book?" I said.

"Wh… What," he stuttered, clearly interrupted and looking at me over his reading glasses.

I chuckled. "Keeps your attention, anyway."

"Oh, yeah, great book; but I'm almost finished. Hey, where're you from?"

His being nearly through *Steppenwolf* was reason enough to talk to him, even though he opened conversations with "Where are you from?" I salivated at the chance to try a German novel in this setting.

We did the compulsory exchange of birthplaces and schools. He was in Germany on a two-month study program and thought it odd I had no Eurail pass or itinerary. I lied that I'd just finished *Don Q* and praised its place in western literature. He said he'd stay up and finish his book if I'd consider trading in the morning. I pondered for a moment, just to mess with him, and then said I'd be happy to help him out.

The next day I took my pack and new novel and, with the weekend crowd, climbed the path to the castle. The day was sunny and the fields along the river orderly and green. My pack attracted comment from a young German-Swiss named Thomas. We spoke, and he said he planned to drive east to Heilbronn after touring the castle. He agreed to take me along and leave me at a road connecting to Würzburg.

I didn't want to pay three marks to go in, and he decided he didn't need to either since he'd seen it before. Instead, we wandered the paths outside the castle. He explained the city hosted the oldest university in Germany. I wondered if Heidelberg had jousting matches against Cambridge in the old days. Across the river the buildings were mostly four or five stories of white brick topped with pointed roofs. The storybook setting was inspiring but diluted by the crying children and cameras clicking all around.

After a half hour we found Thomas's car and started on a winding road along the River Neckar. Low green mountains swept up from both sides of the road, and the sky above the peaks and castle spires contrasted clear blue and pure white like on a crisp fall day. In fair English Thomas said we were driving along the "Romantic Road."

"For myself, romance is doomed," he added.

Nodding appreciatively at my gesture to continue, he said: "I sought to put her in a shrine, to preserve her as a vision of beauty, of female perfection, and she would not have that."

In my own amorous travails I never sought to enshrine Pam, but instead hid how she enchanted me. My troubles came in the end from not being able to make her understand I loved her but still had to leave her behind.

Even Thomas' command of English made him sad. "The Swiss in the west speak French," he said, "and look to France. It is big and gives them a sense of power, of security. In the south they speak Italian and look to Italy. We in the north speak a German dialect, but we do not look to Germany. Our own Swiss language is gone from fashion. Even our politicians only start their speeches in the old language and then switch to German dialect and then to *Hoch Deutsch*. The people laugh but it is sad."

Thomas also thought his military service sad and funny. "In fifteen hundred we had infantry to repel invaders from the hills. But the age of artillery left us behind. Now our generals play games with numbers. In the first two days of war, one third will be lost, but then each man with a personal anti-tank gun will hide behind each tree in the mountains and defend Switzerland."

It was hard to comprehend conscientious objectors in Switzerland. "In my country," I said, "people thought it wrong to cross the world to shoot Vietnamese, who didn't threaten us. But in Switzerland, with your neutrality, soldiers would only have to fight if war came to your own land, when everyone would want to defend themselves."

"I don't know. I think if Switzerland were invaded, I would not fight, and I do not think my generation would fight. Perhaps it is because we are so small and have never had to pay for our freedom with blood. Things go too well."

Thomas was helpful in giving me a long ride but a bit morose. I was glad to move on to a less angst-ridden ride with a stoic carpenter into Würzburg.

The city was smaller than Cologne, and people didn't seem so threatened by my pack. Looming beyond the streets to the west was a large rectangular fort with baroque towers in each corner, encircled by layers of stone bastions. Apparently, a fort was a standard feature in these towns, and this one commanded a low hill across a wide Main River, surrounded by sloping vineyards. Walking away from the river, I passed a beige-colored palace with a central structure and a wing at each end. It also was "baroque," like Bach's music, in its square edges and complex symmetry. Farther on was a cathedral with two rectangular spires and an odd design of alternating beige and red brick.

These forts and palaces seemed like perfect settings for stories. I wished I had the time and the money to learn their history and wander through them. But that would have to wait. First thing was to find Grettstadt and a job. I needed a roof over my head and access to food. Later, I could take in the castles and cathedrals.

I also didn't want to linger in Würzburg while there was daylight. The map in Thomas' car had shown Schweinfurt as barely forty kilometers up route 19 and Grettstadt just southeast of that. At a grocery store I picked up food and directions and walked roughly north.

Where the buildings became lower and more spaced out, I rested the pack against a fence and stuck out my thumb. For half an hour end-of-workday traffic passed, but no one stopped. I got bored and took out a grease pencil to write "19" on the cover of my pad and held it up, resting my thumb.

Traffic thinned but I remained in place. There seemed no advantage in walking up the road, so I just shifted my weight from one leg to the other and tried to think of a song to sing. After a long while a young man approached and glanced at me. He had long, reddish-blonde hair and a mustache and big beard and wore an oversized shirt and blue jeans. A colorful woven bag hung over his shoulder. As he passed, he looked over his red sunglasses and said something in German.

"Excuse me," I said in German, "but I don't understand."

"*Ja, ja...* English?" he said. "You speak better English?"

"*Ja,*" I said.

"What is the number nineteen?" he said, pointing at my sign.

"It's the road to Schweinfurt."

He laughed, looking over my pack. "So, you *trampen* in Schweinfurt?"

"Well, I hitchhike to Grettstadt, near Schweinfurt, but I'm not making much progress."

He reached for my sign and smiled at it. "In Germany," he said, "better you write the place, not the road number. People do not know the road number."

I nodded and took the pad, flipped back the cover and took out my grease pencil. "But this is the way, *ja?*" I said.

He nodded yes and started to cross the road, then hesitated. "Why do you go there?" he said, his smile straightening his mustache and bringing life to his eyes.

"I'm looking for work. A friend is visiting Grettstadt and will find me a job."

Again, he started to go, but paused. "How long you are standing here?"

"An hour," I said, shrugging my shoulders to show time didn't much matter.

"*Vieleicht...* ah, perhaps you come with me? I live in the student housing, just there." He pointed to a string of low buildings across the road.

"The room is not big," he said, "but you can stay in your sleeping bag and go by Grettstadt in the morning."

It had been a long way since Heidelberg, so I didn't need convincing. He seemed like a good guy looking to practice his English.

I didn't notice at the time the pattern in these meetings. Once again I had reached the end of the day or the end of the road or the end of my rope, and someone reached out a hand, someone with long hair and a Moroccan shoulder bag. It seemed I had fulfilled one goal of my younger self in meeting the folks from Alice's Restaurant.

The student's name was Emil. His room was large enough for a bed, a desk and two chairs. When we arrived, he untied a clothesline and folded his wash. The posters on the walls, but for the German words, could have decorated a dorm room at Michigan. An Escher print that had hung in my house in Ann Arbor made me feel at home, and I looked closely at a concert poster for Frank Zappa in Hamburg.

Emil saw me trying to translate and said: "Zappa! You know Zappa!" He said the name in the low bass of Wagnerian opera and added: "I love Zappa, and I know the words... but they make no sense."

He jumped at my offer to translate the songs into English he could understand, and we were soon deep in Zappa's lyrics—a very strange place to be.

"'Dynamo hum' is an orgasm," I said.

He rolled across his bed laughing and then sat back up. "Can you explain the fast words in 'Montana'?"

Emil studied theology at the university and was a communist. His English wasn't good enough to explain that concurrence. It seemed his reality was communism and his escape theology—and American rock music.

"I wish I had been able to join the student revolts of the sixties," he said warmly. His smile then turned to a snarl and he added: "And now we breathe the reactionary air of Würzburg."

"I also missed the protests," I said. "I got to the university a year after we pulled out of Vietnam. The only thing we could find to protest was the CIA recruiting on campus."

Emil went out early next morning, and I lay awake listening to church bells that said it must be Sunday. He brought back pastries and milk for the coffee he brewed on a hot plate.

As I didn't know how long my job in Grettstadt would last, I asked Emil if I could visit again afterwards. He said I would be welcome, but at the end of the week he'd start a month-long holiday. "You will take the address and the number of the telephone in the hallway," he said, and scribbled them on a postcard.

"And remember, put the name on your sign, not the road number," he called out the door as I left.

* * *

The sun was shining when I started for Schweinfurt, but by the time I passed through that town and reached Grettstadt the day had turned cloudy. The tiny village looked like it hadn't changed since the Reformation. Nestled in fields and woods sat a handful of low whitewashed houses with high-pointed roofs and one church steeple.

Children and dogs followed me through the village center. The little ones seemed to think I was from a minstrel show; they giggled and hid. The dogs snarled just out of reach. It didn't look like they got many backpackers in Grettstadt.

Finding the address Victor had given me was easy—there weren't many houses in the village. A couple of kids and a large brown dog watched as I reached the door on a quiet street and rang the doorbell. But it proved impossible to get over the threshold. The elderly woman who answered spoke no English and was openly suspicious. With a sauerkraut expression she communicated that Victor had gone to another town until the next day. She waited sternly for me to take the hint and leave, so I wrote a note to Victor saying I'd made it and would return to see him in the morning.

The lady demonstrated her kindness and regard by taking my note and shutting the door in my face. I turned toward the dog, still standing guard.

"So, what's the best hotel in town?" I asked, but he was not forthcoming with any recommendations.

A road ran out of the village past a narrow wood, maybe two hundred yards across a planted field. There weren't many trees, but it seemed far enough from the houses to hide my tent. Of more concern was the threatening rain.

I hiked to the woods and stepped over fallen branches to a flat clearing in the densest trees. I could still see the village but guessed no one would be looking my way. If only my tent were forest green, like my pack, I'd have been camouflaged. I half-heartedly threw leaves over the orange skin to break up the color, but it didn't help much. Sitting on a stump ten meters from the field, I devoured a chocolate bar and then relaxed with cheese and rolls. I was pleased at having found Victor. The world was not so big after all, and everything was falling into place.

Victor had been a decent boss. I worked in his machine shop during a high school year and a summer. He offered me a promotion if I would stay full-time but understood when I told him there was no way I would give up going to Michigan. Still, the offer told me he liked my work, and he was very friendly when I ran into him again and generous in offering to help me find a job. It was funny how things worked out sometimes. I wondered what kind of work I would do, and if he would convince the sour old lady to let me stay at the house.

When the sun went down, I brought my pack inside the tent and by candlelight finished *Steppenwolf*. I felt like Hesse's wolf of the steppes, who had strayed into town and the life of the herd, an image for his hero's loneliness, savagery, restlessness and homelessness. Well, maybe not so savage.

Actually, the translation of Hesse's writing was well done and his fantasies imaginative but a little lifeless, somewhere between Tolkien's Middle Earth and letters to the *Penthouse* editor. My next goal after getting set up in a job would be to find another novel.

In the morning I hiked back through the waking village and knocked again at the old lady's house. Victor quickly filled the doorframe and stepped out to shake my hand. He was a fit and vibrant fifty-year-old with a white crew cut and sky-blue eyes. I'd never noticed before how Aryan he looked.

"Well, Stephen," he said. "What a surprise!"

"Ah, yeah. Hi," I replied, wondering why this was a surprise. "You said I should look you up?"

"Right. Yes. Let me just grab my keys."

He left me outside, which did not bode well. After a night in the woods, I could have used a bathroom and a cup of coffee. But Victor quickly came out and loaded me into a small white car. We drove to his cousin's gas station while he asked general questions about my trip, but he didn't seem to pay much attention to my answers. At the gas station we both went into the office and he spoke to the owner, who shook my hand and then left us alone.

Victor made a few calls, speaking German in short conversations. He seemed to have trouble reaching people, and I became increasingly uncomfortable with how the cousin and his employees avoided looking at me. Finally, Victor hung up the phone and turned to me with a great sigh.

"No one can hire you because you come from outside the Common Market," he said, with annoying good humor.

"Oh," I said, sensing finality in his tone. I paused, waiting for what would come next, but he just looked at me and shrugged his shoulders. After a few awkward moments, I said, "Have you any other ideas about finding work?"

He shook his head with a smile now plastic. "I'm sorry, Stephen," he said. "I guess there's nothing I can do for you."

I was thinking of maybe a meal, or a bed, or a cup of coffee, but this conversation had turned surreal. He was more embarrassed I had turned up than he was concerned I was thousands of miles from home with no money. How could someone I had worked for and who had invited me be so cold, when strangers went out of their way to help? Disgusted, I wanted to get away. I thought of Emil and asked Victor if he'd put me on a road back to Würzburg.

He jumped at this quick way to dispose of me and drove to an intersection he said was an hour's drive from my destination. He wished me luck, relief beaming through the gleaming teeth of his false smile. When he was out of hearing, I cursed him and all his relations. Then I looked both ways along the empty road.

There was no job; how was that possible? My whole ability to take this trip hinged on Victor finding me work. Where could I go now? What could I do? How long would my money last? Hesse said, "In eternity there is no time, only an instant long enough for a joke." I had both no time and all the time in the world but was having trouble getting the joke.

* * *

Hitchhiking went well and by mid-afternoon I was telling Emil my sad story. His semester had ended, and he was going home for the holidays in two days, but he said I could use his room while he was gone. This solved the roof-over-my-head issue but got me no closer to finding work.

In the evening Emil took me to meet some American exchange students. He introduced me as "a traveler." The students didn't know what to make of that and took their lead from a self-styled intellectual from Santa Barbara. She wasn't particularly attractive but was tall and well-groomed and carried herself with confidence. She offered welcome English conversation but phrased everything pedantically as if to challenge me to understand.

"Germany's guilt retards its capacity to construct a clear world view," she said, "but it is a place *sans pareil* to study the bedrock of philosophy."

"So, you're fluent?" I said, referring to German, though I thought I heard some French in that last pronouncement.

"In German, no, but passable, or I should say *quite* good. But we study in English. It would impede the intellectual discourse to have to translate Heidegger and Nietzsche."

Her reasoning seemed backwards, based on my poor attempts to read literature in the original German. More to the point, Emil couldn't follow her. This clearly didn't trouble her; she turned her entire attention on one person at a time, and it was *my* turn. She was so caught up in her own cleverness that she missed Emil's passion to discuss big ideas. Like George Eliot's Daniel Deronda, I shrank from the notion of a lack of grave emotion passing for wit. I labeled her the "hip-student-abroad" and turned the conversation back to Emil, regretting having to waste time with his American friends.

Relief came when we moved upstairs to watch fireworks to celebrate a music festival at the castle, the structure Emil called "*Festung Marienberg.*" We mounted a wide ladder single file and looked over low roofs into the darkness. Suddenly, flares lit the sky, silhouetting the wide walls of the castle.

The exchange students reacted with cynical oohs and aahs. The couple of Germans and I watched the spectacle of the fireworks and the students. The Germans seemed to share my aversion for the Americans' brazen conduct but were reluctant to ridicule it. These "hip students" got respect despite themselves, while as an American I felt responsible for their lack of tact, just as I was answerable for Jimmy Carter and got undeserved credit for Frank Zappa. At the finale, the students' sarcasm gave way to perfunctory applause. I supposed that kind of meaningless clapping, through years of events, would build calluses against warmth and cold, hard and soft.

Next morning Emil and I walked through town, across the river from the ever-present castle walls. Organ music poured from a church as a weekday mass let out. I went in to listen, but Emil waited in the marketplace, talking with friends. (He disdained churches, another contradiction with his theology studies he couldn't explain in English.) White walls rose to magnificent carved ceiling panels. Behind the altar, framed by white organ pipes, was a rococo painting of the transit between heaven and earth. One organ voice weaved into the next. The fugal form seemed at home here.

When the music concluded, I returned to the marketplace to trade in ideas and realities with my somber German friend. He and I sat on a bench and watched a shady character walk by with a nod. "Ah, this one," he said, "he and I are very different, yet we are not enemies. He is the drug dealer who has made the most money in Würzburg. Do you know Nietzsche? He is a believer in Nietzsche. He is a junkie, but it has been all right because he has enough money. But now the police are too close. Now he is through."

Germans felt life philosophically. I couldn't imagine an American drug dealer following Nietzsche or even knowing who that was, unless maybe they set his writings to a Black Sabbath tune.

In the afternoon we took a bus ride and a long walk to visit Emil's friends, Hans and Ulrike, in their cottage on "the green lawn" above Würzburg. They had a perfect love, nurtured in clean air and hanging grape vines. At center stage was one-year-old Adage. The house was filled with hanging plants and affectionate glances between man and woman and quick kisses from father to daughter. Hans bounced Adage on his knee and gurgled at her and lost track of the conversation, already somewhat out of reach due to his limited English. Emil upbraided Hans that the little girl was too much the focal point, but Hans responded only with dopey, distracted smiles. I wondered at how a grown man could be so lost in the gurgles of a baby.

The sun sank softly beyond the fields. Ulrike took Adage off to bed. The countryside was serene. "Where will you go from here?" Hans asked over bread and cheese and dark beer.

"I don't know," I responded. "I guess to *München*."

"You are welcome to my room as long as you like," Emil said. "But tomorrow night you will have to share. A friend of a friend will stay one night."

"That's no problem," I said. "I'm used to the floor."

The next day Emil snuck me into the student *Mensa* for a cheap lunch and showed me around the university. He translated the school's motto as "devoted to the truth," which he found amusing. I concluded this was one of Europe's newer schools, having been founded only in 1402.

Back at his room he packed a bag, and we waited together for his guest. Meanwhile, he gave me the key and showed me where to leave it. I said I'd probably go soon but would write and tell him where I'd gone. He laughed; clearly, he wouldn't be waiting for my letter.

The guest was a girl named Gita, who knew a friend of Emil's from home and needed to crash for the night. She was about twenty with over-large glasses and unkempt, sandy hair tied in pigtails. She was a bit stout for my taste and spoke almost no English. Emil and she chatted until he left us alone to share his room.

Gita seemed nice enough, though we had difficulty conversing. I felt it was my place to show her around town—or what little I knew. She seemed to appreciate the gesture, and we walked to the marketplace. Since we couldn't speak much, I spent the time wondering where to go next to find work and whether I could pass for Dutch or Danish. I hated the thought of looking like an American tourist and hoped the Germans could sense I was not there to gawk at their old buildings and collect souvenirs. Maybe I was fooling myself.

Gita was distinctly German and so gave me perfect cover on the street. The interesting question, though, was how we would share Emil's room. I looked at her, pondering this. She turned her head and without awkwardness said: "*Essen wir?* Ah, we eat?"

We shared sausages and beer at a shop. I got foam on my nose and she laughed, which broke the ice. I found I had to discard my first impression of her. She was sturdy like an athlete; I pictured her playing water polo. She was also cute when she laughed and a good sport. I was sorry I couldn't understand what she was doing in Würzburg or where she was headed or anything else about her. I was sure she had more of a plan than I did.

After we returned to the street, I pointed out the castle and told her its name. She listened carefully and then corrected my pronunciation. She asked where I came from and brightened with recognition of "New York." We laughed at the kids on their scooters. As we turned for home, we agreed to buy a few bottles of the local *Brauhaus Helles* to drink at Emil's.

Back in the dorm, we opened the beer and tried to communicate. The alcohol loosened things up and our situation struck us both as funny. I'd ask a question and she'd screw up her nose looking at me, and then we'd both laugh. She'd try to make a point using sign language and leave me shaking my head in bewilderment.

"*Deine Augen,*" she said, pointing back and forth between my eyes.

"*Ja,*" I replied. "They are different colors, uh, *andere Farben.*"

I gathered the empty bottles and was about to toss them in the trashcan, but Gita reached for my arm. I looked at her for explanation. She held her hands out for the bottles. I gave them to her, and she pointed to the label, and I saw there must be a deposit. She set them on the bookshelf, apparently for Emil. This was thoughtful, and the least we could do for our host.

To head off any tension as the evening wore down, I showed her my sleeping bag and gestured that *she* should use the bed. She smiled and looked curiously at me.

My comment seemed to decide something for her, and she gestured with her hands to herself and me. "We," she said quietly. "We together?"

This took my breath away. She was tall and hefty, and I wished she wouldn't wear those glasses, but her laugh *had* grown on me through the afternoon. Also, she was not *un*attractive. I smiled, realizing she had me thinking in double negatives. Back to the point, my alternative was another night on the floor.

I hesitated too long. "You also… by the floor," she said, almost apologizing.

Her shyness, following her invitation, moved me. I'd embarrassed her and was sorry. I reached for her hand.

"*Eine schőne Nacht…* eh, one beautiful night," she said, holding up her index finger and beginning to grin.

I smiled and kissed her finger and had to agree.

Chapter VII

The Big Tent

S unlight streamed through the window of Emil's room and woke me. Gita had left a note she would pick up her things in the afternoon. She'd been so warm and welcoming, and it had been great to share the night with her in a real bed. We had intersected at a random moment, and it seemed we each would carry away a smile. The clear light of day could only diminish the moment, though, so I decided to head out without seeing her again.

Gallantry, or possibly just decency, required I leave a note. I naturally verged toward the pedantic, but she wouldn't have been able to decipher something about our "fortuitous trice," so I wrote simply that I had enjoyed meeting her and wished her well. This seemed cold, so I added a poor sketch of myself wearing my pack, hitchhiking with one hand and waving with the other, and left the note beneath a tiny bottle-blue flower from the lawn outside.

Emil had said Munich was a straight two hundred twenty kilometers south and that seemed like the best place to look for a job. So I left Emil's key in the mailbox and set off. The day was clear. A businessman in a brown suit and an Audi took me half way to the city.

His kind but weary eyes showed relief at finding me on the road. He drove this route regularly and was glad for the company and to be able to speak English.

At a rest stop he bought us sausages and beer, my new standard diet. We sat among a dozen people eating and speaking quietly, sheltered from the hum of the Autobahn. He said the hops along the highway would flavor the *Oktoberfest Märzen* soon to flow in Munich.

A tour bus pulled to a noisy stop. In bustled forty middle-aged visitors from Middle America. With chatter at the intensity of a successful cocktail party, they conquered all before them. They were insensitive to anything but lining up for coffee and sandwiches and everything else stopped while they were served. The other travelers watched them without really looking at them. No one who preceded them to the stop spoke over the din.

My D-Day landing in the ferry lifeboat on the way to Holland came to mind. It felt like I owed the continent an apology. But gradually the tourist commotion became the background; like the flowers on an Autobahn island, normal life peeked through. The denizens cast subtle smiles at each other, amused if a bit intimidated, but with quiet dignity.

Back on the highway the countryside was wide-open. I was intrigued by the high wooden supports for hops in fields stretching to distant hills. At home beer was an ice-cold lager from some huge company that splashed its advertising everywhere. In Germany *Bier* was something of the earth, produced in a thousand places with local ingredients and labor. American beer would quench your thirst and five or six would give you a buzz, but a liter mug of *Bier* was a meal in itself and all you needed to take the edge off the day. The German pilsners and lagers also had deep flavor and were drinkable at room temperature, which was *not* how you wanted to drink Schlitz or Budweiser.

In the US I hadn't noticed much difference in hitchhiking from one region to another, beyond the accents of the drivers and the music on the radio. But Europeans were distinct from each other, and hitchhiking gave me a stark view of how different cultures treated the downtrodden. In this measure, the Germans had it all over the English.

Also, at home I always remained part of the world I knew. Even stranded in the middle of the night in some God-forsaken place, I had a job or school and people expecting me. I could always call someone. But in Europe no one waited for me or thought about me or was easily reachable.

Being anonymous might have made me lonely except the people I met seemed so determined to help me on my way. I imagined there was a director in the wings pushing each savior on stage at his cue. I examined the pattern of my connections, which seemed crucial to my comfort and success in stretching out the trip. Wolfgang had found *me* and so had Emil, both only after I was worn out. They noticed me maybe because I didn't notice them—or certainly didn't threaten them. They could see I was American, which made them curious. I carried the pack, so clearly I had no place to leave it. They needed only to confirm I was harmless to feel safe inviting me home.

So far it was working well, the warm couches and hot food and, more memorably, the immersion. Still, there was room to improve my routine of finding refuge only after being ground into the marketplace cobblestones. I needed to skip the miserable stage and get straight to "take me home and feed me."

A hundred kilometers short of Munich, I met a British hitchhiker named Reg. Too thin and pale, he sat on a barrier by an entrance ramp with two shabby overnight bags and a small guitar in a cardboard case.

"Oi, mate," he said. "You heading to Munich? We may as well go together."

We were in no hurry and traffic was sparse. I sat on the guardrail with his guitar and taught him a song from my summers on the beach. Although we hadn't signaled we were looking for a ride, a van stopped. Sometimes things just worked that way.

While we rode in a windowless rear cab, Reg stroked his meager goatee and laid out a plan. We'd reach Munich by early afternoon and play music on the pedestrian mall for money or maybe a meal or a place to stay. "All else fails," he mused, "there's always the big tent."

That reminded me of Montana Bruce's plan to sleep in a circus tent in Amsterdam, but Reg assured me it was no joke. I was to remember the Strassenbahn station Olympiazentrum, by the old Olympic stadium, and meet him there if we got separated.

He told stories about nights sleeping off Autobahn exits but then became quiet. "Sod it if I'm not gone for good," he blurted out, as though continuing a story.

I looked at him, confused.

"I left my mad, Polish wife in Frankfurt," he said.

It was hard not to grin. One of his bags didn't zipper properly and the other bore a cheesy poster for a Pamplona bullfight.

"Right," he said. "It's what I've effin' got here. Or put it bloody this way: what I've left behind, I'm ready to abandon. Well, everything but an old guitar."

We got a ride to the outskirts of the city and walked to a Strassenbahn station, a platform with a few benches and a ticket machine raised above a small parking lot. "I'll play you a Spanish tune while we wait," Reg said. He sat on a bench and took out his guitar.

But before he'd finished his song, the train arrived. It looked the same as those in Cologne, two cars with large windows and no passage connecting them, running off overhead wires. I jumped up and dragged my pack onto the lead car. But when I looked back, Reg was still fumbling with his bags. I tried to get off again, but the doors shut and the tram pulled out. I watched Reg's face as he gathered his things. He was a muddle, but so disingenuous it was hard not to like him.

I got off at the next station, a few stops short of the city center, to see if Reg would show up on the next tram. I wondered if he'd even look for me. After ten minutes the next streetcar pulled up and I boarded at the front. Reg wasn't in the car. I scratched my head, as if this would help me think. At least I knew where to find the big tent.

At the next stop, I hoisted my pack and carried it to the rear car. There was Reg, just opening his guitar case. "Right ho, mate!" he shouted. "Knew we'd meet again."

* * *

It seemed extraordinary Reg could be married; he was so untethered. As we walked toward a pedestrian mall called the Fussgängerzone, he said in Leicester City he'd tried working for a baker and then in a bar. "Loved them Foxes; hated the weather," he said. "And even the bloody football team never won." He paused to survey the scene and muttered: "Story of my life."

We set up to busk along a church wall. Reg sang pleasingly while he strummed major chords. He was no virtuoso but assured me he'd made a living at this. It wasn't clear what he considered "a living."

My voice wasn't very good but I could carry a tune and pronounce the lyrics, so I tried some songs. The Germans liked rock & roll but couldn't understand the words, so it was easy to sing to them. Still, in a couple of hours we made less than two marks.

"Well that be show business," Reg said, frowning and packing up his guitar. "Thought at least I'd run into me mate and find us a squat. Guess it's the big tent for us."

"Sounds good to me," I said, curious to see this apparent fixture of several cities.

He stopped and eyed me with a resigned look. "Right, well you'll soon see. Spent weeks there last summer. Barely an improvement over sleeping in the damp forest and living off chestnuts."

The big ten, or "*Kapuzinerhölzl München*," was at the end of a tramline. Three Marks bought an air mattress, space in a circus tent and tea in the morning. A sign in four languages hung on the mobile hut where tea was dispensed and food sold. The English version said there were four hundred people staying in the camp and continued:

We really hope you don't expect us to keep up a 24-hour service. Running this camp is not our profession. Most of us make the money to be able to afford traveling around like you do. We also enjoy sitting outside, having a drink, listening to musik, talking to people, making connections. We are ready to give you any help we can beyond the routine work of selling food, delivering blankets, cleaning the toilets. So, it depends

on you whether the routine work takes all our time. The service
in this camp is not perfect!! And we don't want it to be!!! We
hope you enjoy your time and let us enjoy our time.

Reg and I each paid three Marks, and he led me under the flap.
We found an empty spot by a post and blew up our mattresses. "I can't
believe I'm back here," he said, "with half the professional thieves in
Munich."

We both laughed, though his expression turned sardonic. He
pondered a moment and said, "Best to start with a bit of grub?"

We each bought a bowl of soup to go with the bread in my pack
and we ate at a picnic table outside the tent. An American boy in jeans
and a button-down shirt introduced himself and before we knew it he
was sharing our bread. Reg threw an exaggerated look behind the kid's
back and pointed at him with his thumb.

"I'll tell you, honestly," the kid said, confidentially, "I'm going
to declare my travel expenses as a tax deduction when I write an article
about what Europeans do to get into college."

It was encouraging to meet a fellow writer, but I was perplexed to
learn he had no novel to trade. He carried only the "exquisitely written"
Let's Go: Europe. I cringed to think the big tent was listed there, as if the
guidebook were haunting me.

*   *   *

It seemed too early when we woke to strange music over the
loudspeakers. The style was early sixties pop but the lyrics modern
and camp. The woman serving tea was surprised I didn't recognize the
soundtrack from *The Rocky Horror Picture Show*. "This young couple
meets a bunch of transvestites from outer space," she said, and paused
for comic effect. "So it works for the big tent."

I nodded and walked off, wondering how that made sense, and
then saw Reg on his way to the road. "Oi mate," he said, "Off to see a
man about a guitar. Careful what you leave in this dodgy flee-bag."

"Yeah, of course. But are you coming back?"

"Left my bags here, so guess I have to. Maybe I'll see you later."

He walked off with a purpose, and I returned to the tent. I packed up, nervous about leaving anything behind after what Reg had said about thieves.

It was a warm morning with a clear blue sky. On the way to the Strassenbahn, I passed sheep grazing in a field and heard church bells. I thought about a camping trip Pam and I had taken on bikes outside Ann Arbor. I had unstrapped my sleeping bag on a hill and it immediately rolled down a path toward the lake. She laughed so hard watching me chase it that tears came to her eyes. Later, we built a fire and cooked hot dogs, and I read to her from *The Fellowship of the Ring*. She didn't know Tolkein and laughed at the descriptions of the hobbits. I didn't tell her the book had long ago filled me with wanderlust, which revelation might have disturbed the bucolic perfection of the day.

There was little chance Pam or Annetta or even my mom would have responded to my postcards. Still, I was feeling detached and hoping for contact with someone who knew me, and so I decided to find the American Express office during the course of the day.

At the Strassenbahn stop I bought a ticket from a machine. When a tram stopped, I hopped on the rear car, stamped my ticket and found a seat. Even at the outskirts, Munich was more alive than the other German cities I'd seen. There were lots of people and bikes. The tram wound through streets crowded with pedestrians. The buildings were mostly four or five stories, some decorated in opulent colors with wooden or plaster ornaments. The sunny day lured people out from arcades and pedestrian passages, their faces filled with joy. I decided I liked *Müncheners*.

The Strassenbahn brought the city up close. Every few blocks the tram barely stopped, and passengers hopped on and off. Some people stamped tickets, but no one seemed to notice. Others, especially young people, didn't stamp anything but acted legitimate. I wondered if I could save the fare to the city. With no job prospects, it already hurt to pay three marks for a bed. For the rest of the ride to the city center, I watched for inspectors in raincoats, like I had seen in Cologne, but saw none. I concluded I *should* try to scam the Strassenbahn.

I got off at Marienplatz, a central square fronted by a large gothic building that was the "new" town hall. Its façade was richly decorated with statues of knights and ladies in allegorical scenes. Nothing about that building looked new.

The day was glorious and sunlight filled the open square. In the center was a column topped with a statue of the Virgin and child, gleaming in gold like a beacon. To one side of the square was a gothic building framing a glockenspiel, a clock with renaissance figures dancing and jousting while chimes tolled the hour. Vendors sold fruit and sausages and liters of beer. On the sidewalk a young artist with hair braided down his back chalked a vivid pastel scene from the ceiling of the Sistine Chapel: muscular images of God and Adam stretching to touch each other's fingers. I wondered how anyone could produce such beautiful images, and in chalk on the sidewalk no less. He passed the hat and looked up at me. I gave an encouraging nod, hoping he'd understand from my pack that I had no money to spare.

Through an archway I wandered narrow, twisting streets. At an open-air market I bought bananas and asked two girls to look up the American Express office in their guidebook. It was close by and easy to find, but there was no mail for me. I wasn't surprised, really; no one could know I'd be in Munich this soon. I thought it might be best not to keep hoping for mail and instead get used to being on my own.

In a cool, dark chapel back toward Marienplatz, I traced the sun's highlights in red and blue stained glass. Tourists paced by and clicked cameras. Something about the stillness moved me to kneel and close my eyes, as if to prove I wasn't there just to check my map. Praying would've seemed hypocritical, but something about the smooth worn wood of the pews and the hint of incense stirred memories that made me feel safe. I thought about Mom more than God. Being in church seemed to bring her peace, especially when the sadness weighed her down. For me, the years of going to mass had bred more familiarity than anything spiritual.

I couldn't decide whether to stay in Germany, keep at the language and look for work. I needed at least to earn my expenses or I'd soon be on a plane home. But the students were starting vacations, and everyone grumbled about four percent unemployment, so what were my chances?

Greece was supposed to be cheap and a few hundred dollars could last for months. This made me consider heading directly south. I could stop to see Annetta and then strike out for Yugoslavia. If I could find relatives in Zagreb, maybe they'd get me a job, if that was even possible in a communist state.

In the afternoon I walked north and came upon the entrance to the Englischer Garten, where lawns stretched beneath stately chestnut trees. On a sunny day, old buildings couldn't compete with lush grass and the deep smell of trees. Water flowed through cobblestoned channels and women sunbathed without clothes. I sat and pretended to write where I had a view of a particularly Teutonic goddess with golden braids hanging over broad shoulders. I kept my Wagnerian fantasy in view as I lay by a narrow channel dipping my heels into the water. Pam and I sometimes dangled our feet like this in the Huron River in Ann Arbor, talking about the exotic places we'd visit someday. But now I sat without her, missing the part of the dream that mattered most.

The sun was warm and the water cool. With my eyes closed, it felt like Jones Beach on Long Island and then one after another like all the beaches of my life. The locations varied but coming out of cool water to lie in the warm sun was always the same. I felt as if I were simultaneously on all my beaches, the universal sunshine seeping into my limbs.

I dozed off, making up for some of the sleep I'd lost among noisy neighbors the night before. When I woke, my goddess had departed and so I walked to a lawn sloping up a hill to a copper-domed monument supported by a circle of columns. The structure looked like a small Greek temple, but recently built. Young people sat in groups on the lawn, and I took up a place among them.

In another imaginary letter to Pam, I wrote of the cool water flowing through the park—but didn't mention the striking sunbathers.

"I dropped a yellow flower into the water and watched it swirl and catch the current," I wrote, "to float round the world and down the stream behind your parents' house."

Two boys got up to throw a Frisbee. They were awkward, clearly not Americans. I wondered if they'd let me show them how to do it. A third bigger boy joined them and could throw the disc far enough to reach where I sat. I tossed it back from a sitting position and the big one motioned me to join them. I pulled out my own Frisbee and stood up. Soon the other two sat and watched the big kid and I throw both discs.

After a while we sat. My partner, Frank, was an army brat from Pensacola and Washington and San Diego and lately Munich. He lived with his parents on the US Army base and came into the city to meet friends under the monument, which he called the "Monopteros."

"Do you think the Army would hire an American itinerant?" I asked.

"Why not?" he said, but he was only sixteen and had no reason to think about working for a living.

Throwing with Frank was more interesting than talking to him, so I coaxed him back to his feet. He had a good arm for a kid.

Afterward, I lay on my own in the sun, listening to a saxophone and then an accordion polka from one direction and sitar music from another, blending as if in a Charles Ives composition. It felt great to stretch out beneath the high white clouds and clear blue sky. Added strains from distant instruments made the full piece sound like prime time in the Fussgängerzone: twenty buskers vying for tips.

Eyes closed to the sunshine, I thought about looking for work on the Army base. How ironic would it be for me to work for the Army? How was it *anyone* wanted to work for the Army after Vietnam? While we had pulled out of the war five years before, the chasm it left behind was fresh.

Politics had meant nothing to me until Edward was called up and I had to watch my mom suffer. Even before those two soldiers in their starched uniforms knocked on our door, the protests had started to make more sense to me than the "domino theory." After Edward was sacrificed to that stupid war, I was convinced the US was the aggressor, our military wreaking havoc where we had no right to be. But my dwindling cash hemmed me in and I decided that, if I didn't find work in the next two days, I would join the Army—at least for a couple of weeks.

Nearly asleep I was roused by the distant sound of an oompah beat. Eyes still closed, I saw Sergeant Pepper in a gazebo. The music continued and finally drew me along a footpath leading to a large beer garden spreading from a central bandstand beneath a canopy of trees. Musicians in lederhosen played polkas and waltzes beneath a five-story pagoda structure surrounded by tables and food and beer pavilions.

I bought a half chicken and sat across from a clean-cut young couple. I nodded to their friendly looks as I inhaled my food and slobbered from my canteen. I laughed to myself, recalling my search for something "foreign." This place more than fit that description with its horse-drawn wagons and crowds drinking from enormous mugs.

I watched a carriage driver give his horse a gulp of beer. When I looked back across the table, the man had returned from the bar with three mugs. He placed one in front of me, and he and his wife smiled. Near as I could tell, he said: "In Munich, we drink together."

I smiled back, thanked them and toasted to Munich. That about exhausted my German vocabulary, and they spoke no English, so I drank my beer and took in the scene while they conversed in intimate tones.

When I shuffled along, a Scot shouted: "Hey, Yankee boy!" and waved me to a table. I joined him, along with an international assortment of young people all drinking beer. The Scot mumbled his name but I didn't catch it. He handed me a beer and, when I said I was from New York, he toasted to "New Hampshire," stretching the long "I" in shire.

We toasted and drank, and I said: "You make New Hampshire sound like where the hobbits live."

"Well, laddie," he slurred, "as to peculiarities of speech..."

"Pe... culiar... rarities," an Irishman named Fergus intoned, stretching out the long "E" and leaning into the Scot. "Not a simple word to say, now would you say?"

"Aye, it is as you say, and we'll be toastin' to that."

The Scot raised his glass and we all toasted to peculiarity.

While I drank my second liter, I traded stories with my new friends. An Irish girl described the castles around Munich, including one in Pullach that housed a youth hostel. Her light blue eyes were unfocused from the drink, but she was sincere. (She had grown up near Blarney Castle and had stone fortresses in her blood.)

A pretty, dark-skinned girl from Turkey was sympathetic about my difficulty finding work. She'd heard there was an "international youth camp" to the west, in a town called Biberach, where you worked four hours a day in return for room and board. I wrote down the name of the town and wondered if I might entice her into sharing her current accommodations, but a dangerous-looking, bearded companion turned up to squelch that idea.

Seeing no prospect of a place to stay, I headed back to the big tent. Reg was snoring peacefully when I arrived, so I pulled out my sleeping bag, blew up an air mattress and collapsed into sleep.

*   *   *

Consciousness arrived, once again, to the "Time Warp." Reg was quickly up and about. "Oi, lad," he said when I opened my eyes. "I've got to run—hoping to find me mate. Catch up at our busking spot."

I nodded and closed my eyes. A half-hour later I got up and went looking for the free breakfast tea. The line at the portable toilets was long so I sat uncomfortably on a picnic table to wait. But the sun shone again, so the day seemed hopeful. An orange Volkswagen was stuck halfway up a dirt mound and three men worked to get it down. Someone commented about the prevalence of beer gardens encouraging that kind of parking.

Again, I took my pack into town in hopes of finding somewhere else to sleep, and this time didn't buy a Strassenbahn ticket. I sat on the tram in a single seat against the window, watching people get on so I wouldn't be surprised. I had a clear picture in my mind of the two inspectors in Cologne and thought it should be easy to spot trouble.

Between two stops I was looking around the car when a short

woman in a raincoat appeared in the aisle beside me. She flashed a badge and asked sternly about my ticket.

I tried to look astonished and not to sweat. I asked urgently if she spoke English. (She did not, thank God.) She tongue-lashed me and threatened me with the *Polizei*. I smiled, trying to look entitled and stupid, and then talked fast and fumbled to take out money.

She didn't buy my act and told me so in quite impolite terms, but I kept asking the fare and trying to look as innocent as a child. She finally threw up her hands in disgust and waved me toward the driver.

"Ah, the *machine!*" I said, eagerly shaking my head and lugging my pack to the front of the car. I could almost feel her make an obscene gesture at my back.

The machine by the driver spit out a ticket, but by that time the inspector had gotten off the tram, so I put the ticket in my pocket unstamped to save for another trip. In the end I managed to ride the Strassenbahn free but for the verbal abuse.

At Marienplatz again I sat in the sun asking anyone who looked like they spoke English if they had a novel to trade. I also splurged on a postcard picturing the glockenspiel and wrote to Pam, keeping it light: "dropping a line so someone knows I'm alive."

My day followed the same plan as the day before: wandering the city, relaxing in the park, looking for handouts in the beer garden. I used my ticket from the morning to get back to the big tent. This time I decided to save three marks by pitching my own tent beside the big top. Once in the bag I fell quickly to sleep. I dreamed of a crowded city festival. Edward and I rode on a horse-drawn cart, looking backward. On balconies pretty young women waved handkerchiefs, but only at him.

While I counted out coins in the morning for breakfast, a man stooped outside my tent and asked me to take it down and pay three Marks for the previous night. So, instead of a substantial breakfast, I pushed off after the free tea and unflavored yogurt, humming a song from *The Rocky Horror Picture Show*.

* * *

Both the army base and the youth camp in Biberach were to the west, so I determined first to plead for a job at the base and, if that was unsuccessful, to push on to the camp. Wherever I ended up, I needed to dry out from all this beer.

This time I bought and stamped a ticket for one Strassenbahn to the city center and another west to the base. There I wandered among olive-drab buildings in the hot sun, looking for a central office. Despite my revulsion for the military, I was sure I'd be welcomed as a prodigal son, as Americans tended to be biblically inclined.

Several receptionists sent me in circles until a gruff master sergeant took pity and explained that anything I could do for the Army would be handled by a local, as this "fostered goodwill."

Next stop would be the youth camp in Biberach. Trouble was I had only a vague idea of where it was and feared it might be too small to find based only on random directions from strangers. It was time to buy a map, so I backtracked to the PX.

The shop was a dream from home: everything American from beef jerky to *Mad* magazine. I reached for peanut butter but then noticed a sign warning the store was open to military personnel only. "The Army," I spat out, "isn't that just great."

Outside, pondering this obstacle, I smiled absently at a young girl going into the store. She was probably fourteen and covered with freckles and wore a Chicago Cubs cap. The same girl made a show of smiling again on her way out and then asked if I wanted her help buying something.

I thanked her sincerely, ready to accept the offer, but then heard someone call my name. I turned to see Frank, my army-brat friend from the park. His parents were gone for the night and he was buying groceries for dinner. I told him about my hard luck seeking work and that I was off to Biberach.

"You can come back with me for dinner and a sofa for the night," he said. "Get an early start tomorrow?"

I'd ceased to be surprised by this kind of invitation and gladly accepted. We dropped off my pack at Frank's apartment, which was in a drab building of little character but was large and comfortable. He suggested I throw my sleeping bag on the sofa, so his parents wouldn't notice someone had slept in their bed. This sounded like luxury to me.

Frank left the room for a moment and returned to find me perusing a bookshelf stuffed with paperbacks.

"Help yourself to a book," he said. "I'm pretty sure my mom's read them all."

I snatched up *The Magus* by John Fowles and stowed it in my pack. I replaced it with *Steppenwolf*, laughing at how his mother would someday find this book and wonder where it had come from. Frank then brought me back to the PX to buy supplies for the road. We browsed through the store, and he couldn't believe the only food I wanted was peanut butter. Then I found the rack of maps and chose one covering Western Europe, which I hoped would tame the cacophony of my journey into a more ordered, perhaps fugal form.

Chapter VIII

Meine Reise

I landed in Biberach by a pile of earth. It covered the driveway and filled my thoughts. It was my earth to move. With each shovel cut, the dirt shifted to cover its wound and I dug again.

Beyond the garage my toil bore fruit. Between the swing set and my tent, a shallow hole became a garden bed. The soil clogged the rake and felt moist to the touch and I could almost taste its richness.

The trees all around smelled of deep forest that called out like a siren. But I had a job to do. I had found my way from Munich to Biberach and stumbled into employment. I knew the next four weeks would go smoother if Pastor Herr Klemperer and Herr Melina trusted me to work when no one was watching.

Ah, but one *was* watching. Young artists sketched on a bridge across the narrow channel banking the River Riss. Trees mostly hid them, but through an opening I saw one young girl focused on me. She looked thoughtfully up from her pad and was startled to meet my gaze. She smiled shyly and turned in embarrassed, fetching profile.

It was concupiscent. My arms and shoulders felt strong from the road. The sunlight glistened in my sweat. I wiped my face and retied the bandana over my hair.

Remembering the Sistine Chapel chalked on the Munich sidewalk, I saw myself as a figure on the ceiling, massive and gleaming in the sun. Each thrust of the shovel was heroic. Each lift tightened muscles from my neck to my ankles. With each turn of the wheelbarrow, I sculpted the perfect arc for the unruly load. And in each sidelong glance from my artist, I savored the roar of the crowd.

The pile of earth had finally shown some effect from my efforts when I looked up and called to the girl: "*Kann ich ihn sehen?*"

She giggled and turned away. I called out again but she wouldn't look. Two other girls looked at her pad and at me and then a mother-hen-of-a-woman herded the class away. I wasn't sure whether I'd said "Can I see the sketch?" or "Can I see you?"

*   *   *

In Biberach an der Riss, someone would always be watching. I was a novelty. No one here went beyond his hometown without a purpose; yet I had landed here with a big rucksack from the land of cowboys and muscle cars. Here, boys started a trade at sixteen; I was twenty-two and wondered what to be when I grew up. A man here worked hard and prayed and then died; I wandered and was excused from attending church.

In stilted conversations, the solid citizens asked where I came from and where I'd go. No one touched the questions I asked myself, like what had adventure to do with sweeping churches and weeding gardens? They wanted to know what my parents thought of my travels, but there was no way to translate my mother's concern or my father deprecation.

The traveling had become a game with "right" and "wrong" moves. This hiatus in Biberach was a timeout, a chance to catch my breath and save money. I had little idea what came next and was grateful I didn't have to think about plans for a month. It was certain I wouldn't have landed in a situation like this if I'd been traveling with Pam or

Edward; this kind of opportunity only opened up because I was alone, and someone took pity.

On our introduction my boss grinned broadly, and his two huge hands engulfed mine. This bear of a man echoed the pastor's introductory "Herr Melina" but then laughed and slapped his chest, saying: "Ernst."

Ernst's open smile won me immediately, and his name conjured up both Hemingway and Shaw's brilliant comedy *The Importance of Being Ernest*. Ernst voiced no end of effusive comments to Herr Klemperer and spread wide smiles all around. Herr Klemperer explained that Ernst couldn't control his joy because his wife had just given birth to his fourth daughter. Herr Klemperer congratulated Ernst, who shook his hand again enthusiastically. It was only when the pastor looked impatient that Ernst took me outside and showed me the pile of earth and the hole that was to be a garden.

As I filled the hole, I wondered if I had dug myself into one. It didn't concern me that Herr Klemperer and I were evading the work laws, but I was nervous that the good minister felt he had to take possession of my passport "for safe keeping." Still, I supposed the church had to look to its security, and at least Ernst clearly had no hidden agenda.

When Ernst picked me up for lunch, he was astounded I had moved much of the pile. With one arm he gave me a sideways hug and squeezed the breath from me. Then he took me to his house, which was part of a low, modern church. After we ate we returned to finish the job together. For three more hours I struggled to keep up, but he-of-the-barrel-chest paused only to suggest I take a break to admire the pastor's house with its columns draped in yellow and red blossoms. With Ernst alongside me, the work went fast. We soon finished, and he took me back to the church for a beer.

*   *   *

Next day, Ernst instructed me to rake up the lawn behind the pastor's house, which made for a leisurely morning compared to the first day. When he picked me up later and headed back to the church, I recalled I needed to mail the postcards I'd written the night before. He spun his Volkswagen on two wheels to return to a mailbox. Once we had stopped, he motioned to see the cards, meaning he'd like to puzzle at the writing, for each pictured the same photograph of his church with its plain concrete walls and unadorned windows.

He screwed up his eyes and then searched the dashboard for a pair of glasses. I had to laugh when he tried to mouth the English words. Finally, I took the cards back and read out loud, to his enormous entertainment.

"Pamela, love," I began, and he roared.

"*Deine Freundin?*" he said, grinning approval.

"*Nein,*" I said, adding mostly to myself, not anymore. I read that I had settled for four weeks working at a church at this address in Biberach, south of Stuttgart. Ernst nodded recognition of the city names. I continued:

Too complicated to explain, but I'm grateful for clean clothes and a mailing address. Also, I might get time to figure out what I'm doing, maybe too much time.

With you always, S

Ernst took the card in his big hand, over-acting his astonishment at how *those* sounds could have come from *that* writing. I found it liberating to read my intimate words out loud without embarrassment, as I knew he wouldn't understand. He was the perfect audience: attentively sympathetic yet unconcerned with the meaning of my words, like a big, faithful dog.

Then he looked at the other cards. This relieved me from dwelling on how I had overdone the salutation to Pam. At least I hadn't signed it "love"; looking desperate wouldn't help my cause.

Ernst was pleased the second card was to my parents and then raised a suspicious eyebrow and insisted I read the third.

Annetta, I've found work and now certainly will visit Turin. I've thought of you often since London and hope you have

recovered from your scare. Please write and say you'll meet
me in Austria or Switzerland in September.

                                        Yours, Stephen

Ernst handled the third card delicately. "*Und... deine andere*
Freundin?" he asked with exaggerated caution.

"*Ah, nein,*" I said, wishing at least one of them actually were my
girlfriend. Ernst's serious expression dissolved into a belly laugh.

*   *   *

Inside a week I was a working stiff. Ernst picked me up at Herr
Klemperer's each morning and set me to raking or sweeping or stacking
chairs. We broke for lunch with the family and, at day's end, Ernst
returned me to my tent in the backyard.

Staples from a grocery store made up my breakfast and dinner,
while my big meal at lunch was always with Ernst's family. The
second morning I realized I could improve plain yogurt by adding wild
raspberries from along the river channel, and so hunting and gathering—
without the hunting—became a part of my routine. Evenings I wandered
through town and then settled into my tent. A wooden box from the trash
became a bookshelf to hold my paperback and pad, along with a candle
and Ubit. By candlelight I became absorbed in *The Magus*. Nicholas
was about to leave Allison in London to teach for a year in Greece and
said that, while he loved her, it would be mad to ask her to wait for him.

It's like putting a girl in a convent 'til you're ready to marry
her, and then deciding you don't want to marry her. We have to
be free. We haven't got a choice.

This struck close to home, and I began composing a letter to John
Fowles to suggest I visit him in England. I thought we might compare
notes on how our respective separations had worked out.

When Ernst picked me up one morning, all I could think of was
the fishy cheese I'd eaten the night before. He said something about my
looking green and asked if Herr Klemperer had let me sleep inside, out

of the rain. I shook my head no and he asked if it was wet in my tent. He waited while I looked up the German word for "lake" to say: "*Ein kleine See.*" He spun on his heels and marched directly to the church office.

Ernst took me home and Frau Melina came downstairs to meet us, wiping one hand on an apron and balancing newborn Regine on her hip. Ernst pointed his thumb over his shoulder at me. She looked apprehensive. I covered my mouth and ran to the toilet.

When I emerged, pale and sheepish, they installed me on a couch in Frau Melina's sewing room. The rest of the day I was conscious of painfully white walls and the little pills the kind lady fed me. I learned "*Zeitschrift*" means "magazine," and I determined to remember *not* to eat cheese that smells like fish. Before the afternoon was done, Ernst told me I would from then on sleep in the sewing room.

A new pattern emerged. Ernst and his wife rose, I assumed at dawn, noses to the grindstone. I was supposed to work from eight to five, but no one ever woke me. When I did stir, word went up the chain of command, from five-year-old Gabi through eight-year-old Nicola and nine-year-old Marie to Frau Melina, and breakfast stood waiting by the time I reached the kitchen.

After I ate I searched around the building for Ernst. When I found him, he'd instruct me to vacuum the sanctuary or rake a yard, and then he'd disappear. I always finished the job long before he returned, and then did whatever else obviously needed doing, and then waited. I did push-ups, so it wouldn't be too hard carrying the pack when I moved on, and looked through the dictionary for a new phrase to spring on Ernst, like "I'm finished."

My main diversion was reading my novel, which had become more essential than ever to my equilibrium. I perhaps over-identified with the protagonist in *The Magus*, despite his misogyny, and felt the mystical Conchis was speaking to me when he said: "You have the one thing that matters. You have all your discoveries before you." But twists in the story began to make me so angry I no longer wanted to visit the author. And more distressing than the story was the prospect of having nothing to read after I finished. Luckily, the pastor's bookkeeper had me to dinner with his wife and twelve-year-old boy. Karl and his wife spoke fairly good English and came to my rescue by giving me English-language copies of *The Ambassadors*, *Madame Bovary* and *The Trial*.

Henry James joined me immediately after dinner. His portrayal of Paris shifted the direction I would take after Biberach. I realized I had wanted to skip France because of what people said about arrogant Frenchmen. It was embarrassing to still be guided by this shallow perception so long after discarding *Let's Go*. Regardless of how the French might treat me, I realized bypassing Paris would leave a gaping hole in my education.

In the evenings I sat in front of the television with my dictionary or walked in the woods or outlined scenes for "the great American novel." By now friends at home would be preparing for grad school. But that world didn't seem real; it was so far away. I had put off writing my letter to the English Department about getting a graduate position for next year but finally mailed off a draft to my mother to type and send in. Writing a cover note to Mom made me wonder how the Yankees were doing and I marveled that, for the first time in memory, I had lost track of the baseball season.

Flipping between sections of the dictionary one evening, I concluded I was not "*ein Tramper*," or hitchhiker, nor "*ein Tourist*." Instead, I fancied myself "*ein Reisender*": one who wanders. I wasn't sure "wanderer" translated to my mode of only hiking when I had to, but I had no one to check this with so simply scribbled it in my pad, knowing at least Edward would have approved. We had often talked about living off the land without focusing on how we'd do that, but this pause in Biberach convinced me it would all fall into place, like in the novels.

Some evenings I went to a pub. Two pints one night stirred the realization I owed Pam further explanation. With a borrowed pen, I squeezed onto a couple of napkins:

Biberach is as real as the muddy workers who drove me into town or the penned young horse with your proud expression we passed along the way. My delivery into real life was typically painful and miraculous. At the youth hostel they said there was no "international youth camp" and offered no sympathy or bed. So I slept in the woods. At a phone booth in the morning I checked a hundred towns in the phone book for an elusive work camp but stepped aside for a lady to use the phone. After her call she asked my problem and sent me to her friend. He headed public works for the region and assured me there was no work camp. He asked what else he could do, and I told him I needed work. Next thing I was drinking coffee with two ministers, who decided I could work four weeks and showed me a backyard for my tent. A stomach issue landed me, instead, with the caretaker's family. I could despair of this life if I weren't so lucky. Write <u>soon</u> *at the address on my postcard and then c/o American Express Paris. I miss you, S.*

Folding the napkins in my pocket, I thought of all the things I missed about Pam and wondered if I could have taken this trip without losing her. If she could only be here, we'd laugh and drink and steal away to make love. But then maybe I was just lonely for some spark of comprehension. If I were with Edward this would all be a lark; we'd drink too much and raise hell and I wouldn't be pining for lost love.

*   *   *

Ernst decided I lacked company "my own age" and enlisted Sven and Werner as surrogate friends. Sven was a baker, eighteen years old. Werner was a year younger, studied metalworking and often drove his car to the church to meet Sven. They belonged to a youth club along with a sixteen-year-old girl named Hilda, who had golden hair and a face innocent and distracting. They took me on drives to pubs, and we made small talk in their paltry English and my worse German.

The local adolescents soon became tiresome, though, and I began exploring beyond town. On weekends and in the evenings the forest became my refuge. I hid there from Marie and Nicola and their swarming friends calling me to meals, hardly noticing how cavalier I'd become about getting enough to eat. I wrote letters and carved branches and breezed through the rest of *The Ambassadors* to begin *Madame Bovary*.

Like this new novel's characters, I kept thinking about my money: how much I would earn and how far this would get me. More importantly, I fell in love with Flaubert's graceful France, which confirmed my intention to visit Paris. Yet the irony didn't escape me: I thought I perceived France through hundred-year-old novels but pitied the Germans for seeing America in modern detective shows.

One evening I met a young girl and her mother as I was about to enter the woods. They had a bottle of beer but no opener. I gallantly offered my knife and turned down their invitation to share, as I also had a half-liter of Biberach's own. Then I followed a route into the woods and turned off the path. Nestled against a log still warm from the sun, I shared a hillside with a squirrel and a pack of brown and yellow songbirds. It was tranquil. The sun warmed my face. I felt that if I had my pack and food, I could have lived there happily for days, as if beside my own Walden Pond. It was a comfort to see that, even on this long-built continent, there were wild places to be alone and at ease. The feeling was spiritual, maybe because of the beauty of the late sun on the dark leaves or because of the stillness. The lack of surface noise revealed that, underneath, the language of the forest didn't change. I thought about Thomas Aquinas's teaching that grace perfects nature but doesn't set it aside.

Ernst continued often to bellow: "Ah, Stephen!" in awe of my industry, when I would remember to set up the chairs for the old folks' lunch, just like last week, or take the leaves behind the outbuilding after I raked the garden. He often remarked that, when the local boys were supposed to work, they only smoked cigarettes.

Every few days I asked Ernst whether I'd received any mail. Two weeks may not have been long enough for letters to cross the ocean twice, but I was anxious. I also had no success getting paid, and it upset Ernst that Herr Klemperer was holding out on me. Ernst offered to lend me money, but I wouldn't take it. I didn't have any expenses other than beer, and so I changed another ten bucks. Anyway, I feared the grief he'd get from Frau Melina for tying up the household cash.

The Frau was quite as strong as Ernst and close to his size. She carried her baby nearly the day through with the other children in tow. But the house was always spotless and mealtimes precise. She spoke in the *Schwäbisch* dialect common to Baden-Württemberg and lacked the patience to converse with me. When necessary she'd speak through one of the girls, who learned High German in school. Or, if Ernst was nearby, he could always phrase the matter with his hands and theatrical expressions. I had no trouble understanding Ernst, and it struck me he'd make an excellent character actor if the *Hausmeister* thing didn't work out.

Yet Frau Melina shared the girls' curiosity about me. She pretended not to see but laughed when Marie and Nicola clung to my arms and chattered for me to say funny English words. She also insisted on washing my clothes and darning my socks.

One afternoon in a storeroom, Ernst stopped tinkering with the plumbing to make a motion like a robot, telling me: "In my job, I'm a machine." He was perpetually in motion, but no machine could communicate the way he did so easily through gestures and grins. Later, he found a miniature pinball machine on top of some dusty boxes. He bellowed and danced it to the workbench, only to became long-faced when it didn't work. But the discovery, he decided, was cause to clear the dust from our lungs. Returning in a flash, he popped open two bottles of beer and dusted off a bench for me to sit.

After a long draught, he slapped my knee. "Stephen, ah Stephen!" he said. He conveyed, mostly by contortions of his pliable features, how he'd been a builder but hurt his back and had to take the *Hausmeister* job because his family could live at the church and there was no heavy lifting. I laughed at the heavy lifting part, recalling his relentless work in the pastor's garden and how his hug had picked me up off the ground.

Ernst gestured to the toy and swung his arms as if they were broken. I understood this to say, in a philosophical manner utterly German: "Life is a game that, for all my trying, I cannot win." But, as usual, he bounced from introspection to joviality. Snickering, he asked about my "girlfriends." I laughed to avoid the gravity of the question. Only one of them might someday again be my girlfriend, I said, and Ernst asked when we would marry and come to Biberach for our honeymoon. I hid behind the language barrier to kill that topic.

*   *   *

Finishing *Madame Bovary* and starting *The Trial* somehow made me thirst for companionship, and the pubs brought no relief. One evening I was walking back to my sewing room early, lonely and bored. A car pulled to the curb and Klaus from Herr Klemperer's office rolled down the window. He asked if I played *Schach*. I looked at him in confusion and he explained: "*Das Spiel der Könige*."

Flipping through my dictionary, I replied that I did indeed play "the game of kings." He threw open the door and we were off to his chess club.

Klaus was a balding thirty-five-year-old with a pointed beard and small, dull eyes. The clubhouse comprised a single crowded room where everyone was intent on play. Only the waiter noticed our arrival. We took seats at a long table where two old men were engrossed in speed chess.

"*Weissbier?*" Klaus said and raised an eyebrow. In a moment we each had before us a tall, narrow glass of beer with a slice of lemon.

The first game proved I was no match for Klaus. But at school I had found I could sometimes beat a stronger player if I moved fast enough, so I suggested we use a clock.

"*Ja: Blitzschach,*" Klaus said, smiling like a carnivore.

The clock didn't help my game, but at least it cut down Klaus's time to think. I forgot my surroundings, as always when I played speed chess, and saw only the board. Still, I dropped another game and then another, barely pausing to taste my second Weissbier in its tall glass.

In the heat of the third game, I spotted an advantage and moved decisively but, when I hit my clock, I knocked my beer onto our neighbors' board and the lap of the man seated next to me.

All play in the room stopped. Everyone looked at the wet and unamused man and at me. I wanted to crawl under the table. The man stood to dry his pants while Klaus wiped his board with a bar towel. The man waived Klaus off from replacing the pieces and announced, with a stony look at me, that he was going home. We watched him leave and Klaus suggested we finish our game. I went down quietly. We ordered no more drinks.

As Klaus drove me to the church, I wished he had a sense of humor. I wanted to laugh at my clumsiness and the old man's startled expression. But I guessed Klaus was embarrassed about bringing a foreign idiot to his clubhouse. I kept a straight face and bid him goodnight with thanks, and he receded into the Biberach background, where people wore plain clothes and led quiet lives.

*　*　*

In my last week I thought I might die of boredom. I felt like Malcolm McDowell in *A Clockwork Orange,* strapped down with my eyes propped open and forced to listen to Beethoven and watch scenes of violence. I actually heard easy-listening music and saw plain, white walls, which was infinitely worse.

Then, at the next family meal, the background eclipsed the foreground. After three weeks of drinking room-temperature soda with lunch, I decided to make use of the ice cubes from the church refrigerator. It was no surprise the ice improved the Frucola. However, I saw nothing to be gained by announcing my innovation and took my drink quietly to the table.

Promptly after the blessing, Gabi touched my glass and her eyes lit up. Nicola exploded at recognizing what I'd done. Marie jumped out of her seat and tried to squeeze past her to run to the refrigerator.

"*Halt!*" Ernst barked and held out his arm for silence. Everyone sat. I looked down sheepishly but noticed Gabi's pout locked on my glass. Ernst saved me from having to say anything by ordering supper to recommence. In the usual frenzy to follow, he poked my arm and nodded at the glass.

"*Eis, eh* Stephen?" he said, as usual making his point with few words.

After lunch I returned to weeding the garden in front of the church. It was gratifying to have a clear task before me. When I pulled an ornery-looking weed at its base, my hand slid into the leaves and my arm went numb. I scrambled up the hill to where Ernst was talking with a parishioner and held up my swollen hand.

"*Nessel*," the old man tittered.

Ernst shook his head knowingly and agreed: "*Ja, Nessel.*"

Back in the garden I avoided the nettles. By the time my hand had returned to normal size, I was lost in the Zen of weeding.

At five o'clock the lady next door came outside, as always, to sound the bell hanging over her porch. She wore a housedress, neatly combed hair and a blank expression. She reminded me of the ladies who planted flowers in front of the church. Did they enjoy gardening or was this a devotional offering? What had arranging flowers to do with religion? I wondered what my communist theologian Emil would say about this.

The last toll of the bell snapped my attention back to the lady. Her grandchildren might clamor to ring the bell when they visited, but what did grandma get out of doing it at noon and five each day? I was sorry she had nothing else to do with her time but recoiled at this indictment of one's later years in the middle of anywhere.

At any rate, work was done for the day. I changed and headed for the forest, hoping to frustrate the little girls who would call me to dinner. Following the sun freshly broken through the low-clouded sky, I approached the woods. The trees were heavy with the day's rain, and the air was scrubbed clean. I walked slowly, hands in my pockets. My fisherman-knit sweater hung a bit long, suffering in shape but not in comfort. I whistled in the still air.

Over a development of new houses rose a rainbow, glorious in the mist and solitude. It arced over a quarter of the sky, and I was sure it must show the direction I should take from Biberach. Recalling the sun's path told me the magic was due west, vaguely the way to Paris. I wondered if this was coincidence.

A few days later I finally picked up my first photographs with the graduation camera. They weren't bad. The Melina clan was fascinated with the campus scenes. But the shots of Pam caused the most discussion, more unintelligible than usual. The one I most prized—showing her holding our stray cat and wearing very little of a bathing suit—I showed only to Ernst. He pulled it from my hand and ducked into the sewing room, his mouth agape. After a moment of silence, he moved as if to put the picture in his pocket, but then returned it to me with a huge smile and a slap on the back.

I remembered my second-floor apartment with Pam as an eternally sunny jumble of bedclothes. I had packed away the tension of the final days and the breakup, and recalled only sun-tanned smiles and laughter. I smiled at how Pam, accomplished in most everything, couldn't tell a joke. She tried the same one over and over but always gave away the punch line. The pressure of me laughing as soon as she started made it even harder for her. Or maybe she just put on an act to keep milking the same joke. Either way, it was endearing how easy she was poking fun at herself.

Having photographs of Pam made it hard to put her out of my mind. The delay from taking the first pictures with the new camera to developing them encompassed our decline and fall, and yet there she was, holding the kitten and trying to mimic a cat face without laughing. It didn't seem fair.

In the afternoon Ernst said, apologetically, that I was to come with him finally to be paid. We spent an hour at Herr Klemperer's office, collecting my money and passport but mostly admiring our blooming plot of grass in the garden and passing time with the secretaries. I also returned to Karl the bookkeeper the first two novels he had given me, knowing I wouldn't want to carry them. I came away with nearly four hundred dollars' worth of solid *Deutschmarks*, enough to last well past Paris before I'd have to find another job.

That evening I packed a wad of marks into my pocket and headed for town. I bought a couple of beers in a pub but found no companionship. Afterward, I wasn't tired and didn't want to return to my sewing room, and so I walked out the forest road. I was unable to decide whether I should go back to Heidelberg and then maybe to the Black Forest and Freiburg or south over the Bodensee to Switzerland. Instead, I sang a repertoire from bawdy drinking songs to classical guitar (which called for substantial imagination). I also did my best to hallucinate a girl walking along with me. I couldn't tell if she was Pam or Annetta, and finally decided she was some other fantasy. Neither of them had written. If nothing came by Wednesday, I'd be off with no hope of mail before Paris.

The command center of my brain solicited damage reports from the little people running each part of my body—an equipment check before the next stage of the journey. The knee, I had come to suspect, would not cure itself. I feared I might spend the rest of my life remembering my first day backpacking in Europe. I chalked that up to a lesson dearly bought. Then there was an invisible splinter in my right heel, which had appeared and disappeared for a week, keeping my footing less than sure. (More disturbing still was the rundown state of my sneakers. I had sewn the top webbing of each and where one sole was coming loose, but I didn't trust my handicraft.) My insides seemed fit. There was no relapse of Bismarck's revenge and, now that I knew to keep my eyes and nose open, I could hopefully keep my digestive system intact. My arms and shoulders felt strong and ready for the move. Luckily, boredom had driven me to exercise, so I wouldn't have to start again in pre-season shape. My skin was no worse than usual, which was to say it could have been better. However, a scab on my thigh wasn't healing. I assumed I'd scratched myself and rubbing on my jeans kept it raw. And a blemish toward the back of my neck had been prominent for... a few days anyway. I touched the spot and found the sore was open.

I stopped walking and touched the spot again. It stung. My craving the day before for oranges popped into my head. I was used to craving chocolate or roast beef sandwiches or cold beer, but oranges? I touched the spot again and realized the fact that the sore made me think of citrus fruit portended ill.

"Idiot!" I groused out loud. Yes, I had eaten with a family and one would think that would keep me healthy, but did I think there was any vitamin C in cake and coffee and noodles? I'd been too stupid to pay attention to what I was eating and too dense to hear my body sounding the alarm.

There was nothing to be done but cut my losses and hope this lesson came less dear than the last. But my self-diagnosis kept me awake when I got back to the sewing room. I slipped into the darkened church and turned the key to open the slat blinds by the piano. Moonlight reflected over the shiny black surface; as an assistant *Hausmeister* I was at least proficient at polishing furniture. I leaned over the keyboard and played a doleful, two-finger melody in a made-up key.

* * *

In the morning before work, I ran to the store for a bag of oranges and a bottle of vitamins. I scoffed at the chocolate display and swore fruit would be my new chocolate.

After breakfast Ernst drove me to a kindergarten. We entered the hallway between four small classrooms and the teachers each stepped out to say hello. Two were close to my age, yet prematurely matronly; they nodded and returned to their students. The third, who seemed to be in charge, was older and very attractive. Ernst and I both shook hands with her and I forgot to let go.

"Helene," she said, as if offering her name would get her hand back.

I laughed, embarrassed, and stepped aside to watch her speak with Ernst. He then showed me to the grass in a field next to the school, which had grown all summer to be waist high. Ernst would mow it with a tractor and I would rake it into piles by the road.

Together we gassed up the tractor and I started raking as soon as he had mowed the first strip. The grass was heavy with dew, and I saw this job would take all day. But since this would be my last work in Biberach, and anywhere for at least a while, I put my back into it. Before long the sun rose into the clear sky, and I stripped off my shirt and tied it over my hair to keep the sweat from my eyes.

Late in the morning the children came squealing out the side door and turned toward my field. The first few saw me and stopped in their tracks, causing a pile-up with those behind. I laughed, and they turned and ran off in a pack. One of the young teachers returned my smile and called out something about it being warm.

It took Ernst only half the morning to mow and he left with a promise to pick me up for lunch. The children went back inside and there was nothing to amuse me except sweating like a farmer. I realized I'd have to ask Ernst for work gloves at lunch to avoid wearing my hands to the bone.

As the noon whistle sounded, Ernst's car screeched to a stop in front of the school. He waved for me and I waded through the stream of young mothers retrieving children. I pretended to forget my shirt on the ground, so I'd have to return and perhaps get another glimpse of Helene. But Ernst beeped the horn and pointed at my shirt, so I had to pick it up. Just then Helene led a little girl to her mother and noticed me. "You return after *Mitagessen*?" she asked, with a strange smile.

"Wild horses couldn't keep me away," I replied but, seeing she didn't understand, I rephrased: "*Ja*, after lunch."

Ernst gave me a wide sidelong smirk when I got into the car. I grinned back and we both laughed. He exclaimed, "Stephen… Stephen," and said I should stay on in Biberach and keep working with him. When I said I must go he made me promise to write from down the road. I agreed but knew I wouldn't write.

After a special lunch of chicken, though in the usual bowls with bones on the table, I gathered a bandana and work gloves and we headed back to the kindergarten with the afternoon session. I thought about bringing *The Trial*, which I had just started, but decided I wouldn't have time to read. Instead, I hatched a plan to pose as a student with separation anxiety, so Helene would lead me in by the hand.

But she was nowhere to be seen, and I had to finish the job, or it would be one more thing Ernst would have to do. He worked so tirelessly and I wanted to help as much as I could. I also decided to buy him and Frau Melina a bottle of wine or schnapps. I wished I weren't a drifter with nothing else to give them. At least the money for my board should help, although I surely had eaten more than two dollars' worth of food a day.

In another hour I was ankle deep in grass. It occurred to me my time in Biberach had come full-circle: from removing a pile to building a pile. I wondered where Helene had gone and found myself singing an Ellington tune: "Over her shoulder, she digs me...." Of course, the words bore no relation to reality. She neither "dug" me nor even noticed I was crooning. In small consolation a passing old man in a pointed hat heard my singing and nodded.

The language barrier allowed me to sing anything at all, in a loud voice, without anyone taking offense at the lyrics or judging me. No one would notice if the songs were lewd or political. I tried Zappa: "I'll take a ride to Beverly Hills just before dawn, an' knock the little jockeys off the rich people's lawn." I felt wonderfully free of the tyranny of my own generation's revolution. I ran down old Turtles' songs and Broadway show tunes and my father's Clancy Brothers ballads. I was so enjoying myself that, when an old couple approached, I assumed they were music lovers.

Instead, they seemed to ask for grass. I scratched my head, wondering if I'd heard right, but they were serious; they'd even brought their own wheelbarrow and rake. With a sweep of my arm, I stepped aside. They waddled around the fence and politely collected several small piles waiting to be joined to my big pile. I left them to it and went on combining piles.

Ernst showed up in the late afternoon, just when I'd finished. It was funny it had taken until my last day for him to gauge how fast I worked. We sat together in the car for a moment without moving, which was odd. I looked at him for explanation and watched a huge smile spread over his face. I gestured to ask what was going on and he waved two envelopes at me.

Letters! I had mail! Contact with the outside world!

I grabbed for the envelopes, but he yanked them away and then, with a belly laugh, handed them to me. One was from Pam; I couldn't believe it! The other was postmarked from Italy and I tore this open first, to put off what I might hear from America.

Inside was a short note from Annetta. Her program would take her to Paris the third week of September, and she would be very busy but thought we could meet there. She wrote a phone number to reach her in Paris and signed off, "Your friend, Annetta."

Ernst was looking at me with a smirk. I finally laughed and showed him I was pleased at what I'd read. I had a goal and a date and a few weeks to reach Paris.

But then he gestured at the other envelope clutched in my hand. I shook my head and stuffed it into my pocket. I didn't want anyone watching when I got the verdict from Pam.

I asked Ernst to drop me at the store. He objected to my buying more food, like the oranges, and insisted it was better for Frau Melina to feed me hot food. I assured him I simply needed things for the road— but mostly I wanted privacy.

As soon as he had pulled away, I found a place to sit beside a tree, opened the envelope and took a deep breath. Pam wrote about our friends at the restaurant and how they'd been scheduled in three shifts a day during the annual Street Art Fair. She had received my cards and my napkin letter from Biberach and thanked me for thinking of her and sharing some of my adventure. She regretted not saying goodbye but hoped I'd continue to write and think of her as a friend. In a p.s. she mentioned seeing our favorite local band in a bar and that she'd been going to the lake with Peter, the cook next door, concluding "He's been *more than* nice since you left, which has really helped."

I stared at the page. I was *not* encouraged to be classified as a "friend," though it was hopeful she'd written at all. As to Peter: I didn't trust him farther than I could throw his Plymouth, and she had to understand her postscript would tear me up. Was that a bit of payback?

After I gathered myself and made my purchases, I returned to the church. Ernst again asked where I would go and wouldn't it be better to stay in Biberach and save more money. I told him I must go and handed him the fifty marks I owed for food.

"*Ah, nein*, Stephen," Ernst said and suggested I make it forty.

I laughed, punched his arm and insisted it would be fifty—and that was not nearly enough. He grudgingly took the money.

I had bought a loaf of bread and half-kilo of cheese. I also chose the most expensive bottle of schnapps in the store, which I knew Ernst would never buy himself, and a postcard to send Annetta to agree on Paris.

My last dinner was a bit somber, but Ernst tried to keep everything upbeat, as usual. Before they went to bed, I kissed each of the girls on the forehead, including the baby, and Ernst and Frau Melina insisted we open the schnapps bottle and drink a toast to friendship and meeting again.

Chapter IX

The Trial

After a farewell breakfast with the whole family, I got lots of hugs, particularly from Gabi, who seemed genuinely sad to see me go. She was so cute; I suspected I wouldn't be her last boyfriend.

Ernst insisted on driving me to the main road. He started the car and then looked at me for instructions. I heard myself say "Schweiz," although I had not consciously chosen Switzerland over the Black Forest. He took off and soon dropped me at a crossroad. He lifted my pack from the trunk, hugged the air out of me one more time and left with a honk and a last big smile.

Before long a red Citröen stopped and I jogged to the car. A young teacher and his wife were headed south. We exchanged introductions and established my destination in broken German and they left me to myself.

I pulled Kafka from my pack. Joseph K had "the feeling of something learned which I don't understand, but which there is no need to understand." This summed up my education in Biberach, just as I found Kafka's writing brilliant, though often obscure.

Bright sunshine and the movement of the car forced my eyes

closed. I saw myself alone on the road, trying to walk faster than my memories. Every few minutes a car passed, leaving a blurry image of a box of dull color in the mist. I scrutinized the silent houses along the road for signs of life. I felt apart from this world, if there *was* a world behind these façades. There was no warmth here, though I was not particularly cold. There was no food, though I was not hungry. No stranger would take me in, though I wasn't sure I should trust a stranger.

There was no reason to choose one direction over another, nothing to do but walk and hope. I looked for something to throw into the air, so it would fall and point the way. To reach a stick in the gutter, I bent beneath my pack and felt suddenly crushed by its weight. I twisted to take pressure off my knee, lost balance, and fell beside my pack.

But somehow I was still walking on cobblestones past low buildings. Gaslight cast deep shadows. I followed one street into another, each narrower than the last. The slenderest streets became alleyways, and these became more and more confined. I quickened my pace, hoping to break into open space. I stumbled on a cobblestone and fell forward into a run and burst onto a cross street wide enough for cars. A street sign on a building read "Juliusstrasse." There were no people toward either shallow vista, but a car stood in my path, its trunk and passenger door open. I knew this was my ride but was afraid to get in and fall asleep before the driver returned. I put my pack in the trunk anyway and closed it but waited beside the passenger door. It seemed odd someone would offer a ride like this, knowing nothing about me and not even seeing my face. I decided to sit in the car but leave the door open, to rest while I considered where the driver might be.

"*Bitte, aufwachen Sie,*" said the driver, forcing me awake. I wasn't sure what that meant, but we pulled to the side of the road and my hosts turned and smiled. I took this as my exit cue and was soon standing on the roadside, continuing south toward the Bodensee and Switzerland. I was glad to escape my strange dream and doused my head from my canteen.

Sometimes I could practically genuflect on the side of the road and no one would notice me, but other times a ride would come from less than a nod. For the second time that day I didn't even consciously nod before finding myself climbing into a car, and soon I arrived at a lake stretching beyond the horizon.

The town of Friedrichshafen on the Bodensee was full of people. I wandered by shops on steep hills and sat in a café. The waiter brought hot chocolate with a bar of marzipan on the saucer. I unwrapped the foil and touched the bar to my tongue. I wasn't sure I liked the sweet almond taste, but it seemed to come with the price of the cocoa so I put it into my cup. The chocolate was warm and soothing.

It was fortuitous that ferryboats put out from this town. My map showed there was considerable water in my way and it would be a long way around to reach Switzerland. Besides, there was something enticing about setting out to sea again, if only over an inland lake. Imagining myself as Ishmael signing on to the Pequod, I thus bought a ticket to Constance.

We soon embarked and I stood alone in the bow, like a masthead, breathing in the pure air and welcoming the spray on my face. There was something liberating about leaving dry land behind. I wondered if it was always an escape of sorts to go to sea.

When we docked in Constance an hour later, I felt I had come to a new land. I looked for a place to change *Deutschmarks* into Swiss francs. In a bank along a main avenue I joined a short line of customers. Each customer had a lengthy conversation with the teller, in what still sounded like German, about the weather or the teller's family and then they transacted business. The teller was clearly an important cog in local life. When it was my turn, I passed a fifty-mark note through the iron bars and said: "Change to Swiss francs, *bitte?*"

The teller looked confused and said something I couldn't understand. It wasn't clear if the difficulty came from my not speaking Swiss-German or my neglecting to first comment on the chance of rain. I said, "Change? Change!" as if repeating myself with more feeling would make me understood.

This propelled the teller, in slow motion, toward his cash drawer.

He placed my German bill in the drawer and, tentatively, handed me five ten-mark notes.

Distraught, I tried again, saying: "Swiss francs. Swiss francs!"

I tried to push my bills back through the bars, but an elegant gentleman with a bushy white mustache stepped forward. He nodded to all and said to me: "You wish to change marks for francs?"

"*Ja, bitte,*" I said and nodded eagerly. The gentleman turned toward the teller, said something about his sister and the gathering clouds, and then gestured toward me and asked about changing currency. The teller was gracious but long-winded in reply. The gentleman finally turned to me with an exaggerated frown: "He says you must change your money at a bank in Switzerland."

Back on the sidewalk, I once again felt rather dimwitted. I was sure the map showed Switzerland south of the lake; how had I misplaced it? I saw a sign to the border, though, and found the illusive country a few hundred meters up the road. I walked into Switzerland before the rain began and stood in a drizzle by the side of the busy road, wondering where I'd left my ball cap.

It was past time to eat, but I wanted to make the most of the weather. From the shelter of a bus stop, I stuck out my thumb, chanting under my breath: "Take me home. Take me home." It seemed impossible this could work again, but my recourse was limited. I couldn't camp in this rain.

Soon a car stopped. A young man waved through the windshield wipers and gestured to put my pack in the back seat and sit in front.

"Where do you go?" he said with a heavy accent when we started to move.

He seemed familiar and I peered at him. "No certain destination," I said. "Do you know where I can set up my tent?"

"But the weather is wet!" he protested.

I shrugged as if to say, "One does what one must."

"You will like to come in Litzelstetten," he said. "*Mein* girlfriend and me stay there, and you stay while weather it is clear?"

I thought he'd never ask, though the phrasing of the invitation was novel.

His name was Birger. He was stern and wore a thin beard and buttoned his shirt to the top. He lived with a girlfriend named Marit. She was short and pretty in a faded print dress that reached almost to the floor. She prepared a sumptuous meal of lamb chops and fresh vegetables. I offered to contribute the bread from my pack, but they laughed and then caught themselves and apologized. I saw this reaction as a way to further ingratiate myself. They had already looked kindly on me; with their gaffe they also felt sorry for offending me. I stuck the bread back in my pack, certain I'd eat it eventually.

After dinner we drank wine and I lost two games of chess to Birger, who openly relished his victories. Posing a challenge to my host and losing gracefully seemed the least I could do. I also had learned to lose nimbly without spilling anything.

Marit studied English and saw literature as a mirror for society. She was eager to trade paperbacks: *One Day in the Life of Ivan Denisovich* for my dog-eared Kafka, so I promised to finish my book quickly. The apartment was filled with her paintings and laughter and Mozart. We talked late into the night, although the limits of Birger's English finally made him quiet and then sullen.

"It is good you travel alone," she said thoughtfully. "This is the way how you feel all that passes."

She was growing on me, and I nodded for her to go on.

"This for you," she continued, "is the time apart from people who rush about with no reason."

She flushed red as she talked, and I wondered if this hinted at her own longing to travel or came from the wine. Whatever the explanation, the late hour brought her to life as it lulled her boyfriend to sleep. Also, it was a relief to hear something approaching my own language. She was sincere and insightful, her lazy smile intoxicating.

Birger went off to bed and Marit showed me to my couch in a small sitting room past the kitchen. When I reached to shake hands, she pulled me toward her to kiss me full on the lips. She stepped back, hiccupped, giggled and disappeared.

I was too tired to sort out what had happened, so I tried instead to picture where I was on a map of Switzerland. But the map kept twisting into Marit's smile. Soon I slept and dreamed, though it seemed much the same as being awake.

Next morning before breakfast I finished *The Trial*. After Joseph K's unfortunate demise, the volume included excerpts from Kafka's diaries, where he wrote: "My talent for portraying my dreamlike inner life has thrust all other matters into the background." Much as I admired Kafka's writing, it was time for me to wake from my dreams and focus on real life. (My father would find it ridiculous I had to come three thousand miles to learn what he told me every day at home.)

In the morning I drove with Marit to the University of Constance, where she worked, to use the library. On the way I learned both Litzelstetten and the university were in Germany, so the illusive Switzerland had again eluded me. We parked and walked through angular, yellow concrete buildings with mismatched façades festooned with odd hangings. At every turn incongruous art installations whirred with the wind. Twisted metal fences rose from a cobble-stoned, lunar terrain.

Marit showed me to a series of large rooms filled with books and unusual art displays but no people except one librarian. "The students, they are on holiday," she said. "You can stay here a short time?"

"I will be fine," I assured her and wandered through stacks and tables of black and white, metal and glass, decorated with bizarre artifacts. Up an antique wooden staircase, I found a desk overlooking the floors below and lighted by a chandelier made of incense holders.

I wanted to learn the French for the essential hitchhiking phrases: "You have a beautiful country" and "Do you know where I can set up my tent?" An English-French dictionary and, surprisingly, also a German-French dictionary, helped in this effort.

Feeling drowsy again, I put down the dictionary and read in Solzhenitsyn: "A warm man cannot understand a freezing man." This didn't help; the concentration camp setting offered stark realism while I needed escape.

Marit drove me home later and started making dinner. Birger was eager to play chess again. I was happy to play and looked beyond him to Marit, searching for anything in her expression to recall our kiss. But she hummed to herself with an indifferent air.

We set up at the chessboard and this time I tried to win. Was I playing for Marit? How nonsensical was that? I dropped a close game and Birger insisted on a rematch. I again concentrated on the game and this time I won, for the first time in Europe, and it felt great. Marit congratulated me a little too warmly, though, and Birger's mood turned sour.

My elation lasted only moments before I saw the cost of victory. In one efficient endgame I had overstayed my welcome. "Just so you know," I said promptly to avoid awkwardness, "I'll be leaving first thing in the morning."

"Where you will go?" Marit asked. Birger seemed less interested in this than in being assured they'd be rid of me.

"I'd like to see where James Joyce is buried in Zurich."

She nodded as if this was a fine reason to pick a destination. "The American playwright Thornton Wilder also wrote in Zurich," she said. "I will drive in the morning and drop you on the road."

Driving next day, Marit smirked as if she and I shared a secret. But she said nothing out of the ordinary and the farewell kiss she blew felt like mostly air.

*   *   *

By early afternoon I had walked from the highway to a tram stop on the edge of Zurich and stood on a narrow concrete island in the middle of a busy boulevard. The road was flanked by low buildings and busy with shoppers and business people. On a red metal post hung a ticket machine and a typed schedule. I tried to make sense of the times and the cost of a ride to the center city.

A man tapped my shoulder and smiled. "Do you need for assistance?" he said. He was shorter and perhaps ten years older than me. He wore a fine burgundy sweater that made his complexion look healthy, but his eyes were too close together.

I nodded and said I wanted to visit the old part of the city. He responded with the kind of laughter with no lungs behind it. He said the time to see the old city was evening and asked where I lived.

"No fixed abode," I said, looking at the low gray buildings along the street and wondering why I had no sense of the time.

He checked the schedule and said I could get a tram on the half hour. "But perhaps you would come with me?" he said. "We could at my home have some meal and come to the city in this evening, when it is being lively."

This was not how connections were supposed to work, and I hesitated. Why had this man approached me when I wasn't yet distraught or even posing as forlorn? And what was with those eyes? Still, it would not do to pass up a place to stay and a guide to the city.

He introduced himself as Georg. He really looked like no threat, so I crossed the street with him and loaded my pack into the trunk of a dark BMW.

"You are English?" he asked as we drove.

"No, American."

"Ah, that is unnatural. I most usually am able to practice English with travelers from Great Britain."

Perhaps sensing suspicion, Georg explained he had traveled widely when he was young and, seeing my backpack, decided to offer the hand that had helped him so many times. This familiar circle-of-life story gave me some comfort, but I remained on guard.

"It was fortunately I even meet you," Georg said. "I was to visit with my girlfriend in Geneva this weekend, but the plans fall through."

Hearing it was the weekend gave me a grip on reality; since Biberach I had lost track of the days. More important was hearing Georg had a *girl*friend, which ruled out lust as a motive for his odd approach.

We drove along a nondescript highway. After ten minutes Georg apologized that it was perhaps farther to his home than I may have understood. Still, he promised we would have a meal and I could bathe and then we'd drive into the city at the best time. I sat, stiff and alert, sensing another deviation from the pattern: instead of inviting me to fit into his life, Georg was planning his time around me.

We pulled into a garage that opened automatically and led into a duplex apartment. The rooms were not large but were clean and elaborately furnished. In the living room, Georg waved at an oversized, dark screen. "This is my television."

He pulled open the blinds. "This is my view."

Opening a wall cabinet, he added: "This is my stereo."

He kneeled, opened a long chest and lifted out a gun. "This is my automatic rifle."

I steadied myself on a chair, reassessing how I'd found myself in this house. Georg's obsession with his belongings was peculiar, his display of the gun frightening.

He laughed. "You wonder I have the rifle, yes?"

I tried to smile naturally.

"In Switzerland all men have such arms. We are trained, if there is war, we must put on the uniform and take our weapon to the mountains."

This story was familiar from the Swiss guy in Heidelberg but I needed no props to get the picture. Calmly, I suggested we continue the tour. He brightened and moved through the kitchen and second floor pointing out additional possessions.

After we had covered both floors, I collapsed in an easy chair in the living room and tried to decipher the television news in German. Georg came into the room and handed me a magazine. I opened the glossy pages and found a pornographic picture story of two women and a man on a sailboat. I struggled to feign indifference but wanted to see the pictures. Clothes were episodically shorn as I turned each page. Feeling the physical effect of the pictures, I wished Georg would go away, but he hovered behind me. I turned the pages until the man on the sailboat stood at full salute before the two kneeling women.

"He is big so here," Georg grinned, holding his crotch with both hands.

I closed the magazine, disgusted but trying to look bored, and handed it back to him. An awkward stillness followed. I turned toward the television but sensed he was disappointed. Finally, he turned to another idea. "We eat a meal now, yes?"

He made a ceremony of opening a can of soup and lighting the stove. He put out a sausage and bread and poured two small glasses of clear liquor. Handing me one glass, he held up the other. "We toast to the helping hand."

After we ate Georg handed me a towel and showed me the bathroom. He stopped the deep claw-footed tub and turned on the hot water. I stood aside and waited for him to leave the room. Once alone, I searched the doorknob and thought it strange there was no lock.

The water was steaming. I dropped my clothes into a dusty pile. Lowered into exquisite warmth, I was ready to stay there all night. I lay back without moving, savoring the heat.

Suddenly the door swung open. I sat up, startled, splashing suds on the floor. Georg walked in naked, holding his aroused organ. I gripped the sides of the tub. My mind raced. He stood in the middle of the floor with a wide, moronic grin.

I fought off an instinct to gag and turned away from him. I stepped quickly out of the tub, refusing to look at him, and wrapped myself in a towel. Without speaking I picked up my clothes and moved to step around him. He shrugged his shoulders and stepped back, saying he would leave while I dressed.

The door closed behind him. I fell back against it.

This was messed up. I struggled to remember his exact line about his "girlfriend." The whole scene felt like a bad comedy, except for the firearms. I grabbed my clothes and opened the door slowly. Georg passed on his way downstairs, dressed for an evening out. I went into the bedroom and sat with my pack, wondering what to do.

Georg called out from halfway down the stairs that he was going to pick up his friend Werner and would be back in ten minutes to take us to the city.

The door to the garage closed. I had to decide quickly what to do. Georg's desires aside, was it safe to stay? I grimaced at an image of him naked with his gun. His bringing another man to the house also could upset the balance if it came to force, but leaving while he was gone meant walking out onto a suburban street where there were no people, with no idea where I was or how to get back to Zurich. Staying could mean getting more to eat and a place to sleep, along with a trip to the old city. I wished Edward were here; he'd know what to do. Time ticked away and then it seemed too late to go. I didn't want him to catch me leaving. I resolved to stay and changed into a clean shirt.

Georg returned and called out. In the kitchen he introduced Werner, who was blonde and slightly balding and probably thirty-five years old. Although he was well dressed, he seemed somehow greasy. Werner said in halting English that his wife was staying home with the baby, which almost caused me to laugh out loud, as I assumed this was Werner's version of Georg's line about visiting his girlfriend. I didn't believe it for a minute.

We drank the clear liquor again, and I watched to make sure they drank as much as I did and from the same bottle. In Georg's car they insisted I sit up front for the view. For twenty minutes they pointed out buildings of note, none of which registered with me.

We parked in the city center and joined the crowds on Nieder-dorfstrasse. Narrow streets closed to traffic wound past cafés with tables on the street. Five and six-story buildings were painted in pastels and crowned in intervals with narrow, pointed towers. We wandered cobblestoned streets and looked over wares on the sidewalk, stopping to drink in cafes where Georg paid the tabs.

"Dadaism," Georg declared as he finished a beer at an outdoor table. "You know the Dadaism?"

Werner smiled knowingly. The question was obviously for me.

"I've heard the word," I replied, "but I don't know what it is. Some kind of art?"

"Anti-art," Georg responded. "Collage and poetry and sculpture. It was born in Zurich, near here in the Cabaret Voltaire. It was anarchy, subversion, from the brutal war in 1916. Art was to be nonsense, to happen by chance."

I was surprised to be interested in something Georg had to say. "Can we see this Café Voltaire?" I asked.

"Ah, no," he replied. "The building is not far, on the *die Spiegelgasse*, but sadly the café, it was unfortunately to close soon when it began."

Art happening by chance seemed right up my alley. I was sorry to have missed the Dadaists by sixty years.

When we got bored walking, Werner led us to a large pub paneled in dark wood and we found seats at the bar. Georg was still buying. I nursed a beer and watched the crowd through the mirror behind the bartender. A dark man with a heavy mustache caught my eye and nodded. I turned away but then it struck me: there were few women in the bar and the men were all thin and suspiciously well groomed.

Georg noticed my unconscious sigh. Then I stood up too quickly and had to steady myself on a chair. I said I had to go. Georg grinned at Werner and they finished their drinks.

We were soon in the car and they let me sit in back. I reached into my pocket and squeezed my lucky peseta. There was no way Edward would have let us fall into this situation, but then I also wouldn't have been afraid with him at my side.

Again, I fell asleep, and this time dreamed I was drinking on a curb with a large rodent in spectacles. I was trying to make sense of this when we pulled into the garage. Georg had already dropped off Werner, which was a relief as far as numbers went. I followed him into the house. He was no match for me physically, but I felt woozy, and he had all that military gear.

He showed me upstairs to a room with two narrow beds along adjacent walls. I removed my shoes but slept in my jeans and tee shirt. I was scared and tried hard to keep my eyes open, but the alcohol shut them.

In the dark I woke, or dreamed I woke, to a wet slapping sound. I knew immediately I was in Georg's house and turned my head slowly toward the room. On the other bed I could make out violent movement. I didn't want to call attention to myself and also didn't want to really see what was happening. Still, the blankets on the other bed fell aside.

In the dim light I saw Georg on his knees with one elbow pumping up and down.

This was nauseating. We had gotten around in the end to *my* fitting into *his* life. I held my breath and lay dead still, closing my eyes to slits so I would only see if he approached. I kept thinking of the gun downstairs and hoping Georg would need no help in satisfying his needs.

When the commotion subsided, the quiet was disturbed only by my racing heartbeat. I remained alert until Georg seemed to sleep.

My next conscious perception was Georg coming into the room, fully dressed and smiling like the sunny day. In his daytime personality, he offered breakfast, which I accepted as if I had earned it. It seemed the worst had passed and I'd make it back to the road intact. I brought the pack down to the kitchen, to keep my momentum headed out. Over a second cup of coffee I relaxed, and it seemed I had chosen right in staying the night.

Georg invited me to visit his friend's house on Lake Zurich. I politely declined. He asked me to reconsider and described his friend's sailboat and the spacious house with lake views and gourmet meals and croquet on the lawn. All I could think of was escaping to the side of a highway. He finally agreed I should continue on my way but only on condition he drop me where I could easily get a ride. "But where do you go?" he asked.

A world of answers spun through my head, but I said: "Paris."

He took solace that Paris was a lovely destination. In the car he insisted on concluding with an "automobile tour" of the city. I felt safe in the car in daylight with my pack near at hand and so didn't object. He drove by a beautiful park and slowed past the Bank of Moscow, explaining the Soviets would never attack because they kept their money in Switzerland.

Seeing two men apparently arriving home from a late night, Georg mentioned that men in Switzerland were open to all kinds of experience. Right, I thought, nothing like a night out with the boys to keep the marriage fresh.

Turning on the charm, Georg told stories of sailing at the lake house. This recurring theme of sailboats was making me queasy. Finally, and resignedly, he pulled to the side of an entrance to a highway to France. I got my pack out of the car before thanking him and then had the urge to push the car with my foot to start it moving away from me.

"Good travels," he called out with a sad smile. I waved good riddance and turned to the road. Once he was out of sight, I spit on the hand he had shaken and wiped it on my pants. It felt familiar and free to be on the roadside alone.

* * *

I leaned the pack against a stone bridge and walked back and forth on the shoulder, trying to solve the enigma of Zurich. People couldn't always be judged right away, but I needed to size up acquaintances more quickly. Georg was a predator and who knew the many ways the night might have gone bad.

The puzzle would have to wait for a leisurely hour, though. I stuck out my thumb, and a ride came quickly. The driver spoke no English so I motioned I would follow his direction west.

Though clouds mostly hid the sun, the road wound through spectacular green mountains, the highest peaks lost in mist. Lone cottages dotted hillsides and even in little villages the houses each stood at a distance from the others. I wondered if this separateness spoke of the severe slope or the same Swiss culture that armed each citizen soldier with a rifle.

After my first ride, I had no more luck. I found myself walking to France, chasing deliverance from the hazy nightmare of Switzerland. I felt an overwhelming need for a friend who would not threaten me *and* who spoke English, or better yet an American with whom I might share humor and sensibility. I laughed that it sounded like I wanted a role in a novel of manners, but my smile faded with the gravity of my encounter with Georg. I had to acknowledge the irony in setting out to follow the protagonists of my novels away from the mundane and into the wide unknown but, having arrived on distant shores, yearning for the familiar.

Hours later, daylight was fading and I was still walking. I finally took a crossroad, turning steeply up a slope to search for a camping spot. It was hard hiking. Each step revealed a broader view of the vast mountains but no place flat and secluded enough for my tent. At twilight I gave up and descended again to the highway. In another half hour a young Swiss couple stopped on their way to Basel, on the French border. I said I, too, planned to spend the night in Basel and wondered if there was a hostel. To my chagrin, the driver's wife knew of a youth hostel in town, and they left me at its door. After I thanked them and they drove off, I decided this was perhaps for the best. I had money for a bed and felt sure I could talk my way in. This might be the place to sort out the real from the surreal.

* * *

The hostel father agreed reluctantly that I could stay the night. I paid in advance and parked my pack in a bunkroom. I took Solzhenitsyn, the bread left from Biberach (the cheese had the warning fishy smell and so went into the trash; maybe I actually was starting to learn something) and two apples from the couple in the last car to a long table in a deserted dining room. The room was clean, almost antiseptic. Stark ceiling lights gave off an electric hum.

"Late dinner," came a voice with an inflection that left unclear if this was a question.

Entering the room came a broad, handsome smile and laughing eyes beneath a mountain of wild brown hair. I was pretty sure I'd found my English-speaker.

"Have a hunk?" I said, breaking off a piece of stale bread.

"Thought you'd never ask," he said and stretched his long legs under the table to join my meager meal.

"Nick Mulroney," he said, extending a big right hand while he picked up an apple with his left.

"Stephen Kylemore," I said and shook the outstretched hand. "British?"

He grimaced. "Australian. And you, it's plain to see, are American."

Once he identified his nationality, I sensed something more musical in his accent than what I'd heard from the Brits. He was tall and hungry, and we soon finished all there was to eat and then lingered to talk. I asked what he was doing in Basel.

"Been sweeping up for my bed and food, waiting for money from home. You see there was a mix-up when I left Paris two days ago. Afraid I was a bit pissed and ended up on the wrong train."

This was a crazy story but in light of my own travels—and his self-deprecating sincerity—easy enough to believe. When he stopped laughing at his own travails, he asked: "What about you?"

"Worked in Germany for a month, but then fell into the Franz Kafka tour of Switzerland."

"Ah, and I see you're finishing up the assigned reading," he said, gesturing at my Solzhenitsyn novel.

"Ah, yeah. I'm due for a comedy. Anyway, I haven't really spoken English in five weeks, so it's good to meet you. I'm on my way to Paris."

"Paris! I love it; just came from there. Maybe we should go together; I've got lots of friends there and probably a place to stay."

This all sounded promising, but I'd become skeptical of people with lots of charm and stories that sounded too good to be true. We agreed it was time for bed and to meet in the morning, and I went off to a blissfully peaceful sleep.

When I came down to breakfast, Nick was helping with the dishes and sweeping the floor. He came by my table to suggest I see the Spalentor Tower and the fountain at the Theaterplatz and then meet him in front of the old Town Hall. This sounded like a plan, but I didn't want to pay for another night in the hostel, so I left my pack by his bunk and took what I'd need for the day.

Nick's directions led me to a medieval structure of two five-story towers with a pointed rooftop between them. A street led beneath an iron gate that looked like it hadn't closed in a century. The structure was imposing, though completely anachronistic, as it wasn't connected to a city wall.

Walking parallel to the river, beneath a red sandstone castle on a hill, I reached the Theaterplatz. There I found a fountain full of mechanical figures swirling about, as if cavorting in the water, joined by two mimes on the plaza. I didn't have much patience for mimes, but these were the ideal link between the cavorting machines and humanity. A plaque said the sculptor Jean Tinguely had completed the fountain the year before.

Nearing mid-day, I took up a spot in the marketplace before the bright red Town Hall and nearly finished my novel before Nick sauntered by, looking like he owned the plaza. We sat together on a bench, laughing at the tourists. It was a great relief to share humor with someone, and I came quickly to trust him and accept his suggestion we visit Paris together. I offered to lend him twenty bucks until we got there so he wouldn't have to wait for his money in Basel. We agreed to take off in the morning, after he spent one more night in the hostel while I slept across the street in the park.

"Something you said last night," he said as we watched a fetching young woman hurry by, "about Kafka and Zurich?"

"Ah, that," I said. "It's kind of a sordid story."

This got his complete attention and he turned an expectant expression toward me. I related the high points of the pickup and the automatic weapon and the bath and the gay bar, culminating in Georg's late-night exertions.

He grinned. "Sounds harmless enough, really," he concluded.

"Yeah but he was the fox and I was the rabbit."

"More like the chicken," he laughed and went on: "You mean you've never tried to seduce some innocent girl with a drink and a meal?"

"Yeah, of course, but this was different."

He looked at me condescendingly. "Different how?"

"Well, the bath, and the gun, and the…"

"And the unfamiliar role?" The amusement in his eyes stopped me from talking. He stared into the distance and seemed to ponder before continuing. "I get it that he was barking up the wrong tree, but at least he knew what he wanted… and where's the harm? You got a place to stay and a meal and he just happened to like… your bum."

There was no use looking for sympathy from Nick. I did think I had to be more discerning in assessing people up front but guessed he might be right that I was making too much of my visit to the dark side.

We lounged through the afternoon and took in the frescoes in the Town Hall courtyard. Later we—or rather I—bought bread and cheese in a shop for our dinner and we spent the mild evening in the park. Later, he retrieved my pack for me and I found some bushes to sleep under without setting up the orange tent.

Chapter X

Maison Fauconnier

Nick was an old hand at hitchhiking and knew the way, and we had an easy time crossing France. We arrived in Paris late in the evening and walked over Pont Marie to the right bank of the Seine and a small hotel for students. The building nestled among others of staid construction on a side street laid in cobblestones. Above the heavy oak door, a sign read *"Maison Fauconnier"* and, in smaller letters, something about being a hotel for international students.

I would learn that student travelers typically occupied eighty of the Maison's hundred beds. During the day a concierge oversaw two women who cooked breakfast and cleaned. In the afternoon another concierge took over. From eleven at night until seven in the morning, charge was left to the night porter, an American named Henry Alcort.

Henry was tall and lean. Dark, wavy hair framed his deep-set eyes, making him look more serious than he was. He had grown up in California and excelled in academics. He started Stanford at seventeen and made perfect grades his first semester. Second semester he punched the teaching assistant who gave him a "B." The university and his father then agreed a leave of absence was in order. He decided on France, where he was soon speaking like a Parisian and seducing young visitors to the Maison.

When we arrived, Henry was killing time before locking up. Nick strutted in with his small bundle of clothes, large wallet and pack of cigarette tobacco, and I followed beneath my mountainous backpack.

"Yes, Henry," Nick laughed before Henry turned to see him. "It's good to see 'seductionism' alive and well in Paris," he said, with his way of raising his inflection at the end of a statement, as if in question.

Henry jumped up and shook Nick's hand enthusiastically and then mine, and then introduced two girls from the University of Florida. Nick greeted everyone, his accent, height and broad smile making him the natural center of attention.

Nick asked Henry if he could put us up, and then noticed how Henry's amused glow turned to bewilderment and said, "Yes well, I guess the Brits'll have to keep that job. Anyway, Stevie and I were thinking of picking grapes."

"*Les vendanges!*" Henry said, and his gaze drifted to a distant horizon, then he snapped to attention. "Yeah, no problem," he said. "Stow your packs in the back room and surrender to 'sleepism' in the cellar." He paused and smiled. "Of course, you'll have to be out before the *concierge* comes at seven."

Nick and I looked at each other and mouthed: "Seven?!"

"But really," Henry continued, "what're you doing back in Paris?"

"You mean the job and all?" said Nick.

Henry took a seat and, with a rolling motion of his hand, gestured to continue.

"Right," said Nick. "Well, after that party last weekend, when we were all pissed, and everyone came to Gare de Lyon to see me off..."

"I slept the next day until dinner," Henry interrupted.

"Well," Nick continued, "I think I remember a number of people helping me onto the train to Calais, so I could catch the ferry and start my new job next day in Birmingham. Bloody thing about the station, though: there was one train going to Calais and another to Switzerland."

He paused for effect. Henry hung on the punch line.

"Woke up in Basel with no money and only clothes for the weekend!"

Henry hugged his knees and rocked as he laughed.

Nick continued even louder: "You bastards poured me onto the wrong train!"

By then everyone was laughing except Nick, who still played to the crowd. When we all quieted down, he concluded: "When Steve came along, I was sweeping the hostel in Basel, waiting for money from Australia."

Henry stamped his heel and shook his head in a laugh now quiet. He was clearly enchanted. I came to see he found his own life, as expatriate-seducer-in-three-languages, dull compared to Nick's.

When the girls had gone upstairs and Nick went to wash up, Henry locked the front door and sat by me. "So, how'd you hook up with the Aussie?" he asked.

I smiled. "Like he said, I rolled into the hostel in Basel one night in need of English conversation. Nick filled that bill in spades." Henry laughed and motioned to continue.

"He stayed up with me until we'd finished my food. Then we hung out in Basel waiting for his money. I spent the next night in a park to save the price of a bed, though Nick had a place to stay at the hostel."

"Nick *always* has a place to stay," Henry said in a stage whisper.

"Yeah, it seems. Anyway, I was headed to France and he said he had friends in Paris, so I loaned him a few bucks until his parents could wire money here."

Before long Nick showed me the baggage room out back and then the cellar. At the bottom of the stairs several old couches lined what looked like whitewashed cave walls. Through an archway was another room lit just enough to show scattered folding chairs facing a small raised stage. Nick and I each chose a couch. I unrolled my sleeping bag, and he unfolded the blankets Henry had loaned him.

After we settled in, Henry bade us goodnight and switched off the light from the top of the stairs. A minute of absolute darkness and silence later, I said: "What's with the ism's?"

"Met a woman last time I was here. Very highbrow. She labeled things with big words: collectivism, social Darwinism, this 'ism,' that 'ism.' Henry and I started adding 'ism' to make nonsense words to rib her—but she never got the joke."

I thought about Dadaism: not a nonsense word, but a movement of nonsense art. After another quiet minute, I said: "You know what I've noticed about France? When I make faces at kids, they laugh. Not like Germany or England."

"There's a real difference. The French are at ease because they know how to live. The Germans live to work, but the French work to live, and it carries over to the children."

After a pause he added: "This was a big breakaway for you: taking off on your own?"

"Yeah. It was hard getting started, but I'd waited too long, and my window was small."

"To tour the world?"

"Well, not 'tour,' but something else. In Germany I called it '*Meine Reise.*'"

"Sounds a bit fascist, kinda like *Mein Kampf.*"

I laughed. "Yes... well, in high school we talked about hitchhiking to Stockbridge, Massachusetts to see Alice's Restaurant."

"Ah, yeah. A mate of mine felt the same about Jim Morrison's grave at Père-Lachaise."

"Well, we never made it to Stockbridge. Then my brother and I talked for years about traveling to Ireland and Spain, but that didn't happen either."

I paused, grateful Nick couldn't see a tear run down my cheek. "So," I gathered myself and continued, "when college was winding down, I decided I had to go for it or I'd *never* get away. I tried my girl-friend and then other friends; nobody would come with me."

"Ah, you're fortunate there; it's not easy moving about with any-one; friends aren't necessarily compatible traveling companions when it comes to it."

"I guess, and it gives me a chance to think about writing it all up as a novel."

"Ah, so I'm slumming it with a swot, am I? Well, make sure you emphasize the panache of the Australian comrade."

"Oh, you can be sure about that," I said. Then I added more seriously: "The hard part was leaving my girlfriend, just when I'd found someone I really wanted to be with."

"Well, the world is full of wonderful women," he said and seemed to fall asleep.

* * *

Henry shook me awake. "C'mon," he said urgently. The bare light bulb hanging from the ceiling was so bright. Henry was still shaking me and said: "You have to split before Fabienne gets here."

Nick led me to the street as my eyes came into focus. We walked a deserted Rue St. Antoine, which became Rue de Rivoli. The sun was barely up, and everything was fresh. A slight crispness in the air was giving way to a warm, sunny day. Shutters opened into ground-floor shops and five or six stories of apartments above. Great stone buildings that seemed to house offices opened on the street between columns or arched passageways. An old woman swept dust from a hallway into the street. A gentleman in a beret nodded as he stepped out of a bakery, two loaves under his arm. The smell of fresh bread followed behind him as he ambled by.

"Up for a baguette?" Nick said. "On me?"

He greeted the woman behind a counter with a wide smile and said: "*Bonjour madame. Une baguette, s'il vous plaît?*" She smiled and handed him a long, thin loaf. He reached deep into his pocket for a franc and thirty centimes, as I tried to memorize what he had said to add to my list of essential French phrases.

We sat in the sun on a street corner by Place de la Bastille. With the crust cracked open, steam rose from the delicious soft bread inside. I asked where the actual Bastille prison was. Nick rolled his eyes and explained the people had torn down the prison in the revolution.

I wondered if he was making that up, given what I'd noticed as his propensity to spin a yarn.

Nick suggested coffee and I agreed. We each pocketed an end of the bread and entered a tiny café open to the sidewalk. Behind a bar of stainless steel, an elderly man with a dramatic comb-over worked espresso machines. Nick ordered two espressos and nodded for me to pay. I grinned at his playing me for our breakfast expenses but laid out the money and then laughed, watching him meticulously unwrap and drop into his tiny cup four lumps of sugar.

"Yes, well," he said, "this stuff is bloody strong. Anyway, I've been on strange diets my whole life to cure being hyperactive."

There was a smile in his eyes and we both laughed. "Guess the diets didn't work," I said, attempting an Australian rise in inflection.

Speaking of diets reminded me of the sores lingering on my wrist and knuckle. Nick examined these and diagnosed a vitamin deficiency and the onset of scurvy. This confirmed my belated fears about my German eating habits. Remembering how Ernst had been so concerned I wouldn't get *hot* meals on the road, I swore out loud at my stupidity and again swore to take vitamin C and buy no more chocolate.

* * *

Breakfast at the Maison ran from eight to nine-thirty. Fabienne was the concierge and oversaw the food service, cleaning and check-ins and outs. She was solid and stern with a stiff black-leather jacket and short, black hair. Emeline prepared the breakfast of coffee and bread with jams and butter. She was petite with a sweet face and short, brown hair in a bowl cut and wore a big apron over a white uniform.

Henry said he generally stayed after his shift for breakfast and then went to nap in his apartment. Nick calculated we should return at nine-thirty, in time to help clean up breakfast and snag some leftovers.

When we entered, a serious-looking young woman sat with a serious-looking book.

"I don't believe it," she said looking up, as if surprised.

"What," said Nick, "you back, too?"

After hellos and quick introductions, Jane Mandel proposed we take the trip to the Eiffel Tower she and Nick had been unable to complete the weekend before. First, however, we ate leftovers in the smaller of the two dining rooms at the front of the building, where guests enjoyed the breakfast that came with a room and fresh linen while they checked their maps and guidebooks.

Jane went back to her reading while Nick and I ducked through strands of colored wooden beads hanging from an archway at the back of the dining rooms. A doorway there led to a rear courtyard, which also led to a storage room—for the baggage of guests who arrived early or had officially, but not actually, departed. There was no lock on the door, which, in any event, would barely close. Inside, the room was lined with rough, wooden shelves and at its end another doorway led to a rustic toilet and shower.

"So, I take it *that* was your erudite girlfriend," I said as Nick took his turn washing up.

"You could tell?" he said as he laughed. He then gave me a quick biography of Jane Mandel. At sixteen she had left suburban Philadelphia to summer on a kibbutz; at twenty she was supporting herself in Europe. She worked at a student hotel in London and saved time off to travel over long weekends. She could get money from home but refused it. She had no patience for women who wouldn't risk even a junior year abroad, or for anyone less engaged with the world than she was.

It sounded like we were in for a fun day. I pulled a clean shirt out of my pack and was delighted to find, folded inside, the Yankees cap I thought was lost. I hoisted the pack to the highest shelf to keep it from the merely curious, but something was in the way. I reached up beyond where I could see to clear a space and pulled down a big dusty paperback *Anna Karenina*. I was thrilled—and only sorry it was too thick to bring on our morning tour.

A quick metro ride brought us to the broad square around the base of the Eifel Tower. The iron monument rose like an enormous braided teepee. We strolled the square among dark black men selling trinkets off blankets, one step ahead of the police.

"You really should see the view," Jane said, mostly to Nick.

"Looks like a lot of stairs," said Nick, eyeing the tower up and down.

"And what does it cost?" I interjected from outside the conversation.

Nick nodded at my point. Jane shook her head and said condescendingly: "You're in Paris; you could pay a few francs to ride a world-famous elevator, even if you have to mix with the *tourists*."

"Well, but those few francs," said Nick. "You see, we're on that 'other' tour."

On cue I added: "They call it 'Europe On No Dollars a Day.'"

Jane sighed and led the way across the plaza. Nick followed, attracted but mostly teasing. I brought up the rear, wondering why.

She paused by a newspaper stand, twirling a finger in her frizzy hair. The headlines shouted about an oil tanker accident. Jane demonstrated her command of French by explaining there had been an ecological disaster off the Spanish coast.

"Capitalism!" she intoned, "and its pollution that dooms the world!"

She stomped off, tossing her cigarette butt into the street. Nick and I looked at the butt and then at each other and laughed, and then we followed.

Jane insisted we walk the Champs-Elysées. "*Très bourgeoise*," she said as she walked defiantly, refusing to step out the way of the well-dressed citizens. She seemed angry, yet fascinated, with this world. I saw only a wide shopping avenue ending at the Arc de Triomphe.

"Must avoid bourgeoisism," I said to Nick, and we grinned at Jane and the other self-important people rushing by.

On the way home, we chipped in for food at a supermarket. At dusk we ate in the square before Notre Dame, watching buskers work clusters of tourists. The immense stone edifice was a striking backdrop for our picnic.

"Have you seen *The Hunchback of Notre Dame*?" I said to them both when Jane stopped talking to chew.

"Thirties talkie?" said Nick. "Teacher in my film class went on about the technical achievement."

"The closing shot backing away from Quasimodo," I said. "Amazing for its time."

Jane munched as if she tasted something sour. I cast her a condescending look and Nick rolled his eyes. She swallowed and resumed lecturing, revealing that her expertise extended to early Catholicism. The name of this and the many other "Notre Dame" cathedrals, she was glad to relate, came from the cult of the Virgin as the "Mother of God," which elevated Mary to the status of a deity in the image of the mother goddess Isis.

I was getting used to hearing Nick make off-handed, outrageous statements as if they were dogma, but much of this was tongue-in-cheek, and he'd capitulate with a self-deprecating laugh as soon as he was seriously challenged. Jane, however, spoke with an arrogance that admitted no doubt, and her equating the Virgin Mary with a pagan goddess spurred in me the urge to come to the defense of my lapsed faith. But confronting her seemed like an awful way to start the evening, so I simply suggested we go back to the Maison.

There was no need to wait for Henry to come to work before we showered. The evening concierge never went near the baggage room. I washed for the first time in days, and dug into my novel, while Nick talked with Jane. Henry arrived, we chatted through the evening and Nick and I descended to our cellar.

Next day we followed much the same pattern: ejected onto a wakening city, early coffee at a café, meeting Jane at the Maison for breakfast leftovers and a guided tour of "significant" sites. On the second day the tour ran from the Basilique du Sacré Coeur in Montmartre to the Centre Pompidou, a modern museum wearing its inside pipes and conduits on the outside, Jane enlightened us, as an expression of "high-tech architecture."

"Functionalism, actually," Nick said under his breath, but then smiled at Jane in mock admiration. She reminded me of the matronly aunt in a novel of manners, entitled to lecture because she's paying the bills.

The next day was Sunday, and her last day in Paris. Admission to the Louvre was free, so she led Nick and me through the main entrance in a wave of visitors. The din inside the museum could not drown out her commentary, so I hatched a plan of escape. As she focused on Nick and he looked at the art, I fell behind and melted into the crowd.

Once free, I stopped and let out a great sigh that attracted curious stares from two ladies. It felt a relief to choose my own direction; the ability to do this had begun to feel essential, a prerogative of my current life. I looked for the *Mona Lisa*, which was easy to find in a front hall. But it hung in a Plexiglas box, Lisa's sarcastic smile an apt comment on her confined display. From behind a crowd of people, I held my camera high, with little notion of how the shot was composed. Just then a busload of Japanese tourists arrived, and I decided I'd had enough "culture."

Outside, at liberty from the crowds and of playing little brother chaperon, I made my way back to the Maison along the quai on the right bank of the Seine, on a street with a succession of names. In a shop I asked the price of an apple, but the grocer pretended not to understand my French or sign language and ushered me out of his store. I walked on, vexed. This wasn't my first encounter with the kind of attitude that once had warned me away from Paris. I often asked for directions in pidgin French and every fourth or fifth person would look at me like I was an idiot and refuse to respond. I couldn't understand this. The Germans were all amused and complemented when I tried to speak their language, whereas Parisians were insulted I didn't do it well enough. Sitting by the river, I reached into my pouch for my good-luck coin and flipped it back and forth over my fingers. I decided Edward would agree: for all its grandeur, the underside of Paris was filthy and cold.

Evening passed to day and to another evening, and one late afternoon in the courtyard, Nick and I sat in the sun. I looked up lazily from my novel. "When will we go to pick grapes?" I said.

"We've got to wait until the harvest works its way up from the south, to Bordeaux; that's the best place to work. Anyway, what's the rush? Our room is free. The living is easy. Not to worry."

"You never worry."

"Yes, well it's the Australian way: no hurry, no worries, and a long life. We may be the most laid-back people in the world, which reminds me of a story." (Almost everything reminded Nick of a story.) "There was this bunch of Aussies at Oktoberfest in Munich. They got so drunk, with everyone partying, that they took a Strassenbahn for a joy ride; took it all over and completely messed up the oh-so-precise German system."

Nick continued but my attention drifted, and he stopped talking to look at me.

"I couldn't leave right now, anyway," I said, distractedly.

This got his attention. He motioned with his eyes for me to explain.

"Well, remember the Italian girl I told you about?"

"Yeah, right, in the London house of horrors."

"It was a church… a shelter."

"Right, but with Bela Lugosi."

That image arrested me for a moment and then I explained: "She's in this program where she visits other universities. I met her after she had finished in London and was staying on for a holiday. Apparently, she's not only stunning but also is really smart. Now she's here for two days, at a technical school outside the city, but she's coming in tonight. Henry called her for me and left the Maison's address."

My thoughts drifted to the mischief in Annetta's eyes. Nick said my unconscious grin was as wide as the Seine and that he must be off. I returned to the Maison to take a shower and see if I had any clean clothes.

When Annetta showed up at the door of the Maison, I jumped up and held out my hands. We hugged. I lifted her off her feet.

When I put her down, we looked deeply into each other's eyes, as if for assurance we were the same people who met in London.

"I'm so sorry…" I began, thinking of Saint Cyril's.

"It's so nice…" she said at the same time, only in the present.

We both laughed and hugged again.

I stashed her shoulder bag in the baggage room. On returning I found Henry had already introduced himself. We chatted a few minutes, and then Annetta and I walked off to a restaurant Henry recommended, assuring him we'd be back before closing.

We held hands and strolled slowly. Her big green eyes gripped me. We kissed. I couldn't believe I'd gotten a second chance and was holding her again. London seemed so long ago.

"My meetings were very long," she said, "and I must return first thing tomorrow."

"No problem," I said, thinking only how good it was to see her. I hadn't yet worked out where we would sleep and was desperate to find somewhere we could be alone. I hoped to convince Henry to switch places for the night or find somewhere else for us in the Maison. There had to be a way to arrange this. But when I was with her, I forgot everything—and left the details for later.

We stopped to watch long, double-decker tourist boats float past the majestic towers and buttresses of Notre Dame as they colored pink from the setting sun. I led her into a dark corner by a bench and took her in my arms.

"I missed you," I said. "I felt so bad about London."

She only smiled. I kissed her lips and her eyes and her neck. She felt small and soft and she smelled of lilacs. Our attraction seemed chemical, a natural reaction. We had not simply carried on directly from where we left off; we had picked up much farther along.

We strolled to the restaurant and sat at an outdoor table. She asked about my travels. She thought the ferry ride to Holland sounded crazy and was not surprised how I'd found help in Germany. "You have a good heart," she said, "and people, they see this."

Lingering after dinner over the last of the wine, I asked about her boyfriend.

"He came to be possessive," she said, with little emotion, "so I leave him. The world is big, but he would make it small."

She leaned into me and kissed below my ear. "I have a small apartment with a window looking at the university. It is very pretty; you must come to see."

"Only money keeps me from going tomorrow. But soon I'll go

south for the grapes, and then I'll visit Turin, and maybe then we'll go together to the Aegean Sea."

She laughed. "I have school," she said. "This is not the time to holiday on islands."

Greece didn't matter or even Italy. I saw nothing but her coquettish smile and visions of us together in some undefined place over the night ahead. When we returned to the Maison, Henry was playing guitar while Nick rolled a cigarette. Nick rose and shook Annetta's hand, saying: "So, the face that launched Stephen across the continent."

She blushed in her way and we all sat around a table. Nick launched into the tale of his day with some friend of a friend in the Montmartre. He told how they met an American artist who had lived in Paris since the 1920s and knew Gertrude Stein because they came from the same town in Pennsylvania.

I was too involved in planning the night to listen to Nick. When Henry rose to lock the door, I followed and pulled him aside. "Henry," I said, trying to communicate my pain, "Annetta and I have only tonight; is there any way we could take your cot and you could sleep in the cellar?"

He sighed. "I'd help you, man—young love and all that—but I'd lose my job. They know I let people stay in the cellar but pretend they don't. Leaving you upstairs would be too much. If a guest came looking for me...."

"Is there any kind of private room at all?"

He laughed sadly. "You think I'd sleep in the dining room if there was anyplace else? No, there's only the bunk rooms, and tonight we're actually full."

I followed Henry as he closed things up for the night, scouting for a private nook or corner. Having no luck, I rejoined Nick and Annetta. She was talking about her conference, something to do with mathematical theory. Nick listened as if he understood, a familiar act. I realized she and I had never talked about her studies while we were snogging in London.

When Henry announced it was time for bed, I brought Annetta to the back room to get her bag. "We have to share the cellar with Nick," I said. "It's not private or luxurious."

She was amused. "At least this time I will not be in the 'girls only' section."

I didn't see anything funny about the situation. I ached to get her alone, and it bothered me she didn't share my frustration. I led her downstairs, where Nick was rolled against the wall, already asleep, and she chuckled at the cave walls and dusty couches.

"Very cozy," she said as Henry unceremoniously flipped off the light.

We removed our shoes and pants in the dark and lay on top of my sleeping bag beneath a blanket. Pushing against her body made me forget we weren't alone, and I reached beneath her sleeping shirt. But she was aware of Nick nearby in the darkness and gently insisted we must wait until next time, in Turin.

"It will be better when we wait," she whispered and kissed behind my ear.

So, my erotic schemes ended in crowded and restless sleep. When Henry sent us forth in the morning, Nick made an excuse, wished Annetta safe travels, and left us alone. I walked her to the train station, exhilarated by her company but unslaked by our confined night.

"You have nice friends," she said. "I am happy you have found your way since we meet in England."

"I'm glad you think so and so glad we got to see each other. After a couple of weeks at the grapes, I'll buy a train ticket to Turin."

"You will love *Turino*," she said, "and we will have the time together."

It was only as I walked back to the Maison that I realized I should have hit up Henry for his apartment. Blinded by love, I thought, mentally kicking myself.

* * *

A few uneventful days later, the cellar light clicked on to reveal someone sleeping on the third couch.

"*Bonjour*. Good morning. I am Claude," he said with admirable good humor.

Henry tossed the three of us into the street together we did the neighborhood tour and returned for breakfast. Then Nick went to see about money from Australia.

Claude was a couple of years younger than me, with shaggy dark hair and a three-day beard I envied. He spoke excellent English and had come to the Maison to meet American students on their way to study at the university in Tours. I admired his initiative in quasi-officially coming to greet the students, which seemed an excellent way to meet girls. I was also intrigued when he said, with a knowing look, that he had brought a little "package" from the countryside, and I accompanied him to a corner park by the Maison.

Like many public spaces in Paris, the park was bordered by a low fence of heavy metal links strung between concrete posts. Claude called it a "romantic gate," meant to define a space rather than keep anyone out. I thought about my ferry ride to the continent, through the romantic gate of the North Sea.

"How did you come to *le Maison*?" Claude asked.

"I seem to live through these loops of hitting bottom and finding salvation. This time I escaped a bit of a situation in Zurich, looking for someone who spoke English. That led me to Nick and then Henry."

"Your loops remind me of Sartre," he said.

To sound clever, I recited my one Sartre quote: "Freedom is what you do with what's been done to you."

Unlike an American, who would simply find this quote odd or pretentious and then move on, Claude heard an invitation to debate existentialism. I'd forgotten how seriously Europeans took philosophy. "Man is condemned to be free," he began.

Seeing the folly in quoting writers I didn't understand, I interrupted: "Ah, Claude, you mentioned something about a 'package'?"

He graciously accepted my dodge and grinned. "We will look at that once Henry arrives."

When Henry showed up, we walked down an overgrown concrete

stair to the path along the Seine. In a short while we climbed to a patch of grass by Pont Sully, in the sunshine with a broad view of the river but out of sight of the road. Claude put hashish into a pipe and we passed it around.

Time slowed and we lingered, enjoying the day as we talked about Claude's plans to visit the United States. Finally, we decided to pursue our respective goals for the day.

"Time for a nap," said Henry.

"I must see what use I can be to my students," Claude said with a grin.

Left alone, I decided to visit the Rodin Museum and wandered off, finding joy in the clear sky and the breeze off the river. I marveled at gothic structures of stone and modern buildings of glass and steel, and was drawn to Art Nouveau elements mimicking the curved lines of plants and flowers. I poked my head inside one chemist shop set on a narrow and deep site. A central stairway rose beneath a high skylight. The floors were supported by slender iron columns in the form of tree trunks, and the mosaic floors and walls were decorated with floral arabesques.

Outside again, I instinctively followed a pair of sandaled legs in a bright summer dress. I lost the girl in a crowd inside Notre Dame as an organ concert began, so I found a seat on the cool stone in the center of the long hall, far beneath the vaulted ceiling. Soft light filtered through intricate stained glass in three magnificent windows, one of which bore a striking design of a rose or a wheel with many spokes.

A massive cacophony from the organ rose up and then evolved into a fugue. I shut out the sound of a paper bag rustling and lost myself in the music filling the enormous space.

After the concert I walked in my best guess of the direction to the museum. In a few blocks I bought coffee at a café opening onto the sidewalk. Sipping the coffee at a table under a tree, I noticed the brass clock over the bar showed it was almost three o'clock. It seemed too late to find the museum and see the exhibits at leisure, so I decided to relax with Tolstoy and try another day.

Paris felt comfortable, like a favorite old sweater. This might have been the pot, but it felt as if someone had rubbed the tension from my shoulders. I relaxed and started moving at the pace of the city and appreciating the good fortune of a free place to stay and friends all about. This was a far cry from the pattern that had marked my earlier travels: exhaustion or despair leading to divine intervention. I thought Edward would be proud to see me figure out how this rambling thing *should* work.

For each of the next few days, Nick, Claude and I returned to the Maison, and then Henry went to his apartment and the rest of us scattered. Nick took in culture and worked on his French. Claude played guitar and read an English version of Sartre, occasionally asking for help translating. I tried to get to the Rodin Museum.

On the way one day I stopped at the American Express office, knowing this was self-flagellation but unable to help myself. To my amazement there was a letter for me—from home. This was the first word I'd heard from my mother in months, and I raced to the steps of the opera house to read it.

She asked how their "intrepid explorer" was getting on. They had received my cards from Amsterdam and Germany and looked forward to hearing all about my adventures. She had typed up my letter to the dean at Michigan and sent it in; reading this, I realized I'd forgotten all about school. Then she dropped the bomb:

We have had a little scare. Doctor Fairborn heard a murmur in Dad's heart and said we would have to keep an eye on that. It is nothing for you to worry about. There is nothing you can do and we do not want you to come home for this, but I thought you should know. We are not getting any younger and this just means your father will have to take it a little easier and watch his weight. He would not want me to tell you this, so please don't mention it.

I stared at the page a long while, looking into the face of mortality. I was angry that my father had kept this from me, in the same way he had nothing to say to me at all, but then I listened to myself and realized it didn't matter what he thought of me; he was my father.

I sought solace in my mother's reassurances and wondered if there really was nothing I could do. I couldn't even write to him about this because then he'd know Mom had told me. I wished I knew for real how serious this was.

The museum would have to wait another day. I was too distracted to lose myself in art and instead wondered back to the Maison. I told Nick about the letter and he assured me heart murmurs were common in people of all ages and nothing to worry about. It didn't matter that he would express an opinion on just about anything; it reassured me to hear someone say with authority that everything would be all right.

"I guess I could call," I said finally.

He raised his eyebrows. "I guess if you could do it *collect*," he said.

A call home was sure to cost at least fifteen francs a minute. People really didn't call overseas except for emergencies, but this felt like an emergency. I'd start with a pocket full of change to get started but call collect when my father would be at work. I could talk fast; Mom wouldn't mind.

With this resolve, I gradually talked myself down from worrying. I would call and send off a postcard saying how beautiful Paris was in September but I missed them both.

Next day I started in the direction of the museum again, but to take my mind off my father I stopped to read *Anna Karenina*. Tolstoy captured me and I read on a bench and later a stoop. I came upon the line: "All happy families are alike; each unhappy family is unhappy in its own way." I thought about Dad and Edward and the whole sorry mess.

I tried writing in my pad thoughts of Turin and increasingly warm impressions of Paris but gave it up and wandered along the Seine looking at prints and postcards. Soon it was time for a baguette and a bottle of wine beneath a tree, and next thing a church bell woke me—too late to visit the museum.

Before bedtime I left Henry and Nick at the Maison and found a telephone booth on a quiet street. I couldn't make the call from the public phone at the Maison because I thought everyone would rib me about calling my mother, while my intention was deadly serious. I lined up all my French coins and it took several minutes before a phone rang and a French operator asked if someone would accept a collect call. Moments later my *father* came on the line!

"Stephen? Stephen, is that you!" he said anxiously.

"Yeah, Dad, it's me," I said, in a panic. Why he was home in the afternoon?

"What's wrong? Are you in trouble?"

"No, no, Dad. I uh…" I was lost at what to say.

"Here, I'll get your mother. Lucille, it's Stephen!"

"Thanks, Dad. You guys are okay, right?"

"Us, yes, of course we're okay. Here she is. Don't stay on. It's expensive."

"Stephen?" my mother said. "Is that you? Is everything all right?"

"Yeah, Mom, I was calling about your letter… about Dad and the doctor. I tried to call when he'd be at work."

"Oh good, honey. Yes, and we're fine too." It was clear Dad was standing by her so she couldn't talk.

"It sounds great," she continued. "And you're taking care of yourself? Good. Please be careful and keep sending cards; everyone loves them."

"Lucille, this is costing a fortune," Dad said in the background.

"Yes, yes Jim," she said to him, and to me concluded: "Well, you know this is very expensive, so if you're okay we'll look forward to seeing you soon."

"Okay, Mom. I love you," I said resignedly. "And tell Dad I love him."

"I will, honey. And we love you too. You take care of yourself now."

So went my first call home in almost three months: no information and not even a reassuring word. I'd have to believe it wasn't serious and there was nothing I could do.

I took a roundabout route back to the Maison. It felt better that I had tried but I was frustrated at how ineffectual my call was. It made no sense my father was home in the middle of the afternoon. I wished that, if Edward couldn't be with me in Europe, he were at least at home so he could tell me what was really going on.

The next day I felt a little less concerned and finally reached the museum, which was after all little more than across the river from Place de la Concorde. It was well worth the effort. A mansion held smaller works and the garden larger-than-life-sized sculptures. *Le Penseur* was the French name for *The Thinker*, but the familiar seated man leaning on his knee was powerful in a way its copies were not. I couldn't help but look at this statue in light of my news from home and the thought we all must face, that someday our parents will be gone. *Le Baiser* dispelled my gloom. The woman reminded me of Pam, and I photographed the embracing figures to share with her, in my dreams. *The Burghers of Calais* again brought me low with its depiction of broken men from a beaten city.

The weight of Rodin's imagination etched in massive stone shortened my breath. While the artist no longer lived, his art held its ability to inspire and move me. I stared through the sunken eyes of his statues into another soul. Rodin, I decided, would be an apt guide for a new stage of *Meine Reise*, when I would look into the eyes of my comrades to see their pain and their passions.

Chapter XI

A Recurrent Feast

The usual crowd sat in the courtyard of *Maison Fauconnier* one late afternoon, half-listening to Henry pick at a guitar. A friend of Emeline's named Jean-Paul joined us and invited everyone to a potluck dinner at his apartment in the Latin Quarter. He was a few years older than the rest of us and dressed more respectably, like someone who held down a job.

As evening approached, we crossed the river together and chipped in for groceries. Up three floors we were welcomed into a four-room apartment with a stereo and a stocked liquor cabinet. Nick volunteered to cook. On his way to the kitchen with a giggling American girl, he caught my eye and we both nodded at the wonder of it all. I looked through the LPs while Claude and Jean-Paul talked cars, and Henry turned on the charm for two girls from Penn State. Soon we spread around the living room, sharing fusilli and wine.

Jean-Paul raised his glass and said, "*Bon appétit,*" sweeping in all the room.

I raised my glass and drank and then said: "We don't toast well in America. Here it's so much more a part of life."

"You Yanks and your 'table manners,'" Nick said caustically. "You care more about keeping your hands clean than you do about the food."

Henry shook his head. "No sense of the fraternal breaking of bread."

"And they call it 'the new world,'" Nick added, with his usual rise in inflection.

Henry left early but the rest of us stayed to listen to music and finish the wine. At eleven-thirty, Jean-Paul drove Nick, Claude and me to the Maison, arriving just before Henry had to lock the door.

For a week we gathered each evening for food and wine, music and conversation. Claude had returned home to Tours. Emeline and her roommate Marie often joined the shifting assortment of Maison guests.

One evening only Nick and I and three coeds from UCLA showed up for dinner, so Jean-Paul suggested a picnic. We stuffed comically into his little car. For once Nick's size worked against him: he sat up front while I had to squeeze into the back with the girls. I maneuvered Audrey, the best looking of the three, onto my lap. She wore a thick brown braid and had sparkling blue eyes. As we settled in for the ride, I got a sense of firm hips and strong legs.

"I must be crushing you," she apologized over the din.

"Not at all," I said, "but hold still and let me guess your weight."

"On no you don't," she shrieked and grabbed the back of the seat to lift herself, bumping heads with her friend and adding to the bedlam.

We stopped for bread and cheese and wine and drove to the Bois de Boulogne. Jean-Paul parked by a secluded circle of stone benches within sound of a small waterfall. When Nick pulled open the back door, the girls and I toppled out, like in a Marx Brothers film.

We opened a few bottles of wine. Audrey gave me a tipsy smile and her friends kidded her about it. But before we had a chance to toast, a tiny white patrol car raced toward us and skidded to a stop, spewing gravel into the air. Two officers hopped out and approached.

We all went silent and looked to Jean-Paul. He stepped forward and the guards said something about "papers." I was concerned my passport and student ID were in my pack at the Maison.

Jean-Paul stepped forward confidently and showed something from his wallet, and the tension eased. Nick said later he was inspired by their casual uniforms and glances at our young ladies to offer each officer a bottle.

The officers hesitated and looked at each other. Then, at the same moment, they laughed and reached for the bottles. They toasted us, we toasted them and they returned to their rounds.

I maneuvered Audrey to a stone bench framed by picturesque vines. The age of the smooth stone and the natural brilliance of the trees made an idyllic scene for seduction. I asked about her trip, and she said they had taken Eurail to Amsterdam, Munich, Vienna and Paris over two weeks. It was a sound plan to skim the surface and notch the belt: the grand tour, check. Still, she was pretty and fun. I decided I'd take a Eurail train with her.

"You shouldn't miss the tour of the historic park statuary," I said, as if I knew something about it.

She stood up and looked like she would accept, but when I reached for her hand she spun away, saying something ending in "Brad."

I followed her back to our friends. After more wine she let me kiss her, but only playfully. Still, I liked that game and her scent reminded me of the beach. She giggled and we drank and the Brad obstacle seemed surmountable. I was sorry she was leaving in the morning.

An hour later the guards returned. "Our patrol this night is boring," the driver said, "so we instead to join with you." Cheers went up and the guards shook hands all around. Laughter and conversations overlapped in French and English. Before long Audrey's friends were wearing the guards' hats, and Nick and I were playing with the blue light on the car. One of the girls dragged the senior officer into the bushes.

"Couldn't resist his cologne," Nick hiccupped, nodding after them.

"It's a Maurice Chevalierism," I replied, wondering if Audrey was familiar with Chevalier. But my reluctant co-ed kept out of reach, and on the ride home switched places in the car with one of her friends.

*   *   *

Audrey departed next day before we returned to the Maison for breakfast. The memory of her smile faded quickly, and the days and evenings again blended together until one day we heard Jean-Paul had to drive to Milan for three days on business. With no prospect of an evening party, Henry suggested a taste of *Louis Quatorze* at Versailles.

Henry, Nick and I started in the morning on the metro, relying on our collective size to buy one ticket for three of us. In line and quick succession, Henry inserted the ticket and stepped *over* the turnstile, I pushed through the turnstile and Nick also stepped over. The attendant heard the turnstile and looked up, but we were through so quickly he shrugged and went back to his newspaper.

We didn't buy tickets when we connected with a train to Versailles. The trip was peaceful, the countryside stretching away in fields of daisies and avenues flanked by cedar trees. Near our destination, however, the door to the connecting car banged open and a *contrôleur* stepped in and began checking tickets. I thought about the lady enforcer in Munich and prepared to jabber in English.

Gazing nonchalantly out the window, Henry hissed through his teeth: "Don't say *anything*. Let me do the talking."

The *contrôleur* looked at our end of the car and took a step toward us. But just then the train slowed to stop at a station and he returned toward the front. We stifled smiles until he was out of sight.

We reached Versailles and walked toward the château. Henry suggested we pick up wine and bread to eat in the gardens. In a tiny shop we bought two three-franc bottles of wine called "Grap" and at the next door purchased two baguettes. We walked up toward the château, but Henry saw attendants at the gate and steered us behind a delivery truck.

"Better stash the food and wine when we pass the guards," he said.

"Is there a charge?" Nick asked.

"Not for the gardens," Henry said, "but they won't let us bring in bottles."

We stuffed the supplies under our shirts and entered the outer gate with no trouble. From the gardens, the château had a wide central structure and two wings, each three stories of white stone covered with dazzling windows. We turned off the center axis of the palace onto a broad avenue of the gardens noted in my art history book for their scale and symmetry. I contemplated how my own life lacked any symmetry, although the scale had certainly expanded.

Henry led us past formal flowerbeds and fountains with sculpted dragons and cherubs. At a spectacular chariot rising from the water, which he called *le Bassin d'Apollon*, we turned out of view of the château and snaked through trees and past statues onto a dirt path, and then turned again where there was no path. We walked up a small hill along an overgrown hedge, brushing aside branches. I felt like a kid on a summer day, on my way to a hideout in neighborhood bushes.

We squeezed through the hedge into a natural amphitheater brilliant with sunshine. The seats were stones, cracked and overgrown with grass and vines. A tiny stream trickled down the worn seats and beneath a large stone stage.

The sun was warm. I took off my shirt and lay back on a hot stone. It was amazing to think members of the court sat here and ate food here (probably better than ours) and watched plays so long ago.

"I do believe," Henry said, holding up the bottle, "that this Grap is the only truly *bad* wine I've had in France."

"The lad has a point," laughed Nick. "It's taken us ten minutes to open the second bottle."

Henry was explaining how the gardens were designed for courtesan trysts, when loud invective crashed over us. Two uniformed guards squeezed through the hedge, both yelling. Henry stepped forward to take the brunt of the abuse, stuttering obsequiously in basic French. I understood none of the dialogue but knew my role was to look serious and confused, which came naturally.

One officer grabbed the bottle and shook his head in disgust. He poured the wine onto the rocks and motioned for us to clean up and leave.

Back at the center axis of the park, Henry summarized: "He insulted our sisters and our mothers, assuming we weren't such shite as to have no sisters or mothers and, worse still, our taste in wine. It was a test: if we understood, we'd have to punch him out, and then he could arrest us."

"He was wrong," I said sincerely. Nick and Henry turned in surprise and laughed at me and then with me.

"What it really proved," said Nick, "is that the French really *can't stand* bad wine."

We moved on, laughing, toward the château. Henry pointed to a wing of the huge building. "Just four francs," he said slyly, "gets you into Marie Antoinette's bedroom."

"Counts me out," said Nick.

"Personally," said Henry, "I'd spend my money on more wine, and this time not 'Grap.'"

Henry offered to spring for a five-franc bottle, so we left the palace grounds to look for a shop. He also had a friend who lived in an apartment behind an insurance office, and suggested we visit. With our bottle not yet opened, we wandered streets much quieter than those in Paris, with fewer shops doing business and much less foot traffic. We found the insurance building easily on streets laid in a grid, but Henry was afraid we wouldn't be allowed to pass through the office during business hours and left Nick and me around a bend in the hallway while he knocked.

Just down the hall was a large window seat carved in dark wood. We made a dent in the bottle, remembering again what wine was *supposed* to taste like. We debated where in the château they had signed the treaty to end World War I. This reminded me America had fought many more wars than those so lately filling my thoughts. Wars seemed to be the inevitable punctuation of history.

I unlatched the shutters of two large windows and pushed them open onto a glorious rooftop scene of angled gables in dark browns and reds.

"Nothing like French rooftops," Nick said and stepped onto the large windowsill. In another moment I looked up to see him gone.

I jumped to the window but saw him standing calmly on a walkway extending to the side. Gazing into the deep earth tones, Nick asked how things went with Annetta.

"It was great to see she was okay," I said.

His expression said his question was more specific.

"Well, as you know," I said and cleared my throat, "we didn't have much opportunity."

"Or imagination!" he laughed, shaking his head. "Wouldn't have stopped me."

This was his usual bluster, but it played into my regret. I had screwed up planning Annetta's visit and wouldn't have another chance until Turin.

"We were only together twice," I said, "but both times we had an instant connection, and I felt like I really knew her."

Nick seemed genuinely interested, but Henry returned and broke the spell. "I can't believe you bastards finished the wine!" he said and added, as if it were the result of our bad manners: "We may *not* pass through the insurance office."

We returned to the streets, which were becoming dark. Though we passed few people, Henry kept a lookout for girls. Nick told us a rumor about Louis XIV's strange tastes in entertainment. My sudden laugh got their attention and surprised me. "Sorry," I said and looked at Nick. "There's something about the way you relate history that sounds like 'Fractured Fairy Tales.'"

"That's *Rocky and Bullwinkle*?" said Nick, not off a beat.

I smiled. I had to admire how he could turn on a dime and laugh at himself. He was *exactly* what I needed after Zurich.

*   *   *

More than three weeks passed. The parties at Jean-Paul's wound down, and it was time to head for the harvest. Nick had received money from home and proposed a farewell dinner. Emeline and Marie joined us along with Henry and Julia, a Duke junior and his romantic project *de jure*. Marie knew a Vietnamese restaurant down a few steps from Rue de Rivoli.

We crowded around a wooden table. Emeline and Marie chattered with the waiter and everyone laughed. Henry ordered for us all, adding Vietnamese to his French to impress Julia. Nick tried to follow the French girls' conversation, but they sped up to tease him. I eyed the odd-looking food at tables nearby. The waiter brought two bottles of red wine and Nick toasted: "To the city of lights!"

With the food and the next glass, Henry toasted: "To our missing friend, Claude: may he return safely from his military service, and thank God the US has no more draft."

"And no more war!" I blurted out in earnest. Emeline and Marie looked surprised I could speak, and then broke out laughing. I fell back in my seat and tried to put off thoughts of war and the ineluctable connection to Edward.

We ate our fill for fifty francs each and the French girls headed home after kisses all around. Nick and I walked back to the Maison with Henry and his date and then left the lovers to themselves. I drifted to sleep in the cellar, wondering what Edward would have done after college if the choice were his.

Chapter XII

Blind Faith

Nick and I said goodbye to Henry before seven next morning. It took a moment to get used to the weight of the pack, but I didn't have to carry it far. We took the metro to an *autoroute* entrance and set up on a ramp to hitchhike.

Time passed but we didn't move from our spot. A succession of cars picked up pairs of girls and girls traveling with boys and I thought about how having Pam along would have made this a breeze. After three hours, we packed it in, took the metro to the train station and bought tickets to Tours, which we reached mid-afternoon. Claude had reported to the army but left a note for us at his parents' apartment giving his friend Denis's address.

Denis welcomed us. He was short and thin, with greasy hair and a mustache. He constantly rolled tobacco or smoked it. He spoke little English but said we should have a cigarette and play records on his turntable. There was no room for us to sleep because two visitors were already sharing the floor, but he invited us to stay for dinner.

We sat in the apartment and talked, and everyone but me smoked cigarettes. When I tired of reading Tolstoy and asked if there was anything to do in Tours, Denis replied we were *doing* what there was to do in Tours. I wondered where young people went to feel energy, as I did in Ann Arbor, and this jolted me to realize I might wander the world only to find myself back where I started. Tap your heels together three times and say, "There's no place like home." But I was forgetting I had no home, not here and not with my parents or with Pam. I cried out loud, "There's no place like *Turino*," which drew an amused grin from Nick.

Staring out the window, I added up my assets, like a character in a French novel. Without the stashed travelers checks, they came to almost two hundred and fifty dollars—and a one-peseta coin. As long as I continued to get by without paying to travel or for accommodations, this should last a while, but I couldn't make it through the winter, especially if I travelled by train.

On the sidewalk outside the window a shapely woman passed wearing a tight white tee shirt decorated with a large Fruit of the Loom logo. It was perhaps the thirtieth such shirt I'd seen in France and evidenced some perverse trend. I wondered if these women knew this label was meant to be worn *inside* underwear. It was disappointing that even French women, with their natural style, could mistake imitation for fashion.

*   *   *

Nick and I camped in a city park by Pont Wilson, a bridge that had been demolished by a gas explosion. In the morning we hitchhiked south toward Libourne to join the harvest.

The day was sunny and clear. Along the road many hitchhikers were headed our way. "The Grapes of Wrath," I scribbled in my pad as we rested in the city square of Poitiers. Nick had gone to scout around. I watched our bags and tried my best Steinbeck:

> *They travel, these young souls from far lands, south from Paris, south from Tours. If it were the 1920s, they would travel by train or automobile through Poitiers to Bordeaux and Biarritz and Spain. But these are no lost generation artists, only post-*

war souls. They gather in small circles at the marketplace.
They eat bread and wine for dinner for the fourth day (and
tobacco, always tobacco, and always the dream of some
intoxicant). They all move toward Libourne, but no one knows
if there will be jobs picking grapes or if only Common Market
residents will be permitted to work.

When Nick returned, he read from my pad and looked at me for a moment as if I were a real writer. Snapping out of this, however, he said he'd met a soldier who thought he might know a place we could stay. He also had learned the place to sign up in Libourne to pick grapes was at the train station.

We bought cheese and bread for the day's first meal. It seemed my stomach had adapted to eating only when there was food before me, and then I'd eat it all. Later, we threw the Frisbee in the square. I was pleased Nick played well, but we attracted the attention of the other itinerants. Two Germans insisted they also must try and each, in turn, threw the disk into the street. School children watched from a safe distance. One pretty young girl slowed in passing to smile at us both with the innocent sensuality of a French girl. A bent old man passed on his way to return empty bottles, hardly noticing us.

When night fell, Nick and I walked along the tables at the outdoor cafés, fishing for a handout. Nick saw his soldier, who was drinking with several comrades at an outdoor table. The soldier waved us over and bought us each a Pernod. Nick spoke enough French to amuse everyone but not enough to get us a meal, and the soldier apparently had changed his mind about knowing where we might sleep. When it became clear we must buy our own second round, we returned to the square.

We split the bread and cheese remaining from lunch and drank from my canteen. Our cohorts huddled in shadows under the trees. A thin Spanish boy came over to bum a cigarette and asked if we had somewhere to sleep. We said we hadn't found anything yet, and he invited us to meet him at ten o'clock, when he would go with a local man to a squatters' house.

After the Spaniard wandered off, the two Germans approached. They were wild-eyed and sloppy and asked about accommodations. Nick said he and I had a tent we would pitch in the woods. They staggered off. "I think they've been sniffing something," said Nick. "Lighter fluid?"

I spit involuntarily. Nick grinned, "Yea, it's not a great high, but it's cheap."

"You mean you've..."

"Tried it?" Nick interrupted. "Yeah, of course, when I was a kid."

There seemed no end of surprises in my Australian friend. I frowned and shook my head.

Nick grinned. "If you aspire to be a 'renaissance man,'" he said, "you must embrace experience."

As the church bell tolled nine, we made one more round of the cafés and at ten met the Spaniard on the appointed corner. He said his name was Marco, which he admitted sounded more Italian than Spanish. His English was halting and his expression innocent. I wondered why he carried no bag and seemed to be trolling for squatters. Marco introduced two others from his country who spoke *no* English, and then waved to another figure emerging from a dark street. With quick nods all around our company set off.

We turned on several tiny streets past shuddered windows. The close-set buildings were no more than two stories high and showed no lights. I walked last, listening to the growing quiet, and then suddenly stopped. I could hear only my companions' footsteps on the cobblestones. Nick sensed I was not following and came back to me.

"What's the matter?" he said.

"I don't know."

"Well, we'd better keep up or we'll lose them."

We each took a step forward, but then I grabbed his elbow and pulled him around a corner down a deserted street. He followed silently until we were beyond the sound of footsteps, and then he stopped me and said: "You look spooked."

"Something's wrong," I said, with quiet urgency.

He looked at me, inquiringly, then said quickly: "That's enough for me, mate." He glanced toward the fading footsteps and then led me back to the square.

I didn't know what had taken hold of me, but the feeling was strong. It was a great relief and surprise how Nick trusted my feeling as I did myself, without explanation.

*   *   *

At the square the café crowds were thinning. The church bell tolled eleven o'clock. The plaza had cleared and we sat on a bench with a young couple from Holland. The girl was cute but very dirty, the boy tall and too thin.

We sat and talked while Nick shared the boy's last cigarette. The couple had a tent and decided to walk away from the town center to the first likely campsite. Unlike the Spanish guides who had spooked me, this couple concerned me for fear they couldn't take care of themselves.

We set out together and walked for a time, debating possible campsites on a wooded traffic island and then in an empty lot. Finally, the girl said she was exhausted and would walk no farther. In frustration, the boy declared they must return to the traffic island. We bid them goodnight and good luck and I lingered, watching them fade into the darkness hand in hand.

Snapping back to our own situation, I said: "We'd better find a place too. We can put the tent anywhere 'til the sun comes up."

"I think we should walk out of town," said Nick. "Never know; get a ride?"

This was a waste of energy—mostly mine. I knew we'd walk for a half hour and still end up in the tent. But something was leading him on, so I set myself beneath my pack to walk the narrow shoulder of the road. I kept thinking how much easier this was for Nick with his small roll of clothes. As I trudged ahead in the dim starlight, he walked behind and occasionally looked into the darkness as if to conjure up a car.

In ten minutes the first set of headlights rose in random angles above the trees. Nick turned and held out his thumb. I shook my head and kept walking. A red sports car convertible went by and then slowed and stopped past us in the empty road. The driver leaned across the front seat. In the light from the dashboard, I could see friendly eyes squint over a bushy mustache.

"Where do you want to go?" he said.

"Just about anywhere," laughed Nick. "Tomorrow we go to Libourne."

The driver jumped out of his car, introduced himself as Jules, and offered us a rug to sleep on in the castle where he lived. While this sounded too much like a fairy tale to be true, anything would beat the dark roadside, so we agreed.

Jules opened the boot, but it was too small for my pack. We stuffed it behind the bucket seats, and I sat on Nick's lap in the passenger seat. When we started up, I did not need to turn around to see Nick's self-satisfied grin.

Intuition had taken us, improbably, from a dicey squat to a castle. More significant than the unlikely plot, though, was that Nick had followed my instinct blindly when we ducked away from the Spaniard, and I had humored him when he insisted we hitchhike out of town. In both cases the most unlikely road turned out best. This expanded my notion of the importance of instinct in surviving on the road: if each traveler knew to follow his own feelings, and two companions trusted each other, then each could benefit from the intuition of either, for twice the advantage. I wondered if anyone had ever written about this.

The car bumped over roads winding through the woods. I thought how I had no apprehension about where we were going. Was this because Jules seemed so amiable, or was I reassured at having someone along I trusted? Is this how traveling with Edward would have been?

Contentment with our prospects, however, did not equate with physical comfort. Nick and I were squashed into the bucket seat and I resorted to the hitchhikers' technique of sleeping to endure an uncomfortable ride, and drifted off, thinking of instinct and fate.

The castle turned out to be middling large and quite run down. Jules and several friends lived in and worked at renovating the monstrosity while they also held regular jobs. Jules' "regular job" was illustrating for magazines.

He showed us to a musty ballroom with lofty ceilings and an enormous fireplace that looked as if it hadn't been used for years. The only "furniture" was a large rug and a pile of blankets. I threw my sleeping bag on top of two blankets and Nick wrapped himself in the rest. I slept instantly.

Through twenty-foot windows without curtains, the sun woke us early, but later and in more gentle fashion than had become our custom at the Maison. Jules was astir, preparing breakfast. We had coffee and tasty rolls, and then he showed us his new cartoons for *Métal Hurlant*, an adult comic book. The draftsmanship in his storyboards was polished, and I wondered if my fantasy literature thesis could be faulted for including no more than a footnote on illustrated magazines.

I asked to take a photograph and went for my camera, returning to find Nick picking at a twelve-string guitar to Jules' rapt attention. Grimacing at Nick's artless playing, I took a photograph of Jules with several pages of frames outlined in India ink, a few filled in with primary colors. The incomplete pictures, lacking captions or words in the bubbles, told the story of a clean-cut young man in a dark dream world, something like *Steppenwolf*. Jules laughed that I was impressed with his drawing and said his real passion was music.

"Well, then you should hear him," Nick said, handing me the guitar. Jules insisted I play.

I sat against the wall and sang a four-chord song. Jules was ecstatic and lamented having himself no gift for music.

"Oh, my guitar playing is less a gift," I said, "than something I picked up to meet girls. It's nothing next to your drawing."

"I must disagree," he said and we argued good-naturedly for a while, but finally agreed we must each use what we have and aspire to what we will.

Jules drove us to a crossroads on his way to meet his publisher. It was still morning when Nick and I arrived at the trailer at Libourne's rail station. Nick got a lead and directions to Château Saint-Hénin. The château was a few kilometers up a hill from the village of Saint-Loubès, which was little more than a wide spot in the road. We hitchhiked, hoping to make the short trip in one ride.

That ride came from a New Zealander named Wally Findley. He was short and wiry and gruff but glad to find mates who spoke English. He was looking for work to buy gas for his beat-up Citroën and took meeting us as a sign he should join us for the harvest. Nick and I reprised our self-congratulatory grin.

We were welcomed with open arms at the château. The proprietor was short and wore suspenders stretched over a round belly. He had large, smiling eyes and insisted we call him "Papa." We were welcome to work the harvest when it started in ten days, even though we came from outside the Common Market. The job paid sixty-five francs a day, less ten francs for meals, a bunk and a blanket. He poured us glasses of wine from an unlabeled bottle and we toasted the success of *les vendanges*.

Back in the Citroën, Wally slapped both hands on the wheel and turned toward us. So where are we off to? Anyone for a tour of the world-famous bordellos outside Bordeaux?"

Nick brightened but said: "I have to conserve cash until we get paid. I think I'll hitchhike back to Paris for a cheap party."

I didn't want to go back to Paris. I thought of Annetta, but Turin would be much better when I had the harvest money and wouldn't have to come back this way. Suddenly it hit me that I was on the road to Barcelona, and I stretched into the back of the car for my map.

Wally and Nick stayed silent as I checked the map and then both broke into laughter. "C'mon, will you," Wally finally said. "Paris or Bordeaux?"

"Spain," I replied. "Jake Barnes and all that."

Wally looked confused and turned to Nick, who shook his head.

"You know, Hemingway?" I said to them both. "*The Sun Also Rises?*"

Chapter XIII

Mise-en-cadre

Summer sun bathed the twenty cottages of Saint-Loubès as the Citroën careened down the hill from the château, raising a commotion of dust. We turned onto the main road and stopped. I got out, retrieved my backpack and swung it easily onto my shoulders. I saluted: "Ten days, then."

Wally tapped the horn and began to pull off. Nick leaned out the window with a wide smile, hair splashing his face, and called out: "I'll give your regards to Henry and the ladies!"

The car disappeared north and the village returned to quiet. Chickens circled and pecked gravel from the shoulder of the road. I walked south, whistling a traveling tune. I had no fear this time about stepping into the unknown, to another place where I'd have no friends and no facility with the language. These were minor obstacles; more important was a renewed sense that things always worked out. It felt like Edward would be along on this trip to Catalonia and would be pleased the Aussie's relaxed attitude had rubbed off on me.

In two minutes I'd walked beyond the village and stuck out my thumb. A car sped by, kicking up dust and pebbles. I turned away and coughed, as the dust sparkled in shafts of sunlight filtering through a great oak tree.

* * *

Later in the day, a radiant sunset lit up the basilica in Toulouse as Gregorian chant wafted on the breeze. On a narrow road paved in cobblestones I could have blended in with the crowd, but for my pack. The passersby glanced up and quickly looked away. Maybe they turned away because of the smudges on my face and whiskers on my upper lip and chin, or because of how I gazed around unguardedly, sucking in the scene like a black hole.

On a road closed to traffic, I leaned against a post. Three- and four-story buildings lined the street in stately old stone, but many of their ground floors were shops done up in gaudy glass and aluminum. Some business people rushed through the Saturday shoppers and over the more static layers of life. A well-dressed woman carried overflowing shopping bags from a fancy store. Two men in suits smoked cigarettes in a doorway, quietly conspiring. A young mother in a long jacket with a kerchief over her head struggled to carry one child and lead another by the hand. I wondered if Henri de Toulouse-Lautrec got his name from this town.

There was no room on the street for me and my pack, so I navigated a tactical retreat. I really wanted, anyway, to cover some more miles before stopping for the day. At a fountain beyond the flow of people, I sat beside the pack. I folded my map to southwest France and eastern Spain, and traced with a finger the route from Paris to Tours, Libourne, Bordeaux and Toulouse. Directly south were the Pyrenees and tiny Andorra, looking like my "romantic gate" to Spain.

A pretty girl with dark hair peeking from beneath a checkered scarf bicycled by with two baguettes in her front basket. A police officer stroked a cat in an open shop door. The cat darted into an alley and the officer laughed and strolled up the block. An elderly man tottered by with a cane and a wide-brimmed hat. I asked directions of a man in a worn blazer repairing a sidewalk, and then swung the pack onto my shoulders and hiked south.

* * *

At twilight I hadn't gotten far from Toulouse and stood in the light of a single bulb hanging from a pole on a country road. I had walked through a tiny village to a crossroad by a stream. In a few minutes the last light faded, and I leaned the pack against a tree. In a few more minutes, car headlights rose into the sky like spotlights and flooded trees across the road at crazy angles. When the lights reached me, I pointed a thumb over my shoulder. The car passed. The dark moonless night closed in again.

In half-an-hour two more cars passed. I rocked on my heels and shook my head, then took out a flashlight and put on the pack to look for a place to spend the night. The narrow border of trees by the stream didn't provide much cover and sloped to the water. I walked back to the crest of the road. It was quiet and dark and then another car approached. I stepped off the road and put out my thumb, but it passed.

It was clear I'd have to sleep nearby and so followed the dirt crossroad between a low wall and a field. A hundred feet from the main road I stepped across the wide grass shoulder. There was no sign of anyone or any sound but a soft breeze. I laid down my pack and thought. With no cover I didn't want to set up the orange tent.

The moonless sky was totally clear and brilliant with stars. I laid the tent on the ground and wrapped it around the sleeping bag, dropped my pants and shoes into the fold of the tent and climbed into the bag. I stuffed my sweater into the pillowcase beneath my head, pulled the poncho over everything and lay on my back, gazing at the sky.

A shooting start carved an arc across my vision and I imagined an orchestral flourish. Other lights streaked in all directions as the music built in a series of minor crescendos. I kept my head still as my eyes darted from one part of the sky to another, my lips mouthing cymbal crashes. I envisioned a silent film zooming in for an extreme close-up of my eyes reflecting streaks of white on black.

* * *

Barking woke me. The sky was clear blue. I stretched my arms but jerked back at the chill of the dew-soaked grass. I yanked the poncho aside to scatter the moisture and laid it wet-side down on the grass. Unfolding the wet tent from my legs, I found my sleeping bag mostly dry. I unzipped the bag and lay back, smiling at the sky.

The dog barked again. A farmhouse stood a quarter mile away over a planted field. I closed my eyes for a moment and took a deep breath and then stood on the sleeping bag to dress. I packed the sleeping bag, then shook some moisture off the poncho and tent and packed them, still wet.

With everything stowed, I took my canteen onto the dirt road. Across the road was a masonry wall topped by embedded shards of colored glass, primitive—and practically permanent—barbed wire. Returning with my camera, I found a toehold in the wall and photographed the sun glittering through the glass, a clinquant portent for the day.

* * *

By late morning I rode in a small van on a winding mountain road as it passed a sign for Andorra. A leather-skinned old man in a dirty straw hat drove with an unlit cigarette dangling from his mouth. I gazed out the window. My fair skin also showed the effects of living in the sun, though for weeks rather than decades. The van's radio alternately caught static and a fast guitar piece that made us both tap our fingers on the doors. As we gained altitude, the air became crisp and broad views of lush mountainsides opened from each curve in the road.

The man pointed a bony knuckle at the first wide spot in the road. The bit of level ground was covered with shops advertising duty-free liquor, appliances and cigarettes. I surmised this principality, or whatever it was, used an exemption from the tax laws to sell goods cheap and attract visitors. I nodded and looked back at the view.

At its scale representing all Western Europe, my map showed only two roads in tiny Andorra, wedged between France and Spain. But we seemed to be on one of these roads because the next wide spot was at the edge of Andorra City. The driver let me out.

The flat ground by the road was taken up by a duty-free store and parking. A young couple emerged from the shop, laden with bags and three identically dressed children. A man with dark, curly hair and olive skin slammed his car door and entered the store quickly and I followed. As if in a moment's dissolve, I reemerged with a liter of Johnnie Walker Black and stashed it in the pack.

Where Andorra City began in earnest, tiny hotels abutted duty-free stores standing against restaurants, with no room to spare. Mountains rose behind the shops to the left, and a wide valley opened behind the buildings to the right. I stopped several times to avoid colliding with people on the narrow sidewalk. A short way into the city, I took one step down to a grocer's door but couldn't fit inside. I left my pack leaning against the outer door and, keeping watch over my shoulder, entered the shop and quickly bought a loaf of bread, cheese wrapped in paper and two apples.

Back in the current of tourists, I had to step into the road to pass knots of people. Before I knew it, I was leaving the city. The last building toward the mountains was a stucco barn, doors standing open on a stack of long leaves that could have been tobacco. Across from the barn a steep dirt road descended to a river running between big stones into a gorge, trees crowding its far bank. A few flat rocks jutted into the water by a strip of grass. It wasn't out of sight of the road but was too long a walk down to imagine anyone would bother with my tent being there for the night.

I hiked down the dirt road to the river's edge and walked upstream. The sun was still high, but the mountains cast long shadows. I laid down the pack and stepped a short way onto the rocks and sat with my food and scotch. I toasted my brother and the mountain, so wild and steep, and set to dinner. I inhaled the food, as if to the frenetic chase-scene soundtrack from a Keystone Cops film. Carrying my life around on my back seemed to sharpen my appetite, and I hadn't eaten anything since breakfast by the glass-crowned wall.

The sun had dropped behind the mountains by the time I unrolled my tent and shook out the morning dew. I set it up on the grass, put on a sweater and grabbed my flashlight and pad. Out on the rocks in the river again, I sipped alternately at water and scotch and wrote:

> *From France to Andorra to Catalonia, my ignorance of languages makes it impossible to converse. I feel like a silent film hero: mute, underfed, weary, but cinematically sincere. I've pitched my tent on the one flat spot in Andorra without a duty-free shop, which comes with majestic views and a rushing river soundtrack.*

The light faded, and I set the pad aside. I bit into an apple as something swooped by my shoulder. Jerking back, I scanned the trees. Another form crossed my vision, irregularly shaped and darker than the sky. A third shape flitted by, and I realized they were bats.

They were incredible fliers and seemed to toy with me, seeing how close to me they could fly. I made no sudden moves, for fear one might crash into me. Their aerobatics made me hum the opening strings of *Flight of the Valkyrie*. The music in my head grew louder as more shapes knifed through the air, silhouetted against the last light. When the music climaxed, I almost applauded, surely a more appreciative audience than they got most nights, and I toasted them as the sky faded to starry black.

Later, settled into my sleeping bag, I thought how Edward must have bedded down with the leaches in the rice paddies, hoping not to get shot, while I could relax with bats and scotch and shooting stars.

*   *   *

The morning was cool. River sounds and the mountains blocking the sun kept me in my bag later than usual. When I finally got up, the sun had dried the tent of two days' worth of dew.

I took my time packing. On the flat rocks I pulled off two shirts at once and knelt to wash. The water was bracing on my arms and shoulders. I brushed my teeth with canteen water and took a long drink. I hated leaving such a bucolic campsite and so sat for a long while reading *Anna Karenina* and writing a description of the air show, trying to be clear and concise—more Hemingway than Tolstoy.

Before leaving I stood on a rock, swinging my gaze back and forth and recalling the bats. I laughed, thinking of when the holy man in *The Razor's Edge* says, "Sometimes strange things happen when alone in those mountains… but what happens depends on you." I felt I had made the most of my night in Andorra.

Back on the road, finally, it felt good to walk. There was little traffic, and the mountains were glorious. My left knee no longer bothered me. I wondered if I'd be spending another night in my tent and stopped a couple of times to enjoy the scenery.

In the late afternoon, a rusty compact station wagon pulled over. The two men inside were tanned and wore soiled shirts with wild flower prints, looking as if they were returning from a bachelor party. A portable cassette player fastened to the dashboard with electrical tape played a quiet guitar piece. The driver had curly, dark hair and a three-day beard. He looked over his shoulder and spoke: "*Mi nombre* Mack. Where?"

Mack added a raised eyebrow like a question mark. I shrugged my shoulders, held my map over the front seat, and drew a broad arc beyond the mountains. "*Mi nombre* Stephen, from USA. I go to *España.*"

They laughed and nodded their heads in agreement. (Apparently that was the only possible destination on this road.) We shook hands all around, and I settled into my seat. The scenery became stark as the road wound through mountains bleached and barren. The second man looked back at me and smiled. I returned the smile. He mumbled to the driver, who nodded and spoke. "We go *a Barcelona? Vendrás?*"

Barcelona! I nodded my head and tried not to look too enthusiastic, but I was almost jumping out of my seat. I left for later the details, like what "*vendrás*" might mean. I heard "Barcelona" and liked the tone of it all. I reached into my pocket for my peseta and rubbed its dull, worn face while I turned toward the mountains. "Thanks for the lift," I mouthed under my breath to my brother, feeling more than ever that he was rambling with me.

After the mountains had turned to plains and the plains to a neighborhood of low residential buildings, Mack parked behind a house. He showed me to a sofa in a large open room and gestured where to leave my pack. Then he brought me onto a terrace overlooking the harbor. We drank a dense red *garnacha* with gobs of fruit and watched the city dissolve into twilight. Then Mack cooked pasta with vegetables and we ate and slept.

In the early morning I read *Anna Karenina* on my sleeping bag on the couch, dressed only in gym shorts. I finished a chapter and copied a quote to send to Pam, maybe: "I think that to find out what love is really like, one must first make a mistake and then put it right." I wasn't sure that was true, but it was certainly opportune.

It felt great to get a solid night's sleep indoors. Sunshine gradually poured over the city. I looked out past the terrace through hair now falling as far as my eyes, three months after my ride-getting haircut in July. I had learned there was no need to cut it short, as it was the most hirsute people who most often offered help.

I went to the WC and, when I returned running hands through my hair, a woman dressed in a towel was making coffee. She was thin and pretty with wild black hair tied in a red ribbon. She looked up and giggled. She pointed at me and then herself and said: "*Stephano*... the *Mara*. Please thank you."

I didn't know if Mara had been in the house the night before or had just arrived. Nodding and smiling, I returned to the living room to roll my sleeping bag. I found a tee shirt by the time she returned from the kitchen. She wore a loose print dress and brought two bowls of coffee to the table along with bread and jam. We began to eat.

Mack emerged from a back room in shorts and sandals. He nodded a greeting to me and looked longingly at the breakfast, then carried a portable radio onto the terrace. Mara laughed quietly, doubled the jam on her bread, and ate with a flourish.

Fast rock and roll in what sounded like Spanish wafted through the doorway. Watching Mack limber up for calisthenics, I chuckled softly. On the way back to my plate, my eyes caught Mara smiling at my amusement.

Later in the day Mack and Mara drove me into town to the Gothic Quarter with a map marked to show the bus route home. Along with bus routes, the map showed a bit of subway. I wondered if I'd have the chance to scam mass transit in Barcelona, just to make the city my own.

The streets and mostly low buildings were rundown but brimming with charm. Men played bocce in the park. On a bench near the sea, I sketched an old woman selling flowers and then bought a pastry to eat while I walked. As the afternoon grew late, many vendors' tables were empty at the flea market on Carrer Comte d'Urgell. I looked at rings offered by a dark gypsy woman who seemed to be dozing on her feet. My interest snapped her to life. She rushed around the table to show how a ring looked on my finger. She spoke fast, then asked a pointed question and waited for my reply.

I shook my head to show I didn't understand Spanish, or Catalan for all I knew, and said: "Two: for a girl and for me."

She shrugged her shoulders and returned to pushing rings at me. I backed off, bowed to her and walked away. I decided it was best not to buy Pam a ring, of all things. Weaving through the crowd, I did buy a Moroccan shoulder bag, rough woven in tan and green. The bag would be practical and put me in the style of my typical savior.

*   *   *

Nighttime had descended and the clock by my couch showed nine o'clock when Mack burst into the room and whisked me to his car. We drove a maze of dark, narrow streets. Twice he ran two wheels onto the cobblestoned sidewalk to pass parked cars. We pulled up by a storefront with a metal security door open a few feet above the sidewalk.

Mack jumped out and rapped on the door, which squeaked upward to reveal a large loft space stacked high with pottery and ovens. The woman who pulled the door open said something to Mack and smiled at me. She had a round, welcoming face with curly black hair tied back and smudges of clay on her face.

Mara turned from a large oven to greet us. She spoke with the other woman, gesturing in the shape of a vase as she removed her cream-colored apron to reveal blue jeans and a loose aqua shirt. Mack pretended to squint at the brightness of her shirt and pulled out his sunglasses. She looked aghast and defended her outfit while washing her hands. After she had thrown a silk scarf of matching aqua around her neck she squeezed by us, pausing to offer the scarf for my approval. My thumbs up made her squeal and dance into the street.

Mack led us around the corner and down a few steps. We entered a big room that looked like someone's home but was filled with six or seven long tables of heavy dark wood. Patrons filled half the seats, eating and drinking. Mack got a kiss from an old woman in a checkered apron, who pointed us to the table against the brick wall at the back of the room. Mack held a chair for Mara and waved for me to sit beside her.

The woman in the apron returned, traded jests with Mack, and turned a knowing smile at me. She walked off as people filled the other seats at our table. The waitress appeared shortly with a bowl of mussels and an oddly shaped wine bottle.

Mack poked my arm and pointed to the second neck angling from the side of the bottle. With fanfare, he lifted the bottle, spread his elbows, and quickly tilted the bottle so a stream of wine crossed a foot of air to his mouth. After a long draft, he righted the bottle without losing a drop. With a self-satisfied sigh, he wiped his mouth on his sleeve.

He smiled broadly and handed the bottle to me. I thought I heard Mara's chair squeak on the floor. Our neighbors looked over curiously. A large, bearded man at the end of the table asked me something. Mara responded for me, and then the whole table stopped talking and paid close attention.

Hearing an imaginary drum roll, and going for style points, I confidently leaned back my head and opened my mouth and then quickly titled back the bottle. A thin stream of wine ran up my shirt and across my cheek to my lips.

Everyone at our table roared, so the rest of the diners looked up. General laughter flowed into lively conversations I couldn't understand. I licked my lips at the taste that had barely reached my mouth.

It seemed my initiation was over, so I focused on the mussels until the waitress brought a great bowl of seafood and rice for us, and a platter of roasted chicken for our neighbors. We all passed the platter and bowl around the table, along with more wine.

With uncalled for drama the waitress brought a ladies' wine glass for me. This was harsh, but it amused my hosts, and it gave me a way to get some wine in my mouth.

Both parties at our table finished at the same time and so we emerged onto the street together. Mara and one of the women strolled arm-in-arm, singing bits of songs to each other until the rest joined in. The two women skipped and danced and the rest of us followed down a narrow street. Across several crooked blocks, strangers joined our parade. Mara called for me to sing along, and so I mouthed nonsense syllables.

*   *   *

When I woke I lay thinking about the night before, how the Catalans really knew how to party. Yet I felt a tear on my cheek. Edward should have shared this with me. He shouldn't have fallen. He shouldn't have been lost to me.

Mack must have gotten up quietly, as he suddenly appeared by my sofa in his workout outfit with the radio under his arm. I quickly wiped the tear from my face but it was too late. In an instant his expression changed from joyful to concerned, and he sat across from me.

"What is…" he said, struggling with the language but with clear intent.

"It's my brother." I could feel tears welling up from just saying that out loud, and paused to hold them in. I knew there was no point; I could never explain this to Mack.

He continued to look at me with great sincerity. I sat up and pulled on a tee shirt and spread my hands to express frustration at not being able to communicate.

"My Brother?" he said, apparently understanding whom I meant and that my concern, or sorrow, was heartfelt.

"Yes," I said, and my eyes went to my pouch on the floor. I opened it and showed Mack my peseta. He held it up with great interest and a slight smile, but then looked at me to explain.

"My brother died in Vietnam," I said, lacking any other way to say it.

He squinted as he processed this and then shook his head sadly. "Ah, Vietnam *guerra*. My, ah, you brother." It choked me up how grief could live in so few words.

I shook my head and sniffed back tears. He patted my shoulder and smiled sadly, then left me to myself.

By the time Mara got up I had washed and tried to look cheerful. They were so good to me and didn't deserve to share my sadness.

My walk later from Mack's house down to the city went in great zigzags. My light brown hair and camera marked me as a visitor passing through the quiet neighborhoods. Edward and I hadn't thought through what we'd do once we got to Catalonia, but I had since done some research. It seems the Catalans revolted against the Hapsburgs in the sixteen hundreds, which led to a siege of Barcelona in 1714. I wondered if I could find remnants of this past. Maybe Edward and I were meant to stoke the embers of Catalan nationalism? It seemed plenty just to join the celebration of Barcelona.

Walking in the footsteps of a fictional character really seemed pointless, when what I wanted was to walk alongside my brother. My arrival and exploration of the city certainly followed the plan of having no plan, but my success in reaching Barcelona felt hollow. I hadn't come to grips with Edward being gone. Visiting places we had talked about wasn't making any sense of my loss.

I reached La Rambla in the center city and walked down Montcada to the Picasso Museum. Everything was closed for siesta, so I crossed into a square, content to read *Anna Karenina* on one of metal folding chairs scattered under the trees.

Hearing shuffling feet, I looked up. A fat old man in suspenders and a straw hat stood before me with his hand out, mumbling. I stood and motioned that I didn't understand. He pointed at the chair, held up two fingers, and then held out his hand again. I shook my head side-to-side and walked off, while he waved his arms up and down.

The museum opened in the afternoon. The exhibit space was intimate. Many paintings were starkly realistic, done when Picasso was quite young. Before one wall I turned back and forth between portraits of a man and a woman so real I imagined their dialogue, although they too spoke Catalan, so I couldn't understand. Seeing how Picasso could paint scenes like photography at such a young age gave me a new appreciation of his later abstract work.

When I returned home in late afternoon, I was counting my Spanish money and realized I'd lost my peseta. This threw me into a panic. I went through my pouch and all my pockets. Remembering my talk in the morning with Mack, I thought I might have dropped it and so pulled the cushions off the sofa.

This was the final affront; I'd lost my brother, and my peace of mind, and now I'd lost even my token of him. I sat on the sofa again, going over my morning talk, when I noticed something beneath a chair. I jumped down on my knees and reached for my coin. With a long sigh, I held it tight between my fingers and then wrapped it carefully in the letter from my mom and jammed it into the bottom of my pouch.

*   *   *

That night the cassette player on the dashboard played a fast tune. Mack pulled to a stop at the end of a pedestrian way. I stepped out of the back door in my crumpled suede jacket and blue jeans. Mack and Mara were still sitting in the front seat laughing when I opened Mara's door. She looked up at me and beamed, then stepped out and curtseyed. Then she pulled each of us by a hand into a trot. Mack and I rolled our eyes at each other and tried to keep up. Very *Jules et Jim*, I thought, wondering why my mind always veered toward storytelling.

The pedestrian way ended at a movie theater. We bought tickets under a marquee showing *"Easy Rider"* in white letters but for two red Rs. We joined a small line along the front of the theater where posters said the movie was subtitled in Spanish. Mack smiled at my relief. He sensed I needed a little familiar comfort.

When we emerged from the theater, church bells tolled midnight. Mara played air guitar and sang a butchered "Born to be Wild," then led us toward a street festival. By the harbor the streets were overflowing with dancing and singing. A red flatbed truck rolled slowly along the harbor road, carrying a band in back wearing what I supposed was traditional Catalan dress. As the truck approached, the music became louder and in my cinematic eye the red of the truck gradually filled the entire scene.

Chapter XIV

Armistice

A red pickup truck rattled through the bright morning. In the truck bed, I leaned against my pack. Over the rail along the sea, a sign advertised the "best" of something on the Costa Brava.

Mack and Mara had been so nice to me I felt bad about being caught up in thoughts of Edward. Their kindness couldn't fill the void, and they knew this even in our silent-film relationship. When I left Barcelona, Mack gave me a hearty two-handed shake and Mara sent me off with a kiss on the cheek and a deep red apple, and they both looked sad for me.

I finished the apple from Mara and tossed the core into the bushes by the road as we passed a sign for Tossa de Mar. I knocked on the cab and the driver let me out and pulled off with a wave. The sun was bright, the countryside dry. I swung the pack to my shoulders and walked along the seaside road to a beach and then turned into the city. The old part of the city, the Via Vella, was mostly medieval stone buildings. Towers punctuated the skyline with tourist signs I later learned meant "Tower of the Hours" and "Tower of Homage." A lone villa commanded the view from a far-off cliff.

Past shops selling food and trinkets to beach visitors, I reached the coarse sand and removed my shoes. Farther on I found a place to take off my shirt and sit on the beach. Three naked four-year-olds—a girl and two boys—made an idyllic image holding hands by the edge of the gentle waves. I watched them against the background of the deep blue sea but passed up photographing the scene. When they ran squealing along the beach, I lay back and closed my eyes.

It no longer troubled me to travel alone where I couldn't speak the language, but this silence gave me too much time to think. If there had been somewhere to leave my pack, I'd have gone for a swim. As it was, I lay with my eyes closed, trying to picture Edward rising from the sea and laughing as he shook water from his hair to wake me. I missed him so much it hurt all over, and I could feel my eyes were moist—yet again. When would this feeling pass?

Something blocked the sun on my face. I shaded my eyes with a hand and saw a young man standing beside me. I propped myself on an elbow and gestured to ask what he wanted, assuming he couldn't speak English. In the glare I could make out he was very thin with a too-winning smile.

"How are ye?" he said, "American, is it? I'm Irish meself. On holiday. Care for a bite t' eat?"

I sat up and rubbed my eyes. The man sat down with his shabby bedroll and continued talking. It seemed too coincidental that an Irishman should rouse me from my Catalonian stupor just as I had been thinking about my lost trip with Edward.

"Eamonn Kiernan," he said in a light brogue, "from all about, but firstly County Westmeath."

"Stephen Kylemore," I replied and shook his outstretched hand. His suggestion about lunch had spoken directly to my stomach, and so we walked together toward the shops.

Eamonn was a bit older and somewhat shorter than me. He wore an Irish cap over a shock of brown hair, even in the mid-day heat. He was not good-looking but his rakish smile had some appeal.

"Aye, there's a one," he commented licentiously, watching a girl walk by on skinny legs barely covered by a skirt. I nodded agreement but turned back to the activity on the streets, hunger holding my attention. He seemed interested in several smaller shops, but I mostly watched the tourists. We bought a roasted chicken hanging in a shop window and a bottle of wine from a bald man with spikey whiskers, and Eamonn suggested we picnic on the large stones by the beach.

We both ate greedily and shared water from my canteen. He said he'd come from Italy and France and was headed toward Madrid. "Good pickin' down that way, I hear," he said. I almost responded I was headed to Bordeaux to do some picking, but then thought that was not really what he meant.

We sank into contented silence. Then he played his harmonica quietly, darting glances around at passersby. Eventually, he napped while I read and the sun fell into the sea.

In early evening, Eamonn suggested we go eat again. He put on a bright red shirt from his bag. I found this outfit a bit flashy and opted not to dress for dinner. We walked back to the commercial center. I suggested exploring a different part of town, but Eamonn said he needed to check on something we'd passed earlier, so we strolled up the same streets we had walked in the afternoon. He seemed preoccupied as we passed a clothing store, which looked deserted. When I stopped up the street to listen to a busker playing a flute, Eamonn turned his attention back toward this store.

"There's a restaurant a wee bit farther on, around this next corner, called Casa Peripecia," he said. "They have great paella. Why don't you get us a nice table *inside*—the rabble get to be troublesome on the plaza—and I'll be along in a flash; have to see 'bout something for a moment."

Regular meals were again becoming familiar and I was ravenous. Around the corner I entered the café. The owner thought it odd I didn't want a table out in the pleasant evening but promptly showed me where I could leave my pack by a large table indoors and brought two menus.

The menu was not making much sense when Eamonn hurried through the door. He quickly sat down, slightly out of breath. I was thankful for someone to order the food and was impressed he removed his cap for dinner. Strangely, he also removed and stuffed his red shirt into his knapsack, revealing the plain brown shirt beneath.

These details meant less at the time, however, than the fact that he could decipher the menu. In short order the waiter served us a big pot of steaming rice, shellfish and vegetables. Adding a bottle of dark red wine, we had a feast. Eamonn asked about my travels and seemed particularly interested in Paris and the Maison, which he called a "sweet dayle." As to his own travels, he talked only about how crowded some cities were and how the local girls compared.

When we had scraped the bowl and finished the wine, the waiter brought the check. I reached in my pouch for cash but Eamonn held up his hand to stop me.

"This'll be on me," he said with a self-satisfied grin.

"But that's not necessary," I said, surprised. "I can cover my half."

"Aye, but you see, you really needn't. I'll explain by and by. Think of it as manna from heaven."

I shook my head to be sure I wasn't dreaming. Surely, my brother had sent this shabby Irish angel to help me make peace with Catalonia. I was quite content. We bid the waiter goodnight and left the restaurant, but then Eamonn sped me quickly through the thinning crowds away from the center of town.

"Are we in a hurry?" I asked after a few blocks, as our pace started to interfere with my digestion.

"Ah, no mate. Just thought it'd be best."

This was confusing. I grabbed his elbow to stop him. "And what were you gonna explain… about the bill?"

He looked both ways along the quiet street and steered me into an alley. "Well you see," he said, "there happened to be an establishment in town that was not, what you'd call, 'well-managed.' In fact, you'd have to say, this particular emporium was crying out for improved procedures in the ways of dealing with an unpredictable public, or let's say, some helpful instruction in the ways 'n means of business, as it were."

I looked at him hard, trying to decipher his meaning, and gestured to continue.

"Well, call a spade a spade. The fact is that bit of jewelry and apparel shop we passed a few times was not at all well-tended, and I felt it incumbent on me to take a bit of a loan, as you might put it, from the till."

I looked quickly around. "You *shit!*" I shouted and then realized our precarious position. In something between a growl and a forced whisper, I continued: "You robbed a store, you jerk, and then joined me?"

"Well, as I say, we'd already 'joined' at that point, and we *did* enjoy a fine meal."

"I can't believe this!"

"Well, there ye go. And to show there's no hard feelings, mate, here's the rest of your share." He took a small wad of notes from his pocket and held it out to me.

I slapped the money to the ground and grabbed the front of his shirt. "You goddamn *thief*," I said. "I am *not* your mate, and I have *nothing* to do with your criminal bullshit! You take your loot and your sorry self and go south. I'm heading north and will kick your ass if you follow me."

He looked astonished, but then his attention turned to the peseta notes beginning to scatter in the breeze and he dropped to his knees to retrieve them. I thought about landing a kick to his belly but was more frightened of the police than angry at him, and turned on my heels to put distance between us.

With long strides and heavy breathing, I hurried through town and onto the coast road. In the fading light a half-mile along the shoulder disappeared, and I spotted a tiny beach far below. There was hardly any traffic and I saw no chance of getting a ride in the twilight. Plus, I was terrified the police would come looking for me, so I found a place to descend. At the first foothold, I stopped to tighten my pack straps and shoelaces and then scrambled, partly on my rear, down a steep path through scrubby trees, ending at a secluded strip of sand.

The beach was so narrow I doubted anyone could see me from

the road. Still, I had the stupid orange tent. I set it up as quickly as I could, close against the overhanging trees. It made no sense, but somehow I felt safer once in my sleeping bag. I didn't use a flashlight or candles, to keep from being seen, and until I fell asleep I strained to hear sounds outside.

I saw Edward hanging limp, held under the arms by two soldiers. A third, leering man jammed a rifle butt into his gut. There was a piercing scream that, as I came to consciousness, I found was my own.

It was pitch black. I jerked up and felt the roof of my tent. The sea lapped against the shore and I remembered where I was. The horror of my nightmare gave way to the nightmare of reality: alone and hiding out from the police. My shirt was soaked through. I pulled on a dry shirt and lay back, listening for sounds until I fell back into uneasy sleep.

Next thing I knew I was bathed in electric orange as sunlight poured into my tent. I cursed the bright color and hoped no one had spotted me.

When I unzipped the flap, I saw the tide had come in so far the sea was within reach. I had to step into four inches of water to get out of the tent. Trash bobbing at the water's edge made me think how my adventure had turned sour. I was in my own private purgatory.

Once I had my bearings, I waded to the tent door and pulled out the pack and sleeping bag. I removed the stakes and pulled the tent up the narrow beach from behind. I quickly packed and contemplated the climb up to the road but just then heard the double-horn siren of a police car approaching from the south. I flattened against the tree line and clenched my teeth until the sound faded away.

"How the hell did I get here?" I said out loud. Scamming subway lines was one thing, but what kind of miscreant robs a poor shopkeeper? And how could I explain I wasn't part of it when I'd spent the day with the only other English-speaker in town?

I wanted to scream. I needed to have more sense.

"Thanks for the angel, *brother*," I spit out.

Then it hit me like a slap. I blamed my dead brother for this mess!

How stupid was that? I thanked him for the good luck and blamed him for all the crap, but he was *dead* and had nothing to do with either.

My breath quickened. I unconsciously dropped to my knees. I wasn't crying, I was sobbing, and I couldn't catch my breath. My hands twisted each other so hard they hurt.

Edward's big grin filled my head: when I finally pitched a strike to him in our backyard; when he teased me for watching Helen McAffery in church; when he convinced me one bad math test wouldn't ruin my life; when he took the blame after I broke the basement window. He was always there, kidding me but protecting me.

Even after he left for college he was with me. Teachers and coaches remembered him and liked me by association. When he called home, I'd talk to him after my mom, and he'd get right to what was on my mind. He talked me through how to stand up to a bully in seventh grade, which changed my whole year—and my self-esteem.

His eyes had laughed so kindly when he told me how to ask Bernadette Barbaro for a date. "There's only a hundred percent of attraction possible between two people," he said, "so you can't let her know how much you like her; you have to act a little disinterested and give her the space to see you." That advice stuck with me all the way to meeting Pam, and even after we moved in together I made sure not to let her know how nuts I was about her.

When those soldiers showed up at our door, my first impulse, after denial, was to console my mom. But I couldn't reach into her emptiness and so had no choice but to face what Edward's death meant to me. There'd be no travelling adventure, and no sharing books and music, and there would never come a time when our age difference faded and we could just be friends. I'd never know what he truly thought about the world, without shielding his little brother. He'd never tell me what really happened in the war. I couldn't share the outrage that grew in me as I came of age. I'd never tell him how my love for him had eclipsed every notion I had of loyalty and patriotism, and set me on a collision course with our president and our dad. We wouldn't grow old together and sit on some porch in the late evening, sipping bourbon and telling the old family stories.

It was idiotic to keep obsessing. He was dead. I couldn't keep carrying him on my back. It was just a fact. For the rest of my life I'd have no brother. This venture to Spain was a tribute, in a way, but it would be *the* tribute. It was time to part ways.

I dug into my pouch and found my good luck coin. "I love you, Edward," I said, still sobbing, looking at the coin that felt like part of my hand, "but this is goodbye, brother."

Stepping into the garbage-strewn edge of the water, I hurled the coin as far as I could and stared at where it splashed into the sea. Whatever else I would accomplish, I had made it to Catalonia and left this monument for all time.

In a moment I snapped to, lifted my pack and started the climb. I wondered if I should have buried the coin, but the sea did just as well— and throwing it was more tragic, which he would have liked. Finding myself joking about this surprised me and lifted a great weight from my chest. I felt strangely free.

At the road I hid the pack behind a bush and climbed a few steps down the cliff face, so I could watch for police cars without being seen. When a small sedan started around the gorge, I stepped up. But in the minute it took the car to reach me, a storm rose in my stomach. As soon as the car passed, I retreated down the slope, found a place to prop on one knee and retched. I caught my breath and then a vision of chickens hanging in a window made me throw up again.

The convulsions subsided. I wiped my bandana across my forehead. An odor of chicken mixed with bile filled my head. The sound of another car came from the far side of the gorge. I rose, stepped from the trees and put out my thumb. Suddenly, I shut my mouth tight and again hurried over the edge and behind the trees.

Sometime later, the sound of another car brought me to my senses, thankful for the notice afforded by the topography. Brushing back a wet strand of hair, I saw a white car catch the gleam of the sun as it rounded the gorge. I stumbled to my feet just before a shiny

Mercedes came out of the last curve. Astonishingly, it stopped and the back door swung open.

The driver and passenger were two young German men, blond and tanned. I lifted my pack onto the back seat beside me and said: "Thank you, ah... *danke sehr*."

The air conditioner blasted, as did music from the car's four speakers. I still felt queasy and watched carefully for police cars on the road ahead and behind, but I hoped my fortunes had changed for the better.

*   *   *

We topped a hill between billboards advertising bullfights and hotels. The Mercedes pulled into a beach parking lot in San Feliu de Guíxols. The town seemed large for the Costa Brava, though the sparse crowd at the beach showed it was past high season.

We parked, and the driver said something and nodded toward the beach in invitation. I looked longingly toward the sea but shook my head, holding two fingers flat on my mouth in the universal sign of digestive problems. They shrugged and helped with my pack and then gathered beach towels from the trunk. We said farewells in German, and I carefully swung the pack to my shoulders and crossed the coast road into the city. I didn't want to be caught out on the road, in case someone was looking for me, and I desperately needed to lie down.

I focused on not getting sick again until I had booked a room in a small pension and lay on top of the cover of a narrow bed. On the wall were framed pictures of bullfights cut from magazines. A thin gauze curtain hung still before the window. On the nightstand was a small lamp, a bottle of sparkling Vichy Catalan and *Anna Karenina*, folded open near the end.

With shortened breath and matted hair, I stared at the ceiling. Suddenly, my cheeks puffed out, and I held my mouth with one hand and felt my way with the other to the toilet behind a partition. When I returned, I removed everything but a tee shirt, took a long drink of water and lay back on the bed, propping up my head to read. My face was flushed and beaded with sweat, but I was relieved to be done with the convulsing and hoped my stomach was finally empty. I slowly turned pages as the afternoon light dimmed. When it was nearly dark, I turned on the lamp, then turned it off again and lay quietly, looking toward the curtain, now faintly stirring. Too soon I jumped up again, knocking the book to the floor, and disappeared behind the partition. On the way back past my pack, I retrieved my pad and wrote:

> *Dostoyevsky makes Raskolnikov sweating in bed come alive for sixty pages, but my reading sixty pages of Tolstoy while hiding out and sweating in bed nearly kills me (or) "How I learned to Stop Complaining and Love Russian Literature."*

Thinking back, I saw a montage of the lamp turning on and off and me creeping back and forth to the partition. By the time I awoke, the sun was up and the water and the book were finished. I took off another soaked shirt that told me the fever had broken. In the small mirror by the toilet, I could again see some difference return in the color of my blue and gray eyes. I washed as well as I could in the miniature sink.

Last thing before leaving the room, I grabbed *Anna Karenina* from the night table, then paused. It was too big to carry just as barter, so I left it on the table. I wondered about this paperback's odyssey: abandoned in a baggage room in Paris, left at a hotel in Spain; where would it go next? I also counted my cash and left my few remaining pesetas on the night table, figuring they didn't amount to much and it would be best to have no Spanish currency if I were picked up for the robbery.

*   *   *

A young couple pulled to the side of the road in a dirty, white Peugeot. The driver had greasy, black hair and an American cigarette behind one ear. Beside him a woman with a tight, black ponytail pushed open the back door. Thin lips made her smile look insincere.

The man reached across to help pull in my pack. When I was settled, we tried to communicate. We shared no language, which did not surprise me. The woman pulled out a road map and pointed to Figueres, north of Girona, and handed me a brochure for *Teatre-Museu Dalí*. I looked at the brochure and nodded agreement. The text made little sense, but a photograph showed a theater or a museum and a photo of Salvador Dalí.

We parked across the road from the museum. I left my pack in the car and condescended with a bow to let the driver pay my admission. It was the least I could do—and I had no Spanish money at all. I was beginning to feel I could stop acting like a fugitive, but the museum was, in any case, an excellent place to stay out of sight.

At the door stood an old man in a gold-braided naval uniform and an officer's hat worn "amidships." He smiled through bristly, white whiskers, tore our tickets and cackled. I relaxed at this bit of satire and from then on gaped and laughed and wondered, to the accompaniment of an accordion tune spiced with dissonance.

Inside the entrance a rope dangled beyond reach. My eyes traced the rope eight meters up to where it was tied to the leg of a table, off of which a pitcher seemed about to topple. I jumped back, then laughed at myself and watched as both the man and woman jumped and laughed as I had. The humor suffered no translation problems.

The woman and I exchanged smiles, viewing the face a lobster sculpted to bask on a telephone receiver. Through an extra-terrestrial landscape was a painting of a huge dog collar that doubled as a viaduct. Upstairs we looked through a keyhole at a giant nose on the floor and next door was a living room designed as Mae West's face, from eyelashes to padded sofa lips. On the ceiling was a painting of a grand ballroom from under the soles of people's feet, the Sistine Chapel of the Munich sidewalk turned upside down and inside out.

Everything had recently seemed so somber. It was a relief that Dalí made me laugh at the world. Nothing was as expected and almost anything could be funny if you looked at it wrong way up. The artist's peculiar perspective of the world also fit my travel plans, and I realized there was humor, not just grief, in my life these days. I felt that my load would be lighter on the road ahead.

The image of the ceiling painting blurred and dissolved in my screenplay vision into a roadside of scrubby bushes burnt by the sun. I was walking a stretch of quiet highway north of Figueres. Traffic was sparse. The day was hot, and the sunlight burnt golden. While I felt beyond any remaining threat from San Feliu de Guíxols, I still wished more than usual to catch a quick ride across the frontier. I stepped heavily, one hand hooked in a pack strap and the other holding a cardboard sign reading "France."

At the end of a long climb, something big and noisy chugged and sputtered behind me. I kept walking but turned my head to see a school bus painted with psychedelic clouds and angels. It pulled over. I broke into my loping top speed and climbed directly into the open door. The driver, a heavy woman in overalls, nodded toward the back and wrenched the bus into gear.

Luggage and camping equipment were piled high in the back of the bus. I lay my pack on the seat beside me. Up front teenagers sang a Spanish song. A boy with yellow teeth and a hypnotized gaze accompanied the singing on guitar. A girl with long braids and the same dazed look kept time with maracas.

Singing continued until we approached a roadside restaurant, where the driver called over her shoulder. A man with a thick mustache and wire-rimmed glasses craned his neck to look out the window while he barked instructions through the side of his mouth. As the bus pulled into the parking lot, the mustachioed man put his hand on my shoulder and spoke quickly. I shrugged my shoulders to show I didn't understand. He tried French, then Italian, and then called something to a skinny girl in a flannel shirt.

The passengers gathered musical instruments and started out the door. The skinny girl pulled me by the hand and said over her shoulder: "You know the busking? We play and the peoples they give the pesetas, si? You, here, hold these bucket."

She led me by the hand into the restaurant. When several of us were inside, my companions began clapping to start a song. I disengaged from the girl and hovered by the door, embarrassed but holding the bucket. The buskers' hoots and clapping filled the two large rooms. The fifty people eating or working froze and looked apprehensive. By the time my companions had weaved to the back of the room and returned to the center, a short fat man in a jacket and vest led a charge of waiters to herd them toward the door. I watched until a waiter waved his arms angrily in my direction and then backed out the door as well. We filed out, some laughing and some still singing, and boarded the bus. I don't think we came away with any tips.

We continued on the highway for an hour or so. I was happy when we crossed into France. I sat on my own, watching the low countryside spotted with trees. Even if I had shared a language with these kids, I didn't imagine they'd have much to say to me, given the brainwashed looks on their faces, and I didn't think it would help to tell them I was on the lam. Soon the bus left me on the road to Carcassonne and continued toward Marseille.

*   *   *

A short ride left me within sight of La Cité, a walled city on a hill. The distant view of medieval stone battlements stirred my imagination and made me think I should stop for the night. There was something endlessly fascinating about walled cities, and I had a couple of days before the grapes. But as I gazed at the city my thumb twitched at my side, and on cue a brown Peugeot stopped. I snapped to attention and moved quickly toward the car, a present ride trumping my historical daydream.

Climbing into the back seat, I smiled and a nodded. The driver simply returned my smile and spoke to the passenger in the front seat, who turned gleaming white teeth on me. His dark hair and beard accentuated the whites of his eyes. Nodding toward the driver, he said: "I am called 'Charles.' He wishes to know where you will go."

"I go to work in the *vendanges* near Libourne two days from now."

Charles spoke with the driver, then turned again to me. "But where will you plan to sleep tonight?"

I shrugged my shoulders.

Charles spoke once more with the driver, then turned and said: "I too hitchhike. I hoped to come together with you tonight. But you will come with me to the house of my friend, near Bordeaux."

Thus, we apparently agreed. When Charles turned to conclude arrangements with the driver, I couldn't hold back my cocky smile. It was good to be back in France.

Chapter XV

Les Vendanges

Making it back to Saint-Loubès in time for the *vendanges* made me feel good about my ability to find my way. I scratched the bristle on my face and hitched up my pack for a short late-afternoon hike up the hill from the village to the château.

At the wooden door of the main house, I met Papa, who reached out to shake with both his calloused farmer's hands. He poured me a glass of wine and then showed me around back to the bunkroom, jabbering in French. As we approached a door standing open next to two open spaces cut as windows in the concrete walls, he patted my back and left me.

There were cots in the room and in the shadows a large figure in recline. Nick looked up with a smile and cheered: "The Yank survives *España!*"

"Hey, I've been in Bordeaux for days," I said earnestly.

Wally poked his head through the far window, pretending to grimace. "We've heard it all before: holed up with some sheila."

Laying my pack on an empty cot, I pulled out my scotch bottle, half gone. Nick bounced into a sitting position and reached out. Wally patted my shoulder and said: "Like I was sayin', mate: great to have you back!"

"He returns with his bottle or upon it," Nick toasted and took a swig.

We talked into the night, by the light of a single bulb hanging from the ceiling. There was no restraining Wally from chronicling his bordello tour. His father had told him this part of French culture could *not* be missed. I doubted my father had this view, or would share it if he had.

Nick said Paris had been "pretty much the same." It was odd for him to pass up the chance to spin a more elaborate tale, but I jumped at the opportunity to put my silent film into words someone could understand. I wasn't ready to share how Catalonia had brought closure to my feelings about Edward. Instead, I told of the stars, the bats and Picasso. Wally and Nick were more interested in the Spanish women.

A knock wakened us at first light. Nick grumbled, threw off his blanket and sat on the edge of his bed. Wally sprang bolt upright calling out: "Breakfast!" I opened one eye on the empty scotch bottle on the floor, which caught a glint of sunlight through the open door.

We joined a dozen workers around the big, oval breakfast table where we had struck our deal with Papa almost two weeks earlier. Maman brought one course after another from the kitchen. Through another door Papa brought wine bottles without labels. Noticing the wine, Wally poked me and winked. Across from us Nick was trying to speak French with the one young woman in the room (and her husband). He too saw the wine, nodded toward Wally and cast a familiar smile at me.

The day was already warm when we reached the fields. The workers took clippers and wooden baskets from a truck and paired off on either side of rows that stretched fifty meters between dirt roads. Nick waved for me to join him. Wally teamed with an old man in a dirty beret. Soon we would all be dirty.

The vines were set in even rows, striping gently sloping hills, heavy with purple-red grapes hanging in bunches almost to the ground.

Nick and I watched how the others cut close to the branch and dropped the grapes into baskets dragged behind them. Then we stooped to begin.

It was awkward. I couldn't reach the grapes without kneeling in the dirt, but it was hard to move forward from that position. I pushed forward as best I could. When a basket was full, the picker would yell "*la hotte*" and a worker with a huge, metal backpack would approach for the picker to unload. Wally tired of "*la hotte*" and began yelling "*le dump!*" Everyone laughed at this and a young boy, and then an old man, shouted Wally's expression when their baskets were full.

Inevitably, I ate some of what I picked. I couldn't be certain if the grapes tasted of the earth or my dirty hands, but it amounted to the same thing. Lulled by the sunshine and the taste of sweat, grapes and earth, Nick and I saw the others leave us behind. We neared the end of our row in about an hour. By that time the others were drinking water and wine by an old pickup truck parked for loading.

Thirst pushed us to finish our row and walk to the truck, wiping our foreheads and well-pleased with our accomplishment. As if on cue, the others grabbed their baskets again. Nick and I looked at each other in disbelief, downed a cup of wine each and hurried to our next row.

Sharing stern looks, we set about showing the Frenchmen how harvesting was meant to be done. I was sure our size and strength would enable us to move faster than the smaller and mostly older Frenchmen. Still, we had to rely on muscle and sweat in place of a subtlety in the twisting and cutting that seemed long-practiced, if not inbred, in our fellow workers.

Regardless of the need to preserve our honor, Nick positioned us in a row that would force him to bump rear ends with the young wife. He was over large for the narrow rows anyway, so crowding couldn't be avoided. I had little time to watch through the vines, but as the pace quickened and the young couple kept barely ahead of us, it was hard to ignore the sound of scraping jeans. There was no doubt I was firmly back in Nick's world.

The married couple was the fastest pair and quickened their pace when they sensed competition. I called "*la hotte*" but didn't wait to empty my bucket before falling to my knees to cut again. Nick crawled forward to avoid the delay of rising. The woman almost sang out in the delight of the race.

I was mesmerized by the rhythmic toil in the hot sun. I saw my Spanish pension with the curtain barely stirring in the breeze and became Konstantin Levin in *Anna Karenina*, a landowner struggling to show his peasants he could harvest wheat as well as they could. Unlike Levin, I didn't have to handle a maladjusted scythe, which would have put all the workers at risk. Like him, however, I suffered for the effort in sore muscles and raw hands.

Coming back to reality, the young couple finished their row just ahead of us. Nick and I lunged to a second-place finish but jogged past the couple to dump our last baskets into the truck and pour the first cups of wine.

"Ah, the sweet thrill of victory," Nick toasted.

"Of sorts," I responded and we both nodded to the wife, who smiled at Nick in grudging acknowledgment of our unorthodox finish.

As the wine coursed down my parched throat, my lower back ached. I was ready for a cold drink and a comfortable chair and tried to recall what Levin did after he lost face with his peasants. Surely, he returned to the big house to put up his feet.

After one more row, Maman called us to lunch. This time we started with a soup she called "*potage Germiny*," sprinkled with shredded sorrel. Everyone inhaled the soup and toasted the morning's beginning. Next came platters of fish roasted with the heads attached and then small bowls of sherbet, both sweet and tart.

Wally assumed the sherbet was dessert and called for more wine. Papa obliged graciously, but Maman was not through serving. She next brought in a large platter of small roasted rabbits. As Nick helped himself, I grimaced.

"Ah, don't be squeamish," he said. "Tastes like chicken."

Maman next served bowls of salad, followed by a plate of cheese. Wally turned up his nose at the salad but sampled each combination of cheese and wine.

With a lemon mousse and nuts, Maman started pushing coffee. Wally protested good-naturedly: "No, no; more wine!" Nick laughed condescendingly but held out his glass to be refilled. I feared we might be making ourselves conspicuous.

Toward the end of the meal, a car pulled up out front and Papa went to greet the arrivals. When lunch was finished, he pulled Nick, Wally and me aside. He explained through Nick's limited French that we couldn't stay to finish the harvest because we weren't from the Common Market. This was outrageous; he knew our nationalities when he offered us work if we would return in ten days. It seemed more like Maman thought the three of us would run Papa out of wine, and a better-behaved crew was at hand. The arrivals from England would take our place and there was nothing we could do about it.

"Bugger it all!" said Wally, shaking his head and steadying himself against a wall.

Nick raised an eyebrow at me. "I was getting tired of stoop labor, anyway," he said, making this sound like a question.

I'd become accustomed to fate guiding my way and simply went along.

Papa said we could work through the day for wages of sixty-five francs, less ten for room and board and another ten for dinner. Nick and I returned to the fields, but Wally opted for a nap. At the end of the afternoon, we decided to skip dinner. Papa paid us and we bade adieu to the *vendanges*.

Wally said he'd drive north and offered us a ride. "What else can we do?" Nick asked, looking at me and the approaching darkness.

Chapter XVI

On the Road

Without pay from the grapes, I couldn't buy a train ticket to Greece and make it to the islands for the winter, not to mention stopping in Turin. But long-range plans were abstract and I faced a concrete choice: walk southeast along the dark roadside, alone, or ride north in a car with Nick and Wally. I put off any big decisions until we reached Paris and hopped into the car.

On the *route départementale* toward Tours, Nick dug through the glove compartment to find Wally's cassettes. "You only have three?" Nick asked, disappointed.

Wally rolled his eyes. "That's right, mate, and I can sing 'em all through by heart."

"Right," Nick said. "Will it be 'King Crimson,' 'Zappa Live in New York' or 'Mix'"? He turned his head to me.

"What the hell," said I. "Roll the dice."

Nick inserted the "Mix" tape into the machine taped to the dashboard. The sun faded to Ian Dury singing a frenetic punk rock cover of a Rolling Stones song.

With only one day's pay from Papa, I'd soon be back to spending

German marks. I saw snapshots of the azure Aegean fluttering out the window. There seemed to be no sense in trying to plan *anything* since my course always decided itself. My German or French hosts would have taken that as an invitation to debate free will versus determinism, but all that mattered to me was the present tense.

Wally said he'd stop in Paris on his way to a manor house in Cornwall where he had worked in the spring. "The lady of the manor's from New Zealand, so she's a bit of all right," he said. "Good bet we could all stay there for a while—probably just kick in for food. And she might put us on the payroll."

The promise of a roof over my head and a potential job was hard to resist. I figured I'd save as much as possible and then head to Turin, whether Greece was to follow or not. There was no assurance what kind of reception I'd get from Annetta, but I was confident in our visceral connection and really wanted to spend some relaxed time with her to give it a chance. I resolved to write to her before we left France to let her know the plan.

We reached Tours a couple of hours after dark and found the apartment of Claude's friend Denis, but he wasn't home. Outside by the car, Wally asked: "So where can we sleep?"

Nick and I both thought of the broken bridge and directed Wally to where we had last camped. Wally pulled onto the embankment and parked in the shadow of the trees. As soon as we got out of the car, three teenagers smoking cigarettes saw us and approached. They spoke little English and were wide-eyed to meet us. The car, such as it was, elevated us from vagabonds into respectable travelers, and our appearance seemed to feed the universal longing of the young to escape the confines of their world.

Wally rummaged in the back of the car and produced a bottle of wine. "Papa's going-away present," he said sarcastically. He handed the bottle to me and broke out a small gas stove to deep fry "chips," which the kids called "*frites*" but declined to share. I opened the bottle with my pocketknife and offered it first to our guests. They politely declined this as well; even at that tender age, French kids knew better than to drink wine from unlabeled bottles.

Nick entertained the kids while Wally tended the chips. Withdrawing a few steps, I watched the peaceful river. Nick said prolonging this aimless life called for spending as little as possible. If that were true, I had to take this ride to all the way to Cornwall, even though this was exactly the wrong direction, away from Annetta and Greece. I'd have to get a train to Turin when I could.

After the chips and wine, the kids left and we prepared for bed. We laid Wally's big, canvas tent beneath our sleeping bags (and Nick's blanket) and folded it over us. The night was mild and the river serene. Though the ground was rocky, it had been a long day, and we spoke little on our way to sleep.

In what seemed the darkest part of the night, we awoke to flashlights in our faces. My eyes snapped open. The lights were blinding. I could barely see shapes of men standing by our heads. I rolled on top of the wallet and passport inside my bag. The darkness and French language added to my grogginess. We stumbled to our feet, asking urgently what they wanted.

As Nick struggled with his French, I scanned the darkness for an escape route. For some reason I focused on the socks on my feet and whether this would help or hurt running up a rough hillside. But then I noticed the leader of the men wore boots and the uniform jacket of some kind of guard or policeman. We might be arrested, I thought, but we should be safe.

Nick turned to us with a frightened expression that melted into a chuckle. "They say we shouldn't leave the car unlocked; we might get robbed."

My grip loosened on the tent stake that had found its way into my hand. Wally went to lock the car. Catching my breath, I drank deeply of the cool night. Nick offered his most embellished "*merci*," and the officer and his friends continued their rounds.

Returning to my sleeping bag, I marveled at our luck. It seemed the percentages would have to catch up with us sooner or later.

The sun had risen early over the Loire and dried some of the dew off our sleeping faces. Wally rose, complaining that a root had dented his back. Nick sat up, instantly awake and hungry. I felt grateful to be through the night with a sunny day and a ride at hand.

Wally cut up and fried more chips and we shared water from my canteen while we packed the car. When I cleared a place for the tent, I found a water-damaged paperback of *On the Road*. Wally said someone at home had told him he must bring a book, and the description on the back cover sounded appropriate, but it had gotten soaked in a mix of rainwater and motor oil before he was half way through.

"You're welcome to it," he said. "All that 'beat' stuff didn't do much for me."

I was thrilled and started reading on the ride north, peeling each yellowed, pungent page from the solid lump of the others. Nick rode shotgun and rolled cigarettes on a map.

We arrived in Paris about noon in heavy traffic and made our way to the right bank. While Nick checked the situation at *Maison Fauconnier*, Wally and I watched girls from a bench. He asked about the nightlife in Barcelona and listened distractedly until an overly made-up woman grabbed his attention.

"Ah, there you have it, mate," he said, resting his case. I watched the woman's exaggerated sway packed into a tight skirt and looked at Wally, confused.

He responded with incredulity. "Ah, now tell me you don't think the French whores have it like nobody's business."

"As to French women," I said, shaking my head in disappointment, "they certainly have something. But as to whores (like that one, who somehow escaped into daylight), I find them pathetic."

Wally raised an eyebrow and dropped his jaw. "Oh, now don't tell me you've never..."

"Never have. Never would."

Wally laughed and sat back. "Well, we'll see about that. My old man's advice about the Bordeaux brothels was the best thing he ever taught me." He had a faraway look and a sated smile seeped across his face. "Finest hospitality in the world."

"Yeah, my dad didn't give me much in the way of tips," I said, envious that Wally and his father shared at least something. Snapping from that depressing thought, I asked what satisfaction Wally got from sex with a woman who was doing it for money, but Nick returned and interrupted, saying with amusement: "Well, there's good news and bad."

"Bugger it all," said Wally. "Start with the bad."

"Well, Henry's off for the weekend chasing a German girl, so we can't stay at the Maison."

Wally and I gestured for the good news.

"Oh, yeah," Nick continued. "But, Emeline says she and Marie will put us up tonight." He paused for effect, then continued: "Their flat's on Rue St. Denis, in the red-light district."

Wally and I burst out laughing. Nick tilted his head, looking at us curiously, but then continued: "We'll meet the girls at their apartment and take them to dinner." Nick was good at spending other people's money, but Wally and I went along since we needed a meal and a place to stay.

Wally and I split the cost of a bottle of wine, yogurt and a baguette, and we all sat by the river to eat.

"I wonder if Jean-Paul's around," I said to myself, but out loud.

"Who's that?" said Wally.

"Ah, some guy who threw dinner parties in his flat when we were here before," Nick said, dismissively. "I'm sure he's got other things to do."

Wally looked at me inquiringly and I shrugged. We had a place to stay and a date for dinner, so it really didn't matter.

"I'm gonna' walk over to American Express—by the opera house," I said.

Nick raised an eyebrow. "Collecting your fan mail?"

"I don't know. Time to kill, and maybe my mother wrote again."

"Now there's a good lad," said Wally. "Who needs a whore when you've got a letter from Mum."

I shook my head, beyond having the energy to defend myself. We confirmed where and when to meet, and I walked to the opera house, through the streets almost familiar. This would be the last chance for mail before I got back to London, and who knew when that might be?

At the office, I handed over my passport and turned to admire the intricate molding along the ceiling. When the clerk and his pencil-thin mustache returned with my passport and an envelope, it didn't immediately register that the letter was for me. I looked blankly at the envelope and then snapped to, recognizing the writing as Pam's!

On the steps of the opera house, I tore open the envelope. The salutation was simply "Stephen," which did not portend especially well, but the important thing was she had written again. I read on. She thought Biberach sounded unusual, which was a funny take on the most "usual" place I'd been. School had started, and she was enjoying her upper-class seminars. She'd moved in with two old roommates and was enjoying their company and the Border collie one of them brought from home. She missed me on weekend shifts at the restaurant and wished me safe travels. Period.

I pondered this, not sure if it was good she missed me or bad she missed me only when she waited tables. Maybe she just wanted company walking home at four in the morning. At least Peter hadn't made it into this letter, and hopefully had stopped being so "helpful." Still there was no "dear" or "love" or any of the other stock terms, normally overlooked, which I would have clung to like a spar floating over my sunken ship. She'd clearly moved on with her life. I recalled Fitzgerald's Monroe Stahr, thinking about his dead wife and forgetting her "lingeringly and miserably again." I would stop looking for mail from home. Letters never improved my day.

Near five o'clock I met Wally and Nick as they reached Rue St. Denis. Wally parked on a small street almost in front of the girls' building. He stayed with the car while Nick and I went to check the address. The narrow streets intersected at odd angles and were lined with low apartment houses.

Workingwomen approached us immediately. The first was large and heavily made up. She took my arm and said incomprehensible words in a tone that communicated clearly. I shrugged my shoulders to say I didn't understand, and she laughed and licked her lips. I directed her toward Wally, grinning by his car.

Nick teased two young girls, who were all skinny legs and makeup, saying in French he and I were prostitutes (for women). They laughed coyly but followed us, pressing to strike a deal. Outside the door to Emeline's building, they looked at him for explanation. He said we were visiting friends, and on cue Emeline called from a third-floor window and we waved. In the blink of a false eyelash, we were all old friends. The large woman moved on and the two young girls assured Wally they'd keep an eye on his car.

Emeline and Marie shared a room barely twice the size of their opened sofa bed, with a tiny room for a toilet and bidet and an alcove kitchen. They greeted us with the bed folded away and on a small table a bottle of sweet Sauternes, which we used to toast the return to Paris.

Emeline was prettier than I remembered. Her short, tousled hair was the same dark brown as her sleepy eyes, and her jeans and loose sweater suited her much better than her uniform at the Maison. But it was clear she liked Nick, as girls tended to, and true to form he teased her. At any rate, the fortune of finding a place to sleep outweighed my budding attraction for Emeline or perpetual envy of Nick. I considered Marie, but she was too large in the hips and quite stern, with severe makeup. Anyway, she seemed mostly interested in Emeline's attentions to Nick, which suggested additional dimensions to the night. All things considered, I felt like the befuddled hero of a Truffaut film.

There was a knock at the door. Marie reached the doorknob from her seat and yanked. In the hall was a young couple, too scrubbed and clean-cut to be French. The boy wore a blue suit and the girl a modest white dress. Marie turned a wicked smile to Emeline and addressed the couple with dripping false sincerity. The couple responded enthusiastically but wouldn't be enticed into the room.

At a lull in the conversation, I asked: "You guys follow baseball? Do you know what's up with the Yankees?"

The young man looked up, surprised, and found my eyes. "Ah, yes sir," he said. "We just arrived from Connecticut, and the Yankees were way behind Boston."

"Damn it," I said, as Emeline said something to the couple and closed the door in their faces.

"Jehovah's Witnesses," Emeline explained. "Marie, she picks at them like bugs on a pin."

Wally said to me: "They must draw battle pay for this neighborhood. And what's with the Yankees? That your team?"

I nodded. "Grew up in New York; they were easy to root for because they always won."

Wally grinned. "But not this year, sounds like."

"Right; probably a good season to sit out."

The girls brought us to a restaurant on Rue d'Enghien. Emeline was a regular and, after a few words with the waitress, ordered for everyone. Nick tried to comprehend what she ordered; Wally and I didn't want too much information, so long as the food wasn't too expensive or obviously made up of animal organs.

Nick talked to the girls earnestly. They giggled and spoke too fast for him to follow. He nonetheless passed on to us that wine and hors d'oeuvres would precede something to do with sheep, which turned out to be lamb stew. With plenty of fresh bread and butter and good merlot, the meal filled us all for three hundred francs.

Afterward, we walked crooked streets, each girl taking one of Nick's arms. Walking behind, Wally nudged me. "The blighter's got a way," he said.

That night Wally and I lay head-to-foot on sleeping bags at the foot of the bed, almost as close together as if we shared my tent. My pack and Wally's luggage filled a good part of the space alongside the bed. Nick, having no sleeping bag, was forced to share the double bed with the girls.

The walls were thin and the windows wide open. Trade continued on the street. The night seethed with sounds of comings and goings. I tried to sleep but unconsciously stopped breathing to distinguish what noises came from *within* the room. I wished I were alone in the woods, away from sordid civilization.

In the morning the girls were sleepy. Marie stayed in bed with a pillow over her head and waved feebly. Through yawns, Emeline helped us collect our things. On the street she kissed each of us on both cheeks and reached up on her toes to rub her hand through Nick's hair.

* * *

Nick said he knew the way to the *autoroute* and sat in front. Wally concentrated on traffic and Nick's erratic navigation. At a stoplight he looked at Nick's tired smile and said snidely: "If we have to look at that canary-eatin' grin all the way to the bleedin' coast, we should at least get the details."

Nick smiled slyly and said: "There was plenty of room if you didn't want to sleep on the floor."

Wally started up again. Nick continued giving directions. I leaned my head against the window, admiring the extraordinary architecture. When we reached the autoroute entrance, Nick changed the tape to King Crimson and I turned to my book. Beyond the outskirts of the city, I looked up, smiling.

"Good stuff?" Nick asked over his shoulder.

I read aloud from a page torn loose: "Our battered suitcases were piled on the sidewalk again; we had longer ways to go. But no matter, the road is life."

Nick grinned. "A bit pedantic."

"Life on the road is a game," I said, ignoring the cynicism.

He smiled, warming to the chance to talk pseudo-philosophy. "How do you mean, 'a game'?"

"I don't know, call it 'EONDAD,' after our budget tour."

Wally turned his head with a raised eyebrow.

Nick explained: "The pure tour: Europe On No Dollars a Day." He then turned back to me: "So if this is a game," he said, "what's the object? What're the rules?"

"The object, first and foremost, is to manage it (which is not always easy). But victory is in the style."

"Style points," Wally laughed, "like bloody figure skating."

"The rules," I continued, "are to move around and amass experience, hedonistically."

"That's rich, coming from the bloke who don't believe in brothels," Wally interjected.

"I believe in them," said I. "I just have no use for them."

Nick and Wally snickered. "What is it then," Nick said. "You bashful—or just queer (given your experience in Zurich)?"

Wally laughed so suddenly he let the car slide onto the shoulder. When we were back in our lane, I said: "No. I should say I don't *object* to them. I find them harmless enough, but I can't understand how they do business, why anyone uses them."

Nick smiled noncommittally.

"Just imagine…" Wally said and then hummed to himself with an exaggerated leer.

"Yeah, as fantasy that's one thing," I said. "But what satisfaction do you get in real life when you know she'd rather be somewhere else?"

A gasoline stop interrupted the debate. Wally and I chipped in sixty francs each. Wally had a ferry ticket for himself and the car but little extra money. Nick said he had practically nothing left and wanted to board the ferry hidden in the back of the car.

I had about two hundred dollars in francs and German marks. I wondered if I should feel guilty not letting on I also had travelers checks buried in my pack. Then I reasoned that my stash was my fare home and my entire stake in life once I got there. I knew Nick had a return ticket and guessed Wally did as well. It seemed to be standard practice to send forth the youth from down under with tickets around the world. Wally also owned his car, which had to be worth something.

We passed by Rouen, but Wally wouldn't stop to see the cathedral. "Who needs to see another church?" he said.

"Monet thought it worth the time," I noted resignedly.

"Monet…oh yeah," he said. "Didn't he play base for the Kinks?"

We caught a glimpse of the cathedral tower over the lower buildings as we drove past and then I lost myself in the flaming sunset. In Biberach, Ernst saw reality as a game he'd never win, but he seemed to have prevailed. And here I was, the thimble piece in the EONDAD game, wondering if it were even possible to win. Perhaps it was all the same: reality is the game, and winning is all about laughing survival.

* * *

By early afternoon we reached Roscoff, on the north coast of Brittany. Wally parked in the ferry terminal lot half-filled with about fifty cars and walked to the office to check the departure time. Nick and I sat on the hood of the car, making quiet fun of a family so pale and pudgy they just had to be British. The air smelled of salt. We heard the cries of distant gulls.

Wally returned with a resigned look. "Well, bugger it all," he said. "The bleedin' French Maritime's on strike. They say we can wait, but they don't know when there'll be boats."

I shrugged and looked about for countryside to explore.

"So when do we eat?" Nick said.

We set about making ourselves at home. After we shared chips from the fryer and water from my canteen, Wally backed the car to a sheltered spot, on the way running over and exploding the canteen. It was comical the way it popped and shot out water, but I was sorry to lose it after all this time.

Arriving in our own car cast us as respectable victims of circumstance, like the other stranded travelers. More importantly, the strikers were French but the passengers were almost all British, sparking Anglo-Saxon camaraderie to which we pledged fealty. Nick played the "stiff upper lip" so well he returned, in no time, with a donated bunch of bananas.

Nick walked with me to the terminal so I could mail ferry postcards. I wrote to my parents again. I also wrote to Annetta, saying I wouldn't be able to visit Turin until after England but I dreamed of seeing her.

"I never send postcards," he said.

"Yeah, well my parents like to hear I'm still alive."

"I reckon they'll figure that out when you get back."

"Right, if you say so. And anyway, I had to write Annetta because she expects me to visit, and I've disappointed her."

"Ah, she'll get over it," he said and walked off toward the harbor.

In the terminal I met a little blond girl as cute as could be in a bright red jumper and overalls. She was about five years old and stretched out on a skateboard. Like me she was happy to be free and easy. She said little but wanted me to pull her with a rope tied to the board. She looked like pictures of Pam as a little girl and instantly won my heart. She rode on her stomach and, though I pulled more slowly and carefully than she wanted, she cried out at every turn. When I photographed her on her skateboard, she was shy but beamed at the camera, and her parents laughed.

The little girl got me thinking of Pam, of course, and how clearly she was done with me. I repeated her line about missing me when she waited tables. I wondered if I should keep writing her friendly cards, at the risk of looking needy.

We ate a dinner of chips, bananas, a chunk of cheese from the skateboarder's mother and candy bars from a vending machine. Wally agreed to drive a couple to the airport at Brest. "They can't wait for the ferry," he said, "and they'll fill the tank."

Nick and I lounged on a pier, enjoying the mild twilight. The ebb tide had left all types of vessels stranded. Sailboats and one large tanker stood on their keels in the mud. Low islands covered with shells dotted a still channel. A red and white lighthouse rose from one of the islands farthest out. I spent a long time setting up a photograph of the grounded boats and the sunset.

"You ought to catch the light reflecting from the mud, with the islands in the background," Nick volunteered.

This technical advice blended with the cries of the seagulls. I ignored them both and continued to set up the shot.

After a long moment squinting at the sunset, he said: "It's like acid."

"I missed the segue," I said, turning back to him.

He said nothing more. He was baiting me but I had to bite. "You mean you've tried LSD?"

"Oh, yeah," he said, clinically. He lost himself in thought for a moment, then added quickly: "Only a couple of times... when I was young. Probably wouldn't do it again; just wanted to see what the fuss was about; Timothy Leary and all that."

"And?"

"It's part mystical and part spiritual. You leave your ego behind and some primitive part of your brain comes through. You see wonder in everything, something like what a young kid feels; it's like floating along in awe of the universe. It's so good it's scary, really."

I turned back to take my photograph, feeling sufficiently captured by the spectacle, but curious about what he'd said. Then we both settled back to watch the sunset.

"So, you'll board in Wally's trunk," I said. "Ever wonder what it'd be like traveling with money? You know: staying in hotels, meals in restaurants?"

He shook his head and smiled. "First, it wouldn't be nearly as much fun. Next, it's a bit disingenuous to pretend we're gypsies or something. There is a reality to privilege. We wander around like vagabonds because we can. Really... we're just slumming."

"Fair enough, if you consider we have the freedom, but I, for one, could not have traveled any other way."

"Oh, me as well. I don't mean it's luxury, or necessarily easy—though it is often easy." He paused to smile knowingly. "I mean we kid ourselves to think we're roughing it or living on the edge or something."

He had a point. I had no money, for certain, but I also had no doubt that someday I would, and I could always go home for a place to sleep and all I needed to eat. It wasn't as if the world had passed us by; our upbringing and background—our class as it were—gave us the prerogative to take a time out, to give ourselves up to this random and revealing season.

Shortly after dark, Wally returned and parked by the flattened canteen. Nick and I went to greet him. His big smile spoke accomplishment and, with little prodding, he produced a small bag of marijuana. "They not only filled the tank, but they left this because they couldn't take it on the plane," he said.

Nick set to rolling the pot with tobacco into a huge two-fisted joint, and then we sat in the car and lit it. I had a hard time with the tobacco and so, with what was left, rolled a smaller, pure joint. We lingered, and smoke billowed from the windows.

Wally looked around the car appraisingly and said: "What we need to make this a real party… is dancing girls."

I clapped him on the shoulder, but felt we had everything we needed.

Afterward we wandered together and separately around the terminal and parking lot. A stout couple from London with two sons at home "about your age" offered Wally and me some wine. Nick said a middle-aged woman wanted him to come out for a drive. "I'd have taken a ride clear to London," he said, "if only she'd wear a sack over her head."

In a few hours the high and the long day left us ready to sleep where we fell. Wally tilted back the driver's seat and slept in the car. Nick and I claimed two benches in the terminal building among our comrades in adversity.

At a comfortably late hour next morning I rose, used the terminal bathroom and reflected upon the accommodations: friendly, unstructured, practically free, with a soft indoor bed and running water. It was an all-inclusive seaside resort, but for the lack of regular meals. It brought to mind the deluxe accommodations on my first ferry trip—in the lifeboat. I thought perhaps I should write a ferry traveler's guide to Europe.

Our fellow passengers, while a bit dull, made an amusing spectacle. I tried to remember a quote from Henry James about poetry in the life crowded around a landing, but I was too lazy to place it.

Back in the parking lot, I found the car empty but for the remains of the joint, which I felt obliged to finish. I changed my shirt and took my pad and bloated Kerouac for a hike.

Meticulously tended fields rolled out from the terminal building.

Stone walls laced hillsides spotted with cottages. The sea lay at the horizon. Billowy clouds drifted toward England. I wasn't sure what was planted in the fields but guessed it was artichokes from overhearing a woman outside a shop. The cottages looked more British than French, probably reflecting some historical English occupation. It was called "Brittany," after all. I described the scene in my pad and tried to remember when Joan of Arc had roused the local populace.

I watched a soccer match from a sunny rock and then finished my sad excuse for a paperback. Kerouac's journey made mine seem tame, and it was hard to overlook that he didn't see it as the stuff of literature. I could have taken a lesson from that had his account not made such a successful novel.

Back at the terminal I walked among the passengers, offering to trade *On the Road* for anything in English. I knew no one would want my book, with its grime and loose pages, but I tried to look sincere and pitiable. An elderly gentleman with a white handlebar mustache smiled kindly at my offer. He taught at a public school and considered it his "duty as an educator" to present me with a slightly used, though entirely intact copy of *The History of Tom Jones, a Foundling*. My eyes lit up, calculating the book thick enough to keep me supplied for some time and yet, unlike *Anna Karenina*, thin enough to fit the outer pocket of my pack. The gentleman brightened at my enthusiasm and patted my back for "minding the classics." I left Kerouac in a trash bin.

At teatime next afternoon, word reached Wally and me that representatives from the ferry line had arrived to "make arrangements" with the passengers. There'd be no departures from Roscoff for days, and the company was reimbursing the price of tickets so travelers could drive to Le Havre for a different ferry. Wally immediately looked for his ticket.

"Say, why don't you come along?" he said. "You waited here to buy a ticket; that should be worth something."

I was skeptical but joined Wally on a line of disgruntled heads of families leading through an open door. Inside a small office sat the graying ship's captain and a greasy, heavy man in a linen suit. Each passenger stood in turn before the table and explained his situation. The man in the suit then made a notation in his book and counted out a refund.

We all inched forward and I scrambled to think of something to say when it was my turn. The ferry line owed me nothing. The company had provided a roof over my head and running water for a couple of days; rightfully I should pay a bill.

When Wally reached the two men, he simply put his ticket on the table. The captain looked at him tiredly and the big man hardly at all, and they pushed toward him a stack of franc notes.

I then stepped up, holding only my passport. Both men looked up quizzically. "You see," I stammered, "well, I don't speak French, I'm sorry, but you see I came here two days ago to take the ferry and tried to buy a ticket but the office was closed, you see..."

"You have not the ticket?" the big man interrupted. "We make the refund to passengers they have the ticket..."

"But you see," I broke in, "when I got here to take the ferry, I had money, but I've had to wait two days and have spent all I had."

The big man cleared his throat and straightened in his seat, becoming imposing. The captain fixed cold sea-gray eyes on me. I sensed I was about to be heaved overboard, and gestured helplessness with my hands.

But before the big man could pass sentence, a murmur arose along the line. The big man hesitated, and the murmur took the form of one angry voice muttering, "Give the lad his money."

The big man looked at the captain, who eyed the waiting passengers nervously. I stood with hands folded, trying to look as angelic—and British—as I could. Quickly, the big man counted out sixty-eight francs to cover the cost of a ticket and asked me politely to move along.

In the lobby I caught my breath and beamed, having just pocketed more than I had earned for a day in the dirt picking grapes. Wally shook my hand, and we were still laughing when Nick arrived. I repeated my story for Nick. His eyes lit up and he disappeared in a flash through the door to the office. In another minute he came back through the doorway counting a wad of notes.

Nothing about this surprised me. I put my money in my pocket and couldn't hide my admiration. "Now tell us," I said, "why they would give *you* money when you intended all along to get on the boat hiding in the trunk."

"Well, that didn't come up," he said. "I rushed into the room, said 'All right, the wife's in the car; the kids are crying; just give the money for the car and two adults and let me get started for bleedin' Le Havre.' And they paid over two hundred thirty francs."

*   *   *

Nick's windfall didn't alter his plans to board the ferry in the back of Wally's car, albeit from Le Havre, but it covered his share of gas and food since Paris and put him a few days ahead. Wally felt cheated, receiving only what he had paid for his ticket, but he found the story sufficient recompense. Nick had stolen my moment of glory, but that was familiar, and I had to admit the episode was a success in the socialist sense: each contributing according to his ability and each receiving according to his need.

Wally put the Citroën on the road to Le Havre. I looked out toward the coast, again recalling my trip across the North Sea in my D-Day landing craft with Montana Bruce and that skinny Spanish kid. That first trip through the "romantic gate" to Europe now felt part of a wave of chaos that had swept me up but that I eventually learned to ride. I gambled innocence for the chance at a clearer view of world. What began as the Hollywood version of D-Day had turned into the real Normandy beachhead, out across the dunes, and along the way I had declared peace in my own war.

Chapter XVII

Ashegrove Manor

In Cornwall, in the southwest of England, an estate called Ashegrove Manor lay outside the city of Truro. While still called a "manor," as in earlier times, the grounds no longer housed tenant farmers and the only agriculture involved fuchsias. The estate still passed from father to son, but it was no longer self-sustaining. Unlike their ancestors, therefore, Reginald Tibbet and his grown daughter, Elizabeth, worked for their living. Reginald was a banker of the City, in a sense little changed in a hundred years. Elizabeth, a new university graduate, worked as a social secretary in the household of the second prince of the realm.

The true personality of the estate came from Lady Margaret Tibbet, or "Maggie" as she insisted on being called. Maggie watched over the younger daughter, Penny, and ruled the household while Reginald tended to business in London. She was close to fifty but remained vibrant. In some ways she seemed younger than Elizabeth. She had a natural style blending casual country dress with a city hairstyle and she glowed with an inner contentment at having the space to raise her fuchsias and her daughters. She also had a democratic, bordering on anarchic, sympathy for those who must do without their own hothouses. While Reginald seemed to think Maggie wanted in reverence for the family's aristocratic station, he should have expected as much in marrying a New Zealander.

Ashegrove Manor was a Georgian house, large but unremarkable, with several wings added over the years to add interior space, with little regard for external symmetry. While the building and grounds had declined from their heyday, they still displayed adornments of grandeur. The linen and china bore the family crest. Reginald spent his leisure hours painting views of the manor house to print on note cards for his personal correspondence.

Our ferry trip from Le Harve had been an anticlimax after the drama at the terminal. Nick managed to conceal his large bulk beneath the tent and our bags and complained of having to hide out in the cold without a jacket until we liberated him when the boat was at sea. We drove from Portsmouth to Truro, arriving at mid-day, and soon I found myself at Sunday tea with the Tibbets. This meal was served in the large dining hall at mid-afternoon to permit Reginald and Elizabeth an early start in "going up to town" (although it seemed to me London must be east, not north of Cornwall). Dark wood rose to a high ceiling and many-paned windows opened on expansive views of the grounds. Hattie, the Irishwoman who had cooked and cleaned for the Tibbets for fifteen years, acted her usual part as server. On this Sunday in late October, Hattie had three extra guests to feed.

Wally was only in his latest incarnation a "guest." The previous spring he had worked in Maggie's hothouses. It appeared he was a bit crude for Reginald's taste, but Hattie obviously liked him, and there was no restraining Maggie from helping a countryman. Wally had returned the evening before, asking for a place to stay for himself, Nick and me.

Maggie's loyalty to New Zealand did not extend to its western neighbor and she seemed cool toward Nick, as if she thought him too sure of himself. Reginald seemed to find Nick rather large and too good-looking, especially after Elizabeth, upon learning he would look for work in London, blurted out an invitation to stay at her place until he settled himself.

Reginald and Elizabeth seemed to find me inoffensive, if not particularly interesting. Maggie, bound to contradict her husband, acted as if I were the most engaging of the three of us. She responded to my attentiveness and complimented my eyes.

"They're different colors, aren't they?" she said when no one else could hear.

I nodded and smiled, putting her to the head of the class. As she turned to Penny, I admired her profile and sweet smile.

Hattie didn't notice my eyes but also took to me, initially for my help with the dishes but genuinely for my Irish name.

Wally explained he had met us picking grapes in France, but we were turned away before we could make any money. He left out the part about drinking too much wine, even in the view of a French vintner. Maggie instantly took us in, as she would any stray, but at Reginald's insistence stipulated we must wash our own linens and contribute one pound each day for food. I had to respect the old boy's efforts to maintain the estate.

Maggie encouraged Elizabeth's invitation to Nick when she perceived animation in her daughter's normally staid expression. As impulsive and irresponsible as he might be, she seemed to think this might be a way to shake Elizabeth of the monarchist views of her father, which she embraced too naturally.

"What type of work have you in mind?" Reginald asked over the roast mutton in a voice sounding a bit like an old wind instrument, perhaps an oboe.

"Ah," said Nick with an impish grin, "I'd be up for most anything… long as I don't have to cut my hair or work for a poofta or anything."

Elizabeth swallowed wine down the wrong tube and coughed until tears came to her eyes. Reginald's hereditary reserve barely masked his disdain. Maggie watched Nick as if he were a child clowning for attention. Wally smiled noncommittally while Penny looked around the table for explanation. I was intent on the food and gave Nick no notice, and Maggie seemed to appreciate this.

Picking up the stalled conversation, Maggie asked Nick what he was *qualified* to do. He said he had finished a university course in medicine, concentrating on astrology, so he could set himself up doing star charts.

Maggie took this as a joke, but Nick insisted he was serious. "Last year," he said, "an American banker from Chase Manhattan hired me to do a chart of the United States, to plot the course of the American dollar."

Maggie laughed and shook her head. Elizabeth had recovered her breath and looked on with renewed interest. Reginald called for Hattie to bring in the trifle.

* * *

I woke up between clean sheets, or at least sheets that had been clean before I slept between them. It wasn't until our first full day that Hattie showed me the bathtub Wally and I were to use, in one of the additions to the rear of the manor. She walked easily through the low doorway and said the one strict rule was never to leave the soap bar in the tub. I went for my towel, eager to bathe for the first time since Barcelona. But my enthusiasm cost me; stepping through the doorway I skinned the top of my head. Clasping my hand on the scrape, I bent and howled. But there wasn't any blood, so I continued to the bath. The heat quickly made me forget my injury and all other troubles.

Living at the manor was quite civilized. A cart left fresh milk outside the pantry door each morning in glass bottles stacked in a metal rack. The cupboards held lots of dry food, most importantly shredded wheat biscuits. I ate four bowls the first morning, savoring the cream at the top of each tiny milk bottle.

After eating, I found Wally lying under his car. For a while I fetched tools as requested but then wandered toward the front of the manor—to survey the estate. A rap on a pair of French doors caught my attention, and I saw Maggie at a desk in the study. She stretched back to pull open the door, holding longer than necessary a pose flattering to her figure. I was surprised and confused by my attraction to her.

"Morning," she said with a sparkling smile. "I trust you found breakfast?"

"I did," I said, "and thank you again for having us."

She paused and tilted her head. "Would you be up for a drive to Falmouth?"

"Absolutely," I replied, charmed she had asked.

Maggie drove a sporty red Aston Martin. We sped over narrow roads sunk deep between hedgerows, her white scarf trailing behind. When we slowed behind a herd of sheep and I could be heard, I asked why the roads were built too low to see over the hedges.

She looked at me like I was a child. "Over the centuries," she explained, "the roads have sunk." She looked terribly amused as she accelerated past the sheep, and I kicked myself for sounding like a yokel.

Falmouth was a harbor town fifteen miles from the manor. Buildings of mostly two or three stories filled a peninsula between the sea and the River Fal. Maggie brought me into a shop and said lunch was on her. "Absolutely whatever you want," she said, handing me a menu listing only sandwiches and soft beverages.

As I stirred my tea I suppressed a smile, thinking about how Tom Jones would have handled this situation. She noticed my amusement but didn't inquire as to the cause. Instead, she asked what I planned to do next. This reinforced my good opinion of Maggie. I found her interesting in many ways and realized I'd never had a one-on-one relationship with a woman so much older than me. I told her I planned to look for work and then head south to Italy and Greece. She smiled wistfully as if she could imagine being young and on the road herself.

After lunch Maggie did her shopping and I followed, dutifully carrying her parcels. In a haberdasher with a small selection of women's clothes, she held against her a golden-brown sweater and asked my opinion.

Her breasts seized my attention for the second time, but I responded diplomatically: "It sets off the hazel in your eyes."

She smiled knowingly and wagged a finger at me, but she put the sweater back on the rack and we continued along the street.

As we started for home, she stopped suddenly and backed onto the shoulder. She asked me to wait, crossed the road and rang the bell at employment office to see about work, but it was crowded with young men and he didn't want to wait. We drove past the cathedral but didn't stop. I only craned my neck as we passed to see pointed gothic spires and long stained-glass windows.

In the late afternoon Hattie served tea in the sunroom to Wally and me along with Maggie and Penny. I thoroughly enjoyed the meal. Maggie was witty and Penny pleasant enough, and I couldn't have purchased all the food I consumed, much less have it prepared and served, for a pound. I looked for some special recognition from Maggie but saw none. Before the sun went down, I found her reading a magazine and asked about my tour of the hothouse.

"Oh yes, Stephen," she said, sounding interrupted. "We shall do… perhaps tomorrow or the next day."

The next day both Maggie and Wally were off doing their own things. I walked the quiet lanes around the estate and into the local village. Sitting in a pub, I underlined a quote in *Tom Jones*: "Her patience was, perhaps, tired out; for this is a virtue which is very apt to be fatigued by exercise." I wondered if Maggie was showing patience or if I had imagined the direction things were going. Or maybe, I thought, she suddenly remembered she had a husband.

It seemed prudent to turn my thoughts elsewhere and so I wrote a Reginald Tibbet note card to my parents saying I'd made it back as far as England. I also wrote Pam that Ashegrove Manor was the perfect place to read Henry Fielding but I sensed a quiet descending, perhaps the natural denouement of autumn. I wrote to Annetta that my plans remained on course and I hoped to visit Italy within the month. What I didn't include in any of these cards was that a true *Tom Jones*-worthy romp through the countryside required a bit more gamesome Maggie Tibbet.

Thursday morning, I woke to learn Maggie had received news from London and left suddenly for town. Penny had been packed off to the gatekeeper's house to stay with a school friend. As a result, Hattie was to have a long weekend visiting her sister; Wally would drive her to the train in the afternoon. This left Mr. Findlay and I as lords of the

a plain-looking little house. A woman in an apron answered and join
Maggie on the porch. They spoke and then together they cut brov
vines growing next to the door.

With the cuttings stored in the boot, we continued along the ro:
and Maggie explained with a swagger: "She had a strain of fuchsia
haven't seen. This could be a find!"

"I'm afraid I don't know what a fuchsia is," I said.

She smiled, though whether at my ignorance or in satisfactic
at her good luck, I couldn't tell. "It's a shrubbery plant of the evenir
primrose family," she said, "with flowers hanging from the ends of i
branches. The flowers are generally pink, red or purple, and the trick
to cultivate other colors."

I tried to look interested. She sighed. "You see, I have one c
the most extensive collections in the country in my hothouse; I sha
certainly show you. Now, this kind woman's fuchsias are nearly don
for the season and need to be cut back. So we chatted, and she kindl
offered cuttings, which I most thankfully accepted."

My face gave away that I still didn't understand her triumph. Witl
a roguish smile, she explained: "Of course, she'd never give me cutting
if she knew who I was."

Maggie was devious, and I was finding her more and more in
teresting.

We drove on, and I was a more appreciative audience for hei
performance when we stopped twice more for cuttings. When we reached
the manor, I carried the plants into the hothouse. Maggie apologized
she couldn't show off her flowers before dinner but promised a "private
tour" later in the week. I liked the sound of that. *Tom Jones* had inclined
me toward amorous elaboration.

The next day after breakfast I shaved for the first time in weeks
and put on a clean shirt. When I went looking for Maggie, however, she
had taken Penny to a school outing. I was left for the day with Wally,
who did *not* notice I had cleaned up. He and I drove into Truro to use
the launderette and have a look around. It felt right out of "Penny Lane,"
in my ears and in my eyes, although more forlorn. Wally stopped at the

manor, with instructions to take in the milk and lock up when we went out. I wondered if I'd ever see Maggie again.

After Wally and Hattie drove off, I wandered around parts of the house I hadn't yet seen. Reginald's small study was comfortable. The leather-bound volumes filling a large bookcase weren't very interesting, though, as there was hardly any fiction. I read *Tom Jones* in a stuffed chair with my feet on an ottoman probably from the nineteenth century.

"Like a bloody bug in a rug," Wally said, entering the room.

"It *is* comfortable to relax on one's own estate," I replied with my best posh accent. "Now if we could only think of some use for the old place."

Wally poured two snifters of cognac. "Have to go light on this stuff," he said. "Reggie marks the bottles."

* * *

Next morning, I packed my novel, pad and camera into my Moroccan bag and set out for Land's End, appropriately named as the farthest point of land before the Celtic Sea.

"Why Land's End?" Wally asked.

"Because it's there," I responded, which was true in a way. There was nothing to keep me on the estate and I felt I would achieve something by reaching a land terminus. Wally said I could borrow the car after he tuned it up, but I didn't want to wait.

My map of Europe barely showed Cornwall at all and noted only two roads in the county. But I found a framed map on a wall and scribbled in my pad a drawing of smaller roads and route numbers. I had to walk a couple of miles to a road headed east and, while waiting for a ride, took note of the position of the sun and direction of the road.

At what seemed mid-day, I was walking a road along the north coast. I didn't feel far enough west to be near Land's End, but I could smell the sea. The weather was almost drizzly, and I wanted to head home well before dark. Beside the empty road, I hiked into low dunes covered with scrubby vegetation, looking for a place to eat. When I found a low point sheltered from the wind, I ate an apple and cheese to a sea gull soundtrack.

After eating I saw a double rainbow to the north. I imagined I might be the only person on this remote shoreline to see the rainbows and so thought they were there for me, to show the way. With no other inspiration, therefore, I set off north.

The dunes were high and blocked the wind from the sea. Near one crest was a concrete bunker that had to be from World War II. At every turn Europe seemed tied to this history. I tried to imagine the Home Guard watching for German U-boats from these dunes.

Almost by reflex my spirit sank at this reminder of war, but I immediately recovered. Something had changed in me. I loved my brother and I hated war, but I was resolved that my life would be enriched, not shrouded, by his memory.

The path ended at a cliff face, where the dune sloped precipitously some seventy meters to a beach. The vantage point confirmed I'd never reach the base of the rainbows, which rose and dipped out at sea. But this didn't lessen my faith in the portent, since this sign had led me to the shore. The cliffs, moreover, reminded me of those along the north shore of Long Island, where my grandparents had lived. My brother and I had often bounded down those cliffs.

Impulsively, I grabbed my bag tightly in one hand and leaped toward the sea with a shout! The wind lifted my hair and filled my lungs with the sensation of flying. In several impossibly long strides, I reached the beach and collapsed on my knees, breathing hard and laughing. I sat to brush off my face and empty sand from my shoes. Although the day wasn't warm, I decided to leave the shoes off and tied them together over my shoulder. The sand was cool and hard.

Out in the water a short way up the beach was a dark shape rolling in shallow waves. Hurrying along the shoreline, I could soon see it was a fish—or more accurately a porpoise. The waves came every minute or so and were no more than a foot high in the shallow water. Yet, the larger of them rolled the huge animal toward shore and then the undertow rolled it back, leaving it virtually where it started, in not enough water to swim.

"Oh, my God!" I cried and looked frantically up and down the beach for help. There was no one in sight. I panicked. There was no one else; I had to do something.

I pulled off my jacket and sweatshirt and threw them with my shoes and bag up on the beach. I rolled up my pants and stepped into the water, which instantly cramped my legs to the knees. I bent to rub circulation into my calves, then gave that up and waded out.

The porpoise was ten meters from shore in shallow water. When I reached it, the sea lapped over my calves. The porpoise lay still, looking at me with one doleful blue eye. It seemed to be crying out. I patted its flank, smooth and cold. "Don't worry," I said, my breath short. "I'll help you."

Porpoises were supposed to be intelligent, but I wondered if I only imagined this one was relieved to see me. I reached down and tried to lift its tail, but it wouldn't budge. It was way too heavy, if I could even get a good hold on it.

I don't know why I decided the porpoise was a male, but I felt certain about this. I thought if I could hold him in position when a wave came, then the undertow would move him toward the sea.

When the next wave rolled in, I got behind and pushed with my knees, but still the swell rolled him over and I had to jump aside. The undertow rolled him back to the same spot.

When the next wave came, I squatted and pushed as hard as I could with my hands above his flipper. I got wet, but the next wave and its undertow again left the porpoise where he started.

The whole time I pushed, I racked my brain for what else to do and kept telling the porpoise I'd get him back to deep water. Then driftwood floated against my leg and I thought of building a wall. I told him I'd be right back and waded around collecting floating wood. He'd done a roll in and out by the time I got back.

After a big undertow, I drove sticks with all my weight into the sand behind the porpoise and cushioned them with kelp. When I was done, my pants were wet over my thighs and I was shivering. I stroked him once more, bade him the best of luck and waded to shore.

At my clothes and shoes, I bent to massage feeling into my legs while I watched the sea. A couple of small waves left the porpoise in place but then came a swell big enough to free him. I stood straight up to watch, eyes peeled, fists clenched.

The wave lifted the porpoise and jammed him against the sticks, which bent but held. The porpoise thrashed its tail into the sticks. Red blood sprayed the foam.

"No!" I screamed and ran toward the water. But then I stopped; it was no use.

My mind exploded. I turned quickly, picked up my things and plodded toward the dunes, tears streaming down my cheeks. I felt brainless and guilty. The porpoise had been better off without me!

I didn't look back until I'd climbed the cliff and sat to put on my shoes. From that distance the porpoise was again only a dark shape in the water. I looked out to sea and noticed the rainbows were gone.

Chapter XVIII

Duplicity

I never reached Land's End. The porpoise was the terminus to the day and to my visit to Cornwall. Hitchhiking back to the manor I decided that, despite having a free bed in a house, a cordial relationship with Wally and milk delivered every morning, it was time to go.

All roads led to London, and it seemed logical to follow Nick's trail. I wanted to find him and get my bearings, so I could figure out what was next. Wally didn't particularly care when I told him I was leaving. "But if you send a postcard," he said with a smirk, "please have the goodness to address it to me as Lord Ashegrove."

Next day Wally dropped me by the main road. I barely had time to breathe in the morning fog before a red two-seater stopped. The gentleman was going "all the way to town" after a detour to see his daughter at her school.

When we stopped at St. Mary's, he told me I should remain in the car, from which vantage point it looked like all ivy, plaid skirts and knee socks. I felt certain Tom Jones would have made something of this younger end of the spectrum but had to admit I was no Tom Jones.

Back on the road I daydreamed I was, instead, Malcolm MacDowell in *If*, wreaking havoc on a stately boarding school. At some point I realized the driver had spoken.

"Oh, I'm sorry," I apologized.

"Nothing at all," he said, "just thought you'd like to know this is the Dartmoor up ahead. We'll be driving through it for a while now."

The moor was in parts barren and wild and in other parts wooded. Farther along, in Wiltshire west of Amesbury, we passed Stonehenge, barely visible over a rise. The intimacy of the exposure to this cultural landmark was right up there with viewing the *Mona Lisa* over tourist heads, through bulletproof glass.

In London I hopped the underground to Kensington Station and easily found Elizabeth's flat, where she lived with another young woman employed by the palace. Nick was sleeping on a couch in the basement, and she offered me a place too, but there was palpable tension in the invitation.

"Well, I guess you felt that," Nick laughed after Elizabeth left him to show me the second couch.

"What... oh, you mean the icy wind?" I said and paused.

He tilted his head with his full smile. "She needs a good lay."

"And you've been here what, a week?"

"Ah, she doesn't *know* that's what she needs. She thinks she must act properly for the sake of appearances. It's all such rubbish."

"I can't believe it," I said sarcastically. "And *you* the model house guest."

"Right," Nick said seriously, and then saw I was teasing. "Well, the house guest part is bad enough, being that we must *never* allow a single thing to be out of place as some palace lackey might stop in, but it's the other part that brought it to a head."

"How did I know there'd be an 'other' part?" I snickered.

"Yes, well, I stopped round to the pub one night and happened to meet a girl from Soho."

"So *ho*," I said, as if separating the syllables made this into some kind of revelation.

"Yes, well, and when I didn't come home that night," he said and then added in a high voice with pursed lips: "and didn't even call."

I shook my head. "Bottom line: where are we?"

"We're welcome to stay a couple more days. Betty—she hates when I call her that—has even given you her seat at a concert tomorrow at the Albert Hall so she won't have to sit with me; she got the tickets from the palace and asked me to go before she realized she loathed me."

Elizabeth later visited the lower depths. With grave courtesy she announced she could not join us for dinner because of something to do with the prince's secretary. By way of consolation, however, she delivered the tickets. She said she loved the symphony but would be unable to attend because of another engagement. Nick rolled his eyes just out of her view.

Nick took me to a shop for fish and chips where I sprung for dinner and to a pub where I bought a round of pints. I told him about Ashegrove Manor but what interested him most was my admiration for Lady Tibbet. He said he had been trying to connect with a job and a place to stay in London, without any luck.

Next day we took a bus to Hyde Park. We had a couple of hours before the concert and the afternoon was almost sunny, so we watched orators on the corner vie for attention, each oblivious to the others.

"It's the dole's ruined this country!" extolled a round belly under a pinstriped suit.

"We are controlled by the international conspiracy of the Vatican and the Queen!" voiced post-graduate angst from atop an actual milk crate.

"Eating animals is eating our friends, our companions on this world!" pleaded a face grizzled with lines of worry.

Having had our fill of oratory, we made our way to the Royal Albert Hall. From the outside this domed structure of red brick and terra cotta looked round, like a Madison Square Garden built during the Italian Renaissance. Circling the building was a mosaic frieze illustrating an involved story with crowds of workers and artists.

Our seats were several tiers up, at about eye level with the indoor fireworks that accompanied the *1812 Overture*. The fireworks were tacky, just as they were at American concerts, although I'd never before seen them indoors. Tchaikovsky supposedly didn't much like this piece and so might have thought the pyrotechnics helped. Despite the composer's view, the overture was a favorite of mine, and I silently hummed along and conducted with an index finger.

Elizabeth joined us at breakfast next morning and asked about the concert. We thanked her for the tickets and the chance to see the venue, and I began animatedly talking about Hyde Park Corner.

"No," Elizabeth said, arresting the conversation, "but what about the symphony? Were they really good?"

Nick shrugged his shoulders and Elizabeth looked fretfully at me.

"Pretty good," I said, "and you can't beat Tchaikovsky. A few sour notes and a bit of smoke at the end."

Nick reached for a roll and nodded approval. "Yeah, you'd think there'd be a fire code."

Elizabeth clenched her fists and rose. She mumbled something in a proper accent and stormed upstairs. I looked at Nick in puzzlement. He shrugged his shoulders. "I guess the London Symphony is sort of the house band," he said, "and we're meant to be grateful."

*   *   *

I soon tired of Nick's job search and the tension at Elizabeth's house. It was time to move.

"I'm thinking of pushing off," I said to Nick as we sat on our basement couches preparing for bed.

"Where to?"

"Well, I had thought about Ireland, but the weather's gonna turn cold, and so I think I'll head south. I feel bad about letting Annetta down. We had such a connection and I *really* want to see her."

"Look, about that," he said and stopped, looking away from me.

"About what?"

"Well, there's something you should know."

The pace of this revelation was killing me, and so unlike Nick. "Out with it," I said impatiently. "What is it?"

"My visit to Paris before the *vendanges*...."

"Yeah?"

"Well, a couple of days in, Jean-Paul had to take another trip to Milan...."

I spun my hand. "I'm sure this is going somewhere?"

"The thing of it is, I rode along and, well, Annetta had left her number in case I was ever in Turin."

The words "Annetta" and "Turin" screeched in my head like subway brakes. I struggled for words. "You said you stayed in Paris!" I argued.

"Look, I didn't mean, or we didn't mean to...."

"We?" I almost shouted. I saw in an instant why he'd avoided talking about Paris. I tried to recall seeing them together and what I'd missed. How could this be?

"You shithead," I spat out. "You haven't got enough girls everywhere you go that you have to chase after mine?"

"Now wait, look, I know it wasn't the best idea, and I didn't mean any harm, and it's not like *I* chased *her.*"

My fists tightened. Sweat broke out on my forehead. I focused on a cricket bat hanging on the wall and thought about cracking him over the head. But while I wanted to pummel him, her betrayal hit me harder. We had a connection; it was almost chemical. The way she looked at me and felt in my arms had been real, hadn't it?

I needed to get away, to be alone. I turned toward the wall and closed my eyes but got no rest. This put Annetta definitely out of the picture. I wouldn't go south again; I didn't really have the money anyway. Finding relations in Yugoslavia was always going to be a long shot, and I wasn't likely to get work there, or in Greece. No, I'd stay close to London, near my ticket home.

But first I had to get out of London, and there was always Ireland. I no longer felt a need to go anywhere for Edward, but the lure remained. This was something I should do for myself. It might also mean something to my father, or at least give me an answer when he asked—as he surely would—about the point of it all.

The next morning was cool. Nick poked his head from under his covers to watch me pack. When I checked my passport and wallet, I noticed Ubit was gone. I figured that shouldn't surprise me. He was always falling out of the pouch and probably decided to give me the heave-ho just like Pam, and Annetta, and Nick.

"I'm going to Ireland," I said dryly.

"The ancestral homeland," he said hopefully and reached out a hand to shake. I ignored his hand.

"I get it," he added. "The whole thing was bollocks, and I'm really sorry. But look me up when you come back. I'll help out; I will. And we'll toast your return."

"Aye," I said like a Scotsman. I scribbled a note thanking Elizabeth and left without looking back.

*   *   *

It felt good to step onto the sidewalk. My knee twinged a bit, maybe from muscle memory of trying to hitchhike out of London, but I felt light walking by stately townhouses to the underground. Annetta no longer drew me south, and Nick could go to hell. Pam had moved on, and I was finally done with mourning for my brother and fighting the Vietnam War. I was unburdened and ahead was only Ireland.

A train brought me to a point along Route M-4 to Wales. It was then slow going through the city's outlying districts. I had to walk along the motorway for a few hours after giving up at one entrance ramp and then another. I wondered aloud about the English, who fell near the bottom of my survey of kindness to hitchhikers.

A blue sedan stopped just past me. When the horn sounded, I looked up, jerked the pack onto a shoulder, and took off in a trot. I laughed to find the driver was Danish. He asked what was funny, and I recounted my hitchhiker's view of Europe. He nodded agreement and suggested Scandinavians would fit the German model. "You also will find," he added, "that the Welsh are more European than the English: warmer and more openly curious."

He dropped me a short walk from the city center of Cardiff, along the coast, and I promptly found his view of Welsh manners sound. I barely had time to set down my pack before falling into conversation with two young men, which landed me an invitation to a couch and a night at the pub with a crowd of their friends. Afterward, I recalled laughter, lots of ale and one girl devoted to The Ramones. I slept on a couch, and in the morning they pointed me up the coast to Swansea, where I could catch the Cork ferry. I also picked up the crucial intelligence that there was *no* youth hostel in Swansea.

Chapter XIX

Sounds & Sweet Airs

I opened one eye without moving my head. I couldn't remember where I was. Beyond a bay window lay a city, and the red ball of the sun on the sea; what city didn't seem important because my bag felt warm and the room safe. It was too early to be awake, but I had to record the spectacle. With one eye closed, I reached for my camera, snapped the sunrise and fell back to sleep.

I awakened again later to a coffee aroma and kitchen sounds. I was surprised to find the camera in my bag with me. In a moment a voice called breakfast was ready and everything snapped into place. My world was in the pack at the end of the couch. I was in Swansea, waiting for the Ireland ferry. A Welsh builder named Garth was making breakfast.

We had met after I covered the thirty-five miles from Cardiff to Swansea and learned the Ireland ferry wouldn't leave until the next evening. I stood on a corner pondering where I might stay and, on cue, a bearded man fairly tripped up the street with a whistle and a grin. His big beard and the woven bag over his shoulder made him an easy mark. I discretely crossed over to his sidewalk and, when he came upon me, looked up in feigned surprise.

"Excuse me, sorry," I said. "Can you tell me where the hostel is?"

He scanned my face and pack and said what I already knew: "Ah, sad to say, there's no youth hostel in Swansea."

"Oh, thanks," I responded, with my best golden retriever puppy face, and added as an afterthought: "I'm waiting for the ferry."

He smiled and shrugged and started on his way, but then hesitated and looked again at my pack and my shoes and my borderline overacted expression—and turned back to face me. I nodded and smiled and began slowly to turn on my way. He hemmed and hawed and finally said: "Maybe you should spend the night in my living room."

Garth and his girlfriend, Annie, talked it over and recommended the Monday ferry, so for two days I witnessed first-hand the warmth and openness of the Welsh. He had backpacked across Africa in his youth and knew exactly what I needed: a pair of high suede shoes for "rainy Ireland." She showed me how to use the washing machine and stuffed me with protein. They both seemed fascinated by how I devoured everything put in front of me, and they introduced me to many friends and pints of bitter. Garth kept everyone laughing with travel stories that ended with the same circle of life: when he was in need, someone helped; now it was his time to put back in. (I loved those stories, which typically led to someone losing themselves in thought and then buying me another beer.)

Next day Garth sent me on a bus to the Gower, west of town. "It's glorious," he insisted. "First place in the UK to be named an 'area of outstanding beauty.'"

I took a bus as instructed on a day sunny but cool. I hiked a breathtaking landscape of green hills on the sea, with the glory of it all to myself except for a gang of brown and white ponies. The animals came close for a look at me but trotted off when I tried to set up a photograph. Instead, I took a close-up of a beautiful red flower with five petals fringed with tiny hairs. There were wildflowers all around so I didn't feel guilty picking a few for Annie. Then I sat on a stone wall, eating Annie's bag lunch, reading *Tom Jones* and trying to make out Ireland over the sea.

I caught a bus back to town, and Annie cooked fish and carrots.

She beamed when I presented the flowers, a bit worse for the trip back to town. Garth said they were scarlet pimpernel, which brought to mind Leslie Howard in the thirties British movie, rescuing aristocrats from "those Frenchies." Supper through, we all stepped out to the pub for a last pint.

Walking down the stone steps to the street next day, a gift of bananas in my pack, I heard Garth call and turned around. He and Annie filled the doorway, a loving tableau wrapped comfortably in each other's arms. "If you find yourself in a fix..." he shouted and nodded earnestly. He had a face for sincere looks.

I smiled and saluted and turned on my way. Three blocks down the great bowl of Swansea, I could hardly distinguish their faces from the crowd of characters who filled my days. I wondered if all this traveling was numbing me. Should I feel guilty if our meeting moved my hosts but was just a stop along the way to me? Garth was so good-hearted, I believed he might shed a tear over my farewell note on the mantel: "Thank you for making your country part of my world."

* * *

A half hour before the ferry set out for Cork, I found a seat on board, gazing at a head of wild, red curls and slender shoulders. She sat in the next booth. We were almost underway and still there was no sign of a husband, but it was certain he'd be off fetching tea.

I feigned a trip to the WC so I could ask if she'd watch my pack. Her eyes pierced, dark brown and playful. She nodded "yes" but seemed distracted and returned to her book. My glance lingered in her tousled hair. I judged she was ten years older than me and out of my league.

When I returned, she was still reading and still alone. I tried a guileless "Thank you." She looked up, amused. The ferry bell sounded and she returned to her book and I rejoined my pack. In a few minutes she rose and gathered her bags. "I'm for the bar," she said with a nod toward the loud schoolboys in the next booth. I smiled and pretended to return to reading. Walking away was arguably her best angle.

My next view of her was through a porthole. I stood on the

observation deck with my pack. She was in the bar and still alone. I could see her in profile with one graceful hand twirling a lock of hair.

Inside, I happened upon her, as if by chance, and asked if I could share her table. Her expression said she wasn't fooled by my awkward approach, but she was entertained. She asked what I was reading. I showed her *Tom Jones* and saw a smirk in her eyes.

When the ferry set off, she stretched back in her seat, a brown cable sweater pulling taut to reveal the shape of her breasts. The bartender had opened up, and she asked what I was drinking. Over my Guinness and her Bushmills, she asked where I would go when we landed in Cork.

"Haven't worked that out yet," I replied, and she let this pass.

When I insisted on buying the third round, she said hers were doubles. I must have looked surprised, despite trying to appear blasé. She grinned. "Someone should have warned you about ladies who travel alone by sea," she said in a theatrically low voice.

I went to the bar and returned with her double whiskey and my stout.

"You won't be tastin' real Guinness until we reach Ireland," she said. "It's part of the magic that doesn't travel."

My stout tasted pretty good, but she continued: "In fact, some people believe you can't get *real* Guinness ten miles outside Dublin. Of course, that's a bit exaggerated, and you'd not convince anyone of such nonsense in Ballycotton, a little corner of Ireland you'd not otherwise see."

I answered with a wanting-to-be convinced look and wondered if I'd heard an invitation.

When the bar closed, she said, "It's too late to return below sea level to a cabin with three proper English ladies."

Against her better judgment, she allowed me to cajole her out on deck. We huddled together against the wet wind. She suggested we guess names for each other. I started, calling her Casamassima after Henry James. She smiled at this and insisted I must be called Tom Jones and not, she said, for the Welsh pop singer.

The hour before dawn we were rocked to sleep together on the carpet in the bar beneath a gallant gentleman's raincoat. The floor swayed gently with the waves. Her touch said warmth, not romance. I wondered if she could tell I kissed her hair.

*   *   *

The morning on board was formal, relatively. We returned the gallant's raincoat and wiped sleep from our eyes.

"They're different colors," she said, looking at my eyes as if discovering a new species of butterfly.

"So I've been told," I said.

She smiled as if this were quite a wonder. She said her real name was Maddy, short for Madeline, and made clear her invitation of a place to stay. I confessed my real name as well and determined to meet my peril head on. I ventured: "You're sure your husband won't mind?"

She acted as if this presumed unfairly. "I'm certain he won't mind," she said, "and why should he?" She let the question stand unanswered for a moment and added: "But, to put your mind at ease, we shall call him."

The husband, Liam, worked at a three-star restaurant called The Fatted Calf from six in the morning until three or from three until midnight, depending on the day. Maddy called him, and he said to come along.

Maddy went below for her bag and we found her car in the parking lot. When we reached Cork, Liam had just started an early shift. We drove straight to the restaurant and sat in an empty dining room. After stilted introductions and fifteen minutes of slow pouring, he handed me a Guinness for my first Irish breakfast. It caressed my throat and marked the inside of the glass all the way down. Then he sent us home to bed with an invitation to dinner at a pub.

At a cottage on a mild bay, Maddy showed me a loft bedroom over the garage. There was a bed piled high with blankets and a paraffin heater I was not to leave lighted while I slept. The room was cold, as suddenly was my hostess. She asked if I wanted tea, but her expression said to decline. She pressed my elbow and said she'd sleep until dinner.

I curled up in my sleeping bag under the blankets. There was no use scheming; it was clearly someone else's move. Instead, I drifted to sleep and dreamed I was on a long train ride beside an elegant woman with a wide-brimmed hat over her eyes. The conductor kept shaking my shoulder, saying I must get off at the next station.

It was Liam shaking me awake. He had lighted the paraffin. It was dark outside. He offered a bath before dinner and walked me to the cottage. Maddy was nowhere to be seen and he explained she was getting dressed.

The bath thawed my limbs and gave me time for apprehension. Something in Liam's tone had been out-of-sync. It was hard to guess what reception I'd get from Maddy. But she appeared in a soft green sweater, cheerful and welcoming. We sat and talked a few minutes and then Liam drove us to a pub in a nearby village. We had a couple of pints and tasty chicken pies listening to fiddle reels. Liam and I split the check.

*   *   *

I'd become accustomed to not knowing where I was when I first woke up. That next morning I knew before I opened my eyes, with none of the struggle between dream and reality. I felt cold and wet air, smelled salt and dark wood, heard creaking beams. There was no doubt I'd landed in "that little corner of Ireland you'd not otherwise see."

At the cottage I found breakfast and a note: "Off shopping. Back at three. Take a bike from the garage."

Then, well, a day 'til three. Three, and that was odd as three was when Liam would be back to work. That must mean she and he were shopping together? But did it mean, as well, he'd be no part of after three? Well, I concluded it was better to be safe and make it a bike ride until three and one minute more.

There was an old tank of a bike in the garage, and I headed off with squeaks and clanks on the only road through Maddy's wondrous corner. Peddling between walls draped with fuchsia and red berries I met wet and warm, greens I couldn't believe, breathing browns and wide tweed smiles. Each sheep and cow, solitary met, paused to watch and reacted confusedly to my barnyard impressions.

Skirting the bay, salty and cool, I sampled berries draping the hedge, finding them tart except for the sweet ones of deepest purple. I confided to a cow closely watching (and whom to trust, if not the local livestock?): "So what of this wild Irish rose? You're Irish, and a female; you might lend perspective."

"Moo," the response.

But what more could I expect? "Moo," I replied.

I passed along, marveling at the verdant countryside and dreaming of what lay ahead.

"Grand day!" came the first greeting from the first farmer.

"It is that," I replied, and he looked like he'd not mind chatting. But I chewed a berry and clanked on. The lane was uneven and my progress slow, in countryside of pure Celtic poetry.

Greetings became the harmony: He, "Grand day"; I, "Beautiful day"; I, "Beautiful day"; She, "Wonderful day." It was no good trying to make them repeat; they'd been at this too long and it suited them, like the dampness in the air suited the lush browns and greens.

Bird watcher clusters. A pub and a pint. Postcards of the Blarney Castle and "the sport of deceiving without offending." A one o'clock rush of "beautiful days" under tweed caps; yes, and a cousin in New York and "sure'n you might know 'im."

Two o'clock came as a turning point, with no need for a second pint in a day already gone edgewise. No, I thought, best to stay alert, in time with instinct. There's danger in them thar hills, sliding into three o'clock and Maddy's little corner.

The road traversed at noon, no surprise, inversely wound at two. Bicycle clanks in counterpoint with wind and sea; a familiar goat and a new friend setter; a "grand day" with two brothers in Toronto.

*   *   *

Rounding the last bend at three ten, in sight and time, I made out her winsome smile through a smoked cottage window. She came out in a jacket and boots. We hunted for beach glass and presented each other with shells. Then we turned inland on the lane and fed each other berries. She placed a red flower behind her ear.

We biked to a fisherman's pub. The regular crowd watched her beat me at darts. She pointed out Louis, the Frenchman who was rich but no one knew what he did for his money. "I only know he wants to bed both my husband *and* me," she whispered and slyly added her drinking without her husband would make a scandal in the village.

Back at the cottage she suggested I start a fire and disappeared to see about dinner. The turf briquettes were strange but easy to light and a warm glow quickly filled the room. She returned with a bowl of pasta, part of a round loaf of brown soda bread and a salad. We toasted with red wine the fading sunlight over the bay and sat long at the table talking books. When I said I'd nearly finished *Tom Jones*, she reached to a crooked bookshelf behind her head, her breasts again pushing against her sweater, and presented me with a large paperback of *Ulysses*. "Now that you've come to the magic island," she said, "you'll want to be movin' up to Irish literature."

I cleared the dishes while she put the food away, and then she chased me from the kitchen while she washed up. I stoked the fire and lay on a thick rug with a pillow under my head. A wind blew through an octave of tones outside, but the room was warm and peaceful. I felt as if I were dreaming, and this time the dream was lovely.

Maddy joined me before the fire and filled our wine glasses. She joked that I took easily to being served. I protested and tried to rise but she silenced me with a finger on my lips.

The wine drained from our glasses. We reclined before the fire. I felt her eyes upon me when I stirred the turf. When I resumed my place on the rug, I felt I was keeping her waiting... and leaned toward her... and softly kissed her lips.

She jerked back, flushed. "My husband!" she said breathlessly. "I can't sleep with you!"

This sucked the air from the room. We both lay still. I wondered how we had leaped to the question of sleeping together and looked at her cautiously.

She threw her arms around my neck. We rolled and scratched, laughed and kissed. Fire filled the room. She held me and pulled me over her and into her with a smoldering hunger. She adored my young body, she said. I devoured her; she was soft and voluptuous, and it had been too long. In the moment of climax, my mind raced in spirals.

Only after we lay quietly against each other did I again think about her husband. What was she like with him, I wondered. How could he have left us alone together?

The glow of the fire was soporific and I lay dozing and dreaming of Maddy's knowing smile, her forest of hair tangled round my fingers. The night crystallized as a new turn. I'd reached past charity and curiosity to a real life. This time the mark I left on my hostess marked me as well.

Maddy stirred in my arms, but I held her tight. The thought of Liam gnawed at me. I was anxious to know how she'd explain to him or *what* she'd explain or *if* she'd explain.

She had said she loved the West, but she hadn't said she'd go with me. Would that make sense, anyway? Did I even need to go west? Would she leave Liam so soon after returning home? What could I offer her? I was a vagabond. I had nothing but a backpack: no car; no bed. She couldn't possibly follow me, or lead me? I could just imagine showing up with her at my aunt's house.

She nuzzled my shoulder. I breathed her in, my guilt building. I had run amok through a marriage and would be off with a jolly nod. I got a notch on my walking stick and Maddy would be left to pick up the pieces. I realized I had too much conscience for this Tom Jones routine.

She looked up, eyes warm and sleepy. I looked away, afraid my expression would betray too much. She touched my chin and turned my face back to her. "What's wrong?" she said softly.

"I don't know how to say this," I stammered.

She looked up with concern and waved me on with a nod.

"I can't stay here."

She rolled toward me, trying to smother a laugh. When she caught her breath, she said in a condescending voice: "I'd have thrown you out anyway in a day or two."

My perspective firmly adjusted, I was embarrassed at having presumed Maddy had an actual attachment to me. I was, I reminded myself, a kid off the boat with no plan and no means of support.

I helped straighten the pillows on the floor and concluded this was the best resolution, although Fielding may have written it differently. She kissed me goodnight, and I retired across the cold yard to my loft.

In the morning Liam, of the ever-unfortunate timing, had gone off to his morning shift. I came to the cottage for breakfast and found no one about. Maddy called down from the second floor. She was finishing a bath and asked me to bring up a towel. I figuratively spat on my hands, rubbed them together and dove back in.

We took another tumble, this time in the light of day and with no morality play. It was more mechanical than romantic but a great workout to start the day. She then fed me a big breakfast of eggs and bacon, coffee and toast, and drove me to the road to the West.

While we drove, she dictated names of friends I should look up. There was Darlene in London, who I shouldn't miss, and Jack Leary, the pub keeper in Cloghane on the Dingle Peninsula, who'd remember Maddy's visit with Liam.

"You should have no trouble getting a lift from here, Stephen," she said, pulling to the shoulder and kissing me on the cheek. As she drove off, she shouted: "Give my best to Jack Leary!"

Perhaps Jack had already sampled Maddy's best? I'd see soon enough, I thought, and started walking west, thinking my grand romantic parting from Maddy had been quite urbane, almost British.

Chapter XX

Wandering Rocks

I stuck out my thumb at a sign for "The West." The third car stopped and carried me on a road parallel to the River Lee.

Past Macroom, I was walking along the road and noticed an old man thatching a roof. He sat halfway up a ladder, grinning at me, in a tweed jacket and cap. I gestured with the camera, and he accommodated me with a perfect Irish pose.

Moving on, I found myself walking alongside a huge yellow Labrador retriever with a need to please. He danced behind me, then in front, then dashed down a gully and over a stone wall, scattering grazing cows. I applauded and he seemed to take a bow, but then an old Saab clattered to the shoulder and a hand waved from within the right window and a black cable sweater.

The driver, by name of Seamus O'Connell, was an artist on holiday. He was a handsome thirty-five, with a strong jaw and wide grin. His girlfriend Nellie rode along on holiday and shared his flat in Dublin. She seemed younger than Seamus and wore her brown hair in a long braid.

Once we started toward Killarney, Seamus spoke over his

shoulder in a low welcoming voice: "That's a mighty big rucksack ye have, isn't it?"

"It's not much," I replied, "but *I* call it home."

Nellie turned in her seat, pretty when she laughed. "Where is it you're going, then?" she said.

"Um, west."

"Um," she exaggerated and giggled, looking to Seamus, "the west."

He turned slightly and raised an eyebrow. "We'll be going the same way, then, won't we?" he said.

I smiled as if to rejoin: isn't life a strange and wonderful thing?

After a bit more introduction, Nellie returned to the subject of my plans and concluded my itinerary was "loose," since my only destination was a pub in Cloghane. I objected and said I was also searching for a cousin in the north. Her smile broke to a sincere look for a moment, and then she laughed again and turned around.

Seamus and Nellie were headed to the town of Dingle, across the peninsula from Cloghane, but they would first spend the night in Tralee. They suggested I stop with them, where surely there'd be a place for my sleeping bag. I bowed my head in gratitude, quietly humming one of my father's Clancy Brothers tunes set on the road to Tralee.

The three-hour drive passed pleasantly. Seamus said he painted mostly abstracts, but he needed a dose of open land and sea now and again "to keep the vision fresh." I said, in more definite terms than I'd expressed before even to myself, that I was thinking of building a novel on scenes from my journey.

"'Build,' you say," laughed Seamus, "as if you'd need an architect to frame your buttresses."

"Now you leave his buttresses out of this," Nellie scolded.

I smiled to be in such easy company and sank into my seat. We slowed, entering a village, and I watched an old woman and her wiry terrier retrieve the milk bottles from beside the door of an ancient cottage.

In Tralee we stopped at the home of Mr. and Mrs. Mead, an older couple who had invited Seamus through a mutual acquaintance. After shaking hands with them both, Seamus said, "This is Stephen, our traveling companion from America."

"Isn't that lovely," Mrs. Mead responded, "and sure we've got a grand sofa for the sleepin' bag you're luggin' about with ye." Mr. Mead nodded agreement; he left the talking to his wife.

I thanked them both and they left us to settle in. A half-hour later Mrs. Mead served tea and currant scones, handed over a key to the back door and again left us to ourselves.

We washed and dressed and left through a garden filled with pink roses to walk the few short blocks to the center of town. Seamus deliberated among pubs lining the street and finally picked one, where he offered to stand the first round. He also bought a packet of salted seaweed and offered it to me.

"Brain food," he said, pointing to his head, "an aphrodisiac to inspiration."

When Nellie finished her half pint, she left to stroll the shops, saying she'd meet us farther along. Seamus kissed her cheek and finished his pint. I jumped at the chance to buy the short second round.

When we were settled in with fresh beers, Seamus said, "So it's a novel you're writing? That's ambitious, isn't it?"

I nodded. "And realistic, I hope."

"Meaning 'realistic' in style or as in 'I really hope I'll write it'?"

"Oh, that I'll really do it. But I have an idea about writing each chapter in a different style. One would be a silent movie, maybe even in the form of a screenplay, to show the hero can't speak the local language. I thought I could add a musical soundtrack to set the mood and insert captions like the old silent films."

Seamus smiled thoughtfully. "It sounds like a massive amount of work."

"But for this night," I said, shaking my head, "the bard must drink and junket."

Seamus smiled and queried with his eyebrows, which were quite expressive.

"Stately, plump Buck Mulligan," I said in an effected brogue.

His eyebrows repeated the question.

"James Joyce," I said, as if all Irishman would know this, and we both laughed.

"Well then," Seamus said and drained pint number two. "We'll be repairing to the next hostelry, won't we?"

Another pint in another pub left my head swimming. Seamus had fallen into earnest conversation about salmon fishing with a man with an impenetrable brogue. I signaled I'd meet him up the street.

A few steps along brought me to McReary's Singing Lounge, where heavy wooden doors stood open to the corner in invitation. I paused where the sound of a fiddle washed over the sidewalk. "As all Ireland is washed by the gulf stream," I muttered and stuck my head into the doorway.

The chairs and tables had been pushed back. A toothless, old man in a tweed jacket and cap played fiddle in the center of the floor. He stamped one foot hard and danced spastically. The patrons, seated or standing, faced the old man with earnest smiles.

I edged toward the bar but stopped to join the applause when the man finished and bowed. Before I could resume begging pardon of a large gentleman blocking my way, a middle-aged woman stepped to the center of the floor. She had a strong, plain face and wore a mid-length dress in a faded flower print. The way she folded her neat hands before her announced she would sing and it would be only respectful to listen. The room fell silent. Her strong voice sounded as if it must have been entrancing when she was young:

> *Oh darlin' boy, the pipes, the pipes are calling*
> *From glen to glen and down the mountainside*

The song reached inside and gripped me. I stared, transfixed. I knew the song, and she sang in my language, but I thought a person like her couldn't exist in my country. It went beyond the accent to the look of both confidence in her place and resignation at her lot; an aging

American woman might have either of these looks but not both at the same time.

The summer's gone and all the roses falling,
It's you, it's you, must go and I must bide

One regular nodded to another and I realized my drunken awe played on my face, like I was a hayseed gaping at skyscrapers. Apparently, the lady was a regular and I the unusual attraction. This was embarrassing, and I knew better than to draw attention to myself, a drunken foreigner with ten quid in my pocket. Backing out the door, I stumbled down the few steps almost on top of Seamus.

"You've had a bit of a sing-along, then, have you?" he said as he squared my shoulders to walk up the sidewalk. We paused to consider but passed up the next two pubs and then saw Nellie's swinging step approaching.

"Well met," declared Seamus.

Nellie flashed her fair smile, took both our arms, and led us along the short streets back to the Mead's. She retired and I kept Seamus company while he smoked "a last fag" in the garden. The night was still and warm. Clouds skittered across the sky. Seamus rolled his cigarette and smoked in earnest, pondering in the way that seemed natural to an artist.

"I've thought about what it would be like to be a novelist," he said finally.

"You'd like to write a novel?"

"Ah, that'd be something, wouldn't it?" he laughed. "No, I don't mean *I'd* write anything, just that I'd thought about it. I'm a painter, not a writer. Still, I suppose I've strong feelings about books."

I hesitated, then said: "I want to write a novel, but I don't know how."

"Well, you must foremostly have something to say."

"You mean a story?"

"Well, not necessarily. Your great novelists didn't get bogged down in story. Your man E.M. Forster—I read him a bit at university—he called story 'the only literary tool for tyrants and savages.' Anyway, didn't some other great thinker observe there really are only two stories: the hero comes of age; and, a stranger came to town? No, it's not so much what happens to your characters as how you say it and the truth you tell."

"But you must make the reader need to turn the page, to find out what happens next?"

"You're burstin' with surprises, aren't you?" said Seamus. "You'd set out to write a 'page-turner,' yet you talk of all different crazy styles and for fun read *Ulysses*, which calls for a trail map, a guide and a gaggle of sherpas."

Seamus decided to smoke one more cigarette while we split the bottle of Harp lager he remembered was in the car. After we finished the bottle, Seamus asked when I planned to begin my novel.

"I'm thinking of it now," I replied.

He nodded in encouragement. "But then it's a bit of a chore with all this movin' about, isn't it?"

I laughed. "I don't know; it seems the moving is what brings it on. Won't you paint or sketch on your holiday?"

"Are ye mad?" he recoiled. "No, when I work, I work; and on holiday, I take a holiday."

After a pause he continued: "Why don't you come back to Dublin? There's energy in the city just now, quite a lot of avant-garde. It's a good place to create: quiet and you could live on very little."

"But it'd take too much time; I'm pretty sure I'll be starting school again next fall."

A chill breeze blew through the garden. "Well, you had me there," he said sadly, stepping on his cigarette butt. "I didn't understand you meant you'd be writin' as a hobby."

That cut deep. I tried to protest but sensed he was no longer interested and gave up the argument. We said goodnight, and Seamus offered a parting word: "You cannot turn inspiration on and off like a spigot. If you've got a novel in you, you should write it before turning to a new life."

On my couch I stared into the shadow where the ceiling would be. There was no way around it: Seamus lived for his art while I played at mine. Could I stop here and forget about school and trying to win back Pam? My fitful sleep deepened in the quiet night.

The morning brought sunshine and cheer. Through the curtain by my couch, the mountains were bright green and soft brown. I walked through the garden toward the kitchen. White scented flowers covered a strawberry bush. I stopped to savor several deep breaths of the cool, salty air blowing from the sea.

Mrs. Mead served up a "fry" of eggs, bacon and sausage, along with brown bread and tea. Seamus and Nellie didn't eat much, which allowed me politely to eat for all under their encouraging smiles.

"It's astounding, really," said Nellie, "how much food you can pack into your skinny frame." I frowned, a bit too thin to find "skinny" a compliment, but kept my focus on the food.

After breakfast, Seamus drove us out the Dingle road onto the peninsula. He seemed distant, and I figured he no longer considered me an artist comrade. Nellie was quite the same as the day before, though, and invited me to join them for lunch in Dingle Town. But sensing I was about to overstay my welcome, I declined. Nellie raised a curious eyebrow but didn't pursue this. She wrote out their Dublin address and kissed me goodbye. Seamus shook my hand firmly and, with only slight condescension, wished me God speed.

*   *   *

I walked a short way out of town along a narrow lane to a sign for the Conner Pass, set down the pack and sat on a rock. On my Europe map, Dingle was the only town marked on the peninsula. I barely had the map stowed when a pickup truck stopped and idled in the road.

"Beautiful day," said the driver. "You'll be going over the mountain, then?"

I threw my pack into the back of the truck and joined the thin, elderly driver in a checkered cap. When he learned I was American, he told me of his brother who had been "almost the police chief of Boston."

The road rose precipitously into the mist. I thought about how Edward would have loved this scene and how, gratefully, this thought now cheered rather than depressed me. My brother would always walk by my side, but I'd come to see this would make me stronger and help me better see the wonder of it all.

After driving a while with no visibility to either side, the old man slowed where the road crested. He waived an arm and said grandly: "On a clear day, you can see England from this spot." He looked at me through the corner of his eye and grinned, as if acknowledging a tale a wee over tall, particularly given that we were on the west coast and England was to the east.

Remembering a postcard in Ballycotton defining "blarney" as "the sport of deceiving without offending," I shook my head and smiled. To one-up my host, I contemplated saying I was a piano tuner who'd lost his perfect pitch and hoped to regain it in the quiet countryside. Then again, there was no reason to compete. If playing the straight man put people at ease, I came out ahead in touching them for a meal or a place to stay or even just a ride over the mountain. Appearing gullible to blarney was no different than laughing along with a Frenchman's American jokes or trying not to beat my Swiss host at chess. I laughed: Eire on no punts a day.

We descended from the clouds over fields bordering the sea, marbled with low stone walls. The driver pointed out a cluster of ten or twelve buildings "that would be Cloghane." He was taking the road east but doubled back to leave me at the only bed and breakfast in the village.

In no time I'd agreed to pay two pounds sixty a night. The proprietress, Mrs. Bamtry, was imposing of figure but disarming in expression. She showed the way through a dark sitting room to a hallway thick with afternoon chill. I left my pack in my small room, washed and changed to my sweater and suede jacket. When I returned, the sitting room glowed with a turf fire. I sat in a tall, cushioned chair with *Ulysses*. A horse-drawn wagon ambled by outside. The turf smell covered me like a blanket.

> *By lorries along sir John Rogerson's quay*
> *Mr. Bloom walked soberly, past Windmill Lane*

After tea and scones that apparently came with the price of a room, I walked a hundred meters to the village pub. The ancient Jack Leary, himself, tended bar for two other relics, Thomas and Paddy Flannigan. They welcomed me to one of the two empty bar stools and Paddy straight away bought me a pint of Guinness.

I passed along Maddy's regards. She and her husband were only a dim memory to Jack, but it was no matter to my welcome. I backed up to the beginning and related the highlights of my trip. For some time I considered and confirmed I was, sadly, unacquainted with each of the dozen individuals my companions knew in the States.

An American botanist named Freeman had over two springs lived in the village, studying plants. "A lovely man," Jack sighed. "Jewish fellah; came with his poor hobbled wife. Thomas there always called him 'doctor.'" Thomas responded to this with the look of a loyal puppy as he laughed and then blushed.

My offer to buy the next round brought a rousing cheer, and Jack toasted: "*Sláinte!*"

"Is that Gaelic?" I asked.

"Sure, lad," Thomas replied, "or as you might say: to your good health."

Paddy then proposed a game of hoops and moved the coat hanging over the board nailed to the wall. He showed me how to toss the thin wooden rings underhand at the numbered pegs. Often enough an errant hoop would roll across the floor and someone would have to squat to retrieve it. Whether born of my youthful impatience or the others' sly exaggeration, I found myself doing more than my share of picking up hoops. In fact, whether I won or lost the previous match, I faced each new challenger, in the guise of welcome but more likely to keep my young back in the game. Jack rewarded me with another pint on the house as "the game of hoops' most promising newcomer."

On my Europe map, the islands off the tip of the peninsula were tiny dots. I asked about them and Paddy gave them the mystical names: *"Baile an Fheirtearaigh," "Dun Chaoin"* and *"An Blascaod Mor."* "In the middle ages," he said, "monks lived on these 'Blasket Islands,' in cells dug into the hillsides."

"That must have seemed like the end of the world," I responded.

"Aye, and wasn't that the point?" rejoined Jack.

It seemed mythical to imagine a monk's journey to the wild outer coast of medieval Ireland and then farther still to a tiny, wind-swept knob. Did sensory deprivation at the raw edge of nature bring them closer to God, I wondered. My times of solitude in these past months suggested the experience would at least bring them closer to themselves.

Before midnight everyone said goodnight, and I walked back along the dark road to my personal turf fire, still glowing. I read myself to sleep in the warm bed in my cold room.

Next morning I had a bath before breakfast. Clean and fed, I hiked toward Brandon Point in a wind that blew clouds skittering across the sky. At the first farmhouse a collie joined me for the walk.

My parents would never keep a dog, though I'd always loved them, so I befriended dogs at every opportunity. In Germany, strange dogs were scary, especially when they saw my pack. Here dogs seemed like those in America, basically trusting and friendly, and they never seemed to be tied up. They also had the Irish ease at introducing themselves and getting to the heart of the matter.

The collie and I walked together for some time and I decided to name him "Leopold," for Leopold Bloom. I was cool but comfortable in a sweatshirt over my sweater as I picked berries from the hedge, talked to Leopold and marveled at the mountains and the sea. The sky was clear blue but spotted with puffy white clouds. I couldn't get over the rich colors, especially the shifting shades as rays of the sun reached different parts of the mountainsides.

Leopold listened while I whistled Beethoven's *Pastoral*, so I jumped at the chance of an audience to try a Clancy Brothers tune:

While going to the town of Dingle,
One fine morning lost to life

The road eventually fell off to a stony beach where a shallow river washed into the sea. The clouds had cleared, allowing sunshine to sparkle in the water as it coursed through large rocks. I spent time setting up a photograph of the river and the mountains and a lone white cottage with a thatched roof. Leopold tiptoed along the sheet of water at the river's edge, splashing after fish.

We stepped across the stones to cross the river and came upon a cluster of six thatched cottages, each at a different level on the hillside. One cottage housed a pub called "Conor's," with a bench outside in the sunshine. Though the door stood open, I couldn't find anyone inside or around back. Leopold watched me circle the tiny building and assessed my defeated look. I wasn't sure if he smirked or just looked like he wanted to help, but he directed a few purposeful barks toward the adjoining farmhouse, which roused Mr. Conor. The proprietor appeared, as if fresh from a nap, calling out "grand day" as he slung up his suspenders and apologized for the wait. He offered no food at this early hour but poured a smooth pint of Guinness. I sat outside in the sunshine and drank slowly, reaching down to scratch behind my friend's ears.

I couldn't shake the feeling I kept leaving behind what mattered most, first the love of my life and now maybe my calling to literature. As the foam of the stout dissolved in the glass, I wondered if either of those dreams were real. Maybe I was meant to stumble along in my career and romances as I did on the road, simply reacting to the bumps and turns.

The evening mirrored the one before. Over tea and scones I wrote a postcard to Pam, which felt like putting a message in a bottle. It wasn't healthy to keep thinking about her, so far away and out of touch, but she felt like my only anchor to that other life.

My thoughts turned to my father, which was hardly more

comforting. He couldn't see the point of traveling to Europe, which he'd known only in war, or to loafing about when I should be working. Ever since we lost Edward and I lost faith in our government, he resented me. Maybe I reminded him of Edward or diverged from his fantasy of his eldest son walking the straight and narrow. My vision of my brother didn't fit Dad's picture, but it was no surprise we disagreed about that too.

And now it was clear my father wouldn't live forever, and here I stood in the land of his mother's family, wondering why he had never reached out to his relations. After my grandparents died in the fifties, before I was born, our only contact with the Irish relatives had come in an exchange of Christmas cards with a cousin named Catherine. The Irish cards were filled with long bleak accounts of death and disease, and my father feared becoming entangled with these poor relations. Still, he was passionate about his Irishness, if he was passionate about anything, and certainly sported a Kelly green tie on St. Patrick's Day and boasted about his Fighting-Irish son.

More important than cards home, I addressed a postcard to Belcoo where each year my parents had sent our Christmas card. May as well go that way, I thought, and maybe send Dad a postcard from the ancestral home. I didn't feel much of a family connection, but then I didn't send much of a card:

I'm Stephen Kylemore from New York, Jim Kylemore's son and your cousin. I'll be traveling up from County Kerry in a few days and would very much like to meet you.

The front shop attached to Jack Leary's pub was also the post office, so it was convenient to mail the cards on my way to the evening's pints and hoops.

As the Guinness poured, Paddy thought again of Doctor Freeman and asked if I'd take a note, in case I should meet him back home. I agreed to do what I could in that supremely unlikely event, and they all three scribbled upon the first thing at hand: a business reply postcard to Irish Merchants (Equipment) Ltd. requesting information on floor care products. Thomas wrote out Freeman's name and "God bless you, Doctor." Paddy sent his best wishes and reminded the doctor he should come back for the calf Tommy Dunn was keeping for him and that she was very fine. Jack started to write they had all had a good time at Thomas's wedding, but he ran out of space. He swore under his breath and called out to his wife for a sheet of paper. When I had retrieved the paper (as clearly no one else would get off his stool), Jack wrote in a steady hand:

Cloghane, 1ˢᵗ Nov. 1978
God bless our native land. May His protecting hand still guard
our shores and may peace and power extend or be transformed
to friends, and nations' rights depend on war no more.

The note was odd but somehow profound. I thought about asking Jack for help parsing *Ulysses* but there wasn't time. After another long sleep in cool, salty air and another large breakfast fry, I settled up with Mrs. Bamtry and hiked east.

Chapter XXI

Times Removed

A quiet Dutch gentleman on holiday took me across the River Shannon. I asked him to drop me in Doolin, on the coast of County Clare, because Maddy had called it "the home of Irish music."

We stopped on the way at the Cliffs of Moher. For a major tourist destination, this was refreshingly underbuilt. The only whiff of commercialism was an old man selling postcards and Irish music cassettes from a small trailer. The scent of the sea filled the mist. A gravel path followed the cliff edge but, because of thick clouds, we couldn't see the water. My driver and the postcard seller both said these were the highest cliffs in Europe. Having seen this nowhere in print, though, I suspected it might be blarney.

We walked a short way along a path with a short wooden fence and then nothingness three meters to our left. At a small ruined stone tower, we stopped and gazed into the mist and then turned back downhill to the car. Just then the wind cleared the air on an apocalyptical scene of jagged cliffs plummeting into a raging sea. I didn't know about the rest of Europe, but these cliffs were immense.

It began to rain as we drove and was pouring by the time we reached

Doolin. I jumped out of the car at a pub called McAns. The wind hurled me through the door, and I dripped a puddle in an entry hall lined with coats on hooks, walking sticks and umbrellas. Through another open doorway came the sound of two men singing to a mandolin:

> *By foreign shores, my feet have wondered*
> *Where the stranger called me friend*
> *Every time my mind was troubled*
> *Found a smile 'round the bend.*

That sounded like my cue, and I entered the room with my dripping backpack. I crossed the open space before the small stage to set my pack out of the way. The mandolin player scratched stubble on a gaunt cheek and looked at my wet footprints.

"You'd best be sitting by the fire, wouldn't you?" he called out.

I turned and raised my eyebrows to inquire if he was speaking to me.

"Yes, lad," said the other singer, older and ruddier than the first. "Sure, you're the only one tracking puddles across the floor, now aren't you?"

I bid them thanks and said I'd first get a pint. They nodded approval of this and the mandolin player launched into a reel, the older man turning to watch the fingering.

At the bar a few men in tweed caps drank stout or whiskey. I asked for a pint and told the bartender to take his time pouring. He smiled approvingly. The nearest man said: "You're on holiday, then?"

"Yeah," I replied, laughing about my likely "holiday accommodations" in the rain beside the pub.

"From America, then?" he continued.

This always seemed so easy. "New York," I said. "Grew up in New York and went to school in Michigan."

Two more gentlemen joined the conversation, and the first paid for my Guinness but mixed himself a "shandy" of bitter and 7UP. We all chatted or paused to listen to the shifting cast of musicians. It seemed no one was paid to perform. Locals and a couple of visitors played just for the music and the camaraderie, taking turns on the instruments at hand. I loved the purity of this.

Along one wall sat five boys and a couple of girls mixing their English with French. I hoped I saw a spark in the big, dark eyes of one of the girls. She sat in a corner, listening to the music, draped like a cat over the shoulder of the other girl. She wore a heavy sweater too big for her, the same dark brown as her eyes.

The rain cleared by mid-afternoon, though the wind continued to blow. I left my pack with the bartender and walked the lane toward the one farmhouse that might offer off-season rooms. I lost my way, which was strange in so small a village. Sensing this, I decided to forget about the B&B and turned onto a narrow road leading to the water, instinct as usual replacing plans in setting my path. I concentrated on Seamus's idea about staying in Dublin; what did instinct tell me about that?

The air was heavy with moisture and a salt smell. Clouds charged in from the sea. Low green bushes and scrubby trees lay back against the wind. I stopped where the lane overlooked the coast, strewn with great boulders. A thundering sea raged against the stones and burst into foam and spray. I huddled behind my arms to watch the waves.

Out beyond the massive and threatening sea medieval monks had clung to tiny islands at the outermost edge of the world. I couldn't imagine how they had dared venture forth from here, or for that matter how my grandparents had the faith to follow vague tales and promises to the New World. It was another loop: their courage—or desperation— came full circle to put me on this coast looking back toward America.

Wind and more rain drove me back into the pub. The bartender greeted me like a lifelong friend. At his recommendation I ordered a hot Irish whiskey. "It'll take the chill out, and no mistakin' it," he assured me.

The bartender knew his remedies, and the pub soon felt warm and inviting. Through the afternoon I heard lots of music and got to know the French kids. They were students on a somewhat organized excursion. They'd come from the north to meet the Dublin bus and were headed to Paris. I traded Paris stories with two of the boys, who spoke good English, and managed to seat myself by the brown-eyed girl, who did not. As evening came on we all ate soup and sandwiches.

The fire, the music, the girl's friendly smile and my sated hunger and thirst left me content to stay where I was for the night, if only I could. Having struck out on a bed and breakfast, I thought about throwing myself on the mercy of the bartender. My pitiful tent would blow away in this wind.

But a Frenchmen handed me another Guinness and the housing quandary slipped from my mind as a guitar commenced playfully to duel with a fiddle. Several tunes later another Frenchman asked where I'd stay the night. I peered furtively at the corners of the bar.

He laughed. "You will come with us," he said. "You have the sleeping bag and we have a little 'barn' where we are invited to stay."

The Frenchmen's "barn" had four ancient walls of whitewashed stone and a low thatched roof over a dirt floor barely wide enough for eight sleeping bags. The roof was too low for us to stand upright. I tried to position myself by my silent girlfriend but landed instead between a Frenchman with a patchy beard and the spiders on the wall. As I tied my bandana over my head, I thought about the girl just out of reach and Paris-bound. I recalled Annetta in London at the start and thought what an enormous shortcut—although maybe an even bigger mistake—it would have been to go with her then to Turin.

When we had all settled in and my closest neighbor was snoring, I pulled up my hood, bunched the bag around my ears, and fell to a dreamless sleep.

Next morning, our exit from the barn was comical, everyone maneuvering at once out of sleeping bags and through the low doorway. Up on the road my acquaintances were eager to be off to their bus stop to the south. I looked hard at my departing girlfriend until she finally smiled. At this small victory, I bid cheerful *mercis* and *adieus* and hiked north. I later wrote in my pad of "waking on the rugged coast of Ireland in a house crammed with worldly Frenchmen."

The narrow road out of Doolin wound through low-walled fields into the Burren, a barren lunar landscape. The road snaked between mountains and sea across sandstone strewn both landward and seaward with otherworldly boulders. It felt good to hike, which was fortunate since there were no cars, and this gave me a close-up view of the countryside.

After an hour, I left my pack by the road and hiked inland to a low hilltop. Cracks in the stones hid tiny pools of life and pockets of brown and electric-green scrub, shielding orchids and tiny yellow roses. A pack of goats appeared on a ridge. I crouched and tried to sneak close enough for a photograph. A lookout goat spotted me, though, and they all scattered down a crevice and up the far side.

Back on the road there were still no cars. I hiked ahead and saw stone houses and a few cows on hillsides. On a promontory beneath a ruined tower, one cow seemed to gaze into the distance, the first bovine I'd ever seen strike such a noble pose.

A car finally approached and, as surely, stopped. "Beautiful day," said I.

"'Tis all that," said the driver. "You'll be taking a trip, won't you?" he said, a sparkle in his blue eyes.

"Isn't that amazing?" said I. "I'm already on a trip."

He let my sarcasm pass with a grin. He was a retired schoolteacher known as Wolfe, after Wolfe Tone, headed to Galway, which was more than halfway to Belcoo. I settled back and ate in the colors of the glorious mountains and loughs. By late afternoon I reached Sligo, only fifty kilometers from my destination. I passed up a search for Yeats' birthplace, hoping to complete my trip before dark.

With the last sunlight, an elderly couple picked me up. I told them my destination and the woman asked whom I would be visiting. I replied with Catherine's family name and address. "Sure, the Donahers are gone from there two years now," said the man, looking to his wife for confirmation. "They're out on the Lattone Road."

I put myself in the couple's hands, and they dropped me before a small, suburban-looking house with flowerbeds and a concrete fountain on the lawn. I waved goodbye, but they waited to see that I got in. Turning toward the door, I pumped myself up for a fast pitch, realizing I'd sent my postcard to the old address so this would be a cold call.

Before I could ring the bell, the door flew open. The doorframe filled with a man's ruddy face and broad smile and around his legs two little boys and a slightly older girl.

"You'll be Stephen from America!" he said. The boys giggled and hid behind their father.

"Yes," I said, astonished they'd heard I was coming and that my own prepared smile felt sincere. In a twinkling I was whisked to the kitchen table and seated before a steak and a glass of Guinness. Aunt Catherine and her husband, Brendan Donaher of the permanent ruddy grin, were probably fifty years old. She hurried about finding more food to set on the table, while he kept my glass full.

My guard let down. The instinct to stay alert and assess my surroundings simply vanished, and this almost brought me to tears. I felt with a certainty there was no need for concern. Compared with every place I'd arrived in five months, this was home.

At their insistence, I outlined my trip and the American lineage. Catherine was fascinated to hear first-hand of relations lost to her after my grandmother died twenty-five years before. When I told them about Edward, she crossed herself and said they had read that tragic news in a Christmas card and kept him in their prayers.

There was no way to reconcile my father's picture of poor, rural Ireland with the Donahers' comfortable life in a modest house on a bit of land, with fishing lodges to let to German anglers. They gave me the daughter Bernadette's room and drew me into this family, my family. This was not just the latest place to crash, where kind people treated me well; this was my cousin's bed, and pouring tea for me was the author of those long, sincere cards that had reached my house every Christmas of my life.

Aunt Catherine answered some of my questions about the family in Ireland but said I should get the details from her mother Ann. She was the last surviving sibling of my grandmother and the matriarch of a family that spread beyond the ends of each of Catherine's stories. She'd been napping when I arrived but was roused and was dressing to meet me. Given my unwashed state, this seemed more ceremony than was warranted.

When I'd finished my meal, I offered to help wash up, but Catherine would have none of that and took my hand to lead me to the front parlor. I was touched at how even my best technique for ingratiating myself with hosts was no use in this house.

"She's nearly blind, Stephen," said Catherine, "and a wee bit hard of hearing, so you'll have to sit close and speak loudly."

Ann sat ramrod straight in an armchair in the front parlor crowded with Belleek pottery. She couldn't have weighed more than ninety pounds and wore a neat, print dress with a lace collar. She smiled softly, sensing rather than seeing my approach.

I was eager for a connection with the grandmother I never knew but was overwhelmed by the glow surrounding this ancient woman. Catherine made the introductions and Ann clasped my hand in her bony, pale fingers with the strength of a vise grip. She held her head high as if peering a great distance.

"Your Granny was coming home to visit, Stephen," she said in a shallow voice choked with emotion, "when the Lord took her to his own."

"I never knew her," I confessed apologetically.

"Sure, but that was twenty-five years ago," she said, as if that were the blink of an eye, and turned toward me.

"Your Granny never made it," she said, patting my hand, "but at least you did." She paused. "You've come in her place."

Chills ran down my spine. My reason for visiting, to find a place to stay or a meal, was suddenly inconsequential and even irreverent. Ann continued to hold her head nobly. The set of her jaw and strength of her grip exclaimed unbounded joy. Her sister had returned from beyond the ocean and this life for a last farewell. I was humbled to see I had closed the circle of her life.

I made up greetings from my father, who could not have imagined this scene. But wishes from distant relations concerned Ann less than what she held in her hands. I asked about her family, and she paused with a pregnant smile and then started to name her children. I begged her to wait until I had my pad and this pleased her, like everything I did. Then she dictated, and I copied furiously. She named her twelve children and their many children and whom they all had married and where they all had settled.

When she had covered her progeny, my hand was cramped and I counted forty-seven second cousins completely new to me. My known family had expanded instantly and geometrically.

Catherine came in quietly, reminded her mother it was time for bed and said: "And you'll have a bit of tea, Stephen, won't you?" Her voice was musical, high notes at the question ending each sentence. "Wouldn't you?" "Isn't it?" "Doesn't she?" She hit her highest note in the earnest long first "E" in "Stephen." No one had ever before said my name that way and it touched me.

"You'll have a bit of tea, Stephen, won't you?" she repeated.

"Oh, no thank you; I've had enough tea today."

"You'll have just a drop, then?"

There was nothing but to give in with a smile.

"And a wee biscuit would be lovely with your tea, wouldn't it?"

*   *   *

I slept soundly in a comfortable bed, but in the morning recalled a disturbing dream. I was speaking on a crackly long-distance line with my mother. She was crying and said my father was dead. I gasped and couldn't catch my breath. I had to lay in bed to collect myself before going to breakfast.

Brendan took time off from work for my visit and suggested road trips through Donegal and Fermanagh. For the next week, my days were filled with magnificent scenery and a dizzying array of relations, each insisting I take some tea. One cousin took me to tour the Belleek pottery factory, where several relations worked, and another took me into the hills beyond his farm on pony-back. I drove with Brendan and Catherine to the lower coast of County Donegal to meet an aunt who ran an inn.

In the evenings after dinner I'd sit and talk with Catherine and Brendan, listen to Bernadette's stories about her school and her friends or play games with Sean and Gerard, who proudly informed me they were six and nine years old. The only troubling note came from the stone-faced British soldiers manning the border checkpoint and riding in the backs of army trucks armed for battle.

We visited the cottage where my grandmother was born, which sat in the North on the border with the Republic. The building looked little changed by the years. The walls were thick, whitewashed stone and the roof thatched. Inside, one large room was filled with barefoot children staring wide-eyed at me. The cousin in residence, Patrick, was ten years older than me. He and his wife were raising the crops and four children. He took me out past the barn to the graves of our mutual great-grandparents.

"It's a free man you are," Patrick said with a crooked grin.

"You mean I don't have to take care of a family and a farm?"

"Oh, for that," Patrick said, shaking his head, "I'd sooner die than give up the land, and the children, for all their mischief, are the true joy of life. No, Stephen, I had my day as a wild rover and don't miss it now. What I'm meanin' is that your America's at peace with herself. You haven't this insanity of one killing another because they attend different churches on Sunday."

"Well, it's only five years now since we were running amok through Asia at war with the world."

"Aye, that was a bad scene. But I'm thinkin' that at least your country is at peace."

"The soldiers here scare me," I said. "It makes me resent the British in a way I'd never have imagined in England."

"Sure, and that's natural, isn't it? But the soldiers were supposed to stop the killin'." He paused and looked into the distance. "We just wish it'd all stop."

He recovered himself and pointed past the cottage. "Can you see, at the dip in the road, there's a gate?"

I nodded. "There's another, forty feet beyond," he said, waving farther away, "and then the Republic. This road past the cottage and our winding driveway has always been rutted because the lorries came through to avoid border duties. Well, two years ago Maureen and I were sittin' by the fire with the wee ones asleep and in come the boys from the IRA. They take out a gun and tell us we must call a neighbor to bring his tractor to pull out a lorry stuck on the driveway. I hadn't a choice and so I called, and they ended by blowin' up a brand-new tractor across from the police station."

"Close to home," I said quietly.

"Aye, and wasn't it a week the wife and I spent in Belfast convincing the authorities we were victims in the affair?"

He slapped my back and led me back the cottage for tea.

I was always the center of attention as my vast new family celebrated my homecoming. They also wouldn't hear of my leaving until I had concocted a story about having to meet Nick in London and wanting first to see Belfast. Aunt Catherine finally consented to my departure only upon my promise to look up a cousin in Belfast and Catherine's sister in Dublin.

Catherine and Brendan talked about Belfast merely as the capital city, if fallen on hard times. To me it was a dark blot on the map. The causes and symptoms of the Troubles seemed to focus there, like Morder in *The Lord of the Rings*. I believed I had to reach the heart of its darkness to begin to understand Ireland.

Chapter XXII

Tale of Two Cities

After goodbyes and a final ardent hug from Aunt Ann, I walked to the highway with Sean and Gerard. They looked at me beneath my backpack as if I were off to slay a dragon and wished me "God speed." I loved the way these people talked.

I feared the Troubles would make it difficult getting rides but found myself immediately in a Belfast-bound lorry, waving goodbye to my little cousins. After quick introductions and my apology that I didn't know his brother in Milwaukee, the driver told me how years back "the boys" had taken his truck to bomb a police barracks. "Twenty thousand liters of whiskey," he lamented, with a doleful smile. I was astonished he harbored no ill will against his kidnappers, though, as "they had the decency to give me carfare home."

We reached Belfast in a couple of hours. The buildings there were grey and packed tightly together. Dark clouds held back the rain. A somber soldier younger than me looked down from a guard tower. Gone were the curiosity and half-serious nods I'd seen all about me. People here went about their business looking at the ground. An open-backed army truck rolled slowly by, soldiers in back pointing guns into the air. I felt as if I'd stepped into *1984* and for once longed to escape this fiction to something recognizable as normal life.

The concentration of soldiers and police thickened toward the city center, but I felt compelled to keep walking. I was convinced I had to reach the core of the malaise before I could escape it.

Police barricades cordoned off a central shopping area stretching away from a grand but grimy official building. To enter I had to snake through a series of fences and metal detectors in a temporary shack beneath a tin roof. The guards ran parcels and bags through what looked like the x-ray machines I'd seen at airports, but they weren't big enough for my pack. I turned up my hands and smiled at the guard, who humorlessly motioned me aside. Two more guards inspected my pack inside and out with what looked like an electric charcoal lighter. I wondered if they'd ask about my pocketknife, but this didn't concern them. One guard tapped his finger on my camera and said they'd confiscate my film if I photographed the checkpoint. I nodded that I understood, thinking I'd heard a dare.

In the gloomy shopping area past the checkpoint, I unslung my camera and carried it in my hand. I backed slowly into a broad doorway and leaned out of sight of the soldiers. Pointing the camera into the crowd, I set the light and focused on infinity. I leaned forward stealthily to make certain no one was watching and then in one motion pulled up the camera, shot the checkpoint, and lowered the camera.

I leaned back into the doorway and waited, my heartbeat drowning out the street sounds. My hands sweated. As moments passed I felt relief and then tasted victory over the darkness. I stowed the camera and hiked up the street, thinking of Joyce's description of British soldiers as a symbol of hatred, violence and history.

In place of pubs with shiny brass doorknobs were ladies in drab overcoats passing noiselessly among dimly lit stores. The buildings were lusterless, the people pale and expressionless. This was less *Ulysses* or *Trinity* than it was *The Trial*.

Having touched what I had sought, I recoiled at an overpowering sense of dread and longed to escape. At the far checkpoint, the heavily armed policemen searched my pack again, presumably to ensure I wasn't smuggling a bomb *out* of the shopping district. Outside the barricades I walked to the first public telephone and leaned my pack against a grimy brick wall.

I dialed the number Aunt Catherine had given for my cousin Bridey. "Hello, Bridey?" I said, swallowing my distaste for her city and pushing the "hopeful well met."

She asked who I was. I explained but she said she knew nothing of a "cousin from America."

"What is your business?" she asked sharply.

"Aunt Catherine sent me…"

She hung up. I stared at the phone and rubbed my chin, my fingers finding and tracing a lump beneath my right eye. In a minute I shook off the trance and found another coin in my pocket. I dialed again and talked fast, but as soon as Bridey heard my voice she slammed down the receiver.

The slam made my eyes bulge. I backed out of the booth with ears ringing. The suspicion in my cousin's voice darkened the prospect of finding anyone to take me in. Again fingering the lump beneath my eye made me wonder what new affliction this announced. I took hold of my pack deliberately and, after a deep breath, swung it wide around my shoulder. The strap pulled loose and the pack flew, landing against the brick building and the sidewalk.

I walked over and leaned against the wall, next to my pack on the ground. "I have to get out of here," I said out loud and then squinted and concluded I first had to do something about my face.

There was a hostel a few blocks away, down the street from a pub wreathed by a twenty-foot storm fence. The receptionist didn't ask for a hostel card, which seemed both trivial and more important than ever in this war zone. After tea and a sandwich, I took a bath and went to sleep, finding no solace in a particularly opaque chapter of *Ulysses*.

Rising early the next day, I followed directions to a doctor's surgery. An hour later Dr. Carmody looked at me through his round, wire-rimmed glasses and said my problem was a lack of vitamins. I panicked and couldn't remember my last orange juice! I felt so stupid to let this happen yet again. All this traveling was teaching me nothing.

The doctor, God bless him, recommended more meat and vegetables and *potatoes*! I had no medical training (on top of having no sense), but I knew I wasn't suffering from a starch deficiency and so questioned this diagnosis. I gratefully accepted the antibiotic prescription, though, and when I asked how much I owed, he was surprised I wasn't English.

"Oh, I don't really know," he said, "You won't be part of the national health then, will you?"

It seemed too late to say I was from Cornwall. Dr. Carmody continued absent-mindedly: "I suppose you shall have to pay something, then; let's say two quid."

An hour after filling the prescription and buying an orange, I stood on an entrance to the Dublin road, the first real highway I'd seen in Ireland. A lorry driver soon stopped and said he was going all the way to Dublin.

* * *

As soon as we crossed into the Republic, the tension fell behind with the murkiness. Fields regained their magic greens. The sun again glinted off rooftops. The wind rushing by my window seemed to carry a distant fiddle reel. In three hours I reached Dublin and began a short hike to my aunt's house in Dundrum.

Dundrum had been built as a separate village but became an outer borough of Dublin. The roads were narrow and full of traffic. Rows of townhouses hid deep, narrow gardens. For this meeting I rehearsed a pitch to explain quickly who I was, but I needn't have worried. Catherine had spoken with her sister who, in any event, was not easily flustered. When I reached Aunt Mary's house, the door opened wide to a big woman's grin.

"You'll be Stephen, then, won't you?" she began and didn't leave off until I was seated to the supper she seemed to have been saving for me.

Aunt Mary was a widow with two sons. Thomas was thirty,

worked in a bank and lived in Cork with his wife and two children. Brogan was twenty-three, lived at home and had worked construction since leaving the university halfway to his degree. Aunt Mary made clear I was to stay a good long while, rely upon her for *everything* and call her "Aunty Mary." This opened theological thoughts about Mary versus anti-Mary, but I had learned there was no resisting the Irish aunts and so simply agreed.

My new routine was grueling. I typically woke around ten to a morning overcast but not cold. My aunt served a big breakfast of eggs, bacon, soda bread and tea (and oranges by special request). While she cleaned up, I planned my day or read the paper or took a bath. At noon Brogan came home for supper and I was summoned back to the table for meat, potatoes and vegetables. By the time Brogan returned to work, I needed a walk in the garden to help me digest all the food. It felt like Ireland was making me soft, and I loved it.

Once ambulatory, I'd take a bus to the city center. I would wander with *Ulysses* and my pad or camera. The weather, I was told over and over, was unseasonably warm and dry for November, though it was not particularly sunny.

I admired the elegant Georgian buildings along the River Liffey. I stuck my finger into the bullet holes in the ionic columns of the General Post Office, stronghold of the Easter Uprising. A tourist brochure said the pediment statue of Hibernia was meant to represent Ireland as the younger sister of Britannia but armed with both harp *and* spear to put to rest any notion of her being helpless.

On the Trinity College campus, my jeans and crumpled jacket helped me blend in with the students, except the serious young men hurried by hard at work while I mostly loafed and dreamed. These students seemed much more serious than the hero of *The Ginger Man*, the American Trinity student whose profligacy and foul language led to the book being banned in the US and Ireland.

I found my way into the library that displayed the twelve-hundred-year-old *Book of Kells*. The illustrations were magnificent and convinced me to hire monks to illustrate my novel—if I actually did settle in Dublin and write it.

Aside from the sites, I mostly strolled the streets and lounged on stoops and benches. Having the leisure to explore Dublin fed fantasies of sharing the streets with Joyce and Shaw, Wilde and Beckett. I also kept hearing Seamus's remonstrance about not waiting to begin writing.

With Joyce in hand I wouldn't need another novel for a long time, but I loved wandering through old bookstores. They were like warm blankets I could wrap around me in the company of so many great writers.

I found several guides to *Ulysses*. While much of this novel confused me, I wanted to read the story, not study it. Still, I was impressed with how much scholarship focused on the book. I skimmed one treatment of Joyce's "Nausicaa" episode—about Leopold Bloom's visit to Sandymount Beach as a parallel to Odysseus drifting to the land of the Phaecians. Bloom's licentious encounter with Gerty MacDowell was less to the point than that he, like Odysseus, was but one step from home. I'd begun to think the ferry from Dublin to England could put me one step from home and begin the final leg of my odyssey.

I searched for a tweed cap to fit my over-large head, despite Maddy's warning that wearing one would doom me to grow old in Ireland. I then wore my cap when I stopped for a beer or tea in a pub, where conversation always flowed easily. A simple nod would start someone discoursing on the weather and, once I spoke, to asking about my home and travels. Taking Joyce from my bag would bring on a passionate debate about literature or expatriate artists. The literary conversations led me to contrast Joyce's leaving Ireland to write with my contemplating settling in Ireland to write. "Contemplation" may have been too strong a word for what was running through my mind, but Seamus had planted the thought, and I found it growing in me.

*   *   *

Late in the afternoon I'd return home for tea and watch the television news with Aunt Mary. She never tired of current affairs. Most of the boys claiming to fight for the IRA were gangsters looking to justify robbing banks. President Carter was a good man, but wasn't he a wee bit simple? European union would be welcome—if only it would bring Ireland financial assistance and get the young ones off the dole.

Aunt Mary wanted to know all about my family. Over tea one afternoon, I found it easy to talk about Mom, a typical mother who spoiled me much the way Aunt Mary did, but who avoided the combustive subjects of war and politics that tore me from my father.

"And then there's Edward," she said with compassion. "Sure, and we heard about him fightin' in Asia; it was all so very wretched."

"I so looked up to him," I said, holding back the tears I thought were done. "I looked forward to the day when our age difference wouldn't matter, when we would be friends as well as brothers."

She spoke volumes of sympathy by quietly filling my cup. When the moment had passed, she turned her attention to my father, her second cousin. I didn't know what to tell her. Dad was so distant from me. She sensed my struggle and gently pulled out of me more than I had ever put into words before.

"He's disappointed in me," I said. "He always thought I was a poor version of my brother, but then Edward was drafted and I became politicized, and everything was coming apart, in the country as well as in our family. When Edward died, it all got worse. Dad and I were caught up in the generational thing. We couldn't sit down to a meal without arguing about the war or music or my hair. When I majored in English at the university I didn't think he'd care or even notice, but he blew up and treated me almost like a stranger."

I realized I'd been ranting, while Aunt Mary had been uncharacteristically quiet. The pause let me reflect on the news about my father's health, which made me feel like the villain in this story.

After a long moment, she seemed to resolve something within herself and spoke softly. "Alan and I were married young and lived a good life. He doted on his first son; he and wee Thomas were inseparable. But, when Thomas became a teenager and started having his own ideas about things, there grew a rift between them. It came to where they were always at each other about one thing and another, things that shouldn't have mattered at all. When the Lord took Alan from us," she said and then paused as if to gather strength, "I was lost in bottomless gloom. But then I saw Thomas was taking it even harder than I was, and he was my boy and he needed me. Brogan was bereaved too, of course, but Thomas was in a dark place. He was racked with guilt at losing forever the chance to make peace with his father." She looked down at the table and I watched a tear fall from her eye.

"One thing, though," she added with a sad smile. "It's helped make him a gentle father himself. Not that Alan ever lacked in kindness to his son."

She grew quiet and we each followed our own thoughts. Dad was my connection to Ireland and this unimaginable family. The emotions that overcame my cynicism would touch him as well, I was sure of it, and I had a sudden longing to share this with him. Maybe introducing him to his family would give me the opening to explain my trip—and myself. I was part of this family, too; he had to see that. My breaking away might be what would bring us all together. I might be able to show him this was important, that far from leading me down a dead-end path, my travels had made us all more complete.

Aunt Mary rose to clear the dishes, insisting I let them be. I walked out to the garden and sat on the stoop. Annetta came to mind; I had to sort out my feelings about her before heading back to London. Realistically, how could I have been surprised she of the revolving "boy-friends" would end up with Nick? For his part, he was just being himself, falling into an opportunity and an eager partner—who couldn't have been so eager if she'd cared much about me. He was just a natural phenomenon, like the rains running into the sea.

It didn't seem important anymore. Annetta had been my island beauty from a distant port of call; I had drowned in her and tattooed her name on my arm. She'd live forever in my heart, but she could never have been real, not like Pam. Pam was home and family and a long life together. If only.

I also wasn't done with Nick. That son of a bitch owed me big time, and I'd find a way to cash in. I just wouldn't turn my back on him again.

*   *   *

The contrast between Belfast and Dublin couldn't have been more pronounced. Dublin was light and humor and so much like home. It took a few days for me to realize, but part of why the city felt familiar was because I'd been working so hard at reading *Ulysses*. Immersed in this alternate reality, I'd awakened weeks before in a dilapidated tower overlooking sunny Dublin Bay with stately, plump Buck Mulligan. Being on site also helped me through several difficult chapters, with Aunt Mary to explain references to Irish history, Catholic ritual and 1906 Dublin.

"Aunty Mary," I said at breakfast one morning, "my university runs trips to Ireland where they track the path through Dublin of Leopold Bloom, the main character in *Ulysses*. Would you happen to know this path?"

"Well, I do know there're all sorts of goings-on each Bloomsday, sometime in June, but I never read the book, to tell you the truth, and couldn't help with the locations."

Thomas came by only once, for an afternoon. Brogan also was gone much of the time, at work or with his girlfriend in Monkstown by the bay. He was always home for the noon meal, though, and one evening took me round to introduce me at the "World Cup," his local pub.

"It's named not so much for World Cup prowess as for the promise," he said, sitting at the bar.

"A sort of World Cup half full," I offered.

He didn't get the pun and turned to introduce me to the bartender.

After our first pint, he said: "So you've been to see the homestead."

I nodded. "Saw the farmhouse and the gravestones of our great-grandparents."

"Ah, it *must* be grand," he said. "Myself, I've never been."

It shocked me he'd never visited Belcoo—only a few hours away.

"Well, you see, we've such a great quantity of relations," he said.

This was hard to fathom, even with Aunt Ann's extensive family tree recorded in my pad. I sipped and pondered my expanded family.

"It's brilliant how you roam about," he added, interrupting my thoughts. "How do you manage it?"

"By hitchhiking and staying with relatives."

"Aye, but have you no work at home?"

"I'm sort of in between schooling. I've finished college and will probably go back for another degree."

"And where will all that learning get you?"

"You're the second person in Ireland to ask me that," I laughed, "and I've no good answer." I gulped some stout and wiped my mouth. "I hope in the end it lands me in a career, maybe teaching at a college."

Brogan was pensive. "I should have kept at the schooling," he said. "But the job is steady, mostly, and then there's Helen, and she's not about waitin'." Helen was his long-time girlfriend, a pleasant girl who didn't seem to display much ambition.

"It's not too late, cousin."

He looked thoughtful, as if expecting me to share some grand wisdom. This made me uncomfortable. If traveling had taught me anything, it was that people had to make their own choices or flow with the life presented to them. But he still looked at me, his eyes gone a little sad.

"You have to think long-range, both of you," I said. "Stop school now and have some kids and you'll close off your options."

He looked at his glass pensively, and I decided to leave off giving life advice and coaxed him up for a game of darts.

* * *

Sometime in my second week in Dublin I called Seamus and Nellie, who invited me to tea. I negotiated the bus lines to their flat near the Royal Canal. Given that I had almost no daily expenses, I bought proper tickets rather than scheme to ride for free.

Seamus welcomed me warmly, though I sensed a ring of solicitude where I'd hoped for camaraderie. The flat was half studio in a ground floor loft, with paintings and artist materials everywhere. Two cats prowled over the furniture.

Nellie remained her cheerful self, with rosy cheeks and laughing eyes, and served up a delicious stew with home-baked bread. I'd brought several bottles of stout, and the meal was relaxed and pleasant. I told them about connecting with my relations, which seemed to relieve their concern for my well-being.

After we'd eaten, Seamus showed off a painting "inspired by the glorious West." The warm colors lit up the room. Nellie said Seamus was unusually proud of this effort, which was painted over a prior composition on the same canvas. "Aye," Seamus admitted, "it's something of a pentimento for my future critics."

This made no sense to me and I looked at it again, ponderously.

"Pentimento," he repeated slowly. "You know, where one painting turns transparent over time and reveals another scene beneath. Happens with the old masters, and with those of us hard-pressed to afford new canvas. They say it allows failure and genius to be revealed in the same frame."

There was a pause. "…Not that I lay claim to any genius," he added in clarification, and we all lost ourselves in his painting.

"So, Stephen," said Seamus, snapping back to the present, "now that you've had a look about, what do you make of all this Republican stuff?"

I paused and thought how politics rather than art had dominated my introduction to Ireland. "The Troubles make no sense to me," I said, "just as it makes no sense Ireland is split in two."

"Aye," Seamus said, shaking his head knowingly.

"What about you?" I said.

"Well, I see it in the artistic sense—how it reflects through my work, and the political sense—how it affects the lives around me, and then the moral sense—which could be the only way that matters, couldn't it?"

A moment passed and I smiled. "So you don't talk politics with strangers?"

He laughed. "You're hardly a stranger, Stephen, but you *are* reasonably perceptive; that'll be handy if you *do* set about writing your novel."

"Oh, I *will*," I said, trying to sound definite.

"When will that be, then?"

"Well, I'm scribbling an outline now; I'll start writing as soon as I get home."

"Is that best, do you think, artistically?"

"As opposed to politically and morally?"

Seamus shook off the joke. "You're here now, aren't you? Dublin's a place of literature *now*, isn't it? If you want to write, if you need to write, then for God's sake write."

"But then..."

"Ah yes, you must have more schooling, for the blessed Lord knows that's how you'll gain the insight to author a great novel."

Nellie broke up the conversation turning contentious, but the evening had nowhere to go from there. I said my thanks and rose.

"Let us know if you change your mind," Seamus said, "and we'll do what we can to set you up."

From the bus to Aunty Mary's, a voice whispered in my ear that I'd never see Seamus and Nellie again. I gazed absently at the buildings I passed and tried to imagine what it would be like to live and write in Dublin.

*   *   *

On Saturday a cousin named Cormac took Brogan and me for a sail in Dublin Harbor. "A wee blow," which felt like a typhoon, kept me half in the cabin of the thirty-foot sloop, looking a bit ridiculous in the kelly-green hat my aunt had given me, which looked like a tea cozy. But Brogan and I survived and were both proud of not getting sick on board.

We were also relieved to make it home to hot baths and the smell of Aunt Mary's roast filling the house. She was eager to hear our seafaring tales and then to opine on the recent news about a gruesome mass suicide in Guyana. Brogan and I were still piling in food when she started cleaning up the kitchen. By the time we had finished, she was in bed.

"Will we have a spot of the old man's whiskey?" he said more than asked.

"Absolutely," I responded heartily.

He brought an old bottle of Gilbey's Redbreast to the dining table. "Da stashed this away," he said, "for *significant* times."

Brogan poured two shots in plain glasses and held one up to me. I touched my glass to his and said, "*Sláinte.*"

He smiled, looking impressed. "You're pickin' up quite a bit of the local culture," he said, "now, aren't ya?"

The whiskey was smooth. Warmth traced a line from my smile to my throat to deep inside me. We both sipped quietly, watching the glowing remains of the fire. The only sound was the wind and a slight creaking of beams in the ceiling.

Brogan seemed to work up to saying: "I've thought on what you said."

I hid my surprise and replied: "About thinking long-range?"

"Aye, and also the *fact* of you."

I looked at him inquiringly. He went on: "You've done with your schooling, and you've taken up and gone, and you believe you have more to do. And that belief, I'm thinkin', is what'll make it happen."

These relations of mine certainly cut to the heart of the matter. I was cautious, sensing he might put too much significance into what I said. "I don't imagine just believing in something will make it happen, but you have to start by believing."

He looked pensive. "It felt like I'd run out of time to get an education and build a real career, but you may be right. First things first, eh?"

I poured us each another shot. I was unaccustomed to the role of advisor, but it made me feel grown-up to think he might act on what I said.

* * *

Several mornings later I lingered under woolen blankets, comparing this to dragging out of bed at dawn in a sagging, wet tent. I was in an ideal physical state: warm all over except my cold nose. I tried to count and left it as more than two weeks I'd been in Dublin. The instinct about when to move on had lost its voice. But December loomed, and I had to go before winter weather swept in.

There was no telling Aunt Mary I would leave. She'd made clear I *must* stay, in all events, until she finished the sweater she'd been knitting for months but now would finish for me. "It really came out too large for Brogan," she said.

I wanted to get back to London, find Nick and figure out if I could hole-up for the winter or would be forced by my wardrobe and slim prospects to push south. So, I picked a date for the Liverpool ferry and then commenced a dozen long goodbyes.

In the end Aunt Mary sent me off with two sleeves to be attached later to my sweater. On the last morning she gave me one more bear hug, and Brogan drove me to the port.

In place of drifting at sea like Odysseus until Athena came to my rescue, I simply had to cash in another travelers check and buy a ticket to Liverpool. My reserve funds were dwindling but I was almost in sight of home if the money ran out. Back on the Irish Sea in yet another capacious ferryboat, I toasted my vast new family and the fading shoreline with my last real Guinness.

Chapter XXIII

Walthamstow Central

The ferry docked at Liverpool and I walked ashore to stand where various highway connections turned off, not sure whether to stick out my thumb. I thought about looking for the Cavern Club, but a kid on the boat had said it was closed and there was no sense standing around *outside* someplace the Beatles once played, just to sniff around for a Liverpool accent. Without as much as a nod from me, a lorry driver stopped on his way to Cornwall. That sounded like a step toward London, so I climbed in.

Since I didn't know anyone else in Cornwall, I decided to see if Wally was still around, or maybe see Maggie again. The afternoon had turned sunny when I hiked the tiny lane to Ashegrove Manor. Maggie answered my knock.

"Stephen," she said after missing a beat. She looked me up and down with half a frown. "You were gone to Ireland."

A statement rather than a question boded ill. I looked her in the eye and said with all acuity I could muster, "I'm off to London. Was just passing by and thought I'd say hello. Good to see you again." I half turned to leave.

"Oh, Stephen," she said, exasperated. "Come in, of course, and put that rucksack down. Hattie will find you something to eat, and I shall arrange transport."

Hattie at least was happy to see me. She brought scones and tea to the sunroom for Maggie and me. Maggie looked good once her comfortable smile returned. She wore a bright orange shirt that brought out highlights in her hair, tied back, I supposed, for work in the hothouse. She said Wally had left the week before. I had the impression the Tibbets had had their fill of rabble, and I couldn't blame them.

"You're a remarkable young man," she concluded, for some reason I didn't comprehend.

"Ah, thank you," I replied and paused, "but between the two of us, you are certainly the more singular."

Color came into her face. "Well, we won't debate it, but leave it where it is." She rose, stopped to gently touch my cheek with her finger and, with an allusive smile, left the room.

Where it was, I thought, was just about right.

Soon and with little fanfare, Lady Tibbet packed me into a neighbor's sedan to be deposited in town. On my way to the car, I thanked her for everything and bowed out. She seemed relieved, which allowed my imagination to concoct a Fielding-worthy cause.

*   *   *

I didn't have much of a plan. Elizabeth wouldn't be happy to see me, but she was my only lead to finding Nick. While I was over Annetta, I was not past being angry with him. But being angry got me nowhere; I intended, instead, to collect on it like a debt.

The Dartmoor reprise was a salted landscape, white flakes swirling over the ground. I was surprised it snowed in England and at first leaped at the wonder, like a little boy aching to go out and play. Then my sock wiggled through a hole in the top of my sneaker, and I saw myself as a Dickensian waif huddling in a doorway against an icy wind. The chill, even seeping into the car, made me feel all the sores and bruises of five months on the road.

England was getting colder. Dublin would be just as cold. That left me with either a long trek to search for my mom's family in Yugoslavia and then on to the Aegean, or bailing out for a warm bed and big Christmas meals with my parents.

I made my way to Elizabeth's house. She had obviously been warned and was girded to meet me. "Nick moved on weeks ago," she said curtly, allowing me only into the vestibule.

"He does tend to move about," I replied, wondering if I should slip past her like a vacuum cleaner salesman and throw my pack on the sofa downstairs. Instead I said, with all the good humor I could muster: "Have you any idea where I might find him?"

"I *believe* he moved from the back of his *friend's car* to the Old Vic," she said, good-riddance peeking through her genetic reserve. "It's a shabby student hotel near the British Museum."

"Ah, thank you, and hey, thanks again for your hospitality on my last visit. And please give my regards to your mom and dad."

She didn't care about my regards. My pack and I did an awkward turn in the vestibule and squeezed out the door to the street.

*   *   *

There was an underground stop by the museum and from there I asked around for the hotel. At a nondescript building with no sign out front, I mounted the stoop and rang the bell. I almost fell backward when Jane Mandel opened the door!

I was shocked, but maybe less than she was. She apparently worked at the Old Vic, so I figured she'd have to let me in. Still, she made no move to open the door any wider.

"Nick's here," she said and then hesitated. "But you know that."

People kept declaring things that should be questions. I nodded my head "yes" and she reluctantly ushered me in and then silently pointed down a hallway. I followed her directions and found Nick in earnest conversation over coffee—what a surprise. He smiled at me without turning his face from his companion, a thin man who noticed me, nodded toward us both and stepped away.

Nick wasn't surprised to see me. He offered his hand to shake and then said he'd go have a word with Jane. When he came back, he explained Jane was assistant manager of the hotel, and he was staying with her. His living off the fat of the land would allow me to pay for a few nights—in what was otherwise strictly a long-term residence.

"Are we good?" he said, gesturing at our surroundings as if to take in everything, including our history. I glanced around the room but said nothing.

"Look, it was a stupid thing," he went on, "and a shitty thing to do to a mate. I'm *sorry*. Are we good?"

There was no way I would make this easy on him. I nodded and half-smiled. He led the way to the stairs and showed me to a bunkroom where I could stow my pack.

I finally turned to him. "I just can't believe you slept with her," I said derisively.

"I never *said* that," he protested.

I snarled, and he stopped grinning and said: "Well, I never said I didn't."

He left me to ponder that and settle in. I kept telling myself it didn't matter, that Annetta was a passing thing. I was glad to have a bed and a few days to sort out what to do next.

Nick later explained that he'd contacted his old traveling mate, working at a shop in Birmingham. But the work had sounded dreary, so he wired home for money and was looking for a job in London.

He was off in the morning looking for work, so I headed out alone to explore Bloomsbury. The British Museum was down the street and was free. I found the Rosetta Stone and wandered through the rape of Ninevah and Thebes. Mrs. Maple, in her cottage in Harwich across from her father's old factory, would have extolled the British as stewards of the world's culture, but this kind of national arrogance made me uneasy. I wondered if the museum director got lots of letters from Thebes and Ninevah asking for their stuff back.

The Vic residents were engaging and often lolled about in the common room. They worked or studied, but mostly they enjoyed the city and each other. During the days I chatted with them or wandered about. In the evenings I wore a comfortable groove in a pub stool around the corner.

The first night at the pub an older and very tall American named Jeff talked about the "hippie trail" he had taken in the early seventies. "They called me 'Big Bird'," he said, which made sense given his height and cartoon voice. "We hopped the Magic Bus in Amsterdam, headed for Istanbul and points east."

We stopped chattering and waited for him to go on. He took a long swig of beer, wiped his mouth on his arm, and continued. "Our plan was to ride all the way to Katmandu. Nepal, man! You know? Thing is, it was exhausting. We took turns sleeping on the floor of the bus, where you could at least stretch out, but the roads sucked, and you couldn't really sleep. We called it 'the urge to go to difficult places by difficult means'."

"How far did you get?" I asked.

"Tehran was cool—but hot, you know. But we finally landed in Kabul. The people were really friendly."

"So, no spiritual enlightenment with the maharishi?" Nick said.

"Oh, man, Afghanistan was spiritual; they took us to a hash farm. It's just, you know, we were almost broke and didn't want to hitchhike home. We caught the Bozo Bus back to Paris. *That* line sure lived up to its name."

It was incredible to think of hitchhiking through Afghanistan and Iran and into Pakistan and India. It made my travels around Western Europe seem so finite.

* * *

One thing left undone was scamming London's underground. What was simple in Cologne and Munich and Paris remained a puzzle in the British capital. The ticket system kept riders honest, and there was no language difference to hide behind if we were caught. But after Nick got us an offer of two days' work, the solution came to him.

Jane's friend had hired us to help set up a stage for a community symphony concert and the next day break it down. The job paid three pounds each day for a few hours work, and we were also reimbursed the fare to the far end of the underground. Explaining the gig to me, Nick's eyes suddenly lit up. He ran both hands through his hair and looked at me like he was bursting to share an idea.

"You've figured it out," I said, bowing to the fashion of asking questions as if they were statements.

He smiled, pondered, and said: "When you enter the underground in the center city, you buy a ticket showing your destination, which is priced by how far you'll travel. When you arrive, they check on your way out that your ticket shows the right destination. Now, at the outer ends of the line, you buy your ticket from a machine and so your ticket is *only* checked for the correct station when you arrive."

He could see I didn't grasp his thinking, so he continued: "A ticket from Russell Square in the center city to Walthamstow Central costs a pound forty, but a ticket from Russell Square to Holborn costs only thirty pence. So, you buy two tickets at Russell Square, a dear one to Walthamstow Central and a cheap one to Holborn."

I began to put it together, but he repeated himself as though lecturing a slow student: "We buy two tickets at Russell Square, one to Walthamstow Central and the other to Holborn. We use the *right* tickets going out and the *wrong* tickets coming back! Our first Russell Square tickets get us to Walthamstow Central, where they check us leaving the station. Then we board at Walthamstow Central with the second Russell Square tickets and ride all the way back to Holborn, where another clerk checks the destination, which is correct."

He had a genius for this.

In addition to our pay and ill-gotten gains for transport, we got the best seats in the house for the rehearsal. I was glad Nick wanted to stay after we set up the risers to hear the orchestra run through "Mars" from *The Planets*. We sat among the empty folding chairs we had so expertly lined up.

It felt like we had come upon music in its natural state. I closed my eyes and rode Holst's muscular horns of Mars "the father" and Mars "the bringer of war" but wasn't sure I could tell them apart. I wondered if that failure should be blamed on my family troubles or my paltry musical training, but it really didn't matter. The music soared, and the planets turned in orbits round the city, loops and orbits.

*   *   *

After breaking down the risers next day, we returned to Holborn Station. Nick had to meet someone, so I decided to give American Express one last try. I headed for Trafalgar Square, laughing at how I had looked for a letter there my first day in Europe.

A clerk took my name, asked me twice to spell it and walked through a doorway. I watched an old man sort letters. The clerk returned, checked my passport and, with no expression, handed me an airmail envelope and a package.

I saw immediately they were both from Pam and almost jumped out of my shoes. I hurried outside to find some privacy. I grabbed a park bench, but before opening anything I stopped, worried about what I'd read. Getting another letter was promising, but there was no assurance what it would say. In so many World War II movies, girlfriends wrote "Dear John" letters to lugs like me fighting in Europe. I saw myself as a beaten-down Van Johnson and this didn't make me happy.

Before I stepped back into that world by reading the letter, I opened the package. I thought that would be safe, and I was right. There were dozens of chocolate chip cookies, an incredible treasure. More importantly there was a note, dated November 30, but all it said was: "It came up tails–P."

The cookies were mostly broken but still a rush of taste from home. I ate three big pieces while I pondered the note. What did it mean? Was she talking about "tales" as in stories? Was that a dig at the literary thing? I was stumped. The letter was postmarked in October, so was sent before the package and probably wouldn't clear up anything. I hesitated, savoring another cookie and a moment of promise and anticipation before reading the letter that would probably shoot me down.

I shooed away the pigeons congregating at my feet to share Pam's cookies. I tried to think of some pressing business I should see to before reading the letter, but I had no business, pressing or otherwise. Finally, I carefully tore open the envelope, as if it were important not to rip it. With no other way to stall, I read:

S - It broke my heart watching your pack disappear up State Street. You took off to roam and left a lonely hole in my life. But as days turned into weeks and weeks into months, I was tortured less by your departure and more by the loss of what we had. Do you remember the kitten that used to visit us on our porch? And the ice cream cones over pinball? And the way you wrapped me in your arms after we made love? I'm torn. I don't know if I can lose myself in that wonder again, but I'm frightened to give up the chance. You wrote about rolling dice to decide your direction. I'm thinking of tossing a coin: heads we each take a sweet memory on our separate way; tails we try again for the magic. I'll let you know how it comes out.

Yours, possibly, P

For a frozen moment I could make no sense of the letter. My brain raced through everything Pam meant to me and what her letter could mean, and then it hit me: the cookie note! It came up tails! Peter didn't matter. No one else mattered. She was mine, my future present! I wouldn't go to Greece. I'd fly home, rest up and clean up and we'd return to Ann Arbor together! In a few short weeks, all would be right with the world.

Walking back to the Vic, even London seemed bright and sunny. I saw Pam's smile and heard her laugh. So much had changed in me during these months, and I wondered how Pam might have grown over this time. For one thing, she had learned how to deliver a punch line!

I didn't tell anyone about the letter—or the cookies. At the pub that night I tried to think of something other than Pam, so I could stop grinning like an idiot. I thought instead of my journey winding down:

what did it all mean? "There's no place like home" had been said before. Like T.S. Eliot wrote, maybe we just "arrive where we started, and know the place for the first time."

* * *

On my last day the inmates chipped in for wine, and we returned for a night in at the Old Vic. The common room was warm and strewn with well-worn chairs. Nick sat on a threadbare oriental rug, reading a horoscope for a Scottish woman named Emma. She was wide in the hips with over-large breasts and a comely face; I wondered how Emma's winning smile would strike Jane when she finished her duties and joined us. Then again, Nick's flirtations only seemed to increase his appeal for girls like Jane. It was hard, in any event, to see her as the abused lover when she was trading room and board for in-house service.

A thin man named Bruce sat in an overstuffed chair pouring for the masses, a green turtleneck buried in his beard. Perched on an arm of his chair as Bruce topped off my coffee cup, I nodded toward the chessboard by the window, thinking I should end *Meine Reise* with a game I actually tried to win.

"So, Bruce," I said, "I hear you're a player. How 'bout a game?"

"Ah, no, mate. *Was* a player. Actually, I was New Zealand junior champion in seventy-one, but I don't play no more."

Nick looked up with an eager smile, sensing competition in the bullshit field. "What, no more challenge?" he asked.

Laughing, Bruce said: "Challenge nothin'. It was the obsession I couldn't stand; what with the tutors and the tournaments, it robbed me of my childhood."

"The solution to a lost childhood is to repeat it," Nick said, "which is more fun, anyway, at a later age." Nick was the poster child for that scheme.

The chessboard brought to mind Biberach and Litzelstetten and the universal game of kings. Maybe it was my sense that the adventure was over that made me seek universality in everything, or maybe it was just that the patterns suggested nothing was unique. Transit scams, promises to write from down the road, music as alternate language, photographic scenes preserved in my mind's eye: it was all ordinary and even fated. The only accomplishment I could find in these months was managing to avoid train stations and picture postcard visits.

Dante said Adam and Eve's paradise lasted only six hours; was *Meine Reise* one night in this musty hotel? Or maybe my moment of truth lasted ten minutes with a big fish?

Anyway, there were the Irish relations. It was beyond even my cynicism to make light of my aunt gripping me like she was holding herself afloat. "Your granny never made it, but at least *you* did." I realized suddenly that Ann and Annetta, bookends with such similar names, had begun and finished the whole show by sending their own distinctive charges up my arm.

Conversation painted the background. I squinted at the dreary window to the street until I could conjure up a sunny Greek beach and Pam looking up through tousled hair to laugh, but I came to perceive the laughter as real. "Sorry, old man," Daniel said in a posh accent. "Didn't mean to shoot you down. Just noticed you needed a bit more wine, wot."

Emma had drifted off and left Bruce with Nick, who pontificated on the astrological signs of chess grand masters. I thought of the light show on the way to Andorra and how Nick's zodiac shtick cheapened the real wonder of the night sky. He saw me roll my eyes.

"And this one," he said, nodding toward me. "Textbook case of one who can't see past his colonial nose."

And if that isn't the colonial calling the kettle black, I thought. It occurred to me Australia had been settled by convicts, which could explain a lot of things.

He persisted, with an appraising look and familiar rising inflection: "Stephen, you fancy yourself a writer?"

"Of sorts," I said.

"And how would you say you go about creating?"

"Ah, usually… with a pen?"

"Very witty," he said with a frown. "I mean do you knock off a story at one sitting, or do you write and rewrite, editing yourself over and over?"

As usual I was engaged, but wary, an instinctive reaction to my cohort. "Well, I've never yet stopped revising a piece until at least the moment it was due," I admitted.

Nick slapped the floor. "Aquarius through and through!"

I shook my head cynically, but they both looked at me, Bruce inquiringly and Nick with the familiar self-satisfied grin.

"Well?" said Bruce.

"January thirty-first," I admitted, flatly.

Nick looked smug. Bruce raised an eyebrow in contemplation.

"You know me enough to understand how I write," I said to Nick, "and probably know my birthday, but my writing has *nothing* to do with how the planets aligned when I was born."

He grinned patronizingly and turned to tell Bruce about Chase Manhattan hiring him to plot the dollar. I'd heard that yarn before and drifted in thought. I noticed the faded print on the wall looked like the mezzotints in the museum, glimpses of clarity rising from the rough surface, and likened this to the nuggets of truth I'd managed to dig up: death on the beach; circles and orbits; snow on the Dartmoor. I reflected on that grand museum, displaying plunder from around the world, as Mrs. Maple would say: safer in Bloomsbury than where it was created.

The doorbell rang and Jane went to answer. The conversation in the front hall was quiet enough to get everyone's attention, and then Jane entered stage right with a guy about my age, lugging two large suitcases. His sneakers and open expression marked him as American.

"Everyone, this is Leo Bankler," Jane said. "Just flew in from New York."

"And man are my arms tired," he said and set down his bags. "Hey, what does a guy have to do to get a drink around here?"

This introduction warmed us all to him immediately. I wondered, though, about how he carted his effects. With those heavy bags and staying at the Vic, he clearly wasn't planning to move around.

Once he had a cup of wine, I caught his eye. "So, you've come from New York," I said. "What part?"

"I lived up by Columbia; graduated six months ago and interned at the public television station."

"So what're you doing here?"

"Oh, got another internship—this time at the BBC. Doesn't pay squat but should be interesting."

He seemed familiar with his dark hair hanging over wire-rimmed glasses. He also wasn't any standard American stereotype: not a hip student or a hosteller or a stonehead. Working in London as a step to other jobs, he was an entrepreneur, like Montana Bruce. It was comforting to find a countryman I could respect.

Time drifted, and I found myself in the hallway. It occurred to me that, if any literature fit Nick's description of an Aquarian work product, it was *Ulysses*. The novel was long and dense, and Joyce was still rewriting while it was being set in galleys. This gave me a way to deflate Nick's astrological ranting. The book in my pack surely must note the author's birth date. I drained my wine and headed for the stairs to retrieve exhibit A, laughing as I pictured waving the book under Nick's nose and trying to anticipate his inevitable dodge.

On the stairway sat a pretty black girl from Nigeria named Diamond. Braids stuck straight out from her head and her skin was flawless. She was leaning on Robin's knee as they talked intimately. I squeezed against the wall and started up the stairs, trying not to intrude.

Robin saluted. "On the bridge, land ho!"

Diamond flashed a glittering smile. "Brother Stephen," she said with a musical British accent, "Robin and I are concerned you seem adrift."

Grateful for the welcome, I sat two steps below Robin and across the worn staircase rug from Diamond.

Robin was Canadian, the daughter of a minister in Vancouver. Her face had the worn but sturdy look of long winters, but her smile was deep and inviting. She settled against the banister on an expanse of haunch and said: "Diamond's been saying how much she misses her mother and her brothers and sisters in Nigeria, which is quite funny, eh, because I've come to London expressly to *escape* my family."

"How is it with you, Stephen?" Diamond asked. "Do you run from your family or pine for them?"

"It's funny you should ask. I was comparing the 'family' here with the dysfunctional family that first welcomed me to London."

Robin's eyes lit up. "Oh!" she said. "This *does* sound good! Do tell!"

"Well," I teased, "there was the exotic lover, the jilted beau, the maniacal uncle…"

Diamond's face screwed up and she said: "I suppose we're an improvement over *that* lot. But what about your *biological* family?"

"Well, I'm surprised to say I've been thinking of them too."

They both looked genuinely interested, so I went on. "My mom supports everything I do; always will. But my dad, he thought going to Europe was just a way of loafing. This, of course, made it even more important I go, to push back against him. And there was this thing with my brother, but that's a long story."

It flattered me how they hung on every word and I marveled at how freely my guarded thoughts poured forth. "But along the way I stumbled across Dad's long-lost relations and found myself tied to him in ways I couldn't have imagined. He's my link, and we're just two in this enormous family."

Diamond was adorably affected. Even Robin lost her smirk.

"I'm actually eager to go home and share it with him," I continued. "It'll mean something to him, in spite of himself, and maybe he'll stop thinking I'm such a wastrel."

Robin was intrigued. "You mean your father didn't know his own family?"

I grimaced. "Well, the Christmas letters we've gotten since my grandmother died made everything sound so dire—this one dying and that one going blind—that my father was afraid to become entangled in all the tragedy. Also, he sees no reason to go to Europe unless you have to fight a war. But I just needed a dry place to sleep and would've been happy with a straw bed in a mud hut."

"And your reception made up for the poor conditions?" Diamond asked.

"Oh, far from that. They live pretty much like we do. And their lives are *not* tragic. Well, first of all, everything is breathtakingly beautiful and the people are as open and kind as they could be. And what we never understood is there are so damned many relations in Ireland that someone had always recently died, or gone sick, and *that* was the important news to tell in the one short letter each year. We didn't need to know there was a big football match or the countryside was glorious in the afternoon sun or we had three brand new cousins. Anyway, they treated my arrival like the second coming. My suddenly copious family embraced me and wouldn't let me leave."

"Sounds like my home," Diamond said. "I'm related to most everyone in my village."

Robin sniggered. "Well, my parents and aunts are so overbearing I couldn't stand many more people watching what I do. Matter of fact, I like the "family" here: easy and nonjudgmental. And speaking of our clan, I hope those blighters haven't finished the wine!"

"I'm with you there," I said, laughing and looking at my empty cup. In a moment I reached a decision and said: "After five months, I think I'm ready to call and say I'll be home for Christmas." I laughed again. "I know how my dad will react: 'Oh Stephen, yes, here's your mother. Now don't waste money on the call.'"

Robin laughed and went in search of the bottle.

"But it'll be nice," I said, "to have someone meet me on my arrival for once."

Diamond smiled warmly and squeezed my hand, saying she needed to find Jane. As she walked down the stairs, I wondered if I'd felt an invitation in that squeeze but realized I didn't care anymore, not after the cookies had arrived. I felt like I did in the early summer, with a serene smile on my face and the prettiest girl in town on my arm.

Left alone, I recalled my debunking quest and continued up the stairs. The room was dark when I pushed open the door. The stillness felt like someone was sleeping, and then I heard soft breathing from one of the beds. I made my way quietly in the dim light from the hallway.

My flashlight and *Ulysses* were in the top of my pack. Sitting on a lower bunk, I paused to taste bitter wine mixed with sweet triumph. With measured breaths, I shone the light on the opening pages of the big paperback. There was a short biographical introduction: "James Augustine Aloysius Joyce, born in Dublin, February 2, 1882."

I quickly shut the book, shaking my head. This proved nothing, of course, and certainly wasn't going to make me hang crystals round my neck and tattoo the orbits of the planets on my back. But, in fairness, the undeceiving *had* failed, despite the one-in-twelve odds. I wondered if I was ethically compelled to report this to Nick but decided I couldn't stand his condescension. "Well of course, Stevie," he'd say, "I didn't make this up, you know." Also, he was the only one to ever call me by that name, and I hated it.

Instead of admitting my chagrin, I returned downstairs hiding behind the box of Pam's cookies. Taking one with a grateful nod, Daniel said, "Nick is revealing the philosophy of travel on a shoestring and your peculiar obsession with transit systems."

Nick put his hand out for a cookie as if this were expected. He looked like he could sense what I'd learned about Joyce. It was just my imagination, though, as he immediately turned back to Daniel and said, "First, the art is to travel on no money at all, which justifies—in some sense—the sociopathic need to dodge paying for anything, tickets in particular." He paused for effect. "The trains will run anyway."

Daniel waved for him to go on. Leo was curious. Bruce slumped into a chair to listen. With this kind of rapt audience, Nick was in his element. I had to admit some pride in how he treated me as his partner among these sympathetic souls. He continued, solemnly, to unravel the underground scam, as though recounting how he had deciphered an ancient rune.

Bruce rubbed his mouth. Daniel looked unenlightened. A smile broke over Leo's face. Nick backed up, like he had when he explained it to me: "We used the *right* tickets going out, but the *wrong* tickets coming back."

Leo nodded, looking at me and quickly calculating. "So you saved…"

"Well, along with our pay, we got an extra two pounds twenty each day in our pockets," I said.

Bruce laughed, "Or in the pub till, you mean."

Stars and planets. Loops over and over to London. Odd place for my trip to center: cold, rainy and ancient. Then again, it was familiar: Dickens, Hardy, *Monty Python*. I could blame it on Freddy Laker that I hadn't come far in five months, from St. Cyril's to The Old Vic. But that was only true as the raven flies; Niall's student shelter of horrors was long ago and a world apart from the Vic.

My gaze drifted across the room and I saw Diamond's profile etched against faded curtains. She was focused on Leo, who was making animated gestures with his hands. Jane entered the room and sat on the arm of Nick's chair playing with his curls. He continued to amuse the crowd and ignore her, while she draped an arm casually around his shoulders.

"The ataraxia of domesticism," I commented. Nick smiled. Jane half-chuckled, unaware she was, as always, the butt of the joke, and probably not knowing what "ataraxia" meant. In that moment Nick and I burst out laughing. Jane sensed an insult and looked to me as the source. I opted for a diplomatic drift toward the stairs. It occurred to me to use up the rest of my film.

Nick saw me return. "Ah, now," he joked, looking at the camera, "I've got to straighten my hair if you're going to do portraits."

"Nah, I've got one shot left, and thought we could get the whole gang."

"Excellent idea!" he said and took charge of herding the crowd around the biggest sofa while I turned on all the lamps.

As I lined up the shot, I said mostly to myself: "I wish I could be in the picture, too."

"Why don't you just set the timer?" Leo asked.

"Timer?" I said, sensing I had been really dumb this time.

In a few moments, Leo had the camera set to take the picture. I didn't think the shot would capture the subtlety of my smile: self-deprecating, yet comforted I had learned in the end that I could have posed in all those photos I had taken of my backpack and the countryside. Leo hit the button and jumped to a place on the sofa and we all said "cheese."

When everyone had spread around the room again, Leo and Diamond welcomed me with contented smiles. She mentioned New York, which reminded me I had missed the end of the baseball season.

"Hey Leo, how did the Yanks end up?" I asked, thankful I hadn't had to watch.

"Oh man!" he burst out. "You don't know? It was unbelievable! We were down fourteen games to Boston in mid-August but surged to tie for the pennant. Then we took a one-game playoff at Fenway."

"Fantastic!" I blurted out. "And then?"

"Spotted the Dodgers two in the World Series... and beat 'em in six."

"World champions!" I whooped. "Two years in a row!"

Bruce sneered at the American delusion of a "world" series. I had to admit the term was a bit myopic, but this was the Yankees we were talking about! I ignored him and high-fived Leo. This was great. I was just sorry I'd missed the excitement. I left them all to go find my baseball cap.

About The Author

William Michael Ried was born on Long Island, graduated from the University of Michigan and Georgetown University Law Center, and has practiced law in New York City for thirty-six years, almost as long as he spent writing this book. He lives with his wife in Manhattan. *Five Ferries* is his first novel.

* * *

See www.fiveferries.com or www.instagram.com/fiveferries for more information and photographs.

* * *

If you enjoyed this novel, let the author know by emailing reviews, comments or suggestions to fiveferriesnovel@gmail.com or posting a review on your favorite website.

57499065R00191

Made in the USA
Middletown, DE
31 July 2019